PRAISE FOR THREE
CHANCES TO CHERISH

"Callaway is the queen of angst and intrigue as well as steamy love scenes."
  – Debbie, *Goodreads*

"A good dose of angst, hot lovemaking, and great characters—vivid, real, and extremely lovable. You'll root for them and their HEA!"
  – Gloria, *Goodreads*

"Experiencing all of the emotions of Evie and James was chef's kiss perfect."
  – Angela, *Goodreads*

"Swoon! I just love this series and the weaving in of the mystery throughout is my favorite aspect! This couple fights hard for their HEA and it is so satisfying."
  – A M, *Goodreads*

"I liked the time Callaway devoted to developing the characters as well as building their romance. The pacing was just right and worked for this couple. I liked that these two fought for each other. Plus all the emotional work really paid off in the steamy scenes!"
  – Gab Reads Romance, *Netgalley*

"Grace Callaway is the Queen of writing troubled marriages on the mend in a way that feels so genuine."
  – Nikki, *Netgalley*

"Right at the intersection of sweet and angsty, this is a heartfelt novel about falling in love well after you thought it was over. With a little ghostly flair. Prepare to be charmed!"
    – Caroline, *Goodreads*

"Lots of fun, wonderful secondary characters, a great plot twist, and lots of steamy scenes with James and Evie. Definitely a 5-star read!"
    – Marilyn, *Netgalley*

"Love the engaging romance and twisty plot."
    – May, *Netgalley*

"Plenty of heated encounters as well as fun kissable moments."
    – Pamela, *Netgalley*

"Grace Callaway delivers another masterpiece. The characters are wonderfully developed, each with depth and personality that make them leap off the page. Their interactions are enhanced by Callaway's signature brilliant dialogue, which is witty, emotionally resonant, and perfectly suited to the tone of the story. The journey concludes with a truly happy ending that ties the story together beautifully, leaving a sense of warmth and fulfillment."
    – Suzette, *Goodreads*

"Well-written, fast paced, and intriguing."
    – M T, *Netgalley*

"A wonderful angst-driven Victorian romance. I loved James and Evie and their journey to reconnecting: slow burn passion and desire, finding love and not letting it go."
    – A J, *Goodreads*

M is for Marquess

The Lady Who Came in from the Cold

The Viscount Always Knocks Twice

Never Say Never to an Earl

The Gentleman Who Loved Me

MAYHEM IN MAYFAIR

Her Husband's Harlot

Her Wanton Wager

Her Protector's Pleasure

Her Prodigal Passion

THREE *Chances* TO CHERISH

BOOK 3

GRACE CALLAWAY

USA TODAY BESTSELLING AUTHOR

Cover Art: Night Witchery

Formatting: Colchester & Page

For Brian,
my forever choice.
Here's to the first twenty-five.

What greater thing is there for two human souls, than to feel that they are joined for life—to strengthen each other in all labour, to rest on each other in all sorrow, to minister to each other in all pain, to be one with each other in silent unspeakable memories at the moment of the last parting?

— George Eliot

Prologue

THREE MONTHS EARLIER

Standing a few feet away from the closed door, Evie was gripped with desire and uncertainty.

She sensed James on the other side, moving around in his adjoining suite. He hadn't yet left for the evening—a rare opportunity, if she had the courage to seize it. With his political star on the rise, her husband was invited to countless affairs. At first, he had requested that she accompany him...but she'd made excuses often enough that he'd likely grown tired of asking.

Or perhaps he has grown tired of me.

She swallowed against the pain and fluttering panic. The truth was she had no one to blame but herself. She hadn't been good enough for him when he married her, and the events of the past year had shown that she would never be. She was cursed. She could never outrun her past. It would poison everything—everyone she allowed to come too close.

Trembling, she retreated a few steps. From this angle, she saw flickering movements under the door. James was getting ready to leave, and Robson, his valet, was putting the final touches on his perfection. She still had a chance to ask if she could join him this eve. She was in full evening attire and had asked her maid to take special care with her appearance. While she was no match for her husband's elegance, she would pass muster. If she was brave enough to make the first move...to break the wall of silence. Even though she shouldn't, she yearned to mend things—to have whatever intimacy she could with him.

She took halting steps to the door. Raised her hand to knock.

Robson's voice filtered through the barrier. "I do believe the diamond stick pin is the correct addition, my lord. It was admired the last time you wore it."

Admired? Who admired James's cravat pin? Who was close enough—bold enough—to remark upon so personal an item?

Evie clenched her raised hand inches from the door, her breaths quick and hot.

"Was it?" Her husband's deep voice came through. "Very well, leave it. It is getting late, and this particular hostess believes in punctuality."

Who was hosting James? Was this a public affair...or a private one?

She had no right to care—not after everything she'd done. But she did care. With every fiber of her being.

"Shall I leave word regarding your return, my lord?" Robson inquired.

A heartbeat passed. Then Evie heard James's distinctive footsteps approaching their shared door. Her pulse racing, she stumbled into a nearby corner, taking refuge amongst the leaves of the *aspidistra*. From the shadows, she saw the moving light under the door and knew that James was standing there on the other side.

Will he come in? Invite me to join him? What should I do?

"No." James's voice was curt. "There is no need to disturb the countess."

Evie listened to his departing footsteps, wetness sliding down her cheeks.

Chapter One

Watching her husband prowl in front of the fire, Evelyn Harrington, the Countess of Manderly, recognized with an uneasy quiver that he wasn't himself. James was always proper and reserved—the perfect gentleman. The perfect husband. Nothing ruffled him; even the most disquieting circumstances failed to erode his composure and rationality. With her, he was courteous and kind, never asking for more than she could give—even if a part of her wanted him to.

However, Evie's polished spouse of over three years was nowhere to be seen this eve. In his place stood a man who looked like James—but his restraint had been replaced by a raw, dangerous intensity. He'd raked his fingers through his thick brown hair, threaded with bronze, disheveling its precise cut. A night beard shadowed his typically clean-shaven jaw. He had shed his impeccable frock coat and cravat and rolled up the sleeves of his pristine shirt. While his physique was naturally brawny, he had packed on more muscle since she'd last seen him from such an intimate distance.

His fitted waistcoat revealed the powerful breadth of his shoulders and the leanness of his torso. Fascinated, she saw the flexing sinew of his hair-dusted forearms as he curled and uncurled his hands. When he prowled away from her, crossing the floral carpet, her gaze caught on the sculpted curve of his backside. Her cheeks warming, she quickly looked away.

While Evie had rarely seen her husband in an agitated state, she also made it a habit not to pry into his affairs. It was better that way—better to keep a safe distance. Although she missed their former closeness, she told herself it was for the best that they did not live in each other's pockets. She couldn't risk letting her secrets destroy the best thing that had ever happened to her.

For his part, James seemed content with the present state of affairs. He never entered her bedchamber without permission and only when he had discreetly ascertained that such a visit would be welcome. In the early days of their marriage, he had knocked upon the door of their adjoining suites at least once a week. But now it had been six months and thirteen days since he'd last ventured into her room for conjugal purposes...not that she was counting. Nor did she blame him for his extended absence. In fact, she was surprised that it had taken him this long to see the truth of who she was: her flaws and shortcomings, the myriad ways in which she was no match for his shining perfection.

Yet things felt different tonight. For one thing, they were away from home. They were visiting Bottoms House, the country manor belonging to James's brother and sister-in-law, Ethan and Xenia Harrington. While the guest bedchamber was well appointed, Evie yearned for her own room back at Grove Hall. Surrounded by her beloved plants and journals, she felt protected. Here, in this borrowed room, she felt the opposite: exposed and on edge.

Of course, the setting wasn't the only thing out of the ordinary. Mere hours ago, she and James's younger sister Gigi had been kidnapped. She herself had been held at gunpoint. To rescue her, James had been forced to take her captor's life. His decisive action came as no surprise. He'd always been the steadfast eldest brother and heir, the one his family had counted upon during times of tragedy and disaster. He performed his duty so perfectly that it was easy to miss that it cost him.

Seeing the rigid expanse of his back, she drew a trembling breath.

Say something, you ninny. You've been a good companion, if not wife, to James...find your way back to that. If you don't long for more than you can have, you will at least have something.

"Are you...are you all right?" Evie asked.

James turned, facing her. She'd always believed "handsome" was too paltry a word to describe a man whose face conveyed the nobility of his character. His blunt, even features exuded uncompromising strength. The unyielding slant of his jaw was somewhat softened by his lips, the bottom one possessed of an unexpectedly voluptuous curve. His steel-blue gaze could express a spectrum of emotions, ranging from wry amusement to stern command.

Right now, his stare was incredulous.

"Am I all right?" he stated.

Although discussing emotional topics was not Evie's forte, she didn't know why he was repeating her question. It was a fair one, given that he had shot someone to save her life. Perhaps he was more rattled than he let on.

"Tonight's events were a trifle disturbing," she ventured. "It would be understandable if you were experiencing a negative reaction in the aftermath."

He continued to gaze at her as if she'd lost her mind. This began to irk her. While she was lacking in many ways, she prided herself on her ability to reason clearly and well. She was a scientist, after all. Her botany experiments had earned her a reputation for intellectual rigor. As a member of the Botanical Society of London, she had written a paper which she hoped to present and perhaps even someday publish.

"You think you understand my current state?" James asked.

She lifted her brows. "Do you disagree with my observation?"

"As a matter of fact." He stalked toward her.

She had the instinct to bolt like a frightened rabbit, yet she held her ground: this was James, after all. The one man she trusted, who'd never done an uncivilized thing in his life...well, except for killing her kidnapper. As far as she was concerned, that act had been wholly justified. Yet did he regret what he'd done? His honor was everything to him, and killing a woman—even a deranged, cold-blooded murderess—would not sit easily with him.

He gripped her shoulders. Pleasure quivered through her at his touch. When she tilted her head back, she was riveted by the blaze of silver in his eyes.

"*A negative reaction* does not begin to describe my feelings."

She collected herself. "It must have been difficult seeing your sister in danger—"

"As relieved as I am that Gigi came to no harm, this isn't about her. Bloody hell, Evie, I almost lost *you* tonight. And you think I am a *trifle disturbed*?"

His tone, while quiet, had the power of a shout. Her pulse raced, and a part of her wished she had run. Not because she feared him, but because she feared herself. For years, she'd worked at keeping her secrets safe. She'd sealed herself inside a shell of prim rationality, never giving her dangerous impulses a chance to emerge. She'd learned to control her yearnings—to stay on the safe path. The only possible path given that she'd chosen to marry the man she loved and did not deserve.

Now James's intensity struck her like a blast of heat. Like the sun's imperious summons to ripen and release. Longing swelled inside her, threatening to burst free.

No, you must not reveal who you are. You cannot hurt him. You cannot lose him.

Longing was a fist around her heart. It was a familiar sensation. She could—and would—manage it.

"Thanks to you, nothing happened." She was surprised by

how calm she sounded. "I am none the worse for wear. I could, however, use a bath."

She prayed he would take the hint. Her gentlemanly husband certainly would. Yet *this* James merely clenched his jaw, a muscle twitching along the chiseled edge.

"The bath can wait until after we talk," he stated.

No, no, no. Why does he have to choose this moment to be stern and commanding?

While James was courteous by nature, he was no milksop. As the Earl of Manderly and heir to the Marquessate of Blackwood, he wore the mantle of lord and master with natural authority. He was firm when required and did not suffer fools readily. Yet with her, he chose to be gentle and accommodating...as if she were a fragile bloom he feared to crush. Even when she showed her thorns, he handled her with care. Rarely did he lose his temper. When he did...she didn't know what it said about her that she found him even more attractive.

It is not fair, how perfect he is. How undeserving I am of him.

Heat pushed behind her eyes. Pushing it back, she took refuge in propriety.

"If you insist," she said coolly. "But do make it quick, for I am quite fatigued."

"You didn't seem fatigued when you kissed me earlier."

She felt her jaw slacken. The husband she knew would not bring up her wanton behavior, which had occurred in the reckless moments after he'd rescued her. He would never embarrass her in such a fashion.

Her lips moved before she could think better of it. "I believe *you* kissed me."

"Can you blame me?"

His intensity released a swarm of butterflies in her belly.

"That madwoman held a pistol to your head, Evie. If I had missed—if my shot had been off by even an inch—I would have lost you."

"You didn't miss." Seeing the tension in his shoulders, she gentled her tone. "You never would. Your aim is as flawless as you are."

"Flawless? Is that how you see me?" There was no humor in his smile. "I killed a woman, and I have no regrets. None. Because she threatened you, and if I lost you, I...I..."

Her breath stuck in her throat. His glittering gaze, topped by fiercely drawn brows and deep slashes around his mouth, set off a wild thumping in her chest. She knew she should run. She should retreat like she always had. But after the months of silence, his declaration, gritty and unfinished, felt like a balm to her soul. While she swayed with indecision, her feet remained planted. Then it was too late. James yanked her into his arms. Enveloped by his strength and the virile scent of sandalwood and male musk that was his alone, she trembled...not with fear but soul-deep longing.

It has been so long. I thought he would never hold me this way again.

"You're my wife, Evie," he said roughly. "*Mine.*"

She tipped her head back as his mouth came crashing down. The impact made her whimper, then moan for more. The scorching kiss burned away her secrets and failures until only a single thought remained.

He needs me and wants me still.

Joy broke the dam in her heart. Desire rushed through her, and there was no way to stem the tide, no way to stop the pent-up need from taking over. She pressed herself against her husband, spearing her fingers into the rough silk of his hair. Parting her lips, she welcomed him in, and the growl that escaped him didn't sound like James. To be fair, she didn't feel like Evie. The months of separation fell away like withered petals, and her restraint followed. In her beloved's arms, she was nothing but sensation. Nothing but endless wanting and heat. The depth of her hunger might have shocked another man, but James...James just kissed her harder.

Wetter. Deeper.

"That's right, sunflower," he whispered. "Open to me."

Sunflower.

The first time he'd called her by this endearment, she'd thought it was silly. Now the whimsy of it dampened her eyes. He hadn't called her "sunflower" in ages, and she hadn't realized how much she missed it, even if the comparison to *Helianthus annuus* was illogical. For she was nothing like the dramatically beautiful bloom: it boldly sought out brightness while she hid in the shadows.

Yet James's desire unfurled her. His possession touched the essence of her yearning until she burned with need. They fought to get closer, tearing at the layers between them. She was desperate and greedy, and his growl conveyed his own urgency. When they were panting and pressed together flesh-to-flesh, she had the giddy, fleeting feeling of being his equal. Even so, in the moment before passion obliterated her, before James shocked her by bending her over the bed and driving into her with a force that pushed a blissful cry from her lips, a thought flitted through her head.

I love you, now and forever. Yet I must keep you safe from the shadows I carry.

Chapter Two

James opened his eyes to an unfamiliar canopy of green silk damask and an equally unfamiliar feeling swelling in his chest.

Hope.

He managed, just barely, to prevent himself from grinning like a fool. Turning his head on the pillow, he saw that Evie was gone. This wasn't surprising. His wife was an early riser, and if this were a typical day at home, she would be puttering in her greenhouse in the ungodly hours before dawn. Yet they weren't at Grove Hall, their idyllic Berkshire estate on the Downs above Brightwalton, and there was nothing usual about what had transpired last night.

Have I finally fixed things with Evie? Is our marriage back on course?

Tucking his hands behind his head, James allowed himself to savor the memories of their lovemaking. Prior to their troubles in the last year, he had experienced his wife's passion...yet even he hadn't suspected the extent of it. Shy and serious, Evie preferred the company of plants over people, a quality he found charming. In truth, he was proud of her intellectual prowess and accomplishments. How many fellows could claim that his lady had discovered a new subspecies of a flower and had written a scholarly paper based on her studies?

Yet, if he were honest, there were times when he wished that Evie would apply the same vigor and curiosity she had for botany to their marriage. The thought was accompanied by a stab of guilt. For Evie *was* a good wife: dutiful and considerate, she ran their household with seamless efficiency. His family and the servants adored her.

As a spouse, she was loyal, attentive, and saw to his comforts. If he complimented a dish once, he would find it added to the regular menu. While Evie could be reserved in public, when it was just the two of them, she never lacked for conversation. True, most of it concerned scintillating topics such as pollination...but he liked her quiet yet passionate ambition. He also liked how animated she got when discussing flora and fauna. Flecks of gold would surface and sparkle in her whisky-brown eyes, and her face, framed by soft blonde curls, would flush a charming peony-pink.

Evie was a good listener, too. When they discussed his favorite subject of politics, he found her mind as agile as any of his male cronies. He valued her opinion and their lively debates when they did not agree. He had also confided in her about his family. She alone understood his close and complicated relationships with his siblings.

Evie had held up her side of the marital bargain. She was a proper countess and a comfortable companion. It wasn't her fault that he wanted...well, he wanted...

More. I want more.

Staring up at the canopy's swirling and inscrutable pattern, he wondered when he'd begun feeling this way. Truth be told, discontent had been niggling at him for months and perhaps longer, yet he'd buried it. If there was anything a Harrington valued, it was loyalty. *Ad finem fidelis—faithful to the end—*was the family motto. His dissatisfaction with his marriage felt like a betrayal of his vows, especially since Evie had been candid about the kind of wife she would be. Indeed, she'd turned down his first proposal.

"You do me a great honor, my lord," she had said with quiet dignity. *"But I fear I am not suited to marriage."*

"To me, specifically, or in general?" he'd asked.

"I have no intention of marrying anyone. I prefer a solitary state, and from what I've observed, gentlemen tend to demand attention. And you, my lord, strike me as a fellow who would expect a union marked by the kind of intimacy that I am neither prepared nor able to give."

He hadn't known whether to be astonished or insulted by Evie's response. There he'd been, one of London's most eligible bachelors, offering for an impoverished lady's companion on the brink of ruin...and she'd turned him down flat. The fact that she'd characterized him, a gentleman vaunted for his self-discipline and restraint, as needful of attention had been icing on the cake. Most men would have washed their hands of her.

James had been utterly intrigued.

Who was Miss Evelyn Ashewood? What sort of woman, with wolves of scandal snapping at her heels, would turn down marriage to a wealthy earl? What lay beneath this lady's dowdy dress, unshakeable pride, and dark, heart-of-a-sunflower eyes?

James had been determined to find out. While he had a reputation for civility, once he set his mind upon a thing, he went after it with single-minded focus. Although it had taken several attempts, he eventually secured Evie's hand. Knowing her skittishness, he avoided talk of love...and contrary to her assumptions, he had no desire for messy entanglements. The few turbulent affairs he'd had as a younger man made him dread dramatics and emotional tempests.

What he wanted was a comfortable marriage. A relationship of mutual respect, care, and trust. At heart, he was a simple fellow, and at four-and-thirty, unnecessary complications held little appeal. Passion was well and good but never at the expense of prudence. He wanted a wife who was a steady partner, who valued duty, honor, and family as much as he did. Of course, physical attraction had to be part of the equation: given his views on fidelity, his marital bed would be his sole sexual outlet, and he intended to enjoy it.

Out of this compatibility, affection would naturally grow. Given his upbringing, he valued love—but he wanted the genuine article, not some trifling imitation. In his experience, infatuation was oft mistaken for love, which required time and commitment. He was a patient man and believed that good things came to those who put in the work.

It had taken a while, but he and Evie had said the words—and meant them...or so he thought. Even if mawkish declarations didn't come easily for either of them, life with Evie was no chore. He should have no complaints, for she fulfilled every requirement on his list. He ought to have been content.

He hadn't realized the extent of his self-delusion until last night.

The memory of Evie bent over the bed sizzled through him. He felt the giving plushness of her hips beneath his hands and the firm bounce of her bottom against his thighs as he plowed her. Her sheath, snug and wet, had sucked him in with sweetly lewd sounds. With a sensual quiver, he recalled the way his veined beast had split her open, her pink petals stretching prettily to accommodate him...

Feeling the gathering heat, he slanted his gaze downward and saw his cockstand tenting the sheet. Waking up in this condition wasn't uncommon, but it was usually due to unsatiated lust. For the last six months, he had used boxing and riding as outlets for his physical needs because he believed space was what Evie wanted. Sports had proved to be a poor substitute for bedding his wife, and he had never stopped desiring her—that had never been the problem. What had been at issue was whether *she* felt the same.

In the early years, he'd caught glimpses of her delightfully wanton streak, but in recent months, she'd been notably reserved.

Cooler. In bed and elsewhere. She favored the greenhouse over his company. He'd tried to draw her out of her shell but to no avail. He didn't know if this was the natural progression of marriage—Lord, he hoped not—or something else.

Something deeper. Some other reason why his wife would hold back...or lose interest.

As lowering as it was to admit, James had wondered whether his love and desire were reciprocated. It was as if an invisible wall had been erected between them, and he didn't know how to knock it down. He'd counseled himself to act like a considerate husband. He had given her space, thinking that she would come to him when she was ready.

She hadn't knocked on his door—not once.

But last night, after months of waiting, he had finally re-established his connection with Evie. Her throaty moans, the way she'd wailed his name as she spent, repeatedly, had eased his doubts. She'd creamed around his cock so delightfully, anointing him with her bliss at least three times, and in various positions...

He was painfully hard now. Seeing the wet spot where his tip jutted against the coverlet, he was tempted to take matters into his own hands. To let off some of the built-up steam. Yet he was a grown man and not some overeager schoolboy. He was hungry for his wife, and the knowledge that she wanted him just as badly made him as randy as a sailor on shore leave.

Yet he and Evie had matters to discuss. First and foremost, he needed to know what had changed for her. Perhaps she had finally recovered from...from what had happened a year ago. While he didn't like to dwell on grief, there was no denying that the loss had pushed them apart, physically and emotionally. Like him, Evie wasn't one to wear her emotions on her sleeve, and he hadn't known how to comfort her...or if she wanted comforting.

Admittedly, discussing the subject of feelings was not his forte. He valued restraint and found excessive displays of emotion distasteful. He supposed he took after Papa...although the latter's stoicism did not extend to Mama. James had witnessed his parents' open devotion with varying degrees of awe, amusement, and embarrassment. Regardless, he considered himself a man of action rather than words, and right now, he sensed an opportunity in his marriage. He was going to make things right—make up for lost time. He was going to make love to his wife until she was hoarse from moaning his name.

Then he would start all over again.

Resolved, he threw aside the covers and got out of bed. He winced as his erect flesh swayed, heavy and throbbing. With any luck, he would find Evie forthwith, and they could take up where they left off last night. Better yet, if he found her alone where he suspected she would be—in the gardens, inspecting this species or that—he might steer her to the woods just beyond. The fantasy was wild...exciting. The image of Evie, her golden hair dappled by the sun and streaming down her back as she rode him like his very own Lady Godiva, made him do the unthinkable: forgoing the assistance of his valet, Robson, he decided to dress himself.

As he headed for the wardrobe, he passed a small table...and saw the folded note addressed to him. He recognized Evie's untidy penmanship; it never failed to amuse him that his precise lady scientist had the handwriting of a tipsy poet aboard a tempest-tossed ship. He reached for the note, wondering if he was about to read his first love letter from her. The notion of his practical girl scribbling some bit of sentimental nonsense gave him an oddly heady feeling. With fumbling eagerness, he unfolded the paper.

James,

I trust you slept well. While I have returned home to tend to my experiments, there is no need for you to hurry back on my account. Stay as long as you wish, and please convey my regards to your family.

Yours,
Evie

As he stared at her messy scrawl, his vision seemed to darken. Just when he thought the door was opening between them, she slammed it shut in his face. Something sputtered, then extinguished inside him. An instant later, rage swelled.

Damn you, Evie. And damn me *for believing that things could be different.*

He hurled the crumpled note. Dragging his hands through his hair, he forced himself to calm down. Not the easiest thing to do when his urge was to drive his fist into the wall. Yet that would require an explanation to his family as to why he'd damaged his brother's property, and he would rather face a firing squad than endure the humiliation.

Like solitaire, rejection was meant to be a solo sport. It took several breaths, but James restored his composure...and his pride. If Evie wanted to act as if last night hadn't happened, then he would oblige her. If she didn't give a damn about their relationship, then neither would he.

If a bloodless marriage is what you want, wife, then by Jove, that is what you shall have.

Jaw clenched, he yanked on the bell to summon his valet. The pull tore, leaving him holding a piece of frayed rope. He tossed it aside with a snarl, pulled on his robe, and stalked off in search of Robson.

Chapter Three

"Wake up, lambkin."

At the familiar voice, Evie opened her eyes. Her cheek was pillowed by her folded arms. The pale petals of a wallflower came into focus. Next to the potted bloom lay the small gold spectacles she used for reading. The familiar fragrance of damp earth and crisp foliage tickled her nose and confirmed where she was. She must have fallen asleep while working in the greenhouse again, as she had most nights since leaving James a week ago. Lifting her head, she winced at the crick in her neck.

"Good morning, Harkness," she said, yawning.

Her former nurse, now her companion, had always gone by "Harkness." The absence of an honorific suited Harkness's no-nonsense style and ambiguous position in the household. Having raised Evie's mama and then Evie, Harkness was a retainer whose selfless service transcended that of a common servant. For years, she'd been Evie's only family.

Since James had insisted upon hiring Evie a proper lady's maid, Harkness now functioned as a companion. Tall and wiry, the latter was like old fencing twisted by time, bending more with each year, yet standing strong. Her salt-and-pepper hair was scraped back from her forehead and formed into steely springs. History was deeply etched upon her narrow face, and her black gaze was a vault of confidences.

Stifling another yawn, Evie asked, "What time is it?"

"It is past eight, pet. When you didn't ring for breakfast, I knew you'd fallen asleep working as usual." Clucking, Harkness draped the velvet cloak she'd brought over Evie's shoulders. "How many times have I told you to have a care? You'll catch your death of cold in this place."

"Since Manderly hired Sir Paxton and his team to install the new heating system, the greenhouse has been consistently temperate."

James had built the octagonal building for her, and it was a marvel. Slender wrought-iron ribs held the glass walls and ceiling in place, creating an ambiance so light and airy that it felt like being outdoors. Raised boxes and ornamental planters held a variety of plants that Evie grew for study and for pleasure. She waved now at the row of prized potted *Ananas comosus*, another gift from her generous husband.

"If an exotic species like the pineapple can thrive in this clime, then a sturdy domestic breed like me will surely survive a night or two."

Harkness snorted. "Plants are your specialty, lambkin. My specialty is *you*. I've not forgotten that time you caught a chill. You were barely seven, and those coughing fits wracked your poor wee body. You couldn't sleep or keep anything down. Your mama was terrified that every breath would be your last. She summoned the best quacks in the county, but all they did was stroke their beards and mutter dire predictions."

Evie hid a smile, for this story was like a favorite old blanket— one that wore well and comforted, despite its many tellings. Though her four-and-twenty years had been marked by ordeals, it soothed her to know that someone had always looked over her.

"Luckily for me, you knew what to do," she prompted.

"Aye." Harkness drew herself up proudly. "I had the footmen carry up a tub of hot water, and I sat in it, holding you, a blanket draped over the both of us to hold in the steam. I didn't sleep for two days and nights, until the steam finally cleared your little lungs, and you could breathe freely once more."

"What would I do without you?"

Hopping off the stool, Evie fondly squeezed her companion's arm, which felt like iron encased in black bombazine.

"You'll never have to find out," Harkness vowed. "No matter what his lordship has to say on the matter."

Evie knitted her brows. From the start, James and Harkness had taken an active dislike of each other. Nothing she said or did could change their mutual animosity.

She strove for a neutral stance. "Manderly knows how important you are to me. He wouldn't dream of separating us."

In truth, James had been more than patient when it came to dealing with her companion. Harkness could be as prickly and tough as a gooseberry bush when it came to people she didn't like. Yet with Evie, the tartness of Harkness's personality was tempered by the sweetness of her care.

"If that were true, his lordship would not have ordered me to stay here instead of accompanying you to Chudleigh Bottoms." Harkness raised her chin. "I should have been by your side, protecting you. If I had been there—"

"You could not have prevented the kidnapping." Evie cut her off. "You could not have fought off a gang of cutthroats, dear. You would have been hurt—or kidnapped along with me and Gigi."

"At least I could have looked after you."

"Dear Harkness." Evie's smile held a touch of wistfulness. "You have always protected me. At some point, I shall have to fend for myself."

"You've been fending for yourself all your life," Harkness said darkly. "My poor lamb, always prey to the worst of predators."

The words released a flood of memories. Through force of will, Evie kept them at bay.

Do not think of the past. It is over and done. Remain in control.

This self-directed counsel usually helped her to maintain her composure. Yet the recent violence had awakened the shadows inside her. Present and past had bled together in her dreams, and she'd awoken two nights in a row, strangled by screams. Her nightmares were not new; the only time she was free of them was on those rare occasions when James spent the night with her.

But he wasn't here. He remained at Bottoms House and had sent no word regarding his return. After her curt note and abrupt departure, his indifference was to be expected.

She told herself she'd done the right thing. Their night of passion had exposed too much—made her *want* too much. It was safer to withdraw and put distance between them. Left to her own devices, she'd been avoiding sleep, focusing instead on work. Here, encased by glass and greenery, no one would bother her—or hear her sob.

"There, there, now."

Harkness pulled Evie into a hug as if she were the small girl she'd once been. The familiar, astringent mix of cloves and camphor burned Evie's nostrils. She allowed herself to be held before pulling away.

"I am fine." She managed a smile. "There is no need to fuss."

Harkness sniffed. "Someone must look after you since your husband seems unequal to the task."

"That is unfair," Evie said hotly.

Despite her marital woes, she would not allow anyone to attack James.

"Manderly has *always* protected me. For blossom's sake, he married me, a nobody, so that I would not have to face the consequences of ruination. More recently, he tracked down the fiends who captured Gigi and me and took a life to save mine."

She paced, hating that James had been forced to commit

violence on her behalf. She brought little enough to their marriage, and the idea of further unbalancing the scales caused a burning in her throat.

"He did what no man of conscience should ever have to do. It pains me greatly, Harkness, that he will have to live with the consequences."

"Your husband did what needed to be done," Harkness said crisply. "The only thing he should regret is not getting there earlier. And what was he thinking, letting you return to Grove Hall unaccompanied?"

"That was not his choice. *I* left when he was sleeping, so don't you blame him for that."

Evie stopped pacing, hugging her arms around herself. Fleeing had been cowardly, and she knew it. Yet the notion of facing James after their scorching encounter had overwhelmed her.

"*If only you could see yourself, sunflower, how beautiful you are.*" His voice had been deeper than she'd ever heard it, his words shockingly wicked—and titillating. "*Your petals spread so prettily for my cock, and your bottom is blushing from being taken this way. Do you like it?*"

She'd *loved* it. And she'd been so lost in desire that she'd told him so.

"*Yes, yes. Take me harder, James. I want you so badly...*"

While James had enjoyed himself—his stamina had been exceptional, even for him—he was not stupid. He would have questions. He would want to know why she'd never been this wanton before. Maybe he would accuse her of concealing her true nature. Maybe, in the light of day, he would be repulsed by the wickedness she tried so hard to hide.

Despite his lapse into carnality, James was a proper gentleman to the core. Recalling the shameless way she'd begged for his attentions sent a hot wave of humiliation through her. True, James had seemed as lost in the moment as she'd been: his earthy vocabulary had been entirely, thrillingly at odds with his character. Yet society harbored a double standard when it came to how gentlemen and ladies should behave, and while James was no hypocrite, he was rather straitlaced.

If Evie were honest, however, she feared his curiosity more than his condemnation. She couldn't afford to have him digging into her past. Her secrets were too dangerous—and could compromise his future. From the start, she'd known she was no good for him, and that conviction had grown stronger as he had begun to pursue his ambitions.

With his charisma and leadership abilities, James had a natural flair for politics. When he spoke, people listened. She'd watched him enthrall guests at balls and supper parties with his proposals to help the working class. One day, James would inherit the right to take his papa's place in the House of Lords; until then, he had other options open to him. Of late, his cronies had been urging him to stand for election in the House of Commons. He'd demurred, yet she understood him and knew where his aspirations lay. For James, privilege was a responsibility: he believed it was his duty to put the power and position he'd been given to good use.

Truth be told, she was proud of James—proud that he wasn't just another louche aristocrat. He could do anything he put his mind to, and he wished to reform the political system to benefit everyone, not just the select few. In particular, he advocated for fair treatment of the working poor, care and compassion for soldiers returning from war, and public health and sanitation for all. Indeed, she had helped him to encapsulate his policies within a single motto: "Dignity for every life touched by labor, by service, or by suffering."

His plans could improve the lives of so many...and she could destroy them in a blink. For as noble as his cause was, it did not stand a chance against scandal. She could ruin him—his reputation and his ambitions.

I will not allow that to happen. If push comes to shove, I will leave him before I allow him to be hurt because of me. Because of the sin I can never erase.

"Men are all the same," Harkness said.

"Manderly is different," Evie insisted. "I wish you would try to get along with him. He has been exceedingly generous to us both."

"I earn my keep and always have." Harkness set her shoulders back. "While I may not have pretty references like your fancy lady's maid, I daresay I can turn you out as well as she can. Moreover, I have looked out for your best interests from the time you were born. When your papa died, I was the one who looked after you while your mama lost herself to grief. I was the one who warned her against remarrying. I was the one who tried to protect you both from Wilmington."

Although seven years had passed since Lord Calvert Wilmington's death, the mere mention of him sucked the breath from Evie's lungs. She flinched as if she were the helpless, terrified girl she'd once been.

"Do not speak of him," she said hoarsely.

"I must, lest you forget the most important lesson of all. Men are the downfall of intelligent women. Look at your poor mama. My Beatrix was so talented and beautiful, yet she fell for that scoundrel Wilmington. Mark my words, lambkin: love is just another name for folly."

Before Evie could respond, she heard familiar footsteps. She whirled around, and her heart thumped recklessly at the arrival of her husband. As ever, he was impeccable. Some men bore the mantle of their station, but James inhabited it. Every inch of him, from the gleaming waves of his bronze hair to the tips of his polished shoes, declared him a peer of the realm.

Compared to him, she looked and felt like a dowd. Hastily, she brushed back the tendrils that had escaped from her untidy plait. She tried to smooth the wrinkles from her skirts, but seeing the dirt stains, she sighed, realizing it was a lost cause.

"Good morning. I didn't know you had returned," she said awkwardly.

"I just got in," James said. "What a surprise finding you here, my dear."

Although his tone was pleasant and tinged with wry amusement, she knew him too well. His blue eyes glinted with steel, a sign of temper held in check. This surprised her. Since her hasty retreat had occurred a week ago, she'd assumed that his annoyance would have faded. Emotions generally rolled off James like water off a richly plumed duck.

"It is my habit to start work early," she said warily. "As you know."

"Your devotion to your studies is, indeed, admirable."

Was there an edge to his tone? His suaveness made it difficult to tell.

"Welcome back, my lord." Harkness's curtsy was stiff and just short of being insolent. "I was about to accompany my lady back to her rooms—"

"I'll escort my wife, Harkness," James said mildly. "You may attend to your other duties."

Harkness appeared as if she might argue. But she couldn't gainsay her employer—or admit that she didn't have much in the way of duties, other than fussing over Evie. Pinching her lips together, she marched out.

Evie thought it wise to change the topic. "Your return journey was comfortable, I take?"

"Quite." James flicked a speck from the sleeve of his Prussian blue frockcoat. "Your company would have made the trip more agreeable."

"I am, um, sorry I left. I had to take measurements of the wallflowers, which were about to bloom. I left you a note—"

"I read it."

He said nothing more, leaving his words swinging like a noose. Any response she could think of seemed like a perilous choice.

Tension bloomed, lush and suffocating. Everything left unspoken seemed to fill the space between them; she was surprised the glass panes didn't steam up with all that was held in. She rubbed her damp palms against her skirts, her heart thumping with the imperative to say something—anything—to relieve the silence.

She wished he would be angry with her. She'd survived being berated, beaten, and worse. Yet this quiet from James was devastating. He'd never looked at her this way before. With such...indifference. The coolness in his blue-grey gaze chilled her and made her feel brittle. Capable of being broken.

She wanted to tell him that she was sorry. That she didn't want to leave. That she had no choice. Yet she couldn't say any of those things without opening Pandora's box.

You cannot let James see the ugliness of who you truly are.

"Then you understand." Her voice tremored. "About the wallflowers, I mean?"

"I am not your keeper. You must do as you please."

The flash of bitterness in his expression jabbed her heart like a pin. The precise and delicate pain spread and spread.

"However, I must ask that you make preparations. The family will be arriving tomorrow."

"Your family is coming here?" she said blankly. "Who—"

"Owen is electing to stay behind. But Mama, Papa, Ethan, Xenia, Gigi and"—James's mouth curled slightly—"that Godwin fellow will be present."

"That Godwin fellow" referred to Gigi's new husband, Conrad Godwin, a notorious industrialist. Since the pair had married in haste and without her family's consent, the Harringtons had yet to make up their minds about him. Evie's impression was more favorable, which wasn't surprising since Godwin had risked his life to save hers during the kidnapping fiasco. Moreover, despite Godwin's faults, it was obvious that he was head over heels for Gigi and vice versa.

As much as Evie adored James's kin, the idea of them

descending upon Grove Hall unnerved her. Her composure was already shaky. Being around people—especially people who were kind and perceptive—would make keeping up her walls even more difficult.

"How, um, long will your family be staying?" she asked.

"They are your family as well," he said coolly. "After your hasty departure, they were concerned for your well-being. That is why they are visiting."

"I didn't mean..." Evie bit her lip as guilt propagated. "They are welcome, of course. I shall make the arrangements."

"Thank you. I won't detain you any further."

He bowed, exiting the greenhouse, and Evie was grateful. Because gazing at his departing figure, she couldn't hide her longing. Despair and desire played tug-of-war with her heart. Drawing a breath, she tamped down her emotions and left her sanctuary to prepare for the guests.

Chapter Four

"I would like to propose a toast to the hostess." Lord Marcus Harrington, the Marquess of Blackwood, raised his glass. "For the splendid repast and hospitality."

Seated next to him at the head of the table, Evie managed a smile. She was fond of her papa-in-law, who had bequeathed his looks and bearing to his heir. Age had added grey to his bronze hair and lines to his handsome countenance, and Evie imagined James would look equally distinguished with time. The marquess's manner was austere and befitting of a military hero who'd fought Boney and triumphed. He was a man of uncompromising principle, and Evie would have found him intimidating if not for his obvious devotion to his lady and their brood. In private moments with the family, his tenderness and wry humor shone through.

"To Evie," the marchioness said warmly. "Hostess extraordinaire."

Positioned beside James at the opposite end, Lady Pandora Harrington lifted her flute with her usual grace. She was the marquess's ideal counterpart: a sophisticated beauty whose gown of violet taffeta matched her peerless eyes and showed off her lush curves. Her midnight curls, touched with silver, cascaded from a topknot and brushed her smooth cheeks.

While Evie was in awe of Papa, she found the family matriarch even more daunting. Mama was blessed with beauty, brains, and a sultry charm that had made her one of London's most celebrated hostesses. With Evie, she was kind and generous, more than once offering to be a confidante. Evie had had to resist the urge to confess her secrets...to beg forgiveness when absolution was impossible. Instead, she had kept her distance. For Mama's warm nature didn't hide another attribute: she had a mind like a steel trap.

"To Evie," everyone echoed.

As the family toasted her, Evie felt like a wolf in sheep's clothing. She was an impostor and didn't deserve their appreciation or kindness. In truth, she owed *them* for sheltering her and welcoming her into their fold, and their beaming goodwill added to her guilt. She risked a glance at James. After their icy reunion, they'd been like ships in the night. He hadn't supped at home last eve. In fact, he hadn't returned until after two in the morning...not that she'd been listening for him.

What he did was his business. She had no right to interfere. She wanted them to lead separate lives, didn't she? It was safer that way. That was why she'd run after their night of intimacy: to keep him safe. His mask of civility cinched her throat. To those who didn't know him, his mood might appear cordial. She knew better. Being a gentleman, he would never air their dirty laundry in public, yet his polished indifference was somehow worse.

Tension whittled away her appetite. She'd chosen the menu with care, but none of the items—which included James's favorite herbed consommé, roast capon stuffed with chestnuts, and veal sweetbread croquettes—appealed to her. She reached instead for her wine glass.

"You shall have to tell me your secrets," Mama declared.

Evie's fingers clenched reflexively around the glass. "I...I beg your pardon?"

"Your decorating secrets, dearest." Mama cast an approving glance around the dining room. "Your style is exquisite."

Evie was glad she'd taken care with the details. The chandelier cast a warm glow over the dark-paneled walls, and nary a speck of dust appeared on the gilt-framed landscapes. The table was laid with the best Sèvres china, gleaming silverware, and sparkling crystal. Bouquets perfumed the air, and the elaborate epergne centerpiece featured a pineapple harvested from the greenhouse as well as other exotic fruits and nuts.

"Thank you," she said. "The credit must go to Hollis."

She nodded at the butler, who was in the background directing the seamless flow of service *à la Russe*. As spindly as a scarecrow, Hollis oversaw the household and kept away chaos. In fact, his wide-spaced eyes seemed never to blink, adding to his air of vigilance. Unused to garnering attention, his weathered features turned the color of beetroot.

He bowed. "My lady is too kind. I merely follow orders."

"Hollis is being modest," Evie said. "Between him and the housekeeper, I barely lift a finger."

"Now you are being modest," Mama chided.

"Not really."

The truth came with a certain relief. There was freedom in airing her shortcomings. Evie looked at her husband again, and this time their gazes met. There was a flicker in his eyes—candlelight or contempt? Whatever the case, it set off a rebellious quiver in her.

"Ask James," she heard herself say. "He will tell you."

Her husband's reply was even. "What do you wish me to say?"

Above his ruthlessly precise cravat, his jaw had a taut edge. She felt the smoldering heat of his gaze across the length of the table. It was a wonder it didn't singe the profusions of petals along the way.

"Say whatever you wish about my performance as mistress of the house," she said.

At her impulsive dare, silver blazed in James's eyes. The intense flash made her breath jam in her throat. It was gone the next instant, covered by cool, restrained blue.

"To Evie." He held up his glass. "For arranging my favorite menu, decorating our home with refinement and style, and entertaining us all with grace."

"Hear, hear, son," Papa said.

The others joined in the toast. While they didn't seem to register the subtle mockery in James's tone, Evie did. His barbed compliment struck the raw and festering part of her that she couldn't reveal to anyone. She felt sick—heartsick in a way that had no cure. What could be worse than being married to the man you loved, knowing that he despised you?

I deserve James's antipathy. I brought this on myself. This is my fault, all of it.

"How are your botany projects coming along, Evie?"

Lady Georgiana, James's youngest sibling, rescued Evie from rumination. Seated to Evie's left, Gigi was a raven-haired, violet-eyed beauty who took after her mother. She had Mama's charm, too: despite Evie's misery, she couldn't help responding to Gigi's inquisitive smile.

"My experiments have yielded some interesting results." Hesitantly, she added, "I have written a paper summarizing my research."

"How exciting. If memory serves, you have discovered a new varietal of some sort?"

Touched that her sister-in-law remembered, Evie nodded. "Yes, I found a subspecies of the *Cheiranthus cheiri*—the common wallflower—growing on the estate. I have been studying its properties and believe it to be unique to the Berkshire Downs."

"How is your wallflower different from others?"

Unable to resist, Evie launched into her favorite topic.

"The blossoms come earlier and are white rather than the usual brighter shades such as gold and purple. What piqued my interest was the strong fragrance this varietal exudes at dusk, which is not typical for *Cheiranthus cheiri*. I began observing it at night and noticed a most intriguing phenomenon."

"Do tell us, Evie." The entreaty came from Xenia, Ethan's lovely redheaded wife.

"It is well known that bees assist in pollination during the day," Evie said. "However, there may be more to the story of fertilization. When I observed my wallflower, I noticed its corolla was closed for most of the day and unfurled at twilight—"

"Corolla?" Gigi's brow pleated.

"I meant the flower's petals." Flushing, Evie reminded herself that this was polite company and not a meeting of her scientific society. "In other words, the flower blooms when the sun sets. Which begs an obvious question, does it not?"

She looked expectantly at her guests; they gazed back blankly.

James came to her rescue. "Bees are only active during the day. Therefore, if your flower blooms at night," he said mildly, "how does it get pollinated?"

Gratitude flooded Evie. Admiration, too. Despite looking like a fashion plate from some gentleman's magazine, her husband was no intellectual slouch.

"That is what I asked myself," she said with a nod.

"And do you have answers?" Gigi wanted to know.

"I have a theory. It may seem far-fetched—"

"Consider your audience, Evie dear," Mama said with a charming laugh. "If you were to say that your wallflower was pollinated by fairies, we would have half a mind to believe you."

"In that case...moths," Evie blurted. "I think moths may play a role."

She held her breath. When she'd tested the waters by sharing her theory with a few select peers in her society, they'd guffawed. Lord Grantwich, a senior member, had patted her on the head, chuckling, *"How very droll, Lady Manderly. Moths pollinating, indeed. When it comes to the garden, we all know those drab creatures are nothing more than pests."*

"How did you arrive at that conclusion?" Xenia asked.

"I've observed *Sphinx ligustri*...the Privet hawk-moth, I mean, visiting my wallflowers. They arrive at dusk when the blooms are unfurling. For some reason, the moths prefer one patch over the others. Over several months, I recorded my observations and noticed that the wallflowers in that area blossomed more prodigiously—twice as much, in fact—as the other sections."

"What a clever deduction." Gigi canted her head. "I wonder if moths pollinate other night-blooming flowers? In our garden at Honeystone Hall, we have several beds of evening primroses. Have you noticed any moths hovering about, Mr. Godwin?"

The last question was aimed at her new husband, who was seated across the table from her. Sleek as a panther in his evening wear, Conrad Godwin was a dashing blond fellow who had a reputation for ruthlessness. Indeed, a few months ago, he had attempted to destroy Chuddums as an act of revenge. Gigi, a steadfast champion of the village and its quirky inhabitants, had locked horns with him, and the pair had ended up falling passionately in love. It amused and reassured Evie to see the powerful Godwin gazing at his bride with undisguised adoration.

"I wasn't aware that we had primroses, duchess." Godwin looked amused. "I'm not the sort of fellow who stops to smell the flowers."

"Maybe you ought to," Gigi said lightly.

"I have no objection to exploring the outdoors with you, my sweet. In fact, it has become one of my favorite hobbies," he drawled.

Evie sensed the flirtatious undertone. Gigi confirmed this by turning a telling shade of pink. Xenia smothered a giggle, and Mama's lips were quivering.

Ethan, James's handsome middle brother, sighed. He had dark hair, indigo eyes, and the sort of brooding intensity one associated with artists. Indeed, he'd once been a renowned piano maestro, whose career had been tragically ended by an injury to his hand.

Since his marriage to Xenia, he'd taken up composing music, and he'd never looked happier.

Ethan lifted his brows. "Must we be subjected to the two of you flirting like newlyweds?"

"We *are* newlyweds. What is your excuse for flirting with Xenia?" Gigi retorted.

Ethan shrugged. "It is not my fault. If you must blame anyone, blame Xenia."

"Me? Why?" his wife squeaked.

"Well, it is your fault, pet. For being irresistible."

He flashed a wicked grin, and Xenia's cheeks turned as red as her hair.

"Really, Ethan," she protested. "What will everyone think of us?"

"They will think that I learned the art of flirtation from the best." Ethan paused, before adding innocently, "Didn't I, Papa?"

"Do not drag me into this, son."

At Papa's grimace, Mama pealed with laughter.

"Come now, Marcus," she teased. "You are charming with the ladies. Admit it."

"Only with you," he replied gravely. "My own lucky Penny."

When she blew him a kiss, the marquess lost his stoicism, responding with a lazy smile that made Evie's heart pitter-patter. Once upon a time, James had smiled at her in that fashion. But he hadn't done so for months...not since the loss. Not since she'd been forced to accept that she was cursed by the sin she'd unknowingly committed—and if she wasn't careful, she might bring James down with her.

"Marrying for love is the Harrington way," Gigi said brightly. "As family traditions go, we could do worse."

"A lot worse." Godwin's tone was wry. "Trust me on this."

Given what Evie knew about Godwin's bloodthirsty lineage, she couldn't disagree.

"*We* are your family now, darling," Gigi said. "Therefore, our traditions are yours."

The tender look Godwin bestowed upon his wife caused a collective sigh.

Evie made the mistake of glancing at James. He'd been silent during the banter, and his gaze was trained on his wine glass. Twin furrows dug between his brows, and Evie could read his thoughts.

If every Harrington marries for love, how did I get so unlucky?

Anguish trickled through her, chilling her heart. The chasm between them felt vast and insurmountable. Surrounded by couples blissfully in love, she had never felt more alone.

"What about you, dear boy?" Mama was also watching her eldest, her gaze astute despite her light tone. "As we are celebrating love, haven't you anything to add?"

The playful and unsubtle nudge had Evie squirming in her seat.

"Some matters are meant to be private, Mama," James said.

His curtness fell like ashes on a fire, snuffing out the merriment in the room.

After a taut pause, Mama murmured, "Forgive me, dearest—"

"There's naught to forgive. Ah, here comes the pineapple gelée, another favorite of mine." James changed the topic, his tone as pleasant and bloodless as if he were discussing the weather. "Evie grew the fruit herself. You must try it."

After supper, the others withdrew to the drawing room. It was Evie's duty to preside over the post-prandial entertainment, but she simply couldn't bear it. Taking Mama aside, she made her excuses.

"A megrim?" Worry shone in Mama's eyes. "It is not surprising, given the stress of what you and Gigi recently endured. Have you seen a physician—"

"There's no need," Evie said quickly. "I am merely tired."

"My maid has a splendid remedy for headaches. Shall I have her mix up a batch?"

"That is unnecessary. A quick nap will, um, set me to rights."

"Get some rest, then. Don't worry about us; we are perfectly capable of entertaining ourselves." Mama paused. "In truth, we should not have intruded, but we were concerned after your abrupt departure from Bottoms House."

With a guilty pang, Evie said, "It was ever so rude of me. But my experiments—"

"You needn't apologize." Mama placed a gentle hand on her cheek. "I hate to interfere, but I must ask...is everything all right?"

She knows. She knows my marriage is a fiasco...that I make James unhappy.

Shame and self-loathing cinched Evie's throat.

Swallowing, she said, "All is...all is as it should be."

The compassion in Mama's violet gaze was almost more than she could bear.

"Go rest," Mama murmured. "If you ever wish to talk, I am here."

Evie fled but not to her bedchamber. Instead, she headed to the greenhouse, where the lush, shadowed silence felt like a reprieve. She could lose herself here, perhaps make further progress on her experiments. During supper, an idea had come to her that she wanted to explore...

As she approached her desk, she saw that the lamp on its surface was flickering even though she could have sworn she'd doused it. Not only that, but her leather-bound journal—the one where she recorded her observations—was lying open. She would never treat her work so carelessly, and frowning, she rushed over...

When she saw the plant clipping that lay upon the open page, her heart jammed in her throat. The purple, bell-shaped flower and trio of pointed leaves looked pretty and harmless, but she knew better. *Atropa belladonna,* deadly nightshade, was the most lethal of poisons. The words, inked boldly on the page beneath the cutting, were equally venomous:

Accidents happen when you least expect it—especially around you, dearest Evie. You know that better than anyone, don't you?

The past rose and enveloped Evie like a cold, dense fog. She tried to breathe, but she was suffocating, smothered by everything she remembered...and everything she did not. Blackness wavered at the edges of her vision, splintering into dots. As her knees buckled, she caught herself against the desk.

Who wrote this? What do they know? What do they want?

Panic swamped her as she gazed wildly around the greenhouse. The flickering wall sconces and faint moonlight revealed that she was alone: the only movement came from the occasional sway of fronds.

"Evie?"

She spun around and saw James striding toward her. He halted inches away, close enough for her to see the lines slashing around his mouth and anger blazing in his eyes.

"What the devil is going on?" he bit out.

Chapter Five

Finding Evie hiding in the greenhouse caused something to snap inside James.

Supper had been an ordeal. All his life, he had striven to be worthy of his family legacy. He lived by principles of honor, duty, and fidelity. He had dedicated himself to his roles as heir, brother, and husband because he believed that was the right thing to do and the path to fulfillment. Yet there at the supper table, surrounded by the people closest to him, he'd come to an ugly realization.

He wasn't fulfilled. He wasn't even happy. Even though he'd done everything right, the true Blackwood tradition eluded him: his marriage was not a love match.

Not even close.

As he'd observed the banter and intimacy between the other couples, a chilly awareness had percolated through him. He had been deceiving himself...for *years*. He'd told himself that he and Evie had what the others had: their version of love was merely more private. He'd convinced himself that, because Evie was shy when it came to personal matters, she felt what she might not say aloud.

She expressed affection in her own way. By running his home with smooth competence. By being a good companion. By supporting him when his youngest brother Owen had returned from the Afghan war a different man—a man haunted by demons that had hurt others, Ethan most grievously. As hard as James tried, there had been naught he could do to help his brothers mend fences. Nor could he ease the suffering of his other family members, who had felt the pain of Owen and Ethan's estrangement keenly.

James's failure had filled him with guilt and frustration. If it hadn't been for Evie, for her steady presence and calm counsel, he would have been rudderless in a stormy sea. He'd been infinitely grateful, and her patience and care had felt to him like love. So what if she seldom said those three little words so commonly associated with devotion? He'd told himself that that was what words were: common.

During the two tumultuous affairs he'd had as a bachelor, the phrase "I love you" had been bandied about—by the women and, he'd acknowledged with embarrassment, by him. He'd said them because that seemed to be the expectation...to be part of the game that his lovers had enjoyed playing. In the end, the words had meant nothing: they were a cheap and trite approximation of the real thing.

Behavior was what counted. With Evie, he'd persuaded himself that he had found true substance. Her actions demonstrated her love for him. They had a genuine bond, the kind that kept a couple together through thick and thin, through sickness and health. And that was enough.

But it's not. It never has been. I've been pulling the wool over my own bloody eyes.

The realization staggered him. It also ripped off the blinders he'd donned for the better part of the year. The truth was Evie had abandoned the pretense of having any interest in him or their life together. She had withdrawn so completely that she was a mere shadow in their marriage. His rationale that her behavior was a natural reaction to grief still held...but for God's sake, it had to end sometime. Enough was enough.

"I thought you had a megrim," he said.

"I, um, did." She bit her lip. "I thought work might prove a distraction."

"Of course." He didn't hide his bitterness. "You find joy in your experiments, but entertaining the family is an obligation. You must suffer through their company until you can make your escape."

"No. That's not it at all—"

"Then tell me how it is, Evie."

He gave her the challenging stare that he usually reserved for political rivals who argued for the status quo. Who buried their heads in the sand and refused to acknowledge the winds of change.

"Tell me," he repeated. "Mama is so concerned that she sent me to check up on you. However, I find you not in your bedchamber but here—buried in your blasted journal instead of carrying out your duties as the lady of the house. Is spending time with the family that repugnant to you?"

The memory of his mama's troubled expression scalded his throat.

"Something is amiss with Evie," she'd said. *"I know how much you value privacy, dearest, but I must ask: are the two of you experiencing some sort of difficulty? You can talk to me about it...or Papa, of course. As he and I have been married for millennia, we have considerable expertise when it comes to marital spats."*

His mama's attempt at lightheartedness hadn't dimmed James's humiliation. He'd thought that his personal problems were inconspicuous—that no one was aware of the distance between him and Evie. Yet Mama had noticed their unhappiness, a fact she'd undoubtedly shared with Papa. Perhaps his siblings also suspected that something was rotten in the state of his marriage.

As the heir, James was supposed to be the role model. Leadership had always come naturally for him, and he'd prided himself on following in his father's footsteps and setting a good example for his brothers. To know that his failure was obvious to one and all came as a nasty blow.

"How could you even suggest such a thing? I like your family... very much. You know that."

Evie's gaze swam. It took every ounce of his willpower not to cave to her pleading expression. His reflex was to smooth things over—to not press her further when it caused her obvious discomfort. Yet what had leaving Evie to her own devices achieved thus far? To his irritation, he saw that her hand remained protectively upon her closed journal, a gesture that conveyed her priorities.

He shook his head in disgust. "I am beginning to think I do not know you at all."

"What...what do you mean?"

Her bottom lip trembled, and he recalled how full and plush it had felt when he'd licked it. When she'd kissed him after the kidnapping as if her life depended upon it...as if she'd genuinely wanted him. The bolt of lust made him angrier. He'd been trying his damnedest to make their marriage work, yet Evie seemed unaware...or indifferent. It was like trying to waltz with a partner who dragged her feet getting to the dance floor.

"Let us give up the pretense," he said sharply. "I have been coddling you for the past year. Since we lost the babe."

Her sharp inhalation stabbed him with guilt, but he was done with allowing her to hide. With pretending that everything was as it should be when nothing—not one bloody thing—was right between them.

"I understand the loss was difficult. However, you cannot avoid me and our life because of it. I will not allow it."

The tears she'd held back slipped down her cheeks, making him feel like a veritable scoundrel. Every gentlemanly instinct demanded that he stand down—that he retreat and give her the space to manage her emotions in private.

"You will not *allow* it?" she echoed.

"It has been a year." He tried softening his stance. "These things happen, and we must move forward. We are young, Evie, and have a future ahead of us—"

"We have no future."

Her vehemence took him aback.

Frowning, he said, "The physician said you are perfectly healthy. As am I. There is no reason we cannot—"

"There are so many reasons, James."

Her laugh, a hollow and mirthless sound, raised the hairs on his neck. Her eyes turned as hard and opaque as bark. She didn't seem like the woman he married...the woman he thought he knew.

"We were never meant to be together." She said it almost casually. "You know that, don't you?"

"I know no such thing." Despite the trepidation slithering through him, he kept his manner firm. "You are overtired. Still recovering from the shock of the attack and now there is an onslaught of visitors. Perhaps I ought to have waited for a more opportune time to bring up—"

"Now is as good a time as any. In truth, I left things too long."

At her dismissive tone, his temper rekindled.

"What *things*?" he said acidly.

A breath passed. A heartbeat.

"Our marriage was a mistake," she said.

Pain pierced Evie to the quick as she lied to the man she loved and saw his gathering wrath. He was going to hate her before all was said and done.

I must keep him safe, no matter the cost. I cannot let my past threaten his future...his life.

The threat was no longer an abstract fear but a real one, indelibly inked in her journal.

Accidents happen when you least expect it—especially around you, dearest Evie.

Years of guilt morphed into paralyzing anxiety. She risked a glance at her journal. How innocuous it seemed lying amidst pencils and plant cuttings, a sprinkling of soil. Yet it was like a gunpowder charge used to blast tunnels for railways: once ignited, it could bring her life crashing down over her head.

Who knows my secret? What do they want? Why now?

The questions raged, yet she had to shove them aside to deal with her husband.

A muscle ticked along James's jaw. "The bloody hell it was."

"I told you from the start that I am not suited for this sort of arrangement." This was true and allowed her to keep her gaze level. "For intimacy with another."

"You didn't seem to mind the intimacy when I tupped you senseless a week ago."

Lust flamed against her skin. She couldn't stop herself from blushing. From wanting.

"I am not referring to the physical aspect of our relationship, although it is ungentlemanly of you to mention that occasion," she said primly.

"Pardon my rudeness. It was a reflexive reaction to being told by my wife that our marriage was a mistake."

If sarcasm could drip, he would have flooded the greenhouse. With his hands braced on his hips and his gaze stormy, he was clearly itching for a fight. Now *that*...that she could give him. Marriage was an education, after all, and after nearly four years, she knew how to play upon his sensibilities.

If I must drive him away with anger, then so be it. Anything to keep him safe.

"Look at your family. Then look at us," she said briskly. "If marrying for love is the family tradition, then it is one that skipped you."

He jerked as if she'd slapped him. Then his outrage blazed, brighter than the sun, reminding her of her first impression of him: Apollo, the Greek god of light and order. Golden, perfect and admired by all, James demanded the best of himself and those around him. He valued civility and restraint, yet when crossed, his passions could be riled and lethal.

"What happened to you, Evie?" he clipped out. "What turned you cold? Was it losing the babe—"

"Perhaps that was nature's way of rectifying something that should not have happened in the first place."

She regretted the vile statement even as she forced her tongue around it. Not because of the grief that lanced her heart: that festering, unwavering certainty that she had deserved to lose the precious life she'd been given. No, her remorse was for the pain that contorted James's features. He looked as if she'd gutted him.

I'm sorry. Forgive me. This is the only way.

Her heart bleeding, she kept her face composed.

"If that is how you feel," James said, his hands clenched, his voice vibrating with quiet, barely leashed rage, "then there is nothing left to say. Our union *was* a mistake. I misjudged you. When we met, I believed you to be a different woman than the one who stands before me now."

She took the blow wordlessly, emotionlessly. Numbness was her shield.

"However, the fact remains that we are bound for life and share a roof over our heads. As a measure of courtesy, I suggest we steer clear of one another until I can come up with a more permanent solution."

He strode out. Only the slamming of the door, which rattled the fragile panes, betrayed his fury. She took trembling breaths to tamp down her sobs. A wild hope struck her: could she have possibly misread the threat? Grabbing her spectacles from the desk, she donned them and reopened the journal to the page...

The poisonous cutting and words remained, swimming in her vision.

Merciful blooms. What am I going to do?

Chapter Six

Past

James left the stuffy ballroom, wishing he had not accepted Lord and Lady Thurston's invitation to celebrate the return of their scion, Thaddeus, from the Grand Tour. The affair was loud and packed, and he was in no mood to socialize. Earlier this week, Melanie Orneville, James's lover of nearly a year, had ended their liaison rather dramatically: she'd flung a book at his head—Macaulay's substantive volume, *The History of England from the Accession of James the Second*, no less. While she'd done no physical damage, she'd staged her theatrics at one of the busiest bookshops in London, probably because she knew how much he detested public displays.

His lack of feeling had been one of her many complaints about him.

While James couldn't claim that Melanie had broken his heart, she *had* shattered his faith in his ability to choose lovers suited to his temperament. His mistress before her had also bemoaned his insensitivity—"an uncaring clod," she'd called him for his indifference when other men flirted with her. Contrary to her accusation, he was not incapable of jealousy; he simply hadn't cared about her dalliances because there had been so many. If she understood him even a little, she would know that he was not one to wear his emotions on his sleeve. His papa was much the same way and shared a long and famously happy marriage with Mama.

Ergo, James was not overly worried. He simply had to find the right sort of female to be his lover...and when the time came, his wife. At thirty, he was beginning to wonder if the inclination to wed would ever feel more like a desire and less like duty. While there was nothing wrong with duty, he liked to think that, as the heir, he would uphold the family tradition of marrying for love.

Perhaps I am too pragmatic to fall in love. To lose myself in another. Perhaps I am too particular to believe that any woman could be my perfect soulmate.

He shook aside the thoughts which, for him, edged uncomfortably close to maudlin territory. He had no reason to feel sorry for himself. He was in his prime, with duty and purpose to occupy him. Rather than brooding over romantic misadventures, he should focus on managing his land and investments and supporting the reformist policies he believed in. However, he couldn't muster the enthusiasm to defend the repeal of the Corn Laws yet again this evening. It was obvious to him that tariffs designed to enrich wealthy landowners at the expense of the working class had no place in a just society, and he was tired of arguing the point.

As Lord Thurston had boasted about the new greenhouse he'd built for his lady, a noted horticulturist, James decided to take a break from the melee and have a look. The beginning strains of a waltz emptied the corridors, and he walked briskly. Truly, he'd exercised poor judgment in coming to this crush when what he longed for was a glass of whisky, a book, and some blessed peace.

Passing a gallery of gilt-framed portraits, he arrived at the greenhouse. The waft of cool, citrus-scented air was a welcome contrast to the stuffiness of the ballroom. His leather soles slapped quietly against the tile floors, the sound muffled by the lush greenery that flanked the winding path. It was like embarking upon a tropical adventure, with discoveries lurking around every corner. Amused at the fanciful notion, he ventured deeper...

"Unhand me."

He stilled at the low, female hiss.

"Don't be coy, sweeting. We are alone. You've been making eyes at me ever since I returned home."

James recognized that drawl. It belonged to Lord Thaddeus, Thurston's heir. In his early twenties, he already had a reputation for being a rake. He was handsome and rich, oozing the sort of charm that James found insincere but which seemed to attract females like flies to honey. Was the present woman Thaddeus's latest inamorata? Was she merely playing the part of a coquette?

"Keep your distance. I am warning you."

"You ladies enjoy your games, don't you?" The lordling's voice was indulgent. "A tease before the tickle. Now be a good girl and show me what you've been hiding beneath that prim get-up, hmm?"

As James stood there, uncertain if he ought to intervene, a high-pitched scream pierced the dense wall of foliage. It mobilized him, and he sprinted toward the sound. He saw them standing by the windows: Lord Thaddeus, holding his right hand, from which a thin line of blood trickled...and the woman.

She was a pretty, plump blonde. Her unfussy hairstyle and plain dress conveyed her status as slightly above that of a servant, most likely a governess or companion. She had a pair of gold spectacles perched on her nose and looked harmless...except for the ivory-handled penknife she wielded.

"Pardon," James said.

Both heads swung in his direction.

"Are you all right, miss?" he asked.

She stared at him, clearly taking his measure. Behind the lenses of her spectacles, her eyes were a rich whisky-brown and would be rounded in shape, he guessed, if they weren't narrowed in suspicion. She didn't loosen her grip on the penknife.

"I mean you no harm," he said. "I came to offer assistance since I heard you cry out."

"That wasn't me," she said.

Her voice was steady, almost detached. They might have been discussing the weather. Yet noticing the bone-white of her knuckles and the rapid surges of her bosom, he felt a tightening in his chest.

Turning to Lord Thaddeus, he raised his brows. "That was you, sir?"

"The ill-bred creature stabbed me, Manderly," Thaddeus snapped. "She drew blood."

"Here." James offered his handkerchief. "Wrap it with this."

Thaddeus snatched the linen and bound it clumsily around his hand, which James noted had already stopped bleeding.

"You're going to be sorry for this, Evelyn Ashewood." Red-faced with outrage, Thaddeus glared at the blonde. "You have worked your last day under this roof and that of any respectable household. By the time I am finished, no one will hire you. You will never find employment in London again."

The woman—Miss Ashewood—said nothing. She kept her chin up and shoulders back, and she didn't let go of the knife. A warm sensation spread in James...admiration, he realized. For her pride and courage.

"Do you really think threatening this lady is necessary?" James inquired.

Thaddeus shifted his pale and spiteful gaze to James.

"She is a household employee and she attacked *me*, her master," he spat.

"You are not my master." Miss Ashewood spoke up, her voice trembling. "I work for Lady Thurston. And I did not attack you: I acted in defense of my virtue when you would not take no for an answer."

Thaddeus sneered. "Why would I bother with you, you common chit? I have my pick of the *crème de la crème*—ladies with beauty, breeding, and fortune. No one would believe that I would take an interest in a nobody like you."

"Nonetheless, it is true."

Touched by Miss Ashewood's raw dignity, James cut in.

"Why not let bygones be bygones, sir," he said. "There is no use in sullying Miss Ashewood's reputation."

"Are you defending the blasted female?"

The scoundrel had the gall to act like the wounded party. Perhaps he even believed he was. James was acquainted with Thaddeus's sort: cads so accustomed to privilege that any deviation from their desires felt like an assault on their liberties.

"I heard the lady refuse your advances," James said evenly. "She asked that you unhand her and warned you to steer clear. You did neither."

The color rose on Thaddeus's high cheekbones. "Think carefully, Manderly. Is our friendship, the friendship between my family and yours, worth sacrificing for the likes of her? I am giving you the chance to walk away. To enjoy the party my parents are throwing. I do believe Mama plans to do some matchmaking as well. You've met my lovely cousin Lavinia, the Duke of Stafford's eldest daughter?"

James had met Lady Lavinia and partnered her for a polka. She had looks and fortune...and was blander than a bowl of blancmange. She was also entirely beside the point.

"I think it would be best if you attended to your guests," he said. "This ball is, after all, being thrown in your honor. There is no reason for a celebration to end in scandal, is there?"

Thaddeus gnashed his teeth. "Have it your way. Our friendship is over, do you hear me? I hope she is worth it." He stomped toward the exit, pivoting to deliver a parting shot. "Rescue her all you like, but she's not the sort to part her legs in gratitude. She's colder than a nun in winter."

James waited for the door to slam before addressing Miss Ashewood.

"My deepest apologies," he said.

"You needn't apologize, sir," she replied quietly. "You came to my assistance."

"Forgive my manners." Bowing, he did the formalities. "James Harrington, the Earl of Manderly, at your service."

"Miss Evelyn Ashewood." Her curtsy was as neat and unaffected as she was. "I am Lady Thurston's companion. Or was, rather." She exhaled shakily. "After tonight, I shall no doubt be given my marching orders."

"Lord Thaddeus will not speak of what transpired. Self-incrimination is not his style."

"You probably have the right of it," Miss Ashewood muttered.

Then she folded the penknife, a sign of trust that warmed James. When she removed her spectacles, tucking them and the tool into the pocket of her skirts, he nearly smiled. What an unusual little creature.

"Lady Thurston believes everything her son says." Miss Ashewood's long lashes veiled her eyes. "In her estimation, he can do no wrong. He will find a way to be rid of me...but no matter. After tonight, I have no desire to stay. I will find employment elsewhere."

James found the injustice of the situation intolerable. "I will speak to the Thurstons, if you wish. Bear witness to what happened."

She lifted her lashes, confirming his suspicion. Her eyes were rounded in shape and uncommonly large. With her spectacles removed, he saw flecks of gold in her rich brown irises.

"Why would you do that?" Twin furrows appeared between her straight brows. "You don't even know me."

His offer of assistance clearly puzzled her, her honesty tugging at his chest. What had this young woman been through to expect so little from the world? He was merely acting as any gentleman of honor should.

He kept his tone light. "I know you are industrious and organized enough to carry a penknife. To open an urgent letter, for instance. Or to defend yourself against an entitled bounder."

She stared at him. Then, slowly, her lips curved. He found himself dazzled...and he wasn't a fellow prone to losing his equilibrium. Yet her warmth was so unexpected, her beauty so pure and natural that his breath jammed, his heart stumbling against his ribs.

"It is not a penknife," she said. "It's a pruning tool."

"All right," he said after a moment. "I shall bite."

His choice of words betrayed his sudden awareness that Miss Evelyn Ashewood was a toothsome creature. He had a baffling urge to nibble on her full lips, the dainty curve of her ear. Despite its prudish cut, her gown didn't hide the tempting fullness of her bosom. Would her skin feel as silky as it looked? He flashed to an image of himself kissing his way down her tender neck and décolletage, planting a little love bite atop the firm swell of her breast...

Bloody hell, what is the matter with me? She is the hired companion of my hostess, for God's sake. Am I no better than that blasted skirt-chaser Thaddeus?

"Why do you carry a pruning tool?" he added hastily.

"Lady Thurston enjoys horticulture. Assisting her with her hobby is a part of my duties. In truth, it is the reason I took this job."

Her wistfulness was nearly as enchanting as her smile. By Jove, what was it about this female? If he were honest, she was neither the prettiest nor the liveliest of his acquaintance, and yet...and yet she struck a chord in him that no woman had before. The awareness had him reeling. It also made him suddenly, inexplicably certain that he wanted to know more about her.

"You enjoy working with plants, Miss Ashewood?" he asked.

"It is my passion. My mama..." She hesitated. "She was an

herbalist and taught me many things. She passed when I was fourteen."

"I am sorry to hear it. Have you other family?"

She bit her lip and shook her head. When she didn't elaborate, he didn't press.

"I am certain you would like to return to the party, my lord," she said. "I should be moving along as well."

He'd nearly forgotten the ball. That was how singular this encounter was for him. Alone with Miss Evelyn Ashewood, he felt as if the rest of the world had dropped away. Yet proprieties were proprieties, and he wouldn't rescue a lady only to compromise her.

He bowed. "It has been a pleasure, Miss Ashewood."

"The pleasure was mine." Her smile was sweet and shy, so captivating that his heart thumped helplessly and his groin flooded with heat. "Although we probably will not meet again, I shan't forget tonight."

She bobbed a curtsy before heading off. He remained, standing alone in the moonlit jungle, bemused and strangely elated. Perhaps the family tradition hadn't skipped him after all.

And Miss Evelyn Ashewood was wrong.

She would see him again...and soon.

Chapter Seven

"Have you come up with a name for the varietal you discovered?" Gigi asked.

On her way to check on the wallflowers in the garden, Evie ran into her sisters-in-law, who'd promptly invited themselves along. Their company was a charming distraction she desperately needed. She'd barely slept last night; the belladonna clipping, threatening note, and row with James had kept her tossing and turning. She didn't know what to do...how to protect her husband.

Whoever knew about her past clearly meant to cause trouble. But what did they want? Did they intend to blackmail her—for money or some other nefarious end?

In the gloomy hours before dawn, Evie had paced her bedchamber, trying to plan her strategy. If money was what they wanted, she had funds. James was a generous husband. She hadn't come to him with a dowry—with much of anything—but he'd given her everything she needed. And luxuries that she didn't need or deserve. Clothing, jewels...and gracious earth, even a greenhouse. On top of that, he provided her with so much pin money that she barely made a dent in it.

Nevertheless, paying off a blackmailer did not seem like the wisest idea. Wouldn't the villain just want more? By acquiescing to the demands, Evie would sink deeper into trouble. She was reminded of the time when, against her mama's warning, she'd ventured too deep in a swimming hole. A vortex had sucked her in, and she'd flailed desperately, trying to stay afloat, to keep her head above the water...

Luckily, Harkness had found her in time and fished her out. Now, there was naught her companion could do for her. In fact, she hadn't told Harkness about the note. If she had, the other would have put them on the first train to some faraway destination, with no return ticket.

Evie swallowed. She would leave James only as a last resort—if there was nothing else she could do to protect him from her past. She could bear his anger, even his hate. But she didn't know if she could bear being separated from him forever.

"Um, Evie?"

At Gigi's gentle prompting, Evie yanked her focus back to the present company.

"Pardon my woolgathering." She mustered a smile. "You were saying?"

"I was asking if you had named your wallflower."

In her walking dress of ivory wool bordered with lavender ribbon, Gigi looked as delicate as the snowdrops they passed. In fact, she matched the freshness of the garden that Evie had had a hand in designing. Together with the landscape architect, she'd chosen plants to highlight the beauty of every season. She had the benefit of Grove Hall's location: nestled on a warm, protected slope of the Berkshire Downs, the estate was already in the throes of spring. Primroses and celandine were showing off their bright petals, and the wallflowers had unfurled last week.

"As a matter of fact, I have," Evie replied. "What do you think of *Cheiranthus cheiri, variety vespertinus*?"

"It is rather a mouthful." Xenia's eyes twinkled in the shade of her bonnet. Dressed in a forest green ensemble that complemented her red curls and creamy complexion, she was as vibrant as spring itself. "May we call it Vesper for short?"

"Yes, I like it. And the 'evening wallflower' could be its common name." Shyly, Evie added, "Whilst I have discussed my research with colleagues, I hope to present the paper I have written at a Botanical Society meeting one day. But women are rarely invited to take the lectern. Or considered for the ultimate honor of publication in the Society's journal."

"I cannot think of a more deserving candidate than you. Heavens, you discovered your very own flower." Gigi twirled her parasol with delicate gloved fingers. "And its unique process of...um, what did you call it?"

"Pollination."

"Most people overlook wallflowers—and certainly the moths that pollinate them. How did you happen to notice it?"

Because I observe the things that go unnoticed. I know what it is like to be overlooked.

An image flashed in Evie's head: her fourteen-year-old self, dressed in black, hiding in the garden after her mama's funeral. In the hedgerows, she'd sought shelter from the pitying glances and trite condolences. She didn't want to be told that she would see her mama again one day...she wanted to be with her *now*. She didn't want to be alone because that was what she was, no matter what people said. And they said things—things she wasn't meant to hear. Because she was so good at making herself invisible, they didn't see her listening from the shadows.

"That poor child. Such an odd, plain little creature. Didn't get Beatrix's looks, did she?"

"Alas, with no looks and no money, what is to become of her?"

"She is fortunate to have Lord Wilmington. Although he is her stepfather, he will settle a dowry upon her, I'm certain. After all, marrying her mama replenished his estate..."

As the months passed, Evie withdrew into the garden. The

plants became her companions, for they didn't care that she was plain and penniless. Moreover, her botanical passion felt like a connection to her mama. Evie was fascinated by every aspect of the flora—how the plants adapted and survived with thorns, camouflage, and even...poison.

Shivering, Evie shut the door on the past.

"I am an observer by nature, I suppose." She cleared her throat. "As a girl, I spent a lot of time in the garden and spotted the moths that arrived at dusk. I remembered thinking they looked like tiny ghosts hovering above the evening primroses."

"Speaking of ghosts and gardens." Gigi's violet eyes twinkled. "When I was a girl, Owen told me a story about a specter that roamed Great Windsor Park at night. He was apparently a soldier who was supposed to deliver a message but died before he could do so. Now his spirit haunts the park, trying to get the missive to its rightful owner." She gave a delicate shudder. "I was afraid to go into our garden for months. You were much braver than I was, visiting your garden at night."

I wasn't brave. I was just more scared of the monster inside the manor than any that might exist outside.

"Must we talk about ghosts?" Xenia's voice was wry. "I was rather enjoying a break from the supernatural."

Evie didn't blame her, for Chuddums had its own resident phantom. For decades, the locals had blamed the village's misfortunes—from its economic woes to its criminal element—upon "Bloody Thom," said to be the ghost of former resident Thomas Mulligan. The scholar had lived there nearly a hundred years ago and had been found murdered in his home...which happened to be Bottoms House, Xenia and Ethan's residence. The legend blamed his death upon a witch, who'd supposedly cursed him and the village.

Through a series of adventures, Xenia and Ethan had discovered that certain sightings of Bloody Thom had been a hoax perpetuated by cutthroats for felonious gain. Nonetheless, the spirit of Thomas Mulligan *was* real: both Xenia and Gigi had had dreams about him and his lover, which led them to unearth clues about what had really happened all those years ago. It was as though the lost lovers had reached out to those destined to bring their love home...

When Xenia and Ethan were courting, they had made the first discovery: the woman in Thomas Mulligan's life wasn't a witch but a beautiful young woman named Rosalinda, who belonged to a traveling family. Thomas and his "darling Rose" fell in love, but they'd been pursued by a dangerous enemy who wanted Rose for himself. During Gigi and Mr. Godwin's romance, they had discovered Rose's journal, which included the revelation that she and Thomas had married in secret before his death.

"Personally, I adore the story of Thomas and Rosalinda," Gigi said.

"You've certainly made good use of it." Xenia's smile was affectionate. "By spreading word of their romantic legend in London, you've helped bring visitors back to Chuddums, and local businesses are thriving. There is a waiting list for water bottled from Miss Letty's spring because you suggested it might be a love potion."

"That was clever of you, Gigi," Evie said with admiration.

"There *is* something magical about Chuddums," Gigi averred. "I want to do everything in my power to restore the village to its former glory."

"Your power is formidable, especially when it comes to Mr. Godwin," Xenia said. "Since you encouraged him to embrace the role of landowner, he has made significant improvements to the square. Rumors are flying that he may construct a hospital and a theatre. Is there anything he will not do for you, dear?"

"If there is, I haven't discovered it." Gigi spoke impishly, glowing in the manner of a woman who knows she is loved. "I am not the only one with an indulgent husband. If you asked, Ethan would pluck the moon from the sky for you."

Xenia blushed. "I am so lucky."

"And James would do the same for you, Evie," Gigi added.

Evie felt a swift and sudden blow to the heart. Her mask of composure slipped.

"What is amiss, dear?" Xenia asked with concern. "Do you need to sit?"

Evie shook her head, uncertain she could speak without breaking into tears. Without making a fool of herself—or worse yet, giving herself away. Her thoughts whirled, and she didn't have the wherewithal to resist when her sisters-in-law led her to a garden bench. They sat her between them, and in the dappled shade of a *Prunus domestica*, Evie tried to pull herself together.

"I-I'm sorry." She scrambled to come up with an excuse. "I'm not feeling well. I...I may have overindulged at breakfast."

She prayed a feigned case of indigestion would throw them off her scent.

"Stuff and nonsense," Gigi declared.

Then again, maybe it won't.

"Something is afoot with you," Gigi went on. "You haven't been yourself since the kidnapping—"

"Gigi, dear," Xenia murmured. "We talked about this. Have a care."

"I do care," Gigi countered. "Treading on eggshells will get us nowhere. If Evie is experiencing distress, then she ought to talk about it. I was there too, after all. Who better to understand what it is like to fear for one's own life?"

"I have a rather keen understanding myself," Xenia said.

Evie knew that Xenia had endured a cruel upbringing at the hands of her mother, an infamous cutthroat. Yet Xenia was a survivor of evil...not a perpetrator of it.

"Well, that's my point. Evie can talk to us because we will understand." Gigi took Evie's hand and squeezed it. "Trust us, dear."

"I do."

It wasn't a lie. Evie did trust them...but she didn't trust herself. She was like a blight, and the last thing she wanted was to bring harm to these kind and gentle ladies.

"I...I haven't been sleeping well," she hedged. "The effect of disquieted nerves, I suspect."

"That is perfectly normal." Xenia nodded.

"And, um, when I don't sleep well, my spirits seem somewhat depressed."

"Then the solution is obvious," Gigi said. "You must get more rest."

"I am certain you are right."

"What have you tried?"

"I beg your pardon?"

"To improve your sleep," Gigi said patiently. "Have you attempted any remedies? As a botanist, you are likely better versed than we are on sleeping draughts and the like."

An icy droplet trickled down Evie's spine. Her palms turned clammy. Skeletons rattled their cages, but she kept them locked away.

"I try to avoid such concoctions. They make me feel buffle-headed, and I prefer to have my wits about me."

"Have you tried a relaxing bath before bedtime?" Xenia asked. "Or a nice cup of hot milk? The latter is particularly nice with a bit of brandy."

Evie managed a smile. "Thank you for the suggestions. I shall try them."

"Vigorous exercise during the day also helps me sleep better at night," Xenia added.

"Not to disagree with Xenia." A mischievous sparkle lit Gigi's eyes. "But I do believe that certain types of *bedtime* exercises are even more effective for sleep."

"Gigi," Xenia gasped. "That is terribly wicked of you."

"Am I wrong?" Pausing, Gigi wrinkled her nose. "On second

thought, let us change the subject since the two of you are married to my brothers—*eww.*"

"There is nothing *eww* about Ethan." Xenia's smile was slow and sly. "As a matter of fact, when it comes to exercising, he is exceedingly vigorous at *any* time of day—"

"Pray cease." Moaning, Gigi covered her ears. "What is heard cannot be unheard."

"If one stirs a nest of wasps, one must be prepared to be stung," Xenia rejoined.

"At least I can count on Evie not to torment me," Gigi said.

Caught up in the lively exchange, Evie gave James's sister an innocent look. "Actually, I was about to say that athleticism must run in the family."

As Xenia burst into laughter and Gigi groaned, Evie couldn't help but smile. At the same time, her heart panged with grief. If she left, she wouldn't just be leaving James. She was going to miss this—all of this—so much.

"It is lovely to have sisters," Gigi said warmly. "In that spirit, I have a favor to ask. Due to the impetuous nature of our nuptials, Mr. Godwin and I missed out on having a true wedding celebration. We would like to make up for it by throwing a ball, but as you know our new home, Honeystone Hall, is currently under renovation—"

"You must have the ball at Bottoms House," Xenia declared. "Ethan and I would be honored to host the event."

"Thank you, dearest. I was hoping you would offer," Gigi said happily. "Mr. Godwin will, of course, cover the expenses. Indeed, he gave me *carte blanche*—"

"Well, there's a surprise," Xenia said.

Gigi dimpled. "He and I plan to invite guests from London as well, and we wish to show them the best that Chuddums has to offer. We were hoping to hold the ball as soon as possible...say within three weeks?"

Xenia's eyes rounded. "That is no trifling agenda."

"That is why I need the both of you." Gigi turned a beseeching violet gaze upon Evie. "Do say you will help with the preparations."

"I'm not sure how I can help." Evie knitted her brows. "The bulk of the planning must be done in Chuddums—"

"You and James are welcome to stay at Bottoms House," Xenia said immediately.

"Oh, but I...I...have work. My experiments—"

"I know you are busy, Evie. But I would be ever so grateful for your assistance," Gigi pleaded. "Couldn't you spare three weeks?"

Think of an excuse, Evie. Get out of this.

However, her mind refused to cooperate...probably because her heart yearned to say yes.

She faltered. "James may be busy."

"If I can convince James, will you help me, Evie?" Gigi clasped her hands together as if in prayer. "Please?"

How could anyone say no to a Harrington? Even with blackmail and secrets hanging over her head, Evie couldn't bring herself to abandon this life. To give up this taste of happiness that fate had bestowed upon her...out of generosity or cruelty, she didn't know which. What she did admit to herself was that she couldn't leave just yet. Not until she was out of options.

"All right," she said. "If James agrees, I shall come."

CHAPTER EIGHT

"Lord Dunsmuir and Mr. Friend to see you, my lord," Hollis said.

James crossed the study to greet his cronies. He'd known Robbie Dunsmuir and Eugene Friend since their days at Eton, and they had all roomed together at Oxford. Like him, the two were firstborn sons who welcomed the responsibilities that accompanied the role. They shared interests in politics, financial matters, and sports, and James trusted his friends implicitly.

"Well met, old chaps," he said.

After the usual exchange of handshakes and jovial thumps on the back, they settled in the tufted leather seats by the fire. Tea and refreshments were served, and James caught up with his friends.

"We saw your brother on our way in," Dunsmuir remarked. "He looked in fine spirits."

Copper-haired and blue-eyed, the Scot was a lanky fellow whose easygoing charm had made him a magnet for females. Barmaids and baronesses vied for his attention, and he'd been a bit of a rake before he married. Now he had a wife and seemed content with overseeing a growing brood. Given Dunsmuir's own contentious relationships with his brothers—he had five of them —he'd been particularly sympathetic to James's dealings with Ethan and Owen.

"Ethan is doing well." With brotherly pride, James added, "He has been composing music."

"That is capital news," Friend said. "Talent such as his should not go to waste."

Friend was Dunsmuir's opposite physically, being dark and heavy-set. His full mutton chops were a point of pride. Behind his gold-rimmed spectacles, his eyes gleamed with a mix of intelligence and impatience. He'd inherited a debt-ridden textile business from his papa; now he owned a half-dozen lucrative factories, with more on the way. He was also the remaining bachelor of the trio.

"I would wager Ethan's pretty new wife has something to do with his mood." Dunsmuir winked. "We met her as well. I've always had a preference for redheads."

"You have a preference for anything that breathes." Friend raised his thick brows. "And isn't your lady blonde?"

"As bright as sunshine is my Eloise," Dunsmuir said smoothly. "While she holds my heart captive, a fellow cannot help but notice beauty. Well, unless he's entirely captivated by ledgers and numbers—like you, Friend."

Used to the back and forth, which had been going on since they were lads, James smiled.

This is what I need. To spend time with old friends. To think about something other than what went wrong in my marriage...

He reined in his thoughts. Since their last encounter in the greenhouse, he and Evie had been assiduously avoiding one another. They crossed paths when necessary: at meals and activities where the absence of either of them might alert their guests to their marital troubles. Despite his conflicted feelings about his wife, he appreciated her discretion. She would never embarrass him with a public display. In fact, he was beginning to realize that with her, he had the opposite problem: she was so contained that he had trouble reading her at all.

What she'd said about their babe twisted his gut even now, his hands clenching around the arms of his wingchair. For months, he'd avoided the topic of the miscarriage, not wishing to cause her pain. He'd held his own grief inside to spare hers. Apparently, his efforts had been for nothing: she seemed to be incapable of feeling.

"Perhaps that was nature's way of rectifying something that should not have happened in the first place."

How could she spew such vileness? He'd wanted to shout at her, shake her. When had she become this bloodless…this cold? Worse yet, what if she'd always been this way, and he'd fooled himself into thinking that she preferred emotional restraint when she, in fact, had no feelings at all?

"Of course, neither of us are as settled as Manderly here." With a grin, Dunsmuir drew James into the fray. "Look at him, with his flourishing estate and accomplished lady. If your fair countess is free, I should like to pay my respects. Having glimpsed your glorious gardens, I would not mind her expert advice on improving my own."

Friend snorted. "I would keep him away from my lady. And my garden."

"Evie is occupied at the moment." In truth, James had no idea what his wife was doing, but he wasn't about to share that. "She will come by if she is able."

"If we are done with the niceties"—Friend gave Dunsmuir a pointed look—"I think it is best to get on with the purpose of our visit."

So there was a reason for the unexpected call. While James didn't mind spending time with his old friends, he'd suspected that it wasn't mere coincidence that brought them to his neighborhood. Perhaps they had a financial venture to discuss or a political tidbit to share.

"I am all ears," he offered.

Friend and Dunsmuir looked at each other.

"This information must remain confidential," Friend said.

"When have you known me to be a gossip?"

"You have always shown unparalleled judgment." Dunsmuir leaned forward. "Which is why you are about to hear what you are about to hear."

James cocked his head, intrigued. It was clear his cronies were bursting at the seams to share the news, whatever it was.

"Henry Gosford is retiring," Friend announced.

"Gosford?" James drew his brows together. "Why?"

One of the Members of Parliament for Reading, Gosford had just turned forty and had served five consecutive terms. His moderate position made him popular with his fellow Whigs, and his jovial temperament had won the hearts of his constituents. He was the sort of politician who visited orphanages and held babies... and made sure the papers got wind of it.

"When Gosford releases the announcement, the reason he will give is ill health. The real reason," Dunsmuir drawled, "is a certain brunette actress at the Adelphi. Gosford, the fool, was spotted in public with her, and someone leaked copies of the lease he paid for her cottage and other damning receipts from jewelers and the like to the papers. The scandal will eat him—and his wife and children —alive."

"That is unfortunate," James said, frowning. "Mrs. Gosford is an amicable lady and her husband's staunchest supporter. She is undeserving of such treatment. The children, too, are blameless."

"Be that as it may, the party cannot take any chances," Dunsmuir went on. "Gosford must go. He has been persuaded that an early retirement from public life is the only way to control the damage."

"You know what this means, Manderly." Behind his spectacles, Friend's forge-dark gaze smoldered. "The opportunity we have been waiting for has arisen. You must take Gosford's place."

Although James's thoughts had traveled in the same direction, he forced himself to take a step back. To consider the situation from all angles.

"It is not that simple." He shook his head. "The General Election is mere months away. I cannot possibly get ready—"

"We will help you," Dunsmuir said. "Friend and I are at your disposal."

"And you have support within the party," Friend asserted. "While Gosford was admired, he lacked imagination. A true vision. Your name, however, comes up repeatedly during discussions of the party's future and who we wish to represent us."

"I am honored. Truly."

The possibility of spearheading real reform sparked excitement in James. Yet the proposed task was enormous...and not just because of the short notice. Running for election would put him, and everyone close to him, in the public eye. His chest tightened as he considered Evie's reaction to this new development. Even before their relationship had disintegrated to its present state, she had avoided the limelight. While she'd played her social role as countess perfectly, she'd done so out of duty. Out of a desire, it had seemed, to please him.

Now that she considered their marriage a bloody *mistake*, he wasn't sure what she would do. Whether she would go along with his plans. Whether he wanted her to.

In either case, I need to talk to her. Even if it's the last thing I wish to do at the moment.

"If this feels like an honor"—Dunsmuir arched his brows—"why the long face?"

James scrambled for a proper answer. One that wouldn't expose his marriage to scrutiny and, at the same time, would allow him to be honest with his friends. He did not wish to repay their trust with deception.

He cleared his throat. "You know as I do that public office brings attention to one's private affairs—"

"By Jove, Manderly." Dunsmuir blinked. "Don't tell me you have a bit of muslin tucked away somewhere?"

"Of course not." James gave his friend a hard stare. "What kind of fellow do you take me for? I would never break the vows that I made as a gentleman—that I gave before God."

"That is precisely the reason why you must run," Friend said with satisfaction. "While Gosford's early departure will reduce the furor, it will not quiet the wagging tongues entirely. Thus, our next candidate must be unimpeachable. He must be a gentleman of high social standing, whose reputation cannot be faulted in any way. In short, he must be *you*."

"I am not a saint," James said dryly.

"You're close enough," Friend declared. "Unless you tell us otherwise."

Caught between ambition and uncertainty, James hesitated. He didn't know how to address his strained marital relations—no, he didn't *want* to. And he was not certain it mattered. Unhappy couples were neither scandalous nor uncommon. If both parties acted with decorum, there would be no issue.

"You know me as well as anyone," he said at length. "I have no skeletons of which I am aware. Nonetheless, when any man's life is placed beneath the magnifying glass—"

"Ah," Dunsmuir said. "I understand what you mean. Completely."

"You, er, do?"

"You are referring to the dreadful circumstances which have affected your family," Dunsmuir said. "The disappearance of Lord Owen during the Afghan War and his, shall we say, *unruly* behavior after he was rescued. Then there was the tragic accident that robbed Lord Ethan of his musical career."

James frowned. He hadn't been thinking of his brothers but of his own weaknesses and how his opponents might capitalize upon them. Now he bristled at the characterization of Ethan and Owen as detriments to his aspirations.

"Owen served this country honorably and at great personal cost," he said severely. "He is not alone in the challenges he faced returning from war: former soldiers endure hardships every day. As a civilized society, we owe them not only gratitude but compassion, and this must be reflected in policies that provide for their care after the horrors of battle.

"As for Ethan, he has persevered in the face of adversity—adversity that would bring most men to their knees. He is a study in determination and grace. I could not be prouder of my brothers. In fact, they inspire me to be a better man."

"He is ready." Friend turned to Dunsmuir, his face lit with excitement. "I told you he was ready, and this proves it."

"That was a pretty speech," Dunsmuir agreed.

Scowling, James said, "That wasn't a speech—"

"Not quite," the Scot agreed. "Yet it has potential. Listen to me, old chap." His expression grew uncommonly serious. "This isn't just about your ambitions. If we do not put our best candidate forward, we will lose the seat...to Ryerson."

"Eustace Ryerson?" The thought chilled James's nape. "Do you think he has a chance?"

"Since the repeal of the Corn Laws, Ryerson's stance has grown increasingly reactionary. His proposed policies aim to punish the poor for their so-called moral failure and to silence reformers—he's taken aim at trade societies and 'strong-minded females' already. Unfortunately, his fear-mongering has gained him a devoted following." Dunsmuir's shrug was philosophical. "You know as well as I do that Ryerson plays dirty. Several of my sources say that he was the one who leaked Gosford's indiscretion to the papers. He will undoubtedly brandish the scandal like a weapon against our party during his crusade for righteousness."

James swore softly. "You think Ryerson could win Gosford's vacated seat?"

"We think that he *will* win if we do not have a stronger candidate." Friend leaned his arms on his thighs, his gaze solemn and unwavering. "Think of what is at stake here. Ryerson wants to reinstitute harsher workhouse rules. He wants to subject poor women and children to his 'morality screenings' to qualify for medical attention. He opposes any kind of electoral reform because, apparently, if anyone but wealthy landowners has a say in the way this country is run, it will lead to mob rule and social collapse."

"Now that is a speech." James tilted his head. "Why don't you run, Friend? Or you, Dunsmuir?"

Friend shook his head. "I'm not good with people."

"And I might be a little too good," Dunsmuir said ruefully. "I've a few skeletons in my closet. From back in the day, of course."

"You are the one for the job, Manderly," Friend said firmly. "When you speak, people listen. Be the voice of change, and we will manage things in the background."

"We've built relationships," Dunsmuir added. "We have people to call upon, people eager to support you as Gosford's replacement. Say the word, and your campaign begins now."

How could he turn down friends who had such faith in him? How could he refuse the opportunity to contribute to the greater good? At the same time, how could he do any of this without Evie's support—without the foundation of a healthy, if not happy, union?

James expelled a breath. "I must consult my wife before giving an answer. This decision will affect her life as much as mine."

"By all means." Dunsmuir smiled. "However, I think I know what she will say."

That makes one of us, old boy.

"Lady Manderly is a sensible female." From Friend, this was the highest form of praise. "During our talks, she has made convincing arguments supporting the rights of women and the working class. You will do well with her by your side."

That depended on the outcome of James's conversation with Evie. He realized that he could no longer allow things to continue as they were. His efforts to protect Evie's delicate sensibilities in the past had backfired. The best option now was to address the issues concerning their future head-on and without further delay.

"I shall speak to her," James said.

Chapter Nine

Evie crept down the corridor like a thief. Stealthily, she opened the door to her bedchamber and peered inside. The low-burning lamps told her that Harkness had not waited up for her, which felt like a reprieve. She couldn't deal with her companion at this moment—couldn't face yet another loved one she was now keeping secrets from. Closing the door, she sagged against it, her heart thudding with a mixture of fear, guilt, and relief.

I did it. I paid the blackmailer.

She drew off her gloves with hands that shook. Going to the fire, she rubbed her clammy palms over her cheeks and tried to calm her nerves. Had she done the right thing? By meeting the fiend's demands, had she simply opened the door to further extortion?

What choice did I have?

When she arrived at the greenhouse yesterday morning, she'd seen with dread that her journal lay upon her desk. She knew she had locked her notebook in the drawer; someone had invaded her sanctuary yet again. Forcing herself to flip through the pages, she'd found a blunt message:

I know what you did, and the world will too. The cost for my silence is a hundred sovereigns. Leave the money in the folly, tomorrow at midnight. Come alone. If you fail to meet these terms, the next note I send will be to your husband.

Panic had smothered her. Who had written this—who knew her secret? The same hand had written the two notes, and while she didn't recognize it, the bold strokes looked masculine. Names and faces, blurred by the passing years, streaked through her head. Why would someone threaten her *now*...when seven years had passed since Wilmington's death, and she'd finally begun to believe that she might be safe?

You can hide, you little bitch. The memory of her stepfather's slurred words, the ominous thump of his footsteps, made her freeze even now. *But you can never escape. Not from me.*

For years, running and hiding had been her method of survival. Yet this time, she wasn't ready to go. She wasn't ready to leave James.

Despite the tension between them, which had worsened since the departure of his family, she couldn't bring herself to give him up. She wanted to remain near him, even if he was chilly and aloof, for as long as possible. She couldn't let him find out what she'd done—couldn't bear his condemnation. Even worse, his honor would dictate that he protect her and stand by her...which meant he would hate her even more when she destroyed his reputation and his future.

Thus, she'd gone to the gothic folly on the farthest edge of the estate. Her heart thumping like a rabbit's foot, she'd ventured into the deepest shadows of the stone structure and placed the purse of coins where it couldn't be missed. She'd paid the blackmailer with her savings—money she'd set aside in case of an emergency. Then she had fled without looking back.

Expelling a breath, she went over to the *Aspidistra elatior*. It was one of the three things she had left of her mama. Along with the worn copy of *Culpeper's Herbal* and a magnificent string of pearls, she had taken the cast-iron plant with her everywhere. It had survived the dark boarding house room she'd shared with Harkness and the windowless cell she'd been assigned in the Thurstons' townhouse. She stroked the edge of the long green leaf, taking heart from the plant's sturdy, indestructible nature.

"We're survivors, you and I," she whispered. "We can withstand anything."

The click of the door caught her by surprise. She jerked away from the plant, shocked to see James standing in the doorway between their rooms. That door hadn't been opened for months, and his sudden appearance in her intimate space unleashed a wave of dread and longing—mostly the latter.

How she missed him. His steady, quiet strength and unshakeable honor.

It didn't help that he looked deliciously masculine in his at-home attire. His burgundy smoking jacket was expertly tailored to his broad shoulders, and his casual trousers skimmed his muscular legs. His shirt was open at the collar, revealing the smooth bump of his throat and the barest hint of chest hair.

"We need to talk," he said.

His sternness snapped her out of her aching reverie.

"Um...what about?" she asked.

He ran a gaze over her, and she was aware of the glaring differences between them. Unlike her golden god of a husband, she was not dressed in a distractingly sensual manner. For her dark errand, she'd chosen a serviceable black dress to blend with the shadows.

"Where were you?" he said abruptly.

Dash it.

Since the departure of James's family, whatever fragile pretense of marital harmony they'd maintained had unraveled completely. Most evenings, he had engagements, usually returning in the wee hours. She hadn't expected that he would be home...much less standing here in her bedchamber. Thus, she hadn't anticipated the need to prepare an alibi.

"I was...I was engaged in my studies," she said.

It was a plausible explanation.

"Try again." The gaze he leveled at her was more steel than sky. "I looked for you in the greenhouse."

Double dash it.

"I was in the garden."

"Past midnight?"

"The moths visit the wallflowers after dusk, as you know. I was taking measurements and lost track of the time."

When James narrowed his eyes, she plunged on.

"I must be thorough in my research if I hope to present my findings to the Botanical Society. No avenue can be left unexplored. You understand."

"What I understand," he said calmly, "is that you are lying to me, and I have no idea why."

"I am not lying—"

"Another husband might wonder what his wife is hiding. He might, for example, suspect that she is having an affair."

The idea was so preposterous that she gawked at him.

"I would *never*—"

"Then tell me where you were, Evie. What you were doing."

"I told you. I was in the garden...studying the wallflowers."

His eyes flared, his jaw clenching. He looked angry enough to shout—to shake her, if his hands weren't balled. Her past had taught her the warning signs of violence, and if it were any man other than James, her instinct would have been to run. Yet she knew with every fiber of her being that her husband would never do her physical harm.

Even when she was hurting him. Guilt wrung her heart, and for an instant, she considered confessing everything: the depraved act she'd committed in the past, the blackmailer she was paying off, and the threat she posed to everything he held dear.

Burning fear kept her silent.

"Fine." His voice was icy. "If you do not wish to discuss your activities, then you will listen to what I have to say about mine."

Recalling his earlier reference to infidelity, a terrible thought struck her. Had he suspected her of having an affair because... because *he* was having one? She wasn't naïve; sophisticated couples often sought pleasure outside of the marital bed. And the fact was that her own had seen little activity of late. Yet the very idea of James being with another set off a blaze of possessiveness.

"What about your activities?" she said tightly.

He straightened his shoulders while her heart hammered against her ribs.

"Gosford is retiring, and I plan to run for his seat," he said.

It took her a moment to register what he said. And another for the pounding in her ears and chest to subside.

"Oh." She drew a breath, trying to think. "Will you win?"

James's mouth twisted. "That is a vote of confidence, isn't it?"

"That is not what I meant—"

"Friend and Dunsmuir believe that I am the party's best chance of beating Ryerson. I have their backing and the support of others. It is my duty to serve the greater good, and now that this opportunity has arisen, I must step forward."

"Of course," she mumbled.

She felt so small, shrinking in the blaze of confidence in James's gaze. Who was she to stand in the way of his ambition—his destiny to help others? And yet...

"We need to discuss this because it will affect you as well."

James came to stand in front of her. His familiar scent of musk and sandalwood tantalized her senses. She was caught between opposing desires: to flee and to fling herself into his arms. She stayed rooted in place, trembling with yearning.

"I know how important your studies are to you and do not expect you to abandon them for the sake of my endeavors. However, I will require your presence on occasion." He glanced at the cast-iron plant, touching his finger to a glossy tip. "According to Dunsmuir and Friend, presenting a united domestic front is essential to my campaign's success. The General Election is only three months away, and during that time, I would appreciate your support."

His request and the careful way he made it pierced her like an arrow. He had no idea what she would do for him—the lengths she would go to protect him. Her dilemma wound around her like a thorny vine: if she stayed, she would be his Achilles' heel. Yet if she left, James would be faced with a different kind of scandal...unless she could think of a way to disappear that wouldn't harm his reputation.

"What happens in private is one thing." He dropped his hand from the plant. "In public, I shall be relying upon you to play the role of a contented wife. This contest will be a close one, and I will need your help to win, Evie. I have not asked for much, but I would have your word now that you will give me your best effort."

If what he said earlier was an arrow, then his present request was like a blade, slicing clean through her.

"You haven't asked anything of me, James." The truth bled from her. "You've given me everything but never asked for a thing in return."

He stared at her. In the silence, her heartbeat seemed loud and frantic.

"What has happened to us?" he asked, his voice hoarse and low. "Our marriage has been blown off-course, and for the life of me, I don't know the cause of it. But I will fix it, if you tell me what needs to be done."

His offer, noble and intense and so very *James*, drew a wretched tear from her. When he thumbed it away, she trembled at the beauty of being touched by him, at the impossibility of her position. There was no winning, only different ways to lose. Telling him the truth would destroy his future for she knew the kind of man her husband was: a captain who would go down with a sinking ship. Yet she couldn't bring herself to continue pushing him away. The agony of doing so was becoming unbearable, and she was hurting him too.

So she took the only avenue left. A path that drew them away from secrets and shadows and toward a truth beyond words. She threw her arms around his neck, pulled him close, and kissed him.

Of late, James didn't know what to expect from his wife. Her shifting moods had kept him on his toes, and he was now more certain than ever that she was hiding something. He meant what he'd said: if there was a problem, she had only to tell him. Instead, she was kissing him, and he was staggered by her. By the lush hunger of her kiss. By the yielding softness of her curves pressed against his rigid edges. She tasted like she had that night at Bottoms House—wild and sweet and alive with desire. She was a different woman and yet the same. A bud bursting into full, honeyed bloom.

When she parted her lips...well, he was only human, after all, and randy as hell. The days of tension morphed into sudden, unstoppable lust. Palming the back of her head, he took her mouth the way he wanted to. Fully, deeply, completely. She whimpered, melting against him. His kiss turned into one of possession, and when she not only welcomed his driving tongue but suckled it, a bolt of heat shot straight to his groin.

Despite her outward shyness, Evie was not reserved in bed, praise God. Before the recent cold spell, when she'd seemed to lose all interest in him, the heat between them had been heady and undeniable. He had enjoyed peeling away the prim layers of his lady scientist to discover the sensual vixen beneath. Her complexity had aroused and challenged him, and although she'd been a virgin on their wedding night, she'd proved a quick study. With her, there were endless avenues of desire to explore.

While he enjoyed her mouth, she was doing some exploring of her own. Her touch, reverent and eager, never failed to stir him. Beneath his shirt, his muscles flexed as she slid her palms over his chest. She made a sound in her throat, one unique to her: half-purr, half-moan...all sweet. She reached lower, tracing the jutting ridge of his erection. Pleasure seized him as she caressed his bulging tip through his trousers, circling her thumb until his arousal seeped through the wool. When she cradled his stones, giving them a light squeeze, he took control before it was too late.

"Tell me, Evie." He captured her jaw in one hand, holding her gaze. "Tell me what is troubling you. Whatever is wrong, upon my honor, I will remedy it."

She stared at him, then averted her eyes.

"Nothing is troubling me," she said.

Fury surged with a force that he'd never experienced before. He grabbed her hand, which still gripped his cock, and removed it from his person.

"Do not touch me," he bit out.

Red splotches stood out on her pale cheeks. "I...I thought you liked it when—"

"Do you know what I like, Evie? What I truly prefer?"

She swallowed, her eyes wide.

"Honesty," he said in disgust. "Just the bloody truth. If you cannot give me that, then I want nothing from you."

He walked out, slamming the door behind him.

Chapter Ten

A few days later, Evie wandered into Chudleigh Bottoms. The morning was warm, and she'd enjoyed the mile-long walk from Bottoms House. Villagers were out and about in the square, and several called out friendly greetings, which she shyly returned. James's siblings were highly regarded amongst the locals, and she didn't want to ruin their reputation.

The way I ruin everything.

The three days since her arrival at Chuddums felt like the longest of her life. After the devastating row with James, she'd expected he would call off the trip. Instead, he'd remained committed to supporting Gigi's ball. She'd also overheard his cronies endorsing the trip, saying that Chuddums's central location in the county would be the ideal place to launch James's campaign.

Evie had never been to the Outer Hebrides, but she imagined it couldn't be any colder than the atmosphere during the carriage ride over. In the past, she'd appreciated that her husband seldom lost his temper, yet she was beginning to realize that there were more painful alternatives. His chilly politeness cut like a blade. He shut her out completely, treating her as if she were a stranger or acquaintance he had to tolerate. She almost wished he would shout at her—maybe that would stoke some righteous anger in return. Instead, his indifference pruned her self-confidence, and she felt smaller with each passing moment.

While they could avoid each other at home, doing so in the current situation was trickier. Xenia had assigned them the same bedchamber where they'd had their night of passion—and the memories and close confines added fuel to their tension. Since requesting separate rooms would undoubtedly raise questions—especially in his family, where couples preferred the intimacy of a shared bedchamber—they implicitly divided the space. James slept on the sofa in the attached sitting room and set up a makeshift office there as well. To minimize their interactions, they adapted their schedules. Evie went to bed early (or pretended to, at any rate) while James stayed up late with his brothers.

Feeling more alone than ever, she slept poorly, which did not help her mood. In her lowest moments, she contemplated leaving James. What good was she doing by staying? In fact, she was making things worse. He despised her now. Yet her departure would surely cause a scandal and destroy his chances of winning the Reading seat. She wished being squashed between a rock and a hard place didn't feel so familiar.

Moreover, she had the blackmailer to contend with. The possibility of his return kept her in a constant state of vigilance. Her initial relief at delivering the hundred pounds had long faded, replaced by a horrible certainty that he would contact her again. She wished she could confide in Harkness, who'd insisted on coming along, but she knew the solution her friend would propose and she wasn't willing to run...yet.

Thus, she stayed, paralyzed by dread and anxiety, waiting for the guillotine to drop.

In her current state, Evie found it difficult to focus on the ball preparations, but Gigi seemed to have everything well in hand. Gigi's effervescent spirit camouflaged the fact that she had the organizational skills of a general. Her airy charm and generous purse had tradesmen and servants eager to do her bidding. When she ran into a snag, Mr. Godwin was there to assist...even if they didn't always agree on things.

This morning, Evie and Gigi had been discussing the speeches to be given at the ball when Mr. Godwin came in. Gigi had informed him of her plan to invite the village nonagenarian, a fellow named Wally, to make a toast.

To which Mr. Godwin had replied, "Duchess, if Wally gives a speech, we shall still be standing there when our grandchildren get married. Absolutely not."

Gigi had argued, the two bantering back and forth. Finally, Mr. Godwin had silenced his wife...by kissing her. The newlyweds had been so lost in each other that they'd forgotten Evie entirely and hadn't noticed her slip out. While she was happy for Gigi—no one deserved happiness more—seeing a couple so much in love amplified the misery of her own situation. She had fled the manor, seeking out fresh air and distraction in the village.

She had errands to run, and luckily, she knew she wouldn't bump into James. His campaign was already in full swing. Two days ago, he'd toured a hospital in the neighboring village of Chudleigh Crest, examining the facilities and visiting with the patients. Yesterday, he'd done the rounds in Chuddums, talking to shopkeepers and listening to their concerns. Today he'd gone to a pottery to learn more about the goods it produced and the potential for exports.

James had not invited Evie on any of these excursions. Instead, he'd been accompanied by his stalwart cronies, Lord Dunsmuir and Mr. Friend, and some local Whig matron of influence. Evie had learned of his activities during the supper conversation with his family. She understood his decision to exclude her: their discord had grown difficult to conceal. Having seen the looks exchanged around the supper table, she knew it was only a matter of time before one of the ladies broached the topic with her. She didn't blame James for not wanting to put their fractured marriage on display during his campaign. At the same time, his rejection hurt because she wanted to help...wanted desperately to be the sort of wife he deserved.

Well, you're not. You never will be. So stop crying over spilt milk.

She felt a warning pulse at her temples. Since headaches had been a regular visitor, she resolved to ignore it and focus on her outing. Throughout the square, she saw signs of bustling commerce. Cheerfully painted signs and tidy storefront displays declared that the village was open for business. She peered through the sparkling windows of several establishments that she'd previously visited with Xenia and Gigi.

In Mr. Khan's bookshop, patrons occupied brightly upholstered chairs, nibbling on sweets as they perused a paper or the latest novel. The drapery appeared packed, with matrons circling around its owner, Mr. Duffield, an affable blond Adonis who was a particular friend of Gigi's. As Evie didn't share her sister-in-law's interest in fashion, she continued past the draper's as well as the dressmaker's atelier and a newly opened millinery.

Unfortunately, her megrim was getting worse, and she hadn't come across an apothecary which might have a remedy. Getting back to Bottoms House on foot was going to be a problem. She navigated a section of the path that was cluttered with stacked crates and barrels of produce. When a fellow suddenly stepped from behind a towering heap of lettuce, she collided with him.

"Oh, dear," she gasped. "I beg your pardon, sir."

Flustered, she looked down to meet the man's gaze. He was a shade over four feet tall, with brown hair and piercing blue eyes. He wore a crisp white and green apron that matched the colors of the painted sign above the shop, which announced that this was "Pickleworth Produce—Purveyor of Berkshire's Freshest and Finest."

"I didn't see you," she said apologetically.

He raised his brows. "Haven't heard that before, have I?"

Before she could think of a response, he held out a green sprig. "Try this," he said.

Since it didn't sound like a suggestion, she took the leafy stalk and sampled it.

"The watercress is delicious, sir," she said sincerely. "Crisp and fresh, with a peppery bite."

"It was harvested just this morning." He gave her a look of approval. "Liam Pickleworth, at your service, my lady. Go on inside, and my Loretta will wrap some up for you."

Since it seemed rude to decline, Evie entered the shop. The softer light eased the pounding in her head, as did the scent of fruits and vegetables. The walls were painted a calming shade of green. Wooden shelves displayed baskets of the season's harvest, which included stalwart carrots, tender cabbage, and forced rhubarb. A long table offered a plethora of prepared treats, from pickled vegetables to jams and honey. Bouquets of herbs sat in vases of water, and Evie paused to smell the peppermint, inhaling the fresh and cooling scent.

"Good morning, dove. I'm Loretta Pickleworth."

She turned at the approach of a petite, rosy-cheeked blonde. The greengrocer's wife also wore a striped apron, but hers had a fanciful green frill along the pockets and hem.

"Oh, hello. I'm Evelyn Harrington."

"I know who you are, my lady." Mrs. Pickleworth smiled. "How may I help you?"

"Um, Mr. Pickleworth said I was to ask for watercress."

"What my Liam says and what the patron wants isn't always the same, is it?" The proprietress's emerald eyes twinkled. "I'm pleased to fetch the watercress, which is greener than a schoolboy on his first day. But perhaps you were looking for something else?"

Evie was unable to resist the lady's smile.

"Actually." She peered around the shop. "You wouldn't have any willow bark on hand, would you? I have a bit of a megrim and didn't see an apothecary in the square."

"The nearest apothecary is in Chudleigh Crest, my lady."

Evie's temples throbbed in protest.

"Luckily, I have something better than willow bark," Mrs. Pickleworth said. "We'll have your megrim fixed in no time. Come along now."

As her head was fuzzy with pain, Evie didn't put up a struggle. She simply followed when Mrs. Pickleworth led her out the back door. She blinked at her new surroundings. The pretty, sun-drenched courtyard had been transformed into a physic garden and was filled with troughs of plants. Despite her headache, Evie identified most of the herbs immediately.

"Chamomile and meadowsweet," she murmured. "And, over there, is that motherwort?"

"Indeed, my lady. Are you interested in herbs?"

A memory flashed of opening her mama's carved wood case, a spicy, floral scent tickling her nostrils. She saw herself picking up one of the tiny tincture bottles. The drops fell like tears into the glass, vanishing in the amber liquid...

"No." Evie slammed the door on the past. "Not specifically. But I have a general interest in botany."

If the tremor in her voice betrayed her, Mrs. Pickleworth didn't seem to notice. The lady led her into a small shed; inside, the space seemed to expand as if by magic. Somehow, there was ample room for wood cabinets, a drying rack, a small hearth and sink, as well as a seating area. At her hostess's bidding, Evie sat at the cozy table, examining the packets of herbs scattered across its surface. Spotting a familiar book, she ran her fingers lovingly over the worn cover.

"*Culpeper's Herbal*," she said. "I have my mama's copy."

Mrs. Pickleworth looked over from the hearth, where she'd set a kettle over the fire. "Mine belonged to my grandmama."

"Do you come from a family of herbalists?"

"Well, we never called ourselves as such." Mrs. Pickleworth opened a cabinet, revealing narrow shelves lined with jars and tincture bottles. "But the womenfolk in my family have a talent for kitchen physic. There hasn't been a resident physician in Chuddums for as long as I've been alive, and when the villagers aren't able to make the trip to Chudleigh Crest, they come to me."

With expert flair, she sprinkled herbs into a teapot. To that, she added drops of an amber tincture and other mysterious ingredients. Finally, she poured in steaming water, swirling before straining the contents into a cup. She brought the drink over, setting it in front of Evie.

"Try the tea, my lady," she said.

Evie lifted the chipped cup, prettily painted with cornflowers, and sniffed at the murky brew.

"May I ask what herbs you used?"

"It's an old family recipe." Mrs. Pickleworth plopped into the adjacent chair. "The mix includes feverfew and chamomile to relax the nerves, mint to revive, and honey to hide the bitterness. Drink up, dove—before that megrim worsens."

Since her head was pounding, Evie took a cautious sip. The tea had an earthy but not unpleasant taste. She took another sip, then another. By the time she drained the cup, a pleasant warmth had settled inside her. The tightness at her temples began to ease.

"Thank you," she said in wonder. "Your remedy is quite effective."

The good lady beamed. "In a few minutes, you'll feel right as rain."

"You've been most kind, Mrs. Pickleworth. I don't know how to repay you."

"You can start by calling me Loretta, as most folks do. And there's to be no talk of debt after all you've done for the village."

Evie furrowed her brow. "But I haven't done anything."

"Of course you have. Chuddums was on a downward spiral until the Harringtons came along. Your family has restored our hope and faith in ourselves...but don't just take my word for it. Look around you, and you will see the pride proprietors take in their shops, the way everyday folk whistle a merry tune as they make their way through the green. For the first time in decades, they believe that they have a chance of prevailing over the curse."

"Lord Ethan and his wife were the ones who ousted that gang from the village and began unraveling the secrets of Thomas Mulligan. The Godwins helped to revive the spa and other businesses. As for me"—Evie shrugged—"I haven't done a thing."

"You were abducted right here in the village."

The reminder chilled Evie's nape, her hands curling on the table.

She tried to make light of it. "Not precisely helpful behavior on my part."

"On the contrary, Lady Manderly."

Mrs. Pickleworth placed a hand over Evie's. The lady's warm, firm squeeze was a stark contrast to Evie's cold and trembling fist.

"The villagers rallied to search for you and Mrs. Godwin because we admire your courage. And we know that both of you belong here."

Evie felt a wistful pang. *I've never belonged anywhere. The only place I've felt safe is with James...and he no longer wants me.*

Swallowing, she said, "Gigi deserves your friendship, but you hardly know me."

"Do you know how Chuddums came to be?"

Evie shook her head.

"Its founders were men and women who marched to the beat of their own drum. In life, they'd always been outsiders with their heads full of dreams and hearts full of passion. Take my own great-great- grandparents. They were both in service in London, but they wanted to grow cherries. People thought they were stark, raving mad, but they invested their life savings to buy the only patch of land they could afford and started a farm here in Chuddums."

"Did their plans come to fruition?" Evie couldn't help but ask.

"They had years of success and years of failure too. Such is life," Mrs. Pickleworth said philosophically. "The important thing is that they lived their dreams. That is what people come to Chuddums to do."

Is it possible? Is Chuddums a place where dreams come true? A place where I could be free to love my husband—and become a wife who is worthy of him?

A tear escaped, sliding down Evie's cheek.

"Are you in pain?" Concern creased Mrs. Pickleworth's features. "Is the megrim worsening?"

"N-no." To Evie's dismay, her voice hitched. "I-I'm fine."

Mrs. Pickleworth took her hand, unfurled her fingers, and massaged her palm until she felt herself relaxing.

"I've found that a good chat can sometimes ease a headache as well as herbs. Especially when one has been through an ordeal." Mrs. Pickleworth studied her with earnest eyes. "If there is anything you wish to speak about, I am here to listen."

Evie knew the lady was referring to the abduction and wanted to confess the truth: she'd endured far worse. Right now, she was being extorted by some mysterious villain from her past, and the only thing keeping her here was her love for her husband...who despised her. Words crowded her throat. She sprang up before they —or the tears pushing behind her eyes—could escape.

"You have been kindness itself, Mrs. Pickle—I mean, Loretta," she said in a rush. "I cannot thank you enough. But I'm feeling much more the thing, and I must get back. The others will be wondering where I am."

"Of course, my lady." Mrs. Pickleworth was on her feet as well. "Would you like Liam to drive you back? We've only a cart but—"

"I'm fine. Truly. Thank you...thank you again for everything."

Evie dashed off while she still could.

Chapter Eleven

Upon her return to Bottoms House, Evie was greeted by Brunswick, the butler with mastiff-like jowls and a gruff but kindly manner. He informed her that the master and mistress were out with the Godwins, and she tried not to show her relief. Although her megrim had subsided, she felt shaky and unsettled and had no desire to socialize, even with family. She wished she was at home, where she could escape into the greenhouse.

At least the other couples were gone. And, after the visit to the pottery, James and his cronies were supping with the Whig widow, who'd apparently invited the local gentry so that he could promote his cause. He would be out late, and Evie was glad for it. She simply could not manage another frosty marital interaction.

She hurried to the bedchamber, locking the door behind her. She rested her back against the solid barrier, closed her eyes, and let out a sigh. Solitude had never felt so welcome. With her eyes still shut, she began untying the ribbons of her bonnet. She was dusty from the walk back and needed a bath. Soaking in warm suds struck her as a perfect way to unwind—

"Evie?"

She jerked against the door, her eyelids snapping open. James was standing in the doorway of the connected sitting room. He was in his shirtsleeves, his collar open, and his shirt untucked. His thick bronze hair was mussed, and he looked groggy...which was unusual. Unlike her, he didn't need much sleep, and he awakened with an energy that had always baffled her. During their better days, when he'd spent the night, he had put that vigor to good use. He'd lured her into wakefulness with warm kisses, his rampant manhood wedged against her bottom...

Remembering those times made her heart contract with helpless longing. Her breathing quickened as he crossed the room toward her. He'd taken off his shoes, and her belly quivered at his casual state. The contrast between his elegant clothing and large bare feet was strangely arousing.

"What...what are you doing here?" she said stupidly.

"I am staying in this bedchamber if you recall."

His obvious irritability gave her pause. James tended to be suave; even his attacks were smooth, slicing to the bone before one realized one was bleeding. She took a good look at him. His hair was sticking up on one side, and sleep wrinkles marred his cheek. His face had a slight flush that enhanced the glitter in his eyes. For once, he didn't appear calm or collected.

"What has made you grumpy?" she asked.

He stared at her. "I am not grumpy."

At his annoyed tone, she merely lifted her brows.

Frowning, he ran a hand through his hair. "I was working and didn't expect an interruption."

"I didn't think you would be here." Awkwardly, she added, "I thought you would still be at the pottery."

"The visit ended early. I came back to catch up on a few things before supper."

"Like sleep?"

"I wasn't sleeping."

"Then why has a pillow left its impression upon your face?"

"I was working on a speech and decided to rest my eyes...never mind." He braced his hands on his hips. "Where were you? Ethan said you weren't at luncheon."

The problem with the silent treatment, Evie reflected, was that it put you out of practice for normal conversation. She and James hadn't had a civilized exchange for days, and she was rusty. Her husband wasn't at his best either. Instead of a casual inquiry about one another's day, their exchange felt stiff and accusatory...like they were spoiling for another fight.

"I went into the village." She strove to sound neutral. "I met the greengrocer's wife, who happens to be a gifted herbalist. She showed me her physic garden..."

Should I mention my megrim? Will he care? What if it reveals too much about my state of mind?

"One thing led to another," she finished lamely. "I lost track of time."

"Plants." His mouth curled. "I should have known that would get your attention."

The barb dug into her, as it was no doubt meant to. While James had a temper and could be as righteous and aloof as the mythic Apollo, he was rarely mean. Evie knew that not all husbands would be as supportive of their wives' interests as he was —her stepfather being a case in point. After marrying him, Mama had had to carry on her studies in secret for fear of inciting his temper...not that that had taken much.

In contrast, James had never questioned Evie's passion for botany. He listened patiently every time she brought up *Cheiranthus cheiri, variety vespertinus*—which, heaven help him, had been often—and had even read her paper, providing honest and helpful comments. And, by the blooms, he'd built her a greenhouse and supplied her with anything and everything she needed for her work. Remembering his kindness allowed her to tuck away her hurt and resist sniping back at him.

Instead, she asked, "Is something the matter?"

"Nothing is the matter."

His curt reply confirmed that something *was* wrong. Studying him more closely, she saw the sheen of sweat on his brow. The flush on his cheeks had heightened and spread down the corded column of his throat.

"You're acting strangely," she said. "Are you feeling unwell?"

"I am perfectly fine."

His eyes were bright...glassy.

Anxiety prickled her. "I don't think you are."

"Perhaps you don't know me as well as you think."

Concern prompted her to ignore his snide remark and take a step toward him. When she reached for his forehead, he slapped her hand away in the manner of a virgin protecting her virtue. She would have laughed if she weren't so worried. Instead, she evaded his attempts to wave her off and managed to press her palm against his brow.

Alarm shot through her. "You are burning up."

"Hot, am I? Well, it's your fault I am like a banked fire with no vent..."

His smirk slid into a frown as he suddenly swayed.

"You're ill," she said fretfully. "Get into bed, and I'll send for the physician."

"Nonsense. I am never ill. We Harringtons have strong constitutions..."

His gaze grew unfocused, and he went pale as a sheet. She cried out a warning even as he toppled. When she tried to catch him, his dead weight was too much, and together they crashed to the ground.

Chapter Twelve

PAST

"Do you like it?" he asked.

The question was unnecessary because Evie's expression was, for once, completely unguarded. The shadows had left her eyes, and there was just bright, shining joy as she twirled under the sky of glass. The finishing touches had been put on the greenhouse yesterday, and now it stood like an empty jewel box of glass and iron. The arched roof was composed of slender, white, wrought-iron ribs that secured the sparkling ceiling panels. Green and ochre tiles covered the floor in an elegant, geometrical pattern. Pots and raised beds were empty and awaiting his countess's whims.

As Evie dashed around the room, talking to herself as she made plans, James was amused and satisfied, like a man who knows he's given the perfect gift. Shopping for Evie required skill. During their year together, he'd discovered that frocks, jewels, and other feminine luxuries held little appeal for her. Yet he had noted her delight and wonder when they'd visited a friend's conservatory and decided then and there that she ought to have one of her own.

"Oh, James. The greenhouse could not have turned out better. It is perfect."

Evie's glowing excitement justified the extravagance.

"We used your ideas for the design," he reminded her. "Your suggestion to steepen the slope of the ceiling to allow in more light quite impressed the architect. I do believe he wishes to hire you on."

She giggled. The sound was so carefree, so unlike his wife, that he felt a pang in his chest. As he'd predicted, married life with Evie was never boring. He enjoyed discovering her quirks and complexities. He'd learned, in bits and pieces, about her past and knew that she'd weathered difficult times. She'd lost her papa early on and her mama at age fourteen. Left in the care of her stepfather, Lord Calvert Wilmington, Evie hadn't mourned when he died three years later—and James didn't blame her. The profligate bounder had gone through her mama's fortune and her inheritance, leaving her destitute.

To survive, Evie had taken whatever work a seventeen-year-old gentlewoman could find, from sewing to selling arrangements she'd fashioned from dried flowers. She and Harkness—the battle-axe's loyalty to her charge was the sole reason James kept her on— had shared a room in a boarding house, pooling their earnings to scrape by. When Evie had landed the job as Lady Thurston's companion, she had believed her fortunes were finally improving.

The image of Evie warding off that scoundrel Thaddeus with a pruning knife smoldered in James's memory even now. She'd been making her own way in the world from a tender age, and it showed. She didn't trust readily. She expected little, and when she received anything, even the smallest boon, her stunned gratitude cut him to the quick. It made him want to give her more—every-thing he could. He was determined to show her the bounty of life and take away her fears...even if he didn't know their full extent. Despite their flourishing bond, she had hidden corners, places she didn't want him to see.

Well, he was a patient man, and his wife was worth the wait. He wanted her to willingly yield her secrets. He wanted everything of her—especially the three words she'd yet to say. To be fair, he hadn't said them either. As delightful as their maiden year of marriage had been, the time hadn't felt right, and he didn't want to scare her away. Yet the feeling was there, at least for him. He was certain of what was in his heart and yearned to know what was in hers.

Evie was affectionate, in her own way, and delightfully sensual. He thanked his lucky stars that his prim and intellectual wife enjoyed making love as much as he did. But did the pleasure they share transcend the physical for her? Did she feel...*bound* to him? The way he felt bound to her?

"Well, he cannot have me," she said.

James cleared his throat. "I beg your pardon?"

"The architect," she said coquettishly. "You may tell him I will be otherwise occupied now that you've given me this magnificent greenhouse to conduct my studies in."

"Will I come to regret giving you this retreat?" Unable to resist her rare playfulness, he tugged on a blonde ringlet by her ear. "Have I built a greenhouse, only to lose my wife?"

"You could never lose me."

Even as she drew her brows together, looking faintly startled by her words, he felt a jolt of pleasure. Giving in to the impulse, he cupped her cheek.

"Say it, Evie," he said huskily.

"Say...what?"

"Those three little words. I know you have thought them. And I want to hear you say them aloud."

Her flush gave her away. He could scent her nerves along with her fresh and subtle perfume.

Leaning down, he murmured against her ear, "They are only words and little ones at that. Give them to me, my sweet."

A pulse leapt in her throat.

"Thank you?" she said breathlessly.

"That is only two words."

"Thank you...kindly?"

She jolted when he nipped her tender earlobe.

"Try again, darling." He ran a thumb over her plump-as-a-peach mouth, his groin heating because he knew how sweet she tasted. "You've come close to telling me. Last night, for instance. When I was inside you, you looked at me, and I saw your lips move as your pussy clasped me in that special way when you're on the cusp—"

"James."

"Have I embarrassed you, Evie?"

Enjoying her blush, he couldn't resist swooping down for a kiss. The flavor of her—nervous, eager, and needy—went straight to his head. Or both his heads, rather. He was already hard as a rock as he explored his wife's mouth until she was panting, moaning, melting against him.

"Say it," he urged.

She gazed at him. He'd dislodged her hairpins, and her cornsilk tresses were tumbling over her shoulders. Through her thick lashes, her whisky eyes were bright with desire and trepidation.

"Why?" she whispered. "Why do I have to say it?"

"Because I want to hear it."

He took her mouth again, reveling in her hot, lush response. The adage about still waters applied to his Evie utterly. He wanted to plumb her hidden depths...figuratively and literally.

"And because," he murmured against her plush lips. "I want to say them back."

"You...you do?"

Her surprise roused a mix of frustration and tenderness. Whatever had happened in her past had made it difficult for her to trust him. He thought it was the height of irony. As a fellow for whom most things had come easily in life, he'd failed at that which mattered most to him: protecting his family and winning his wife's trust.

Pulling back, he gave her a somber look. "Why does this surprise you?"

"I...I don't know." She bit her lip.

"Am I failing to demonstrate my regard for you?" he pressed.

"*No.*" Her vehemence was, at least, reassuring. "You cannot possibly believe that, James. After everything you have given me—"

"I am not referring to things," he said impatiently, "but how I treat you. Have I done anything to make you doubt my feelings? Is there anything I could improve upon to gain your trust?"

"No." She sounded desperate now. "I have never doubted you, James. Never. You have given me...you've *been* everything I could hope for in a husband. From the start, I didn't deserve you. Didn't deserve your noble offer—"

"Noble?" He drew his brows together. "Are you implying that I offered for you out of honor?"

"You are a gentleman, James," his wife said earnestly. "The finest gentleman I know. It is your nature to protect and to see justice done. Although it was not your battle to fight, you could not stand by and allow Thaddeus Thurston to ruin me. So you married me."

"I married you because I wanted you in my bed."

She blinked.

"By Jove, Evie." Exasperation took hold, and he was tempted to shake some sense into her. "After a year of marriage, surely you cannot doubt my desire for you."

"I don't doubt it." Her cheeks pink, she mumbled, "But you are, um, a man in your prime and it is your duty to—"

"Devil take duty."

Words he'd never uttered before. Yet his wife had a way of bringing out his primitive side—the part of him that acted on feeling and impulse rather than logic. And right now his instinct was telling him that Evelyn Ashewood Harrington needed to have her knotty logic untangled, and talking was not the most expedient way to accomplish that goal.

"You don't mean that. You are a gentleman of honor—"

"Devil take that too."

He yanked her toward him, and she gasped.

"What...what are you doing?"

He continued undoing the buttons on the back of her dress. Luckily for him, she preferred practical styles, and there was a minimum of frills and fuss to get in his way. He had her frock pooled around her ankles in no time.

She swatted at him...rather unconvincingly, he thought. Her surging bosom gave her away. Framed by the neckline of her corset, her décolletage had a delicate flush that heated his loins. Before Evie, he'd considered himself a general admirer of the female anatomy. His wife, however, had made him a devout man when it came to worshipping one specific part: bloody hell, Evie's breasts were magnificent.

The firm, plump mounds strained against their confinement. With each breath, the rounded tops jiggled enticingly. He would wager his fortune that beneath her corset, her nipples were ripe and fully budded, ready for his tongue.

By Jove, the woman has me panting like a dog for a taste of her... and she thinks I bed her out of duty? Because I'm honorable?

The notion was so ludicrous that he might have laughed. Instead, he finished freeing her from her corset. It hit the floor with a clatter, and her rustling petticoats soon followed.

"It is fairly obvious what I am doing," he said calmly. "I am going to make such thorough, convincing love to my wife that she will no longer be able to spout nonsense about marital obligations."

Clad in a thin shift and a pair of drawers, Evie crossed her arms over her chest.

"We cannot do that *here*," she sputtered, her eyes huge. "What if a servant comes in? It is the middle of the day, and we're in a public room...one made of glass, for blossom's sake!"

His lips twitched at her gentle expletive. Like everything about Evie, it was unique and adorable. And contrary to her intention, pointing out the naughtiness of what they were about to do only made him harder. His erection was clearly visible, a thick ridge that marred the smooth placket of his trousers.

"All the better to prove my point," he said.

"What is your point, pray tell?" She scowled. "That you're a troglodyte?"

If the shoe fits.

He reached between her crossed arms, grabbing the neckline of her shift. He jerked downward with concentrated force, and the sound of ripping linen was surprisingly satisfying. Perhaps there was a bit of a cave dweller in him, after all.

"James Harrington."

She sounded genuinely shocked...although not as offended as she was pretending to be. The bright gold flecks in her eyes and roses in her cheeks betrayed that she was enjoying this new game. Then there was the way she was covering her exposed décolletage. Instead of shielding her breasts, she was cupping them like a bloody offering. When he spotted a plump pink nipple nudging between her slim fingers, his mouth watered.

"I cannot believe you ruined my chemise," she scolded.

Her raised chin and coy challenge tugged on his cock. Energy crackled between them, a palpable sense of excitement. James marveled at what he was discovering about his little minx of a bride...and about himself. Primal heat sizzled through his blood. The sense of freedom was exhilarating—like stripping off one's cravat after a long day.

He yanked her into his arms. "It seems you need convincing that I am more than a gentleman."

She didn't push him away. Instead, her arms wound around his neck. Her tits pressed against his chest even as her smile curled against his heart.

"Why don't you show me?" she whispered.

Devil and damn.

Crushing his mouth to hers, he dragged her down to the tiles.

CHAPTER THIRTEEN

"Oh, merciful petals," Evie gasped. "This feels...strange."

"Ride me, my love."

Out of gentlemanly consideration, James had arranged for his wife to be on top. Truth be told, he benefited from this position as much as she did. He barely felt the tiles of the greenhouse beneath his back, so captivated was he by his very own Lady Godiva. Sunlight, diffused through the glass ceiling, turned her tumbling hair to spun gold. Her brow furrowed with concentration as she slowly screwed herself onto his cock. Her solemn, nearly studious expression jolted him with a wicked fantasy.

One of these days, I'm going to make love to Evie with her spectacles on.

For now, he enjoyed his unobstructed view of her big brown eyes as she slid down his staff. Her careful pace beaded his brow with sweat, and the feel of her hot, tight pussy taking him inch by inch was an excruciating pleasure. The sight of her bouncing tits was an added stimulation. Aiming his gaze lower, he watched avidly as her petals spread to accommodate his girth. Because of her petite build, she looked stuffed full even though he was only halfway in. He tightened his grip on her lush hip, guiding her down.

"All the way, Evie," he ordered. "You can do it. Take every inch of my cock."

He could tell she liked his naughty vocabulary, and he wished he had used it earlier. He'd never been particularly vocal during the act, and with his wife, he'd had a vague notion that he ought to protect her delicate sensibilities. Yet there was nothing delicate about the way Evie was attempting to impale herself upon his rod...praise God.

"You're so big," she whimpered.

From another woman, he would have assumed the praise was practiced flirtation. Yet Evie's sincerity, coupled with her wide-eyed expression, nearly unmanned him. He'd never felt bigger—never wanted a woman the way he wanted her. His sweet and unpredictable countess, who was tightening up due to nerves and the novelty of the position.

"Your pussy is lovely and snug," he said. "Perhaps this will help."

Releasing her hip, he reached for her downy blonde thatch. Finding her hidden nub, he circled with his thumb. She wriggled and gasped, but he kept diddling her until he felt a gush of liquid silk.

"That's nice," he said huskily. "So nice and wet. That's better, isn't it?"

"Yes. Oh, James..."

She made a sound, half-moan, half-sigh, as she sank down to the hilt. *By Jove.* He was engulfed by her lush heat. When her pussy gave a voluptuous squeeze, he bit back an oath and willed himself not to come. Not yet. Not now, when they were exploring this new variation of intimacy.

Evie's knees dug into his hips as she tried to find her rhythm. She'd always been a quick study, and in no time at all, she figured out how to drive him mad. With her cornsilk waves tumbling down her back, her golden-brown eyes bright with desire, she rode him like a goddess of sensuality. She was fire and rain, heat and wetness, the priceless gem in this jewel box of glass.

In other words, she was everything...*his* everything.

Her eyes on his, she pried his hands from her hips.

"Let me," she said.

Her sultry request set his blood on fire. He was hot—bloody sweltering—as she rose, keeping just his tip inside her. He groaned as her cunny tightened around his sensitive knob, bliss blazing through his veins. Before he could recover, she sank all the way down, taking him to the root and swiveling her hips until he saw stars. He had the urge to flip their positions, to plow his naughty girl until she screamed his name. Despite the molten pleasure pouring through him, he needed more. Wanted more.

"Give me the words, Evie," he rasped.

The flames in her eyes turned to shadows. He sensed her fear—felt it in the way she froze.

"You don't want them from me," she whispered.

Egad, the woman was a mystery to him.

"I do," he insisted. "Say them."

For an instant, she said nothing, biting her bottom lip. Despite the scorching pleasure of their joined bodies, he felt emptiness swell inside him.

"I love you." She sobbed it. "I love you. Always and forever."

Joy exploded. "I love you, Evie."

He bucked his hips, driving into her while pulling her down. His need for her was visceral, endless, the pleasure beyond imagining. He felt her come and groaned as her pussy milked him. His eyes closed, he pumped into her, chasing his finish—

"You will regret it."

"Regret what?"

Frowning, he opened his eyes...and the sunlight refracting through the glass made hers blaze too brightly. Her gaze was so painfully intense that he had to look away. Confused, he felt desire morph into a different kind of heat...one that was searing him from the inside out.

Alarm and bewilderment spiked. *What the bloody hell is happening?*

His blood was boiling in his veins, his skin steaming. His head pulsed, and when he tried to move, the floor of the greenhouse fell away. He plummeted—into a boiling vat. Groaning, he flailed in the punishing heat until it vanished. A chill took its place, shaking him until his teeth rattled. Then a new pain began. The ache started inside his bones, burgeoning until he felt his spine begin to crack. Agony fissured through him, reaching his head. He groaned as a hammer pounded inside his skull, threatening to break it wide open—

"James, darling. Don't leave me."

The sobbed words came through the haze of pain. He tried to open his eyes, but they were crusted shut. The razors in his throat shredded his voice.

"I'm sorry." Evie's voice drifted to him like a buoy. "I love you...more than anything. You know that, don't you?"

Did he know that? He wasn't sure. Everything was a blur.

"Don't leave me, James. Please don't go. I love you so much—"

Was he going somewhere? He didn't want to. Yet his head was spinning, his body burning, and suddenly, he found himself at the very edge of a cliff. For a moment, he teetered and glimpsed what lay below: a fathomless void.

Then he plunged.

Chapter Fourteen

Evie awoke with a start.

The light from a lamp warded off the darkness before dawn. She was in her night rail, curled up in the chair by James's bed, where she had fallen asleep. She'd kept vigil for the last three days while her husband battled what the physician had diagnosed as influenza. A severe fever had seized James, followed by bed-shaking chills. He had been out of his mind and unable to keep anything down. Evie had tried to make him comfortable, applying cool washcloths that steamed against his burning skin.

Evie had never seen him in such a state. Normally, he was as robust as an oak, but the physician had said that the hospital James had visited had experienced an outbreak of similar cases. The doctor had cautioned Evie to have the sickroom linens changed regularly and to keep the windows open to dispel the noxious miasma. She was to alert him if any other household members developed symptoms.

Xenia and Gigi had visited frequently, offering to relieve her. While Evie appreciated their support, she refused to leave James. Seeing him in this fragile state terrified her. It also made her realize the extent of her self-delusion: she could never bring herself to leave him, under any circumstances.

Please God, keep him safe. I'll do anything in return. Anything at all.

Thus far, her prayers had not been answered. The lamp's glow revealed the toll of the illness on James. Days of fasting had sharpened his cheekbones and deepened the shadows beneath his eyes. The dark scruff along his jaw was juxtaposed with the pallor of his skin, which had lost its vital glow. Save for the shallow surges of his chest, he lay frighteningly still.

Despair clutched her chest, and she took his hand in both of hers, bringing it to her cheek.

"Don't l-leave me." Her voice hitched, tears sliding from her eyes and dampening his knuckles. "I could bear anything but that."

A dreadful certainty fell over her like a shroud. This—all of it —was her fault: James falling ill, the destruction of their marriage, the loss of their babe. Even their last row had been her doing. Now he might die and their last memory of one another would be of anger and pain. Unable to bear it, she shut her eyes, held his palm against her cheek, and prayed. Even though she knew it was useless, she poured her heart and soul into a bargain with God.

Heavenly Father, I know I have committed the gravest of sins, but James is a good man. He has done nothing wrong. I am the one who must atone. Punish me, not him. I will do anything you ask, anything at all. Or...or take me, not him. I would gladly go in his stead—

"Evie?" James's hand twitched against her cheek.

She opened her eyes. James was staring at her groggily.

Have my prayers been answered?

"James," she breathed. "Oh, my darling. You're awake!"

"Have I..." His voice emerged as a croak. "Have I been sleeping?"

Seeing his grimace, she released his hand and hurried to fetch him some water.

"You must be parched. Drink something before you try to talk."

Helping him raise his head from the pillow, she held the glass to his cracked lips. He took a sip, then another. When he began to drink greedily, she controlled the flow with careful tilts of the tumbler.

"Slowly now," she said. "One sip at a time."

After he finished half the water, she set it aside.

"Let us see how that settles. You haven't kept anything down in days."

"Days?" His voice was still hoarse, but his eyes seemed more alert. "What happened?"

"You've been ill, darling. The physician thinks you caught a case of influenza, perhaps from visiting the hospital. You have had a terrible fever for three days."

"Three days?" James looked confounded. "But I am never ill."

Given the severity of his illness, his conviction in his invincibility made her sigh.

"Nonetheless, you were this time. You had everyone worried." When her hands trembled, she put them to use tucking the sheets neatly around him. "You fainted right here in this chamber. We tried to rouse you and couldn't. Your brothers lifted you into bed, and we've all been taking turns keeping watch. We sent word to Mama and Papa, but they're away visiting their estates and may not have received the message."

He frowned. "I don't recall any of that."

"That's hardly surprising, given that you were delirious with fever."

She pressed a palm to his forehead: it was damp but cool. Relief billowed through her like smoke from an extinguished fire, the intensity nearly smothering. She took several breaths before speaking again.

"The physician said that once the fever broke, you would make a speedy recovery. How are you feeling now?"

"Fine."

At the habitual reply, she lifted her eyebrows and waited.

"Perhaps my head has a slight ache," James muttered.

"Well, that's to be expected. The physician left some willow bark, and a good lady from the village shared an effective remedy for megrims. I'll have both brought to you, along with some nourishing beef tea. And perhaps a dish of blancmange."

"Blancmange?" James grimaced. "Being temporarily indisposed does not make me an infant."

The fact that he could complain about the menu was a positive sign. He'd always been specific in his preferences, especially when it came to food. The return of her husband—her honorable, stoic, exacting spouse—made her feel almost giddy.

"The doctor advised bland foods to start," she said. "Perhaps buttered toast would be more agreeable?"

"God, yes."

He said it with such feeling that she laughed.

"Beef tea and toast, then." She couldn't resist brushing a bronze lock from his forehead. "Would you like anything else?"

"Actually." He cleared his throat. "I could use the necessary."

"Shall I summon Robson—"

"I can handle it myself. It's only a few steps, and getting up will do me good."

Evie hastened to help him sit up. Seeing how much the effort cost him, she again suggested ringing for his valet. Instead, the stubborn man got to his feet and immediately swayed. She ducked under his arm to steady him.

"I've got you," she said. "Are you certain you can do this?"

"Bloody certain." He clenched his jaw in that determined way of his. "I'm going to the commode, not Timbuktu."

Well, that's that, I suppose.

Once James decided upon a course of action, he was like a dog with a bone.

He regained his balance and made it to the commode cabinet behind the dressing screen without issue. Afterward, he insisted on doing his ablutions at the washstand, brushing his teeth and splashing water on his face. When he started fussing about finding his shaving implements, she drew the line.

"The shave can wait," she said firmly. "Robson will assist you with that later, when you're steadier on your feet. For now, back to bed."

He grumbled, but the fact that he acquiesced spoke volumes about how he was feeling. Once he was settled again, she fluffed his pillows and pulled the coverlet over him.

"I shall send for what you need and let the others know you're awake. They've been ever so concerned. I'll be right back—"

As she made to leave, he caught her hand.

"You look tired."

Flustered by his perusal, she tried not to squirm. She knew she did not look her best. She'd had little rest and hadn't looked in a mirror in days.

"I haven't slept well," she mumbled.

"You've been here with me, haven't you? I heard you."

With sudden panic, she tried to recall what she might have said when she thought he was comatose. When anxiety and exhaustion had lowered her defenses and led her to pour out her heart. Her memory was a blur of desperate thoughts and frantic rambling, and she couldn't definitively separate the two.

Merciful petals, did I bargain with God aloud? When I prayed, did I name my sins? Did James hear me...does he know that I did something terrible?

"I was here." Her heart racing, she wetted her lips. "You were, um, feverish most of the time, and I didn't think you could hear me."

"I don't recall your precise words, but I felt your presence.

Your support by my side." He squeezed her hand, his eyes the tender shade of the horizon at dawn. "Even half out of my mind, I knew you were looking after me. You gave me strength, and I wanted to thank you."

"I am your wife." Emotion clogged her throat. "You don't have to thank me. It is my duty to look after you."

"Duty. Of course."

She couldn't bear his disappointment, the return of the flint in his eyes.

"Not only that." She expelled a breath. "I was worried for you...out of my mind with fear that I might lose you."

He tightened his grip on her hand. "You are not going to lose me, Evie."

"I don't deserve you."

Out of nowhere, a dam burst inside her, and she couldn't hold back what she'd feared she might never have the chance to say. The regrets that had consumed her while she'd kept vigil by her husband's side.

"I haven't been a good wife to you. I've said horrid things—"

"We both have. That happens during a row. One says things one comes to regret."

"I didn't mean it," she blurted. "The awful thing I said about... about losing our babe. I don't know why it happened. I've asked myself over and over again, but I still don't know why, and I refuse to believe that nature would intentionally be so cruel. All I do know is that I wanted our daughter. Oh, James, I wanted her more than anything—"

She didn't know when she began sobbing. Or how James had the strength to pull her into bed and tuck her against him. Yet lying in the shelter of his arms, she felt safer than she'd ever been, even as the grief she'd buried surged like a storm. It whipped through her in a rage of tears and shudders even as James held her tight.

When her tears finally slowed, she felt as wrung-out as a rag.

"I'm sorry," she whispered against his chest.

"Don't you dare apologize for your honesty."

Beneath her ear, his heartbeat went from steady to thundering, and she raised her head. His eyes were blazing—and, she was stunned to note, wet.

"I want the truth, Evie," he said tightly. "You don't have to hide things from me, no matter how bad they may seem. In fact, the worse they are, the more we need to share the burden. Did you think I didn't grieve our little girl? Did you think that I wouldn't understand your pain—that I didn't share in it?"

She thought back to his reaction—to that period she'd shut out entirely because it had been too painful. She let it all come back: how full of expectation he had been for the birth of his heir. Being James, his exuberance had taken the form of preparations. He'd started renovating rooms for the nursery, interviewing nursemaids, and planning out an educational curriculum that spanned from birth until the day their child graduated from Oxford, his alma mater.

When the blow came, he had gone...quiet. He had put a halt to the projects. He'd tried to console her, but she'd been so consumed by grief and guilt that she'd pushed him away. Physically and emotionally, she now recognized. She hadn't done it on purpose; she'd simply gone numb. While she'd gone through the motions, she hadn't been truly present—as if a part of her had floated away.

Moreover, her husband had always been a pillar of strength. She hadn't considered that he might have needed comfort himself. Seeing the sheen of pain in his eyes, she realized that she'd mistaken his equanimity for lack of feeling.

"I'm sorry that I pushed you away." She touched his stubbled jaw, her voice quavering. "I didn't mean to do it. I think I...I was so wrapped up in my own sorrow that I failed to see yours."

He took her hand, kissing her palm before placing it over his heart. Feeling its strong and steady rhythm, she snuggled closer.

"It was a painful time for both of us." His admission was raw and worlds away from the polished and aloof god she likened him to. "I wanted to comfort you, but I didn't know how. Simultaneously, I was wrestling with my own demons. I kept ruminating over what I did wrong—what I could have done to better protect you and our babe."

"There was nothing you could have done." Aghast at the unfair burden he'd taken on, she lifted her head and looked into his eyes. "It wasn't your fault. The physician said that...that such things happen without rhyme or reason. There was nothing you—or anyone—could have done."

"And yet." His gaze held hers. "The heart...it is not quite so logical, is it?"

She swallowed, feeling transparent beneath his scrutiny. James had an uncanny ability to read her. It was as if he knew she felt responsible for the loss of their babe, although he did not know the cause. She couldn't—wouldn't—share with him her reasoning: that the death of their babe had been punishment for her sins. But she could give him a part of the truth.

"No, it isn't." Her voice trembled. "I...I carried her, James. I would have given my life to protect her, but I failed."

"You didn't fail, sunflower. Neither of us did. We did our best, and there will be other chances."

His tenderness filled her with breathless hope.

"Will there?" she whispered.

"Without a doubt. You have my word, sweetheart."

Cupping the back of her head, he brought her mouth to his. The kiss soothed like a balm and stirred like a promise. She let herself sink into it, into the succor and seduction of his strength. Their mouths clung and explored, their hunger reignited by their new intimacy. Desire drizzled like hot honey over her senses. Beneath her, she felt the virile leap of his response, and it made her blood burn.

She was so lost in passion that she didn't hear the door open.

"Evie? We heard voices and wondered if James—"

Startled, Evie jerked her head up and saw that Gigi and Mr. Godwin had entered. James's sister's face was bright with relief while her husband looked like he was trying to conceal a smile.

"It appears that all is well, duchess," Mr. Godwin said.

"Thank heavens." Gigi hurried toward the bed. "James, dearest, you had us ever so worried. How are you feeling? Are you recovered?"

Blushing furiously, Evie realized she was sprawled wantonly over her bedridden husband. When she tried to roll off him, he prevented her escape by placing a possessive arm around her waist.

"I am perfectly well," he told his sister. "I've never been better, in fact."

The steely ridge beneath Evie's thigh attested to this, and her cheeks grew hotter. Twisting her head, she saw that Gigi was beaming, and Mr. Godwin was no longer bothering to hide his grin.

"That is splendid news indeed," Gigi said. "We shall have to let Ethan, Xenia, and Owen know. They've been beside themselves with worry—"

"Glad to have you back, Manderly." Slinging an arm around his wife's shoulders, Mr. Godwin tugged her closer and murmured, "Why don't we share the news with the others and leave these two to their reunion?"

With strength born of desperation, Evie pulled free and stumbled to her feet.

"Please stay and visit, and I shall let the others know," she said with as much dignity as she could muster. "Mind you don't tire James. And do not, under any circumstances, allow him out of bed."

She headed out, but at the door, she couldn't resist looking back. Gigi and Mr. Godwin were flanking James's bed, catching him up on the plans for the ball. James, however, was staring directly at Evie. He gave her a wink that made her insides flutter, and she left, floating on a cloud.

Chapter Fifteen

As the physician had predicted, James made a full and rapid recovery. To celebrate, his brothers and brother-in-law took him to supper at the Briarbush Inn. Located on the corner of High Street, the popular establishment had a comfortably shabby ambiance. The ceiling sagged between heavy oak beams stained by soot. Plaster crumbled from walls mellowed by time. The air was redolent of baking bread, roasting meat, and beeswax polish.

This evening, the public room was as packed as a market at noon. Competition for the dining tables was fierce, especially for those close to the giant stone hearth that held a kettle of simmering mulled cider. Owen's attempts to secure a table had been foiled twice: first by a rector who'd sped by on winged feet, then by a spinster who'd simply knocked him aside with her cane.

Rubbing his side, Owen muttered, "Care to remind me why we are dining here?"

"It's Thursday," Ethan said.

Owen drew his brows together. "What is special about Thursday?"

"It's Pie and Fool night. And no one makes a pie or a fool like Mrs. Thornton."

"What kind of pie? And what flavor is the fool?"

Despite his gangly build, Owen ate like a horse...which came as a relief to James and the family. Following his return from Afghanistan, Owen had gone through years with little or no appetite. That, combined with too much drinking and not enough sleep, had turned him into a walking skeleton. Since his arrival in Chuddums last fall, he had filled out. He would always be lanky, but his enjoyment of the hearty country fare and working outdoors had toughened his physique. His brown hair was overdue for a trim, but he looked rested...which owed less to the bucolic setting and more to burying the hatchet with Ethan.

Watching his brothers banter, James felt a weight lift from his shoulders. As the eldest, he had a duty to look after his siblings. Witnessing their rift and being powerless to fix it had been excruciating. He'd feared that their relationship might never be mended, but then a miracle happened. Ethan had purchased Bottoms House, and in this downtrodden village in the middle of nowhere, he'd found Xenia. Or at least, he hadn't pushed her aside when James had suggested that he hire her as a housekeeper.

Xenia had restored more than Ethan's manor. Her love had healed Ethan and allowed him to forgive Owen. Even if Owen hadn't forgiven himself for injuring Ethan, the two had reconciled. A few months later, Gigi found her soulmate as well. Initially, James had had doubts about Conrad Godwin, but he now saw the man's devotion to Gigi—and to rebuilding Chuddums.

Maybe this place does possess some sort of magic. Maybe my siblings and I were destined to come here for a reason. Maybe there is hope, not just for them, but for me as well.

Thinking of the conversation with Evie, James felt a surge of hope. It had been their first honest conversation in nearly a year. She'd been open about her feelings in a way she never had been before. Recalling her anguish, his throat tightened. The grief she'd bottled up had been like a poison and needed to be purged. Truth be told, he'd been surprised by his own show of emotion. By expunging the past, they could move on. The loss would always be there, but they could face the future together.

He recalled her wistfulness regarding a second chance, and determination welled inside him. Now that there were no longer secrets between them, he would show his wife the sort of marriage he desired. He hadn't made his move yet; he wanted to be strategic. To choose his next steps with deliberation and care. Although their tension had improved since their talk, Evie remained skittish around him.

Last night before supper, he had tested the waters. Dismissing his wife's maid, he'd helped her put on her mama's pearl necklace. She'd shivered when he'd slid those cool pearls around her neck, and he couldn't resist kissing her—a simple brush of his lips beneath her left ear.

Color had flooded her cheeks. She'd twitched as if she'd touched an electrifying machine.

"We...we can't be late for supper," she'd stammered.

As excuses went, it was a transparent one, but he had let it go. Throughout supper, he'd watched her, the way those pearls bobbed upon her magnificent breasts, the sweet curve of her cheek when she smiled. Several times, their gazes had collided, and she'd averted hers, with an endearing shyness that made him grow hard beneath the table. That night, it had taken considerable willpower not to climb into bed with her.

He was recognizing that passion wasn't their problem. Looking back, that had been the one area where their connection had always been robust. True, she'd pushed him away physically for a time, but her explanation had made sense. He believed that she hadn't meant to do so—and now the heat was back between them, stronger than ever. Yet he sensed there was still something holding her back.

A remnant of grief, perhaps, or the natural awkwardness that came with getting reacquainted? Lying on the lumpy sitting room sofa, he didn't know what the problem was, precisely, but he knew he needed to take things slowly with Evie. They needed to get to know one another again...or perhaps for the first time.

That didn't stop him from fantasizing, however. The images of making love to his wife while she was clad in only her pearls and spectacles had made his blood rush. Like a damned greenling, he'd been forced to take matters into his own hands, stifling his groans with a pillow. The release had cleared his head and clarified his plan.

He would court Evie again, get to know her body and mind. He would secure her love. By doing so, he would steer their marriage back on course...and finally fulfill his family legacy.

"The filling and flavor depend on Mrs. Thornton's mood," Ethan was saying as he clapped Owen on the back. "A word to the wise, lad. Whatever you do, do *not* ask the good lady questions about the menu."

Owen frowned. "Why not?"

"Just trust me on this—"

"Good evening and welcome, sirs."

The booming voice belonged to Mr. Thornton, the proprietor. The fellow's chest was as wide as the barrels of ale lined up behind his bar, and his rolled sleeves revealed bulging arms that would make a guest think twice about unruly behavior. His hair was concentrated on his bushy mutton chop whiskers, and his bald pate gleamed as he bowed.

"Good evening to you, Mr. Thornton," Ethan replied. "We were in hopes of securing a table, but it appears you are fully occupied—"

"Never too occupied for the Harringtons," Mr. Thornton declared. "Or for you, Mr. Godwin. The improvements you've made to the square have already brought new business to the village and my establishment. As landlords go, you are a breath of fresh air. Especially after the last bloke."

"The investment is of mutual benefit," Godwin replied. "And when it comes to cultivating Chuddums, my wife is never short on inspiration."

"Gigi says the village needs an apothecary, a theatre, and a hospital," Ethan said wryly. "I don't suppose you're going to build those for her as well?"

His green eyes glinting, Godwin said nothing.

"Bloody hell," Ethan grumbled. "You are going to spoil our sister rotten."

"She could never be anything but sweet."

Hearing the former cold-blooded rake utter those words with absolute conviction, James felt his lips twitch. Yet he wasn't surprised. His baby sister could melt a heart of stone.

"Lord Manderly, you are an esteemed guest this eve." Mr. Thornton's gaze turned speculative. "If you don't mind my saying, your bid for the Reading seat is a topic of great interest to many here."

"I never object to the truth," James said easily. "I would expect, nay hope, that there would be curiosity about my candidacy and the upcoming hustings."

Friend and Dunsmuir had gone full steam ahead with the campaign. Their most recent plan involved hosting a hustings in Chuddums. They'd argued that holding a political rally here—the first of its kind in Chuddums's history and one that would bring visitors to benefit the local economy—would signal that James was no aristocratic snob, but a man of the people. The fact that the formerly downtrodden place was undergoing a renaissance, thanks in no small part to James's kin, was visible evidence of what he stood for: progress and prosperity for all.

While James had to admit the plan was sound, he had to prepare with haste since the hustings was to be held in three weeks' time. His rival, Eustace Ryerson, had already agreed to debate him —and planned to preach fire and brimstone, no doubt. Ryerson was also spreading coin to win favor, and rumor had it he meant to pack the hustings with hired supporters. When Dunsmuir suggested copying that strategy, James had unequivocally refused. He was going to win by honest means—or not at all.

As the innkeeper led them through the crowded public room, James did indeed draw his share of attention. He exchanged pleasantries and answered questions. Whether these men had the right to vote was irrelevant: everyone had the right to be treated with respect, and their concerns mattered as much as any landowner's. As he'd expected, people's main worries had to do with putting bread on their tables and caring for their families, and he took the time to explain the benefits of his proposed reforms in plain and simple terms.

At a prime table by the fire, he found himself face to face with the village's oldest resident and pillar of the community. Mr. Walford, known simply as "Wally," had a shock of white hair and more wrinkles than a laundry. His coat was a blazing shade of magenta, and his dark eyes were magnified by thick spectacles. He was accompanied by two ancient cronies, and the collection of empty tankards suggested the trio had been there awhile.

"Lord Manderly." Wally drew himself up. "I would like to pose a question."

"I shall be happy to answer if I can, sir."

"What will you do about the curse?"

James paused, nonplussed. "I beg your pardon?"

"Are you not familiar with the legend of Bloody Thom?" Wally smacked his lips, as if preparing for a delectable dish. "I shall be happy to enlighten you—"

"That won't be necessary, Wally," Ethan cut in. "My brother knows about the curse."

Frowning, James said, "I am acquainted with the legend, yes. However, I wouldn't say I know all the specifics—"

"Of course you do." Godwin, known for his composure in any situation, was suddenly as jittery as a kettle on the boil. "Mr. Thornton is taking us to our table, and we mustn't hold him up."

James glanced at the innkeeper, who was leaning on a table, chatting with a patron.

"He doesn't appear to be in a hurry—"

"He's being polite. Best not take advantage." Ethan addressed Wally and his friends. "Enjoy your evening, gents—next round is on me."

As Wally and his pals stomped their feet and waved their canes in appreciation, Godwin pushed James forward. Before James could turn to scowl at his brother-in-law, Ethan grabbed his arm, and James found himself being herded away between them.

"What are the two of you doing?" James demanded.

"Saving your hide," Ethan muttered. "Or, more precisely, your ears."

"They begin to bleed," Godwin explained. "By the time Wally gets into the tenth hour of his story, and you realize that he's only on the prologue."

"He seems like a decent old chap—"

"He is, and that is how the trap is laid," Godwin said darkly. "One minute, you are being courteous to the kindly old codger. The next, you're being led around the village on a tour...*that never ends*."

A few moments later, the innkeeper seated them in a private parlor, hidden behind a tatty blue curtain. The cozy table had just enough space for the four of them, and a mullioned window offered a blurry view of the dark square. A buxom serving maid brought them foaming tankards and a trencher of bread and cheese.

Ethan broke a piece of hot, crusty bread, slathering it with butter. "If that was any indication of how the hustings will go, you appear to be in fighting shape."

"Looks can be deceiving." James sampled the ale, which was full-bodied and creamy. "No matter how prepared one is, one never knows how such an event will go. Crowds are wildly unpredictable. A single comment or heckle can turn a supportive audience into a mob out for blood."

"Why expose yourself to potential violence?" Owen studied the slice of crumbly cheese on his plate. "There are better ways, surely, to win votes."

"With only three months until the General Election, this is the quickest path—and an exercise to separate the wheat from the chaff." James exhaled. "I have significant backing from the party, but I haven't won everyone over yet. I must prove that I am the worthiest replacement for Henry Gosford."

Dunsmuir had put it bluntly. *"You're in the lead, but you haven't secured the nomination yet, old boy. Influential members, including our lovely patroness Lady Morgana Vernon, want proof that you have what it takes to beat Ryerson—and that you don't share Gosford's Achilles' heel for scandal. The hustings will be your chance to show them your mettle."*

Or a chance to fail spectacularly.

James shoved aside the thought. Doubts got one nowhere. Preparation was the key.

"Assuming you haven't set up a love nest with an actress somewhere, these are not hard shoes to fill," Godwin said.

"It is not enough to be free of scandal. I must be worthy of representing the people who have placed their trust in me. I want to be a catalyst for meaningful and lasting change—"

"Save your campaign speech for the hustings, brother." Ethan feigned a yawn. "You already have our votes. The reason we proposed tonight's outing wasn't to discuss politics."

James quirked a brow. "There was an ulterior motive for the invitation?"

"There's nothing ulterior about it."

The looks Ethan exchanged with the other men put James on edge.

"To prove it, I shall inquire plainly." Ethan cleared his throat. "Is everything all right between you and Evie?"

By Jove. That is forthright.

"While I appreciate your concern, my marriage is a private matter." Deflecting was a reflex, as was the lofty tone he'd honed during his lifelong tenure as the eldest son and heir. "I will not discuss it."

"I hate to puncture your hot-air balloon," Godwin drawled. "When ladies are involved, there is no such thing as privacy."

"Evie would not speak of—"

"According to Gigi, your countess is as much of a clam as you are. But females, they have a sense about these things. Gigi is worried about your happiness." Godwin shrugged. "As I do not wish for her to be troubled for any reason, I agreed to broach the topic with you."

James found himself grappling with the fact that his baby sister was aware of his marital conflict...and that she'd sent her husband to investigate.

"Xenia noticed as well," Ethan said.

His middle brother's assertion ended the battle, giving mortification a decided victory. As an artist, Ethan had a habit of focusing on his music to the exclusion of all else. The fact that he was now willfully—nay, cheerfully—sticking his nose where it did not belong was a blow to James's pride. Was his relationship with Evie so obviously strained that *everyone* had noticed?

"There is naught for anyone to be concerned about," James said stiffly. "All is well."

"You can talk to us, you know."

Oh, for bloody sake. Now my youngest brother thinks I cannot manage my own affairs?

Looking into Owen's earnest grey gaze, James sighed.

"I know," he said. "There is, however, naught to discuss."

"Xenia thinks your troubles could be related to the prophecy," Ethan said.

"I don't have any troubles," James said testily.

"If you did, Xenia has a theory as to why. She thinks that all four of us—you, me, Gigi, and Owen—were destined to come to Chuddums to find love. When we do, we unravel a piece of the mystery regarding Bloody Thom."

James was about to express his opinion that the theory was absurd, but Godwin spoke first.

"Gigi agrees with her, and so do I." The magnate, whom James had formerly thought of as a sensible sort, stroked his chin as he addressed Ethan. "When you met your wife, you discovered that Thomas Mulligan wasn't killed by a witch. Indeed, the 'witch' was a beautiful traveling woman named Rosalinda whom he fell in love with. During our courtship, Gigi and I uncovered more of the story, including the fact that the pair had wed before Thomas was murdered by some bastard who was after Rosalinda."

"You think I am going to fall in love?"

This came from Owen, whose face showed both unease and wistfulness.

"You're a Harrington. Of course you will," Ethan said. "But I don't think it is quite your turn, lad."

All attention turned to James, and he fought the rising heat in his face. He wasn't about to share the intricacies of his marriage: that after nearly four years, he and Evie remained on shaky ground when it came to love. As the eldest, he had always handled his own affairs—set a good example. There was no reason to reveal his shortcomings.

Luckily, the curtain parted, saving him from further interrogation. It was not the serving maid but the innkeeper's wife who brought in their supper. Mrs. Thornton, a pug-nosed lady with frizzy ginger hair barely restrained by her cap, thumped platters of food onto the table. Mouth-watering aromas came from the massive golden brown pie and the bowl of spring peas and carrots swimming in butter and herbs.

"Supper smells delicious, Mrs. Thornton." Ethan's voice was reverent.

"It *is* delicious," she said matter-of-factly.

With an expert hand, she cut a generous slab of pie, plating it along with a scoop of vegetables. Over this, she ladled a spoonful of rich, thyme-scented gravy. She repeated the process, plunking dishes in front of James, Ethan, and Godwin. As she was working on the final serving, Owen peered at Ethan's plate.

"What kind of pie is that—*ouch*." Owen glowered at Ethan, rubbing his side. "Mind your bloody elbow."

It was too late, however. Mrs. Thornton pinned Owen with a gimlet stare.

"What did you say?"

Ethan shook his head in obvious warning, but Owen answered anyway.

"I was wondering what kind of meat is in the pie, ma'am."

His polite inquiry had a remarkable effect on Mrs. Thornton, whose complexion went from ruddy to florid. She dropped the serving spoon with a loud clatter. Bracing her hands on her hips, she glared at him.

"Are you questioning my cooking, sir?"

"Um, no." Owen looked confused. "I just wanted to know the ingredients."

"The ingredients in this pie," she said in a dangerous tone, "are what I chose to put in there."

"I didn't mean—"

"You don't come to my establishment to *know*. You come to eat—or starve. It's up to you."

Owen frowned. "That hardly seems hospitable."

Even James, who didn't know the woman, could tell that the reply was unwise. Like a pot left too long on the fire, she blew her lid.

"Hospitable?" she exploded. "I'll show you hospitable. No pie for you!"

She snatched the half-filled plate and slammed it back on her tray. The rest of the pie and vegetables followed. The curtain flapped angrily behind her.

Ethan spoke first. "I warned you not to annoy her, lad."

"I didn't do anything," Owen protested. "I just asked what kind of pie it was!"

Ethan shoveled a forkful into his mouth. "A delicious pie, that's what. Best I've ever tasted."

Grabbing a fork, Owen aimed for Ethan's plate. "Give me some of that."

Ethan kept his plate out of reach.

"Sorry, lad," he said with a smirk. "*Ad finem fidelis* has its limits. When it comes to pie, it's each man for himself."

Chapter Sixteen

She was running...running as fast as she could.

The forest floor was dewy beneath her feet, the night fog weaving thickly between the trees. Even with her lantern, she could only see a few inches ahead. Yet she wasn't afraid of the woods. For the monster didn't live in nature's labyrinth but in the lavish manor ablaze with light.

Why, oh why, did I take this position?

She cursed her stupidity and her arrogance. She ought to have listened to her mama, who'd warned her that no good would come from putting down roots. Her folk had traveled for generations, yet in her conceit, she'd believed that she could do better. That she was meant for more than the simple life her family led.

Shame choked her and shaped her breath into sobs. Because of her mistake, she had no one now. She was shunned and disgraced and so very alone. The fog drifted, and through the veil of tears, she saw a web of moonlight draped across an entrance...a shelter in the woods. A place where she would, at least temporarily, be safe.

Right now, the monster would be climbing the steps to her attic quarters. Night after night, trembling in her cot, she'd listened to the menacing thump of his boots. She'd screamed the first few times—loud enough to wake the dead. Yet no one came to her aid. When she'd summoned the courage to tell the lady of the house, she'd received a beating for her trouble.

Shut your gob, you troublemaking slut, Mistress had hissed. *My husband is an important man of the highest standing. If you dare to slander him again, he will see to it that you pay...you and that stinking, no-good, peddling family of yours.*

She had no choice but to run. One day, when she'd saved enough, she would get farther than the forest. She would run and run and run...so far that the monster couldn't find her.

When will I ever be free?

For now, she would hide in this cave. She entered warily, in case this was the refuge of other frightened animals. Raising her lamp, she saw that the snug space was empty...and gasped when she saw a dazzling wall of pearls. Astonished, she went over and touched her fingertips to the glowing spiral embedded in the rock.

Not pearls, she recognized with wonder. *These are shells. Hundreds of them.*

The circular pattern covered the entire wall, flowing with a continuity that seemed to have no beginning or end. It seemed to move, a line of light twirling against the dark, and it filled her with a strange sense of hope.

Outside, the monster howled. "There is no escape, Rose. You are mine."

But for now, concealed in her hideaway, she was safe.

Evie shot up with a gasp.

She was alone, in bed at Bottoms House. James must still be out with his brothers; he'd said not to wait up. Bringing her shaking hands to her face, she dashed away the wetness clinging to her cheeks.

A dream. It was a dream. It didn't really happen.

Yet her heart was thundering because it had *felt* real. Frighteningly familiar. Even though she hadn't suffered the same violation as Rose—who must be the Rosalinda of legend—she *had* known the same fear. The flavor and texture of it coated her tongue, dripped sickly over her insides.

She, too, had run. Shackled by her gender and youth, she'd never gone far. Most times, she'd favored hiding, and she was good at that. At making herself as unnoticeable as moss on a stone.

If Wilmington cannot find me, he cannot hurt me.

That had been her motto. Even so, evading him completely was impossible. He would hunt her down, and in his mild, matter-of-fact way, tear her confidence to shreds.

"What a disappointing investment you are proving to be, Evie." He would say it almost conversationally. *"Fat and plain, a four-eyed blemish on womanhood. You've inherited neither your mama's charms nor her pleasing demeanor. You will end up on the shelf because no man will want you. And even though you are not of my blood, I shall have to bear the burden of your existence."*

That was Wilmington at his kindest. When he was drunk and raging, the monster would truly emerge. *"You're an ugly, useless cunt. A worthless bitch."* Red-faced, spittle flying from his lips, he would cage her against the wall and spew vitriol at her while she cowered. She'd learned to endure such moments by reciting plant taxonomy in her head.

Plantae... Tetradynamia... Siliculosa... Cheiranthus... Cheiranthus cheiri... the common wallflower.

Over and over again, so that while her body trembled, inside she felt nothing at all.

The change from girl to womanhood, however, had made the situation intolerable. Then, she'd had no choice but to fight back. To do...what she'd done.

The fact that she'd been under duress didn't stem the flood of guilt and dread. Did the dream portend that her sins would soon catch up to her? She hadn't heard from the blackmailer again—had buried the whole business in a pit of denial during James's illness. But the extortionist could demand more money at any time, and God help her, she didn't know if she could make good on her vow to leave James, even to protect him.

Not now, when he was smiling at her again. When he'd held her and listened while she purged her regrets...some of them, at least. Their talk and the kiss that followed had sown seeds where hope had lain fallow.

"There will be other chances," James had said.

He'd given her his word—which, for him, was as unbreakable as a vow. True, he hadn't done more than that yet...but he was still getting his strength back. Moreover, she felt as if they had been given a fragile second chance and knew, intuitively, that he felt it too. If they were to make their marriage work this time around, they couldn't rush things. They couldn't make the same mistakes as before. She didn't know how she would manage her secrets, but knowing how much her husband valued honesty, she resolved to be as truthful as she could.

In the meantime, James had had heaps of visitors. Mr. Friend and Lord Dunsmuir had been practically glued to his side, pestering him about the campaign until, finally, she'd set her foot down and told them her husband needed rest. They'd left him with a pile of speeches and notes for the hustings. She'd argued that James oughtn't push himself so soon, but he had insisted he was up to the task.

It was good to have her bull-headed husband back. So good that abandoning him and the life they shared seemed impossible. Perhaps her dream hadn't been an omen about her blackmailer, but about something else. Xenia and Gigi had alluded to the dreams they'd had of Thomas and Rosalinda. Their visions had started when they arrived in Chuddums and started falling for their respective mates. Both ladies were convinced that by finding their own true love, they were helping to undo the curse. By exposing the truth of what happened between Thomas Mulligan and Rosalinda, they would finally bring Bloody Thom peace.

Could it be that James and I are a part of this? Is a happy ending possible for us? If he knew my secrets, could he still love me?

Rosalinda's question echoed in Evie's heart.

When will I ever be free?

The next morning, James left for an early ride with his brothers. Which was just as well since Evie had a list of tasks to tackle. She and Xenia accompanied Gigi to Chuddums, where market day had taken over the square. Stalls were overflowing with produce, freshly caught fish, and assorted local specialties. She met with the flower seller to make the selection of flora for Gigi's ball. Evie carefully chose flowers not only for their aesthetic value but also for their meaning: garlands of myrtle and ivy to symbolize fidelity, pink roses for admiration and joy, and orange blossoms for eternal love.

She and the ladies also stopped at the dressmaker's shop. In addition to her own ball gown, Gigi had insisted on ordering ones for Evie and Xenia, and during their fittings, the trio enjoyed tea and gossip with the talented modiste, Mrs. Sommers. By the time they returned to Bottoms House, the men were back. Xenia went to assist Ethan with his latest composition, and Evie headed to the drawing room, where the butler had said James was entertaining guests.

At the door, Evie hesitated. She wanted to support James in his ambitions...to be a true helpmeet. A politician's wife was an important partner in his success: her social savviness and influence could make or break a campaign. While Evie couldn't claim to be a skilled hostess, she was willing to try to be what her husband needed.

Yet James hadn't invited her to this gathering. Beyond her presence at the hustings, he hadn't asked anything else of her...of a public or private nature. He had been kind and gentle, but he had made no marital overtures, which she'd attributed to his physical recovery and the demands of the campaign. But perhaps it was something else—something to do with her.

Maybe he no longer desires me. Maybe he realizes that I am not pretty or popular enough to stand by his side. Maybe he thinks I will dull his shine rather than enhance it.

Self-doubt coiled around her like a vine. She saw herself as others had seen her: awkward, plain, worthless. She nearly turned around and left. Then she heard a burst of laughter and exuberant exclamations. She recognized the voices of Mr. Friend and Lord Dunsmuir...but who did that sultry female voice belong to?

Before she could think twice, she opened the door and entered.

James was standing by the window, and next to him was the most stunning creature Evie had ever seen. The woman was statuesque...and the statue she resembled was that of Venus. Sunlight brought out the auburn in her brown hair, giving her curls a fiery sheen. Her upswept coiffure exposed the graceful arch of her neck and the generous swell of her bosom.

While Evie's own figure was rounded, this lady had both curves and height, resulting in a voluptuousness that Evie could never hope to achieve. The newcomer looked as if she'd been poured into her emerald-green walking dress, so flawlessly did it cling to her figure. Even Evie, who was no arbiter of fashion, could tell that the frock was the product of some Bond Street genius. However, with her sculpted face and rose-tinted complexion, this lady would look exquisite in rags.

That wasn't the worst of it. The ravishing female was flirting with Evie's husband...*and had her hands all over him.* Evie watched with a spark of outrage as the woman reached out and *caressed* James's arm.

"I have saved you from a speck of dust, sir." The lady's voice had a teasing purr. "You know I have learned my lesson and prefer my candidates—and their reputations—spotless."

Red bled into Evie's vision; she marched toward them.

"Good afternoon."

Her tone had enough bite to startle her husband, who twisted his head in her direction.

"I am Lady Evelyn Harrington, the Countess of Manderly." She addressed the woman, whose surprise was deftly masked by amusement. "I do not believe we are acquainted."

"I did not realize you were home, my dear," James said hastily. "Allow me to make the introductions. This is Lady Morgana Vernon, whom I have mentioned is a patroness of my campaign."

You failed to mention anything important, you lummox. All you said was that she was a widow with political influence. You did not say she was a toothsome siren who wants you in her bed.

Jealousy was new to Evie, and she couldn't say she liked it. Yet she was powerless to stop its molten bubbling when Lady Vernon spoke.

"A pleasure, my lady." Her manner was as smooth as her porcelain skin. "May I call you Evelyn? I prefer to dispense with formalities when it comes to my intimate acquaintances."

I wager there are quite a few pesky formalities you would like to dispense with when it comes to my husband. And that will happen... over my dead body.

Evie's smile was mostly a baring of teeth.

"Lady Vernon has been instrumental to your husband's cause, ma'am." This came from a beaming—and rather oblivious—Mr. Friend. "We have been working with her closely. In fact, she came today to present her ideas for the hustings."

"And to meet you, of course, my dear Evelyn." Lady Vernon had the assured manner of a woman used to getting her way. "In my experience, a statesman's surest support must come from his own hearth. Any cracks there will eventually compromise the foundation of his campaign...as evidenced by Henry Gosford's regrettable situation."

The keen analysis revealed that the lady possessed intellect as well as beauty.

Evie lifted her chin. "You will not find any cracks here. I intend to support my husband to my utmost ability."

"I am glad to hear it. Given the short time before the General Election, Lord Manderly will need the assistance of a dedicated partner."

The fact that she had left the identity of that "partner" open-ended did not escape Evie. An ember smoldered in her chest as she thought of the worldly brunette "assisting" her husband—spending time with him, dazzling him with her beauty and sophistication, seducing him.

Keep your hands off James. He is mine.

"I am more than capable of assisting my husband."

Evie's tone came out sharper than she intended, cutting through the layers of politesse. Lord Dunsmuir cleared his throat, and James sent her a strange look.

"I do not doubt your abilities," Lady Vernon said, unperturbed. "Indeed, I am an admirer of your work. You have an interest in wallflowers, do you not?"

Evie stared at her. "You are familiar with my studies?"

The way Lady Vernon lifted her shoulders elevated shrugging to an art.

"When it comes to research, I daresay I am as thorough as you, my lady."

The notion of this woman *researching* her made her heart thud with anger...and fear.

How dare she? How much of my past has she excavated? A sudden suspicion chilled Evie to the marrow. *What has Morgana Vernon uncovered...and could she have anything to do with the blackmail?*

The connection was unlikely, she told herself. Lady Vernon

was a wealthy widow who had no need of money. But had the timing of the lady's "research" dovetailed with the arrival of the blackmail note? If so, it was probably a coincidence...and yet. As Evie struggled to summon a suitable response, one that wouldn't give anything away, James spoke.

"I will not have my wife's privacy disturbed." His tone brooked no refusal. "For any reason."

"Chivalry suits you, my lord, and will serve you well. Crowds like their knights in shining armor. You must play up that role at the hustings." Lady Vernon's mien was coy and considering. "However, you must also have a mind to how the game is played—and won."

"My bid for the seat is not a game. Nor am I some actor performing before a crowd," James said dismissively. "At the hustings, I will present the case for my reforms and lay out the irrefutable logic—"

"None of that will matter if people fall asleep during your speech." Lady Vernon studied her rose-tinted nails. "Lord Dunsmuir, you claimed that your candidate was prepared for the public stage."

"He is," Dunsmuir said quickly. "Friend and I have been preparing Manderly for the debate, and we are confident he shall best Ryerson—"

"On the issues, perhaps. Which no one cares about at a hustings, and Ryerson knows this. You do realize how he's made a success of himself?"

When Dunsmuir and Friend exchanged uneasy looks, the widow sighed.

"Idealism is well and good in the clubs, gentlemen, but when it comes to the real world, one must be prepared to make compromises. Being logical—being *right*—is no guarantee of winning, and Ryerson knows this. He will not debate Manderly on the issues. Instead, he will employ his favorite tactic of flinging dirt at his opponent until something sticks. And something will, eventually.

It matters naught if most of what he says is utter rubbish: he knows how to smear opponents with aspersions and lies. If he gets a whiff of scandal, he will fan it until it rivals the worst miasma the Thames has ever produced. Mark my words, he is behind the downfall of Gosford and countless others as well. Which is why I want you, all of you"—while she addressed the room, her gaze lingered on Evie and James—"to be prepared."

What if Ryerson knows what I've done? It would give him the power to destroy James's ambitions...and his honor and reputation. How could I have exposed James to such danger?

You're a blight, a curse. The past escaped its cage, slithering through her head. *You're nothing but a burden. Worthless, worthless, worthless.*

Fear burst inside Evie like a dandelion. The fluff clung to her throat, choking her. She couldn't speak...could barely breathe.

"We shall be prepared."

James's conviction and the way he circled an arm around her waist, as if they were a united front, heightened her anxious misery.

"I have dealt with bullies and cheats, and I am not afraid of the likes of Ryerson," he said firmly. "In the end, truth and integrity will prevail. They always do."

Chapter Seventeen

"It's a pleasure to see you again, my lady," Loretta Pickleworth said warmly.

"The pleasure is mine, ma'am."

Evie spoke shyly, even though the good lady's beaming welcome felt like sunshine on this dreary day. Morgana Vernon's visit yesterday had tied her up in knots. Like a coward, she'd avoided her husband, afraid she might reveal too much. At the same time, a wild part of her wanted to shake the tree of her past and let every rotten fruit tumble down at once.

Would James stand by her, then? When he'd spoken of other chances, he had been referring to conceiving another child together...not forgiving her for a heinous crime. Would he defend her if he knew her secret? If her scandalous past brought his dreams crashing down? She didn't know what he would do, but of one thing she was certain: if she lost James, there was someone waiting to take her place. Her petty thoughts made her feel even worse, and she'd fled to Chuddums in search of distraction.

"I wanted to thank you again for the herbs. They worked like magic," Evie said sincerely. "For me and my husband."

"Ah, yes. I heard his lordship came down with a touch of the ague. But I don't have to inquire after his health, do I, since he and his brothers were down at the Briarbush. By all reports, he appeared hale and hearty whilst enjoying a pint at Pie and Fool night." Seeing the widening of Evie's eyes, Loretta laughed. "That's village life for you, dove. News travels faster than a locomotive."

Evie managed a smile. "I imagine Manderly is a topic of conversation these days."

"Oh, everyone is on pins and needles to see him speak. A lot has happened here in Chuddums, but we've never hosted a hustings. Puts the village on the map, doesn't it, and good for business too. In fact, I've been preparing my special jam to sell during the event. Visitors might like to take home a souvenir, don't you think? A taste of Chuddums."

"I think that ought to go on the label," Evie said with a smile.

"Well, then, it just might. Now, will you join me for a dish of tea? I'll ask Mr. Pickleworth to mind the shop while we have ourselves a chat."

Without waiting for Evie's reply, Loretta hollered the request to her spouse, who hollered back in the affirmative.

"That's settled then." Loretta beamed. "Off we go."

Evie found herself back in the cozy courtyard shed, taking tea with her friend. She sampled fresh, fluffy bread slathered in ruby-red jam.

"Your rhubarb jam is delectable," she said. "The perfect balance of sweet and tart."

"That it is." Loretta smiled as she stirred her tea. "I come from a family of fruit farmers, you see, and that recipe was handed down from my great-great-grandmama. They say her jam was even more delicious, but I had to substitute rhubarb for the ingredient she used, which is no longer available."

"What was the original ingredient?"

"Cherries." A dreamy look softened Loretta's comfortably

worn features. "My family had orchards of the plumpest, sweetest cherries, a variety not found anywhere else. In fact, back in the day, the village was so famous for its cherries that it was dubbed 'Chudleigh Blossoms.' Visitors came from near and far to see the trees in bloom and to sample delicacies made with the fruit."

"If the cherries were so popular, why did your family stop growing them?"

"It wasn't by choice, my lady. The trees stopped producing fruit, you see. Year by year, despite my family's best efforts, the crop dwindled, and not only theirs. All the local cherry farmers in the area were affected until, finally, there was no harvest left."

Intrigued, Evie leaned forward. "Was there a blight? Some sort of infestation?"

"That is the mystery of it," Loretta said somberly. "To this day, no one knows what caused the cherries to fade. The trees had no visible signs of damage or disease, appearing healthy while producing no fruit. Indeed, my brother still maintains a few trees on his property, in hopes that he may one day coax a crop from them."

"I should like to have a look," Evie mused. "At the trees, I mean. I have some experience with botanical matters, and perhaps fresh eyes might reveal a new clue regarding the crop decline. Would your brother mind a visit?"

"Quite the opposite. There's nothing Ned enjoys more than waxing on about his orchard." Loretta patted her hand. "It's kind of you to take an interest."

"Think nothing of it." For Evie, praise had always felt like an ill-fitting coat. "I'm unlikely to discover anything new. And I am in your debt for the herbs—"

"It's the thought that counts. And friendship isn't tit for tat, dove."

Loretta's declaration was like her jam: simple and sweet.

"Now I hope you won't find this impertinent." She studied

Evie with a kind yet astute gaze. "You look like you could use some rest—all that fretting over your husband, no doubt."

You have no idea. While Evie knew that her friend was referring to James's recent illness, she was now fretting for an entirely different reason. Her reaction must have shown for Loretta frowned.

"His lordship is fully recuperated?"

"Oh, he's fit as a fiddle." Unable to help herself, Evie blurted, "In fact, his renewed vigor has, um, not been entirely overlooked by others."

She couldn't say more and was surprised she'd said as much as she did.

"I understand." Loretta had a knowing gleam in her eyes. "My Liam, he draws glances aplenty. And quite a few females have come to shop for more than turnips, if you take my meaning."

Relief at being understood percolated through Evie.

She released a breath. "What did you do about it?"

"What any self-respecting wife would do." Loretta's chin angled up. "I chased them off with a broom."

Picturing herself waving a broom at the glamorous Lady Vernon, Evie had to laugh.

"That certainly would get the point across."

"If it didn't, the toe of my shoe against their backside certainly did."

Evie's chuckle faded when she saw her friend wasn't jesting.

"A woman has as much pride as a man," Loretta said stoutly. "If some chap made eyes at me, Liam would be after him with more than a broom. If it's sauce for the goose, why not for the gander?"

Evie couldn't argue with that logic.

"If a fox were to wander into your henhouse, my lady, would you look away and pretend it wasn't there?"

"Um, no. I suppose not."

"There is no *supposing* about it. Of course you wouldn't. You would chase it off, protect what's yours. The same applies to marriage. It does nobody any good to stay silent and hide their feelings—not when it comes to the things that matter."

On the way back to the manor, Evie decided to take a detour through the woods. The visit with Loretta had put her in a contemplative mood, and the forest, padded with leaves and moss, enlivened by birdsong and the burbling stream, was the perfect place to lose herself in thought. Her friend had presented a perspective that she hadn't considered before. She did have her pride, just as James had his. If he felt some fellow was encroaching on his territory, he certainly would not stay silent.

Then why should I?

The question opened corridors of the past from which she usually ran. Yet this time, in the safety of the forest, she let herself venture through the dark halls, seeing all the places and ways she'd hidden herself from the terror of her stepfather's power. Maybe, she realized with a jolt, she'd never stopped hiding...even in her marriage.

The awareness tingled through her that perhaps it was time to do something different. Was there a way to test the waters...to see what part, if any, of her past James might be able to accept? Furthermore, it had been more than a fortnight since she'd heard from the blackmailer. It was possible that he was satisfied with the payment she'd made. Possible that he might leave her alone. Without that menace looming over her head, it might be easier to reveal some of her secrets to James. He was an understanding and tolerant husband, after all.

Stop trying to pull the wool over your own eyes. It is one thing for James to tolerate your quirks and another for him to accept that you killed a man.

A rumble sounded, jolting her from her thoughts. Looking around, she realized that she'd wandered off the path and deep into the forest where the terrain had turned hilly. Water rushed downstream, churning as it hit the rocks. As thunder sounded again and agitated birds shot into the swirling sky, she hastily searched for shelter. She noticed something up ahead...a pale arch in the hillside, visible behind some overgrown brush.

Is there a hollow in the rock behind those shrubs? Perhaps I can wait out the storm there.

She dashed over, clearing away the brush. To her surprise, the arch wasn't a natural formation of rock but stone that had been worked by hand and embedded with...*shells*. A tingle tiptoed up her spine, and with dawning wonder, she passed under the arch and into a chamber the size of a church's apse. No more than a dozen feet in any direction, the cave had a niche in the entryway and, on the other side, a stone bench in a recessed alcove. There was a little hearth, with a pile of kindling that someone had left behind. The scents of decay and growth reminded her of her greenhouse, another solitary retreat.

I wonder how long this hermit's grotto has been here?

Wealthy landowners oft constructed such dwellings on their estates, and some even hired hermits to occupy them. The hermits often wore robes like monks, with long hair and beards, and dispensed advice or philosophy. Their presence was intended to give the estate a fashionably romantic ambiance.

As Evie examined the grotto, her tingling sensation grew. Her breath quickening, she traced her fingertip along the familiar pattern in the wall. A single shell at the center, its rings spiraling outward in such fluid circles that the entire design seemed to have no beginning or end.

"The spiral of shells," she whispered. "I saw this in my dream."

She gazed at the pattern for a long time, trying to puzzle out its meaning before she noticed the markings carved into the adjacent wall. Moving closer, she saw they were words. Squinting in the dim light, she read them aloud: "You are mine, and I am yours. Not only for ease, but for every trial. This is the way of love: to stay, to forgive, to begin again."

A lover's vow—was it Rosalinda and Thomas's? Or had it been added by others who had visited this place in the intervening years? Evie didn't know, but the sentiment stirred something deep in her...something she was not yet ready to examine.

Was my dream of Rose actually a vision? Did she find refuge here in her time of need? Am I standing where she once stood...did she bring me here for a purpose?

Trembling, Evie pressed a hand against her thumping heart.

As soon as the rain let up, Evie left behind the hidden hollow and returned to the manor. She felt shaken...and exhilarated. A part of her had attributed her dreams to an overactive imagination—and, perhaps, a desire to be part of the romantic legend like Xenia and Gigi. But Rose's visions had led her to the grotto, which meant they were real. Evie knew she had to share this with the others so that they could put their heads together and figure out what it all meant.

Exhaling, she climbed up the front steps. First things first: she wanted to rebuild the intimacy between her and James. He would be dressing for supper now, and instead of avoiding him, she could waltz into their shared chamber and ask him how his day had gone. She could make pleasant small talk while making wifely adjustments to his cravat and lapel.

Her splendid plan and gathered courage came to naught when the butler informed her that the earl had gone out. He hadn't left word of his whereabouts, only that he would not be taking supper. Deflated, Evie trudged to her room alone. When she was greeted by the lingering scent of James's cologne, longing and frustration welled inside her. Tossing aside her bonnet and gloves, she wandered listlessly to the sitting room that James had taken over.

Seeing the papers scattered across the escritoire, she went over with a faint smile. A messy desk was one of James's foibles, which she secretly found endearing. She tidied up newspapers, correspondence, and notes he'd jotted down for his speech. She found a cream-colored envelope with a broken seal; the paper was smooth, with a luxurious heft, and she turned it over. A pulse throbbed at the side of her throat when she saw the unmistakably feminine hand that had addressed the note to her husband.

She paused, debating the merits of what she was about to do. Her sensible side argued that this was James's private correspondence: she had no right to pry. Her primal side drove her shaking hands to extract the note. Attar of Roses, which she'd always found cloying, wafted from the paper. Unfolding it, she read the lushly penned message:

My dearest Lord Manderly,

I hope you will join me for a private supper at my home this evening. I wish for us to become better acquainted and to discuss our future plans without interruption. Too many cooks can spoil a dish —or a campaign, don't you agree?

I eagerly await your reply.

Yours,
Morgana Vernon

Better acquainted? Our future plans?

Was the woman hinting that she and James had started a liaison...or that she wished to?

An image blazoned in Evie's head: James alone with the ravishing widow, drinking champagne and dining by intimate candlelight. This very moment, they could be laughing, flirting, and doing heavens knew what else.

Not if I have any say in it. Loretta was right. I must protect what is mine.

Crumpling the note in her fist, Evie stalked off to find her husband.

Chapter Eighteen

The journey to Lady Vernon's estate took over an hour. The rain was a steady thump on the carriage roof, fat drops pelting the windows and making muck of the roads. Halfway there, Jeffries, the driver, inquired if Evie wanted to continue; she gave him a decisive yes. Having set her course, she had no intention of turning back.

What if I am too late? What will I discover when I get there?

Her thoughts raged as powerfully as the winds outside, but she refused to give in to despair. She had to hope—to believe that despite everything that had gone wrong in her marriage, James would not betray her.

At her destination, Evie wasted no time gawking at the magnificence of Lady Vernon's manor. She already knew her rival had wealth, beauty, and influence. Yet that didn't give the woman the right to dally with *her* husband. Jealousy and righteous indignation prompted her to open the carriage door before the wheels came to a full stop. Despite Jeffries's pleas for her to wait while he fetched an umbrella, she raced up the front steps through the whipping wind and rain.

She didn't care about getting wet—didn't care about anything but stopping the seduction of her husband. She rang the bell as lightning cracked the sky, releasing sheets of water. A few minutes later, the butler answered. He stared at her, his expression going from startled to dismissive.

"Deliveries are to be made at the back entrance," he said coldly.

Given that she was drenched and still wearing the simple walking dress she'd worn to Chuddums, she didn't hold his mistaken assumption against him. She set her shoulders back and summoned a commanding manner.

"I am the Countess of Manderly," she said. "I believe my husband arrived before me."

"I beg your pardon, my lady. Please come in."

The butler's composure was a testament to his skill, especially when she handed him her soaking bonnet and stood dripping on the marble floor.

Bowing low, he said, "Allow me to inform the mistress of your arrival."

Evie dashed water from her cheek. "Are Lady Vernon and the earl at supper?"

"I believe they are enjoying pre-prandial drinks in the drawing room—"

Evie did not wait to hear the rest. She headed toward where she thought the drawing room would be. The butler hurried after her, his long stride allowing him to reach the door in the dark-paneled corridor first. He gripped the knob as if he feared she would wrestle it from him.

"If you will allow me to announce you, my lady—"

"I will announce myself. Please open the door. Or I shall."

Looking horrified, the butler quickly opened the door. Before he could open his mouth, Evie swept past him. Her heart plummeted at the intimate scene. James and Lady Vernon shared a cozy loveseat. Their backs were to her, their heads bent close together.

A dull roar filled Evie's ears.

"What is going on here?"

She didn't recognize the growl in her voice, nor the mad beat of her blood.

James twisted his head around, his expression one of utter surprise...the *bounder*. Did he think she wouldn't catch him in the act? Frowning, he got to his feet.

"Evie?" He ran a baffled gaze over her. "What are you doing here?"

"I am your wife." She lifted her chin. "It is my place to be here."

"How lovely of you to join us, Lady Manderly."

Lady Vernon rose, the movement as sensually elegant as her rose-colored silk gown. Her neckline trod the precise line between fashionable and scandalous. Her chestnut hair was upswept, with a single plump curl left to dangle coyly over her shoulder. She did not look surprised, nor alarmed, to be caught *in flagrante*. Her lush mouth, tinted the same shade as her dress, tilted upward at the corners.

"Please, do have a seat." She gestured at the seat beside her, the one James had vacated, before addressing the butler. "Aston, see that another place is set for supper."

Evie scowled. *What is the blasted woman up to? If she thinks I am going to pretend to be civil while she entices my husband, she is sorely mistaken.*

"I am not interested in your games," she said tightly.

"Evie. What is the matter with you?"

James had the gall to look mortified. Instead of waiting for her reply, he turned to Lady Vernon.

"Pray forgive my wife," he said in a low voice. "She has been under a great deal of strain, between caring for me during my illness and—"

"Do not presume to speak for me." Evie clenched her hands, unable to bear the humiliation of her husband apologizing to this...this interloper on her behalf. "Or treat me as if I am some naïf. I may not be as worldly as Lady Vernon, but I know what I see with my own eyes."

"By Jove, Evie," James said in a warning growl. "Have you gone mad—"

"Pray allow your wife to continue, Manderly." Lady Vernon's eyes gleamed. "I am interested in what she has to say. Especially since, unlike most acquaintances, she has the courage to say it to my face rather than whisper it behind a fan."

Understanding the unspoken challenge, Evie squared her shoulders and summoned the image of Loretta's broom. She stalked over to her rival, ready to defend what was hers...but came to an uncertain halt. When she entered, she hadn't seen the coffee table in front of the loveseat. A large map of Chuddums was spread on its surface. Diagrams had been drawn on the map...what appeared to be plans for the hustings. Boxes labeled "dais" and "audience area" had been sketched over the village square, with additional notes scribbled along the margins.

"As you can see, the earl and I have been working," Lady Vernon drawled. "A hustings doesn't plan itself, after all."

Heat rushed into Evie's cheeks. She recognized James's handwriting on a separate sheet of paper: tasks to accomplish before the debate. His pen, moist at the tip, lay next to the list. Simultaneously, she registered the beverage sitting next to it: coffee, not champagne. The stage wasn't set for seduction...but business?

Lifting her gaze to her hostess's, she saw amusement laced with understanding, and her humiliation grew. She'd acted like a jealous fishwife...like the veriest *fool*. She'd shown up uninvited to a lady's house, looking like something the cat dragged in—literally—and made rude and unfounded accusations. In the taut silence, she heard water plop from her gown onto the pristine Aubusson.

By the blooms. What have I done?

She risked a peek at James. He stared back with scowling displeasure.

The butler returned. "Supper is ready to be served—"

"Thank you for your hospitality, Lady Vernon." Steel threaded James's voice as he gripped Evie's arm. "Regrettably, my wife and I will not be staying. It is late, and we have a rather long journey ahead of us."

Back in the carriage, Evie's courage deserted her, and she retreated into silence. Grim-faced, James also said nothing. The storm outside matched the one brewing between them, thick and charged and impossible to escape.

The storm kicked up its heels and did a mad jig across the countryside. Knowing when to concede defeat, James directed Jeffries to stop at the nearest lodging. The inn they came upon was like a barrel of lamprey, with rain-slicked travelers crammed together and vying for one of the last chambers.

James secured the last suite. It cost double the usual, but he didn't give a damn. His inner tempest was fiercer than the storm. Alone with Evie in their cozy quarters, he didn't know where to begin. She, on the other hand, seemed utterly calm—practically detached. She toweled off her hair and explored the snug space, as if she'd never seen a finer chamber in her life.

As he fought to control his temper, she fetched a fresh cloth and held it out to him.

"Would you like a towel?"

It was the politeness, the *wifeliness* of her inquiry as if everything were normal between them, that made him snap.

"No, I would not like a bloody towel," he bit out. "What I would *like* is to know why you behaved like a Bedlamite this evening."

Her eyes went huge in her pale face. "That is uncalled for."

"On the contrary," he said severely. "How else would you describe your behavior? You show up uninvited to Lady Vernon's tonight. Then, when she graciously overlooks your appalling manners and invites you to supper, you *insult* her."

"She was not being gracious. She was showing off," Evie argued. "Flaunting her poise and sophistication."

"You are being ridiculous," he said shortly.

"And you are being an idiot." Evie had the audacity to glare at *him*. "How is it that you are a brilliant man when it comes to politics, but an absolute *lummox* when it comes to women?"

That hit a nerve. The truth always did.

"You are not the only one questioning my judgment when it comes to females," he shot back. "I've been questioning my own choices of late."

Evie jerked as if he'd slapped her.

"It is too late for regret, isn't it?" she said bitterly.

"Do you regret marrying me?"

He fired the question like a bullet. It was, he realized, the one he'd been afraid to ask. But now he would have the answer once and for all.

"Are you angry with me, Evie? Have I failed you in some way?" he pushed. "Is that the cause of your coldness? At times, you seem to hold some affection for me. But at others...like tonight." He raked a hand through his hair. "You know I need Lady Vernon's help. Her support is critical to winning the election. Why would you try to sabotage this?"

"Because Lady Vernon doesn't want to see you get elected, James. She wants to see you get undressed."

At his wife's acerbic reply, James stilled.

"I beg your pardon?" he said slowly.

"You heard me." Beneath her lowered brows, Evie's eyes blazed with passion. "I read her note. I know she wants to get *better acquainted* with you—to discuss your *future together*."

"Now wait one minute—"

"She was certainly dressed for the occasion."

"Christ." He threw his hands up. "What does her bloody dress have to do with anything?"

"It has to do with *everything*. She sent you a flirtatious note. She dressed in a provocative gown, one she was practically falling out of, and arranged for the two of you to be alone at a cozy supper. I might not have caught you *in flagrante*...yet. But the intent was there."

Rage surged, darkening the edges of his vision.

"How dare you," he thundered. "Do you think so little of me that you would accuse me of such sordid trifling?"

"It is not you. It's *her*. I know what I saw—"

"Devil take you, Evie. I am done."

He paced away from her and shoved at a chair, sent it toppling over before whirling to face his wife. She was wide-eyed, white-lipped...and beautiful. A beautiful stranger. One who did not know him—at all. Even as fury had a stranglehold, it was despair that knocked the breath from him.

"This isn't about Lady Vernon. It is about you," he said. "About the contempt you hold for your own husband. How long have you despised me? How long have you thought me a man without honor —a scoundrel capable of breaking his word and his vows?"

Evie wetted her lips.

"You had the right of it after all." Weariness dragged at him like a sodden cloak. "I am an idiot for believing that, despite every-thing, there was hope for us. How could there be a future when you hold so little feeling for me? At least now I understand your indifference. From the start, you did not want this marriage, but fool that I was, I thought I could win you over. That you had a heart to win over. Now I see that I was wrong, and you were right. You don't care about our marriage or me. You are not suited for intimacy, and I am done trying to make this work."

He turned to go.

She grabbed his arm.

"*No.* That's not true."

He steeled himself against her pleading. "It is over, Evie."

"I do care. I care *too much*."

Clenching his jaw, he shook her off. "It is too late."

He headed for the door. Evie somehow beat him to it, barring his way.

"Please listen," she begged. "I know my behavior tonight was unseemly, but it wasn't because I doubted you. I know you are a man of honor...how could I not when you married me because of it? When I see, day after day, how good and noble you are. To your family and friends, to the constituents you want to help. And most of all, to me."

He quelled the quickening in his chest. He couldn't allow himself to be pulled back into the cycle of hope and disappointment. He was *done*.

"I am not what you need," he said flatly. "Perhaps the reverse is true as well. We have had our chances and failed to make each other happy."

A tear trickled down her cheek.

"You are *everything* to me." Her voice hitched. "The failures are mine, don't you see? I have never deserved you, and I knew that from the start. That is why I refused you...because I knew I was not good enough for you."

That had to be a lie, for it made no bloody sense.

"There is no need to grasp at straws," he said curtly. "Let us give each other the courtesy of ending this with honesty."

"I *am* being honest. I swear it, James. Why are you so dashed oblivious?"

The flare of temper, the way she glowered at him, oddly convinced him more than her words or tears. This side of Evie he was familiar with: the forthright and sensible woman who suffered no fools.

"You cannot possibly still harbor the illusion that I married you out of honor," he said bluntly. "We settled that years ago. Emphatically, I might add."

The words slipped out, and he cursed himself for bringing up their passionate interlude in the greenhouse. The first time he'd tupped her outside a bedchamber—and the first time they'd exchanged words of love. The memory had snuck up on him, but perhaps she'd forgotten. Perhaps she would think he was referencing something else, a conversation—

"Making love doesn't settle anything. We are living proof of that."

Her honesty riveted him. Yet he remained wary that this was yet another diversion that would lead nowhere. Braced, he said nothing and waited.

"I have never felt like your equal, James." Her manner was steady, even if her voice quavered. "From the start, I knew that you were—that you *are*—too good for me."

"That is nonsense," he said dismissively. "Your family is as old as mine. And you know I've never cared about the financial arrangements of our union."

"The fact that you've never held my lack of a dowry against me is what makes you so good," she said wryly. "But I am not referring to social status or even wealth."

"Then what, Evie? What is this perceived difference between us?"

"I am not a good person," she whispered. "Not like you, James. You are perfect in every way."

He studied her pale features and realized that she was in earnest.

Flummoxed, he said, "I am far from perfect. And you are a fine woman, Evie. Why would you think otherwise?"

"I...I just do." Gold flecks shimmered in her eyes. "I knew from the start that I didn't deserve you, but I selfishly married you anyway. Because I couldn't help myself. You were everything I wanted—honorable, intelligent, and kind. Not to mention absurdly attractive. Why would a fellow like that, who could have any woman he pleased, want a fat, plain lady's companion with nothing to offer?"

His instinct was to argue that she was none of those things. Yet he felt a prickling awareness as he viewed their past interactions through this distorted lens. Was this why Evie had acted so hot and cold? Not because of indifference or faltering affection...but because of her own insecurities?

"Even if you felt this way initially," he said, "surely those feelings changed with time? We have been married nearly four years. If I failed to demonstrate my regard for you—"

"You didn't. You have always shown me the greatest care and respect. I was the one who failed, don't you see?"

"No. I don't see..."

Then the realization dawned, puncturing his anger. He hadn't been fighting his wife, but a shadow—the ghost of grief and loss. Tenderness welled, and he didn't stop to think before closing the gap between them. When he took her hand, he found it cold and trembling.

"Evie, we did discuss this recently. Losing the babe was a tragedy. But neither of us could have done anything to prevent it."

"I know that now. Intellectually speaking, at least." She drew a shuddering breath. "Yet there is a part of me that wonders...did this happen because of something I did? Not during the pregnancy, perhaps, but in my past. Was this my comeuppance for mistakes I've made, sins I may have committed—"

Unable to bear her self-recrimination, he pulled her into his arms.

"There now," he murmured against her hair while she wept. "That is foolishness talking. In the absence of reason, the heart searches for fanciful answers."

"You are the b-best thing that has ever happened to me, James. And I am afraid. So afraid of ruining our m-marriage the way I ruin everything else."

Her aching confession wrenched his heart. He bled for her—for the unnecessary burden she'd been carrying all this time—even as relief blasted through him.

She was never indifferent. She was afraid. Afraid...because she cares too much.

Women, he marveled, were a mystery, and his wife especially. Even if he lived to be a hundred, he would never understand the workings of her mind. As long as she was his, however, he could make things work.

Stroking her back, he said, "You haven't broken anything that cannot be fixed."

"I am sorry that I acted like a madwoman." Her voice was muffled against his chest. "I let jealousy get the better of me and jeopardized your campaign. It was poorly done, and I hope you will forgive me."

Her sincerity washed away the residue of his anger.

He tipped her chin up. "I do, darling, but I am not the one to whom you owe an apology."

A hint of mutiny entered Evie's expression.

"As my behavior was unbecoming, I will apologize to Lady Vernon," she said stiffly. "However, I am *not* wrong about her, James. Her designs upon you are more than political. A wife knows these things."

It was small of him to enjoy Evie's jealousy. He would chastise himself later. For now, he allowed himself to take secret delight in her possessiveness—in the revelation that it was an abundance, rather than a lack of, feeling that drove her actions. While they still had problems to work through, he could fix them knowing that he was not alone in this marriage. Evie was as invested in their relationship as he was; he mattered to her. Mattered so much, in fact, that she'd boldly staked her claim.

He understood her reaction, for he'd never been one for sharing. If the situations were reversed, he might have acted as impetuously as she had. And probably with a great deal of violence.

He caressed her cheek. "You have nothing to worry about, trust me."

"I do trust you. But Lady Vernon had better beware if she tries to take what is mine."

Evie huffed, a dangerous sparkle in her eyes. Only she could make jealousy look adorable, and he couldn't resist the lure of her pout. He kissed her, and her sweetness unleashed his hunger. She pressed against him, soft and yielding and *needy*. She moaned, fisting his lapels as he deepened their connection. The wet, hot mating of their mouths set off a fever in his blood. A condition for which there was only one cure.

My wife. My Evie. Always mine.

Chapter Nineteen

Buttons went flying. Fabric tore.

Finally, Evie managed to get James's waistcoat off.

In those same breathless moments, he'd managed to strip her down to her chemise. She moaned as he fisted a hand in her hair, yanking her head back so that he could ravage her mouth. His roughness thrilled her and stoked the wildness in her blood. Tonight, in this moment, there was no need to hide herself or her desire. There was only the brilliant truth that even the darkest secret couldn't dim.

He was hers, and she was his. It was as simple and complicated as that.

When his teeth grazed her neck, her knees wobbled.

He caught her, carrying her to the bed. Lying on the mattress, she gazed at him with open adoration while he stripped off his shirt. His brawny shoulders gleamed in the firelight, his chest a wall of muscle dusted with hair. The ridges of his torso flexed as he bent to remove his shoes. His hands went to the waistband of his trousers, unfastening them and pushing the fabric past his lean hips. Her breath caught when his manhood sprang free.

By the blooms, he was ready. His cock hung thick and heavy

between his carved thighs. She saw the smear of wetness on the broad tip and felt an answering trickle between her own legs. Then he was looming over her, his hair like polished bronze and eyes gleaming like moonlight on a stormy sea. A wave of yearning crashed over her. What had she done to deserve such a fellow?

"My bright-eyed god," she said without thinking.

He cocked his head. "Pardon?"

Since her new policy was honesty whenever possible, she decided to confess.

"You have, um, always reminded me of Apollo." At his blank look, she said, "You know...the Greek god of the sun?"

"I know who Apollo is." He drew his brows together. "The statues of him always make him look like a milk-fed youth who never lifted anything heavier than his own lyre."

At his appalled response, she giggled.

"He is also the golden boy," she said, smiling. "Admired by all, he establishes harmony and order. He is lofty in his ideals, perfect and untouchable."

"First off, I am no boy. Secondly, I have plenty of flaws. And thirdly..."

He planted his hands beside her shoulders. The heat emanating from his disciplined form electrified the space between them, and her nipples reacted, tightening and throbbing until they poked visibly against her chemise.

"I am definitely touchable." Sensual invitation gleamed in his gaze. "Care to see for yourself?"

She didn't need to be asked twice. Reaching up, she ran covetous hands over his satiny shoulders and down the long, sculpted muscles of his back. She loved the feel of him, hard and warm, the contrast of his smooth skin with the virile scratch of hair. When she scraped her fingernails over his flat nipples, his pupils flared. Emboldened, she slid her palms down his taut abdomen, loving how he quivered at her touch. She traced the arcs of muscle from his hip bones to his groin, then hesitated, recalling his rejection when she'd last touched him here.

"Don't stop, sunflower," he said huskily. "I want your hands on my cock."

Merciful petals.

His wicked permission caused a flutter between her thighs. She reached for his shaft, curling her fingers around its substantial girth. He throbbed and strained against her fist. Her eyes locked with his, she pumped him slowly, firmly, adding that squeeze at the tip that she knew he liked. He groaned, his approval slickening her palm.

"Devil and damn, I've missed this. I've missed you, Evie." His gaze, steel-blue and earnest, pierced her heart. "This is what I wanted: nothing but honesty between us."

There are still secrets between us.

She shoved aside the thought. She'd revealed more than she ever had, and for now, that was enough. While she hadn't told him all the details of her past, she had let him see the truth of her heart. Right now, she felt freer with James than she had in ages...perhaps ever.

"I've missed you, too," she whispered. "I hated fighting with you."

"Fighting isn't all bad."

"It isn't?"

"No. Because now..." His smile had a wolfish edge. "We get to make up."

He kissed her, and her thoughts melted. When he finished ravishing her mouth, he searched out the sensitive places that made her writhe and pant. The plump lobe of her ear, the tender line of her throat. He cupped her breasts, and his eyes went heavy-lidded as he played with her nipples, setting off pulses of pleasure. When he bent his head and licked the budded tips through the linen, she moaned his name.

"Your tits are so pretty," he muttered. "I cannot get enough of them."

He reached for the neckline of her chemise. She expected him to draw it over her head; instead, he tore it straight down the middle. The sound of rending fabric took her back to that time in the greenhouse, when James had first shown her his primal side. She adored the hot-blooded lover beneath his civilized polish and tingled from head to toe as he raked a greedy gaze over her nakedness.

"That is more like it," he said.

When he fell upon her, she speared her fingers through his hair, holding on as he devoured her breasts. He layered sensation upon sensation, lashing with his tongue, scraping with his bristle, and grazing with his teeth. She squirmed, squeezing her thighs together, wanting more yet not knowing how much more she could take. When he pinched one nipple and closed his lips around the other, she felt a liquid tug at her core. He suckled her forcefully, and she gasped at the sudden flood of bliss.

He looked at her with glinting surprise. "Did you come, sweetheart?"

Embarrassed, she couldn't answer him. It had never happened this way before. She'd never been this terribly eager—

"Well now." His mouth formed a sensual curve. "What a delightful surprise."

"For me too," she admitted.

His smile deepened. "I wonder what else we shall discover."

"Oh, God," Evie chanted. "Oh, my goodness. Oh my *God*."

"James will suffice, darling."

He would have said more, but his mouth was otherwise occupied. Eating his wife's pussy was a treat, one he'd allowed himself to indulge in on occasion. For despite his enjoyment, Evie had always been a bit bashful about having her cunny licked. Sensing her discomfort, he'd backed off. He'd done a lot of that, he realized. Of retreating...out of courtesy or to preserve what he'd perceived to be his wife's delicate sensibilities.

Not tonight. Tonight, Evie was different—they both were. The conflict that had nearly torn them apart had instead torn down the barrier between them. Their argument had left him feeling raw...and strangely free. It was as if he'd shed the cloak of responsibility and restraint he'd worn all his life. Apollo, his foot. Tonight, he was nothing like that aloof and disciplined god. If anything, he felt like Bacchus, wild and maddened by sensual desire.

Spreading Evie's plump crease with his thumbs, he feasted his fill. Her wanton flavor and desperate cries were the most potent of aphrodisiacs. His granite-hard cock throbbed with a heartbeat of its own, and he ground against the mattress, just enough to relieve the pressure. He didn't want to go off like a Roman candle when there were things he burned to try with Evie—fantasies that had teased his imagination but that he'd suppressed for one reason or another.

Like this, for instance.

Stiffening his tongue, he pushed it inside his wife's passage. When she responded with a squeak and a lush squeeze, he grunted with delight. Soon another part of him would be buried deep inside this lovely hole...

Evie jerked her head up, her dazed gaze meeting his. "Should you be doing that?"

"Most definitely," he said thickly. "You are delectable, meant to be savored inside and out."

To prove his point, he swiped his tongue up her slit, using the tip to tickle her pearl. She went stiff as a board, then let out a wail. Weaving her fingers into his hair, she arched her needy little pussy against his mouth. By Jove, she was a vixen. Why the bloody hell had he held back before?

Then and there, he came to a decision.

There will be no more holding back—for either of us.

He replaced his tongue with his thumb. Rubbing her slick bud, he licked inside her again. Her taste intoxicated him and drew a spurt of early desire as he thrust against the mattress.

Her head rocked side to side. "By the blooms. I'm going to... to..."

"Do it, love," he growled. "Spend in my mouth. Let me taste your pleasure."

Her spine bowed off the bed, and she gave him what he asked. Her nectar anointed his tongue, her abandon an unspeakable delight. Prowling over her quivering body, he kissed her deeply, sharing the taste of her bliss. She moaned, rubbing her tits against his chest, twining her tongue with his. The fact that she was still needy, still hungry, made him wild with lust. Nudging her silken thighs apart, he fitted his tip to her opening.

"You're mine, Evie. Say it."

"I'm yours. Take me, James. Please."

Sweeter words he'd yet to hear. His eyes fastened on hers, he drove home. Lush heat surrounded him, gripped him, pulled him in deeper.

"Christ, I love being inside you." A guttural sound worked up his throat as her sheath tightened exquisitely around him. "You're so snug and wet, made to take my cock."

"When you're inside me, I feel like I belong to you."

Her surrender caused something to snap inside him.

"You are mine," he snarled. "Every part of you."

He pulled back, only to slam in. He gave her no quarter, and she wanted none. She dug her fingers into his bunched biceps, arching to meet his thrusts, moaning as his stones thumped against her mound. Feral with lust, he grabbed her delicate ankles and slung them, one by one, over his shoulders. He saw Evie's eyes widen, for this was new to her. He lunged, and they both gasped for this felt new to him too. Not the position, but the pleasure... the thrilling intensity of it. He'd never been in so deep. Never been stripped this bare. Never been so entangled, body and heart.

He gazed into Evie's flushed face.

"I'll never get enough of you," he said hoarsely. "I'll always want more."

Planting his forearms on the bed, he drove into her, deeper than before, as far as he could go. Buried to the bollocks, he ground his rock-hard shaft against her peak until she writhed and whimpered and begged. The pressure gathering at the base of his spine told him he wasn't going to last, and he wanted one more thing.

He looked into her eyes. "Come for me."

"Oh, darling," she panted. "I have. Several times."

He knew this, and if he didn't, her satisfied blush would have given her away.

"Do it once more," he coaxed. "With a little help."

Balancing himself on one arm, he took her hand and placed it where they were joined.

"Touch yourself while I take you."

She bit her lip. "I couldn't possibly..."

"Like this."

He moved their hands together, showing her.

"I can feel you tightening around me," he groaned. "Keep doing it, Evie. Don't stop."

He started thrusting again. The feel of her fingers, the shy movements and juicy sounds, stimulated him beyond bearing. Then there was Evie's expression—her helpless desire as she frigged herself while taking his cock. Maddened with lust, he pounded into her, and within moments, he felt the beginning flutters of her climax.

"There's my good wife," he growled. "Squeeze me just so."

"Oh, James. That's so...so...*oh bless the blooms.*"

Her lips parted, her spine bowing off the bed. Her spasms rocked her—and him. Throwing his head back, he buried himself to the hilt. He erupted, his bliss blasting from him in voluptuous surges. Shuddering, he continued thrusting, letting her milk him of every drop.

Then he cuddled her close, nestling her head against his shoulder. Contentment filled him as he saw that Evie looked well loved. Damp tendrils clung to her forehead, a blissful smile tucked into her flushed cheeks. He traced a fingertip over her bottom lip.

"What are you thinking, sunflower?" he murmured.

"That you were right." Her eyes gleamed. "We should fight—and make up—more often."

Chapter Twenty

"Are you awake, sweetheart?"

Evie surfaced on a disorienting wave of pleasure. Blinking at the strange room, it took her a moment to recognize the inn where she and James had spent the night. She was lying on her side, and James was behind her. If the stiff rod wedged against her bottom was any indication, he'd been up for some time. He'd pulled her top leg over his hip, and his hand was busy between her thighs. She didn't know how long he'd been at it, but she felt how wet she was. Her desire was simmering and nearing a boil.

His husky words heated her ear. "I have been thinking."

"Is that the name for what you are doing?"

"Vixen." He nipped her earlobe. "You know full well this is called frigging. After all, we did it to each other—and ourselves—throughout the night."

She blushed at the reminder of their wickedness. They'd been insatiable for one another. While she'd never doubted James's virility, his appetite had stunned her because he'd never been one for overindulgence. He was moderate in his drinking habits and rarely had a second helping at meals. Yet he'd spent himself numerous times in the past few hours—and made *her* come even more than that.

Thinking of his potency sent a fresh wave of heat through her. Although a part of her regretted her rash actions at Lady Vernon's, she couldn't regret the outcome. She and James had finally connected...in a way that felt both familiar and new. They'd navigated the pitfalls of misunderstanding and explored new territory—intimacy that was both physical and emotional.

"Moreover, I am capable of doing two things at once." Amusement entered his voice. "I can think whilst petting your sweet pussy."

She squirmed, inflamed by his words and his jutting hardness. In the past, he had occasionally said naughty things during moments of passion, but never as casually as this. Come to think of it, the way he was touching her, in that lazy yet proprietary manner, was new too. She had the sudden insight that this was the reward for honesty. James was lowering his guard and showing her more of his true self.

"What are you thinking about?" she asked.

"That I like waking up next to you."

When he nuzzled her neck, she sighed.

"Especially when there is nothing between us."

Even as he brushed his lips against her shoulder, her heart stumbled. Their incendiary passion had allowed her to forget, for a few precious hours, the terrible thing she'd done. Yet her sin could never be erased—would always be there between them. For an instant, she contemplated confessing everything to him...

"What's the matter, sunflower?"

His endearment heated her eyes, made her tremble with yearning.

If only I could be that bright and beautiful. If only I could seek the light rather than hide in darkness. If only I weren't so...so afraid.

"Nothing." The word abraded her throat. "Nothing is the matter."

James turned her onto her back so swiftly that her breath whooshed from her lungs. She was pinned by him, body and gaze.

"I felt you stiffen," he insisted. "Tell me what went through your head just now."

She couldn't bear to see the suspicion clouding his vibrant eyes.

"I was just thinking..." She searched for an innocuous excuse. "About Lady Vernon."

It wasn't a total lie. Her thoughts had wandered in that direction. Admittedly, some of them had been petty in nature, but she'd also worried about the damage she might have done to James's career.

He furrowed his brow. "I thought we settled this last night. Upon my honor, there is nothing going on between—"

"I trust you."

While she didn't trust Morgana Vernon, she did have faith in her husband. And she wanted to support his dreams the way he'd always supported hers.

"I was thinking..." She drew a breath. "I could ask Gigi to invite Lady Vernon to the ball."

Surprising James was no easy feat, but his stupefied expression indicated that she'd managed it.

"Forgive my slow-wittedness," he said. "I was under the impression that you had no particular fondness for the lady."

"I don't," she said candidly. "But she is important to your campaign, and I know how much winning the seat means to you. I will support you, James, in every way I can. Even if it means making amends with her. I will add a personal note of apology to the invitation."

While humble pie was not Evie's favorite dish, she would force it down, for his sake.

"You are too good to me, love."

He brushed his lips over her forehead, nose, and mouth. When he smiled, his eyes crinkled at the corners, his mien so tender that her heart sang.

"While you are in a charitable mood," he said, "I have a favor to ask."

She looped her arms around his neck. "What is it?"

"It concerns a certain comparison you have made."

When she gave him a blank look, he prompted, "To Apollo?"

"Oh. Right." She arched her brows. "What of it?"

"Could I persuade you to compare me to a less callow fellow?"

When she realized he was serious, her lips twitched. "He's a deity, for blossom's sake. The epitome of light, reason, and moral balance, not to mention masculine grace. Why, he's perfection itself. Surely that should satisfy your vanity?"

"He's as hairless as a cherub and looks as if he might be blown away by his own sneeze." James was clearly disgruntled. "And Ethan is the one with the musical talent, not me. What the blazes would I do with a lyre?"

"Fine." Laughing, she framed her husband's hard, bristly jaw in her hands. "If it makes you happy, I shan't compare you with a god."

"I didn't say that. Just not *that* god."

"Do you have another in mind?"

"As a matter of fact, I do."

At his smug look, she rolled her eyes.

"Well, don't keep me in suspense."

"I shall give you a hint. He and I share a lot in common. He often sports a thunderbolt—and lo and behold, so do I."

Her giggles melted into moans when James thrust his staff against her mound. Pleasure sizzled, lightning-hot, as he teased her sensitive bud with his hardness. He swiveled his hips, sliding against her until she was panting.

"What do you think? Aren't I more like Zeus?"

"You just want to be king of the gods."

His smile was slow and suggestive. "I would settle for being *your* king."

Quick as a flash, he rolled her atop him. Even as she planted her palms on his chest for balance, he grasped her hip in one hand, lining up his cock with the other. In a single motion, he impaled her, thrusting up while pulling her down. She gasped at the decadent stretch. There was nothing but him: the way he filled her, the way she held him. Gazing down into his brilliant eyes, she felt...complete.

"Aren't you a pretty sight sitting on my throne?" he murmured. "Ride me, Evie. Show me what a good queen you are."

By all that blossoms.

And she did.

"You should have taken me with you."

Seeing Harkness's sulky features, Evie sighed. The return to Bottoms House had marked the end of her and James's blissful interlude. The manor was a flurry of activity; with the ball only days away, every corridor hummed with preparations. Lord Dunsmuir arrived to whisk James away on some critical errand. Her husband barely had time to kiss her before he left. Once she was alone, she managed to dash off a note to Gigi about Lady Vernon's invitation before her companion cornered her.

"I was not in a clear state of mind. But it was for the best," Evie said brightly. "The time alone was good for Manderly and me. We worked out our differences."

Harkness's brows shot up. "Did you tell him? About Wilmington?"

Fear nipped at Evie. Even though they were alone behind closed doors, she glanced around to ensure they had privacy.

"No," she said. "But we cleared the air, and I think things will be better from now on. He believed that I thought he was unworthy...can you fathom that?"

Harkness harrumphed.

"Anyway, I shall endeavor to be clearer in my feelings. I want to be a good wife. To show him that Morgana Vernon isn't the only one who can help him with his campaign."

"That tart is interested in more than his campaign," Harkness said with a snort. "He's either blind as a bat or doesn't want to see her intentions."

The comment gave Evie pause. "Manderly is honorable. It's difficult for him to fathom that others might be less so. At any rate, I trust him."

"Does he return the sentiment? *Should* he?"

The pointed question felt like a jab.

"What do you mean by that?" Evie asked.

"This came for you earlier."

Reaching into her bombazine skirts, Harkness removed a note. Evie snatched it, her heart racing when she saw her name written in the blackmailer's hand. The seal was broken.

"You opened it." Her voice shook as badly as her hand. "You had no right."

"It is my job to protect you. How long has this extortion been going on? How could you keep such a thing from me?"

Evie felt herself falling, slipping into the shadows.

"It happened one other time."

"Do you know who the dastard is?" Harkness demanded.

"No. I thought...I thought maybe after I paid him, he would go away."

"My poor, innocent lamb." Pity replaced the hurt in Harkness's dark eyes. "Blackmailers never go away, not until they bleed you dry."

Her heart hammering, Evie forced herself to read the note.

Silence is a rare commodity, and the price for mine has gone up. Deliver your mama's pearls to the stone gate on the northern side of the estate this Saturday at midnight. You will see a rock unlike the rest, white and free of moss: deposit the necklace in the gap beneath. Come alone...or your husband and the well-heeled guests at the ball will be amongst the first to learn of your sin.

"He knows about Mama's pearls," she said through numb lips. "And about the ball. How does he know so much?"

"You've worn Beatrix's necklace to many affairs. If he has seen it, he has been close to you at some point. He could be a servant... or a lord," Harkness said darkly. "Either could learn of the ball as well. But the true question is, how does the blackguard know about your past?"

"I don't know." Coldness seeped through Evie. "What am I going to do?"

"You will start by telling me everything." Harkness's face was set in severe lines. "Then we will do what we've always done: work out a plan to survive."

Chapter Twenty-One

When James entered his wife's bedchamber two nights later, Evie and her companion were standing by the dressing table, their heads bent together. They spun around at his approach, their expressions alarmed.

He halted. "My apologies for startling you. Am I interrupting something?"

"No." Evie's smile didn't quite hide the flutter of nerves. "Pauline just finished dressing me, and Harkness was, um, adding the finishing touches."

"My lady has an important role to play tonight. She must be perfection itself."

Given the stony stare the old bat aimed at him, James guessed that Evie had told her companion about Lady Vernon. He suppressed a sigh, wishing Harkness wasn't quite so informed about his private affairs. Yet he wouldn't begrudge his wife a loyal confidante. He came forward, taking Evie's hand. Cold, he noted. And she was a trifle pale.

Poor thing is truly nervous at the prospect of dealing with Lady Vernon.

The fact that she was doing so anyway, for his sake, filled him with tenderness.

He brushed his lips over her knuckles. "You are perfect as you are, my dear."

Roses bloomed in her cheeks, filling him with satisfaction. While he enjoyed making his wife blush, he wasn't lying: she was a vision tonight. Her golden hair was smoothly parted in the middle and drawn back in glossy twists that framed her face and wove into an intricate coil at her nape. Her coiffure was adorned by a small cluster of orange blossoms. The simple style suited her, drawing focus to her large brown eyes, pert nose, and full lips.

Her gown of lilac taffeta left her pretty shoulders bare and showed a modest amount of décolletage—which was his preference. He didn't need other men ogling what was his. Of course, any discerning fellow would take note of her delightfully curvy shape, but imagining wasn't the same as seeing. Call him old-fashioned, but James liked having the exclusive privilege of viewing his wife's charms. He liked that Evie chose to save the best for him and only him.

He noticed that she wasn't wearing much jewelry tonight. Her diamond engagement ring and matching band sparkled on her finger, but her throat was bare. He considered this a stroke of luck. She usually wore her mama's pearls, and knowing their sentimental value, he hadn't wanted to ask her to take them off. Now he wouldn't have to.

On that note, he said to Harkness, "If I may have a moment alone with my wife?"

When the woman hesitated, Evie gave her a nod. "Go on and finish getting ready. I shall see you downstairs."

With clear reluctance and a lingering look at Evie, Harkness departed.

"What was that about?" He quirked an eyebrow.

"Nothing. Have I ever told you how handsome you look in formal evening wear?"

Evie's flirtatious smile distracted him.

"Er, I don't believe so."

"Well, you do." Her expression was guileless. "Even without your lyre."

"Vixen." With a grin, he pulled her close. "Must I remind you again of the instrument I carry?"

Gazing into her warm whisky eyes, he had the mawkish thought that he would happily drown in them.

"I am still sore from your reminder this morning. Or reminders, rather."

"Poor wife." He rubbed a thumb over her lower lip. "I have been rather greedy of late, haven't I?"

"The feeling is mutual."

Her sincerity drew a laugh from him. It also puffed his chest... and other parts. To distract himself from his insatiable desire for his wife, he focused on his purpose.

"I have something for you." Releasing her, he reached into the inner pocket of his tailcoat and removed the jeweler's pouch. "I had intended it for our anniversary, but I thought you might find use for it tonight."

"You needn't have," Evie protested.

She always became charmingly flustered whenever he gave her a gift. He'd always assumed that her reaction was due to the financial hardship she'd endured. The years when she'd had to scrape by had naturally led her to question extravagance. However, their raw emotional honesty at the inn had made him consider another explanation: did Evie's insecurities make her feel unworthy of presents?

This he would not stand for. His wife deserved the best of life, and it was his privilege to provide it. Loosening the strings, he removed the riviere necklace and let it dangle from his fingers. The diamonds formed a loop of flashing white fire, the fluid movement of the setting a signature of Garrard. The sparkling gems were graduated, with the largest trio, each over five carats, positioned to hang just beneath the collarbone.

"James." Evie's voice was choked, her gaze wide and fixed on the glittering strand. "It is far too much."

"It is just the beginning."

He meant it, metaphorically and literally. He planned to create a parure for her. A full set of jewels that he would present to her, piece by piece, occasion by occasion, to commemorate their life together.

"This is a symbol of our fresh start. We have both made mistakes, but we have a second chance. A chance to rediscover happiness"—he strove for a casual tone—"and love."

Despite their passionate reconciliation, love was a topic they had yet to broach. This wasn't surprising: communicating about emotions was a forte neither of them could claim. For his part, he could debate politics for hours, yet discussing what lay in his heart was a different matter. He had no talent for expressing himself. And he didn't know if Evie returned his feelings.

He remembered the first time they'd said the words in that sunlit greenhouse, a year into their marriage. He had believed them, then. Since he and Evie weren't prone to dramatic declarations, they'd doled out those words sparingly, making them all the more precious. Yet after the miscarriage, Evie had withdrawn into silence...and so had he. Somewhere along the way, those three simple words had been swallowed by grief and distance and secrets. Now he no longer knew where she stood.

Stop being a namby-pamby. She is your wife, for God's sake. Tell her how you feel.

Even as he summoned his courage to say more, he saw it: the flash of dread in Evie's eyes. As if she feared what he might say next...as if she didn't want to hear it. His gut sank as the logical conclusion slammed into him.

The only reason she would wish to avoid the conversation is if she does not love me.

He knew that desire was not the same as love. He'd had lovers before Evie, and none of them had grabbed hold of his heart. None of them had made him yearn for intimacy the way she did. He knew Evie desired him and cared for him. Yet physical attraction and affection weren't the same as love—and they weren't enough.

Could I be misconstruing her reaction? Perhaps she needs time to assess her feelings. After all, our reconciliation is new, and I sprung the topic of love on her like a blasted idiot.

He said as neutrally as he could, "Is something the matter?"

"No." Her smile was clearly forced.

Why is she lying? Because she doesn't want to admit that she's fallen out of love with me?

Her gaze didn't quite meet his. "The necklace is lovely. Would you help me with it?"

She turned her back to him. Numbly, he draped the cold stones around her throat. And wondered what the bloody hell he was going to do next.

"Gigi is glowing with happiness, is she not? Mr. Godwin cannot take his eyes off her."

"Yes."

James's mama had asked him to fetch her champagne, and now the two of them were standing in a corner shielded by potted palms, an oasis amidst the glittering throng. He watched as his sister floated around the dance floor in her husband's arms. The two were laughing, Gigi's cheeks flushed a charming pink. Evie whirled by after them, partnered by some fop. It wasn't jealousy James felt but something deeper. It started in his gut and spread like a blight that caused hope and joy to wither.

"Xenia was such a dear for offering up Bottoms House. She

handled the arrangements beautifully," his mama went on. "Ethan must be so proud."

"Yes."

Did I make a mistake marrying Evie? Have I been fooling myself from the start?

"And Evie is in splendid looks. That exquisite necklace from Garrard was an inspired choice. You have your papa's knack for finding the perfect gift."

He nodded absently. He couldn't even blame Evie, for she'd been honest from the start. She'd said she wasn't suited for marriage and intimacy, but in his arrogance, he'd assumed he could change her feelings on the matter. If he wooed her, did his best by her as a husband and lover, then he would win her heart.

Failure had never been an option. Why should it be, when he'd managed to achieve most things he put his mind to, if not easily, then through sheer grit and will? Instantly, the exceptions clawed at him, leaving bloody trails: he was successful at most things... except in his closest relationships.

With his brothers. With his wife.

By Jove, he'd failed them. His brothers, at least, had found their own way to heal. But Evie...he didn't know where he'd gone wrong. What else he could do. What it would take to earn her love —to earn the right to be part of his family legacy.

"I think I shall take a dip in the champagne fountain. Make a splash."

"Yes."

When silence greeted him, he forced his attention back to his mama.

"Er, pardon. Did I miss something?"

"You haven't heard a word I've said, have you?" His mama studied him with keen violet eyes. "What has you so distracted, my dear?"

He forced a smile. "My apologies. I was woolgathering."

"Does it have to do with Evie?"

While his mama looked like a glamorous society matron in her blue-and-silver shot silk gown, nothing got past her. She'd always had a sixth sense when it came to her children. Her Achilles' heel was her soft heart, which his siblings—Owen especially—hadn't been above manipulating when they were caught in some mischief. However, even at a young age, James had understood that the heir must take responsibility for his actions. He loved and trusted his parents, yet he preferred to keep his own counsel.

"It is nothing to concern yourself over," he said smoothly. "Shall we join Ethan and Owen by the buffet table?"

"After."

"After what?"

"After you tell me what caused the row you are having with your wife."

"We are not having a row," he said curtly.

That was too paltry a term for their impasse. At the same time, he didn't know *what* he and Evie were having. Was there a name for lusty coupling combined with fluctuating emotional distance? A crisis, perhaps...but even that didn't necessarily apply. He knew plenty of couples who would be satisfied with such a scenario. One that would make the begetting of an heir a pleasant exercise, and after that duty was done, allow each partner to go his or her own way.

Why am I not satisfied? Why must I want more?

"Well, something has upset you. You can confide in me, you know."

"I'm fine."

"How like your papa you are." Mama's expression was both affectionate and exasperated. "When it comes to discussing emotions, the two of you are peas in a pod."

"There is nothing to discuss—"

"Then why are you moping instead of dancing with your wife? Why has she been avoiding you?"

He stiffened. "I do not mope. And it is not fashionable to live in each other's pockets—"

"Since when have you cared about fashion? James, tell me what is bothering you."

His mama's heartfelt plea undid him.

"I may have made a mistake." The admission tightened his chest. "I misjudged a situation. I thought one thing to be true, and now I realize that it isn't. Or maybe it is...but I don't know how to ascertain that either. By Jove, I'm not explaining this well, am I?"

"You're doing fine, dearest. The situation you misjudged. Do you wish it to be true?"

Yes, I want my wife to love me. But I am not sure she does. She is holding back—and I don't know why.

He gave a terse nod.

"Then make it so."

"If it were only that easy." Looking down at his hands, he saw that they were clenched. "I am not certain that I can fix this."

"Then don't try."

He drew his brows together. "You told me to bring about the outcome I wished for."

"To do so, you must abandon the notion of single-handedly *fixing* the problem. Marriage isn't meant to be one person's labor. You and Evie must work together."

"I don't know if she shares my view on the matter."

"Have you discussed it with her?"

"Not precisely," he admitted. "I wanted to be sure of a solution before I broached the topic."

I wanted to be sure of her before I spilled my heart.

"You do take after Papa." Mama sighed. "Honorable men who hold the world on their shoulders. Even as a child, you would try to mend what was not yours to mend. While your sense of responsibility is admirable and has allowed you to accomplish great things, you must also learn to share the burden. To acknowledge your own vulnerability. Otherwise, despite your strength, you risk crumbling under the weight of all you carry."

Her wisdom shifted something inside him. He exhaled, feeling some of the tension leave him. His mama was right: marriage was a shared responsibility.

"I shall speak to Evie," he said.

"Good." Mama patted his cheek. "Now tell me about your campaign. Papa and I should like to help in any way we—"

"There you are, Lord Manderly. I wondered where you were hiding."

Lady Vernon glided over in a swish of crimson taffeta, her rosy scent tickling his nose and making him want to sneeze. He was about to introduce her, but Mama spoke first.

"I don't believe I have had the pleasure."

"The pleasure is mine." Lady Vernon sank into an elegant curtsy, diamond-tipped pins glittering in her elaborate coiffure. "Your reputation precedes you, Lady Blackwood. If I may be so bold, talk of your grace and beauty is not exaggerated."

"Mama, this is Lady Morgana Vernon," James said. "She has been a great supporter of my campaign."

"Has she?" Mama's smile was pleasant. "How generous of you, Lady Vernon, to volunteer your efforts on my son's behalf."

"I consider myself a patroness of worthy causes, ma'am. My dearly departed husband left me with an abundance of time and resources, and I like to put both to good use. There is much at stake when it comes to the next election."

Mama sipped her champagne, watching the other over the flute's rim. "On that, we agree."

An awkward silence fell. Some unspoken message seemed to pass between the two women, which James knew better than to try to decipher. Before he could offer to fetch Lady Vernon refreshment, she tilted her head.

"I do believe they are playing my favorite waltz. Alas"—with a mournful sigh, she waved at the dance card secured to her wrist—"I am without a partner."

This cue James understood, as any well-mannered gentleman would.

Politely, he offered his arm. "If I may have the honor?"

"I would be delighted, my lord."

As he led her to the dance floor, he glanced back at his mama. She was watching him, twin lines between her brows, and he thought he heard her mutter, "Peas in a pod, as I said."

Chapter Twenty-Two

Heart pounding, Evie exited the ballroom onto the back terrace. She grabbed a lantern from the stand by the doors, then raced down the steps into the manicured hedgerows. Fortunately, the threat of rain kept the guests inside, and she hurried along without interruption as rising winds scattered leaves and debris. It was a quarter to midnight; she had barely enough time to meet the blackmailer's demands. With each step, she felt the weight of her mama's pearls concealed in her skirts.

A tear leaked, rolling down her cheek before she could stop it.

Stop feeling sorry for yourself. You must do what needs to be done. You must save James from scandal...even if you cannot save your marriage.

The image of James waltzing with Lady Vernon blazed in her head. Their dance had delayed her exit. She'd halted in the shadows by the terrace door, unable to tear herself away while her husband danced and enjoyed another woman's attentions. To be fair, Lady Vernon had been doing most of the flirting, but James had asked her to waltz.

He didn't ask me. He barely spoke to me at the ball.

The wall was between them again, more insurmountable than ever. Even worse, she had only herself to blame. When he'd given her that priceless necklace as a symbol of their second chance, she'd simply...frozen up. Guilt, shame, and despair had paralyzed her. She'd resorted to pretending nothing was wrong, because how could she tell her husband, who was speaking of love and happiness, that she was about to pay off a blackmailer who knew she was a murderess?

She didn't know if James would give her another chance. Right now, she couldn't worry about it. Couldn't worry about anything but protecting him from the most imminent threat. As she and Harkness had planned, the latter was making excuses for her at the ball. If anyone inquired, Harkness would say that she'd gone to the retiring room or come up with some other pretext to explain her absence.

Evie left the garden, heading toward the wooded area behind the property. She spotted the gamekeeper's cottage hidden amidst the oak and beech trees, her lamp illuminating the higgledy-piggledy silhouette of its thatched roof. Xenia and Ethan had recently restored the building, and although Evie had never been inside, she knew Owen sometimes stayed there because he liked the privacy.

Wind rustled through the woods as she continued past the cottage toward her destination. A snapping twig made her start; when she whipped her head in the direction of the sound, she saw glowing, unblinking eyes...an owl. Exhaling, she forced her feet to keep moving. Drops of rain hastened her pace, and she arrived moments later at the stone wall. The lantern's light licked over the row of wet stones, and one gleamed, white as bone and bare of moss.

Setting down the lamp, she gripped the slick rock. It shifted readily; beneath was a gap, just as the note had described. She took out the velvet pouch that held her mama's heirloom; pressing it briefly to her lips, she placed it into the hiding place and slid the rock over it. Before she could change her mind, she grabbed her lamp and began the trek back.

As luck would have it, the sky spilled over. She dashed wetness from her cheeks as the teeming rain turned her gown into a sodden mess. She had no idea how she would explain her bedraggled state back at the ball. By the time she reached the gamekeeper's cottage, water was coming down in sheets, and her lamp had gone out. She had no choice but to take refuge. Finding the cottage door unlocked, she felt a surge of relief.

She entered the rustic abode, flickering with shadows, and smelling of linseed oil, smoke, and peat. Seeing the figure standing at the blazing hearth, she halted.

"J-James," she stammered.

His damp hair curled on his forehead, and his eyes were bright with righteous fire.

"No more lies," he said grimly. "I will have the truth or, by God, I am done."

As he confronted his wife, James realized that he'd never been this angry. Self-control had never been a problem for him, but right now he wanted to drive his fist into a wall—better yet, into the face of the bastard she was meeting.

How could I be such an idiot?

Twice now, when he'd married Evie and during their recent reconciliation, he'd believed that they would overcome all odds. He'd thought that love would be theirs at last...that the years spent building a proper foundation, allowing things to unfold in their own time, had not been wasted. He'd striven to be a patient and supportive husband. And his reward?

The knowledge of her betrayal would have crushed him if he

allowed it. Instead, he used his molten rage to forge pain into armor. This time, he would not be swayed by her lies.

Enough is enough.

"Who were you going to meet here?" he demanded. "Who is he, Evie?"

She blinked at him. "I...I don't know what you mean."

Her hair hung in wet tangles around her face, and her eyes were huge in her pale face. She looked like a bedraggled orphan, alone and afraid—

Afraid of being caught in the act. The duplicitous bitch.

"Stop lying." He bit out the words. "The game is up. Why else would you sneak out of a ball and show up here? I *knew* you were up to something—you've been acting strangely for weeks. That night, when you came home late and lied about being in the greenhouse, I suspected you had taken up with some bounder. Yet like a witless dupe, I believed your excuses. I thought that whatever you might have been up to, you were not capable of infidelity. When you told me you were still grieving our lost babe, I believed that too."

"That wasn't a lie," she whispered. "I do grieve—"

"Grieve?" he said mockingly. "You are not capable of feeling—of caring about anyone but yourself. Clever of you, by the by, to feign jealousy over Lady Vernon when you, yourself, were engaged in adultery. When I saw you leave through the terrace, I knew you had something nefarious planned. Unfortunately, the dance detained me, and you had a head start. Then I thought of this cottage—the perfect place for a tryst. I was surprised when you were not here; did you get lost in the storm? I assume that is what prevented your lover from showing up as well. No matter, I shall deal with him soon enough. Now I will have the bastard's name before I decide what to do with you."

"Please, it's not what you think," she pleaded. "I would never betray you—"

"Give me his *damned name*."

She jerked at his roar but held her ground. She took a shaky breath while he clenched and unclenched his hands, struggling for self-control. His gaze shot to the door when it suddenly rattled… but it was only the raging storm. He almost wished it were his wife's lover—then he would have the satisfaction of tearing his rival limb from limb.

"I…I don't have a lover." Evie licked her lips. "I swear upon my honor—"

"Your honor," he said bitterly. "Do you think that means anything to me now? You have destroyed everything I thought unshakeable. Everything I held dear. It is over between us, and there is no going back. Tomorrow, you will return to Grove Hall. I will stay here until I figure out a permanent solution for our living arrangements."

"P-permanent solution?"

"I want you out of my sight. If I had my way, Evie, I would never see you again."

Even through his shield of anger, he felt piercing anguish.

How could she have done this to me—to us? She treated our marriage like a tot treats a toy. She smashed it to smithereens for sheer pleasure.

The heat in his chest was matched by the heat behind his eyes. By Jove, he would not unman himself. He would not give her the satisfaction of knowing the wound she'd inflicted.

"James." Her eyes, big and *deceptive*, beseeched him. "I never… I never wanted this."

"You don't wish to tell me his name? Fine. I shall find out another way." He couldn't bear to be in her presence a moment longer. "Goodbye, Evie."

He strode past her.

"Wait," she choked out.

Unwilling to hear more lies, he reached for the doorknob.

"I'm not having an affair. I…I am being blackmailed."

Her heart raging louder than the storm, Evie waited for James's response. He remained where he was, his hand on the knob, his shoulders rigid. When he said nothing, she realized that he was waiting—was still poised to leave her...for good. To cut her out of his life with a surgeon's precision.

You have nothing to lose. He despises you. At least let him do so for the right reason.

Her pulse jittering, she forced herself to finish what she started.

"It began a few weeks ago. Someone left me a note in the greenhouse. He knows—I believe it is a man—a secret about my past. He is threatening to expose it if I do not pay him. I did, once. That time I lied to you about being in the greenhouse, I was at the folly. Delivering the hundred sovereigns he demanded."

Slowly, James pivoted.

"Tell me you are joking," he said.

She shook her head.

"You risked your goddamned neck—no, we'll get to that." He pinned her with a burning gaze. "What hold does he have on you? What is this secret?"

"You will hate me," she whispered.

"You will tell me. Now."

Fear had an icy grip on her throat. Despite everything she'd survived, she'd never been as afraid as she was now: this moment when she would have to bear her husband's judgment. Her hands were shaking, and she twisted them together as she forced out the truth.

"I killed my stepfather. I...I am a murderess."

Even with the horrible fact dislodged, the pressure in her chest remained enormous. James stared at her, expressionless. She couldn't tell what he was thinking...if he was horrified, disgusted, or simply stunned. It was his politician's face, calm and unflappable.

"Calvert Wilmington died of an apoplectic fit," he stated. "When you were seventeen. That is what you told me. If what you say is true, then the scandal would have rocked society, and I would have known."

"Only if people knew what I did," she whispered. "I never told anyone—except Harkness."

"Yet this supposed blackmailer knows."

He didn't bother to hide his skepticism, but at least he was giving her a chance.

Swallowing, she said, "Yes. I think...I think he must be someone from that time in my life. Lord Wilmington had a valet, Merrow, who was his loyal retainer. And there were other servants who must have known what...what went on in the household. They might have guessed that I had a reason to hurt my stepfather."

"What reason?"

James's expression was harsh, without a trace of tenderness. He was cold and distant, and if it had been anyone other than him, she would have clammed up. But this was her husband, who'd given her his protection and care for years. In return, she'd given him nothing; honesty was the least she could offer now.

"Lord Wilmington came into my life when I was ten. My papa had died two years earlier in a boating accident, and my mama missed him desperately. She was lonely and lost. Wilmington came along and swept her off her feet. He was handsome, charming, and seemed kind. He expressed interest in raising me as his own. Mama married him within months of their meeting.

"Things seemed fine, at first. He was attentive to both Mama and me. He showered us with lavish gifts...gifts he purchased with Mama's money. When Papa died, he'd left Mama with a stipend that would allow us to live comfortably, but not extravagantly. Wilmington, as it turned out, was penniless and riddled with debt.

He'd hidden his financial situation from Mama during their whirlwind courtship, and when she found out the truth, she would have accepted and helped him...if he hadn't continued to incur debts."

"He gambled?" James inquired flatly.

"On everything," Evie said. "Cards, dice, horses. He squandered my mama's income. She tried to stop him, but she was afraid of him...we all were."

James's jaw was taut. "He abused her?"

"Not in a physical sense." Evie exhaled, unsure how to explain. "It was more that he controlled her...reduced her. With Papa, Mama was always full of life and passionate about her study of herbs. With Wilmington, she became a shadow of who she once was. In public, he was the perfect husband, gallant and generous. Everyone thought he was devoted to her, but in private, he was different.

"When my mama became with child, he took over and made all the decisions. *'So as not to trouble your delicate constitution, my dear,'* he would say. *'Your focus must be on nurturing my heir.'* When she...she lost the babe, things got worse. He took full control, not just of her finances, but of everything. He cut her off from friends, saying she was too weak to visit, and dismissed the servants who were loyal to her. Harkness only escaped the chopping block because she was willing to stay on for a pittance and kept her opinion of him to herself."

"Harkness holding her tongue? Now there's a first."

James's wry comment made it easier to go on. To delve into the rotted guts of the past.

"After the miscarriage, Mama was different. She lost interest in the world and stayed in her bedchamber most of the time. Wilmington encouraged this. He hired a physician who insisted that she take laudanum instead of her own herbal tinctures and confined her to bed rest. She never recovered. She died when I was fourteen."

The loss cut like a dull knife. She'd grown used to the pain, even if sharing it was new. She forced herself to go on.

"I was left in Wilmington's care. Whilst he maintained the façade of being a caring guardian, he resented me—resented the expense of raising a young girl. *'Your dress, your meals, and your very existence are the result of my generosity,'* he would say. *'Never forget your debt to me.'*" Shuddering, she said, "What made it worse was the pleasant, mild way he would say such things. It made me *feel* ungrateful...as if I wasn't doing enough to please him and earn my keep."

"He was manipulating you," James said curtly. "A fourteen-year-old girl who'd lost both her parents and didn't know better."

Evie nodded, grateful that she wouldn't have to explain. "He did the same thing to me as he did to Mama: he cut me off from friends, controlled everything I did. When I displeased him—or if he was in a vile mood for some other reason—he would berate me. Say that I was fat and worthless. He called me a bad investment because I had none of my mama's beauty and would never land a rich husband. I was lucky to have him because no one else would want a pathetic creature like me."

"The bastard," James gritted out.

"I grew terrified of displeasing him, especially when he was in his cups. He was..." Her pulse spiked at the memory of objects and expletives being hurled at her. "He was unpredictable when drinking. I learned to hide from him, to make myself as invisible as possible so I wouldn't catch his notice. I became quite good at it. Hiding, I mean. Until I turned sixteen, and things changed. In the months that followed, his attentions grew increasingly... unnatural."

Unable to meet her husband's gaze, she stared instead at the hearth. The sight of the flames made her tremble, for fire and brimstone would one day be home to her immortal soul.

"I was a late bloomer, but that year I became a woman. And Wilmington noticed," she said in a low voice. "When some young man sought an introduction after seeing me at church, my stepfather accused me of wantonness. He went through my belongings, read my journal, burned my correspondence. One time, I was reading, and he came up behind me and...and he touched me." She hugged her arms around herself. "He rubbed my shoulders and said that a bluestocking wouldn't fetch much on the marriage mart. Afterward, I told myself what he'd done was innocent, but I couldn't stop my skin from crawling. Then it happened again.

"He gave me some trinket and bade me to thank him by sitting on his lap and giving him a kiss. I was too old to do such a thing, but I feared his wrath if I didn't. So I did. And when I tried to kiss him on the cheek, he turned, and his lips met mine. Shocked, I realized that he...that his hand was on my breast. I managed to get free, and he blamed me. Called me a slut, for tempting him.

"After that, there were other instances, mostly when he was drunk. The final time, he cornered me in the stairwell. He started... started pawing at me. He said that since no man would want a nobody like me, he might as well enjoy what he'd paid for. I was lucky that a servant walked by, and I ran to my bedchamber. Harkness was there, and she helped me to bar the door. Somehow, we managed to keep him out."

Fear and shame poured through her in waves. Her insides churned, and she wondered if she was going to be sick. Then James was there, in front of her, lifting her chin up.

"I wish Wilmington were alive," he said. "So that I might kill him."

His face was radiant with rage. That rage was somehow cleansing, cutting through the filth that clogged her throat and letting her breathe again. It gave her the strength to let out the rest.

"While I appreciate the sentiment, it is unnecessary. For I did the deed myself."

"You had sufficient reason," James said starkly. "Nonetheless, I should like to hear the rest."

"I didn't intend to take his life," she blurted. "I only meant to drug him so that he...he would be too lethargic to pursue me. He'd trained me to bring him his after-supper brandy, and it was a simple matter of adding a few drops of my mama's valerian tincture, which induces sleep but is otherwise harmless. At first, my plan seemed to be working. The tincture made him too sluggish to harass me, and sometimes he dozed off. I thought I'd come up with the perfect solution...until I made a mistake."

"What happened?" James asked.

"I am not sure exactly." She wetted her lips, her heart racing as the memory flooded her. "I brought him the brandy, which I'd doctored as usual. After drinking it, he...he *collapsed*. He lay shaking on the carpet. I froze, but then I came to my senses and called for help. His valet, Merrow, ran in. He...he pinned me to the wall, shaking me and asking me what I had done. I couldn't respond. He tried to revive my stepfather. But it was too late. Wilmington had stopped breathing. I'll never forget the way he looked: bone-white, utterly still. He was dead—because of me. I murdered him."

"Evie, look at me."

James held her by the shoulders. His touch was gentle but firm. He was an anchor, grounding her back in the present.

"What did you give him?"

"I thought it was valerian. But when I took the bottle from my skirt pocket, it wasn't the sleeping tincture but *Atropa belladonna*. God help me, I'd poisoned him—with deadly nightshade."

"It was an accident. You didn't do it on purpose."

"I don't know if that's true," she whispered. "I hated Wilmington. In my head, I had wished for his demise countless times. And then...and then I made it happen."

James caught her chin, made her look at him.

"Did you knowingly give him the belladonna?"

"No. The tincture bottles were similar, but I don't know how I could have switched them. I think...I think I am cursed, James."

"There is no such thing. That Bloody Thom nonsense has gone to your head."

"I *am* cursed." A tear rolled down her cheek as she finally bared the hideous truth of who she was. "I am a harbinger of ill fortune, and you would do well to be rid of me. I should not have married you—it was wrong, selfish. Then, when the blackmail started, I should have left. But I couldn't leave when you are every-thing...everything I ever wanted. I tried to protect you the only way I knew how: by paying the blackmailer. If I didn't, he threatened to expose what I'd done and ruin your name and political future. How could I let that happen?"

"What price did he demand this time?" James said tersely.

"I gave him my mama's pearls."

Another tear escaped, and she dashed it away in shame. Wilm-ington was right: selfishness was part of her nature. After the harm she'd caused, she had no right to feel sorry for herself, to grieve the loss of a mere piece of jewelry.

"Where? Where did you leave it?"

Sniffling, she told him. And froze when James grabbed his hat and strode to the door.

"Where are you going?" she asked.

"To fetch the necklace. Stay put—I mean it, Evie." He'd never looked sterner—lordlier. "I expect you to be here when I return."

"You mustn't! If the necklace isn't there, he will expose everything—"

"Let him," James clipped out. "You will not bow down to this coward."

"It could ruin you," she said desperately. "Ruin everything—"

"Bar the door behind me. And Evie?" His gaze was more powerful than the winds, whipping her emotions into a frenzy. "You had better be here when I return."

With that, he walked into the storm, leaving her trembling and uncertain in his wake.

CHAPTER TWENTY-THREE

J ames returned to the cottage, his emotions barely held in check. At least Evie was where she was supposed to be. God help him if she'd decided to disobey him. As she fumbled with the wooden bar to let him in, he reminded himself to remain calm. To not frighten his wife, who had already been through enough—nay, too much. More than any lady should have to endure. He had to approach the situation logically and find the best solution to the unfolding disaster.

Evie opened the door, and he entered, removing his outer garments and shaking off the rain.

"You were gone so long," Evie said in a small voice. "I was worried something had happened. Did you...did you find the pearls?"

Her timidity raked the coals of his anger. Now that he knew the root of her insecurities, he wanted to howl with rage. If Wilmington weren't already dead, he would murder the bastard—slowly and with great pleasure. Instead, he battened down the hatches and contained the violent urge that would not help his wife.

"I was too late." He slapped his gloves onto the table. "The scoundrel must have been watching you, snatching up his prize the moment you left."

He saw her shiver at the notion of being observed by the villain. It gave him a horrible satisfaction to know that she did, at least, have some regard for her safety. Thinking of the risks she'd taken behind his back made him thirst for blood. Those opposing desires—to lash out and to protect—were tearing him asunder.

He exhaled through his nose. "I also went back to the house. I asked one of the footmen to convey our excuses, so no one would worry about our absence."

"Of course." She bit her lip. "That was thoughtless of me, disappearing like that."

Acting without thinking seems to be your modus operandi.

He wanted to shout at her. He wanted to pull her into his arms and hold her tight. He did neither, going to dry himself by the fire.

Evie drew closer. "Thank you for looking for the pearls. You needn't have."

For some reason, that was the straw that broke him.

"Devil take it." The words left him in a roar. "You are my wife. It is my *duty* to protect you—and it is yours to let me know when you need protecting!"

Seeing her flinch, he bit out an oath and stalked toward the cot in the corner, putting distance between them. He braced his hands on his hips, stared at the ceiling, and tried to find his composure.

"I would never hurt you," he said finally. "No matter how angry I am. I am not like that bastard Wilmington—"

"I know that. By all that blooms, you are *nothing* like him."

Evie tugged on his arm, and he turned to face her.

"You are the opposite," she said fiercely. "Honorable, protective, and kind."

"Yet you lied to me." The betrayal seared through him. "For nearly four years, you've carried the burden of this secret. Rather than confiding in me, you chose to suffer in silence. Am I so unworthy of your trust? Did you think I could not help you—that I would not?"

"There is no man on earth whom I trust more." Her eyes shimmered. "But it wasn't about you, it was about *me*. How undeserving I am of you. You already made a poor bargain in this marriage—"

"I won't have you saying that." He cut her off with a glare. "Or believing such nonsense."

"It isn't nonsense," she insisted. "You might be blind to the truth, but that doesn't mean the rest of us mere mortals are."

He shoved a hand through his damp hair. "What the bloody hell is that supposed to mean?"

"You are *perfect*, James."

He found her tone—and the way she waved at him—oddly insulting.

"Your virtues are countless, and your honor is unimpeachable," she went on. "How was I supposed to tell you that I am a murderess?"

"Stop calling yourself that," he snapped. "You didn't murder that bastard. It was an accident—and, in any case, he deserved what he got."

"That doesn't make me any less guilty."

"It bloody well does." He checked himself. "You are deliberately missing the point."

"No, *you* are missing the point."

The spark of battle was in her eyes, and strangely, it soothed the beast in him.

"It was wrong of me, beyond wrong, to keep my past from you. I regret it more than I can say, and I cannot begin to apologize for dragging you into this. For betraying your trust and ruining your future. However..."

I should have known a "however" was coming.

"However, why is it that you refuse to see the truth?"

"What damned truth?"

"That I am not your equal," she shot back. "Not in station or wealth, looks or character. You are Apollo, and I am some lowly acolyte who doesn't deserve to kiss your feet. How am I supposed to then say, by the by, I killed my stepfather who tried to molest me?"

She was mad, he decided. Stark, raving mad.

"You will cease with this comparison to Apollo," he commanded. "It is demeaning to both of us."

"If the sandal fits."

His blood went from simmering to boiling.

"Fine. If you wish to pursue this ridiculous metaphor, then by all means. You are not an acolyte—if you were, you would be subservient, meek, and adoring, and you are none of those things. What *you* are is secretive, inconvenient, and reckless. If I am Apollo, then you are bloody Daphne." He jabbed a finger at her. "You are impossible to pin down and conceal yourself with plants instead of dealing with reality. I offer you my heart, and you bolt as if I carry the plague. I am tired of chasing you—tired of loving you when you make no effort to love me back."

His chest heaving, he glowered at her. Evie's jaw had gone slack, and she was staring at him as if he'd descended from Olympus... Christ, now she had him thinking in mythological terms.

"How could you possibly love me?"

The crack in her voice punctured his self-righteous anger.

"It would be easier if you didn't lie to me at every turn," he said shortly.

Seeing the disbelief in her eyes, he threw up his hands.

"Devil take it, Evie. We've been through this. Why do you think I married you?"

"Because you felt sorry for me." She bit her lip. "And we had a physical attraction...but that is not the same as love."

Knowing her past allowed him to quell his impatience. Now he understood why it was difficult for her to accept his love—to see her own merits the way he and others did. Wilmington had distorted her view of herself from an impressionable age, deliberately whittling away her confidence and sense of worth so that he could better manipulate her.

I hope the bastard is rotting in his grave.

"I fell in love with you the moment I saw you holding Lord Thaddeus at knife-point," James said bluntly.

"You didn't let on." She blinked. "Not for an entire year."

"It took me a while to realize the nature of my feelings. And, if you'll recall, you expressed no interest in a love match." He gave an irritable shrug. "Things were fine between us, and I saw no reason to upset the balance. Emotions are felt, even when not articulated. You weren't declaring your undying devotion to me...but your actions conveyed your affection. You gave me your unwavering support during the trying time with Ethan and Owen and saw to all my comforts. When I was reasonably certain you felt more than affection for me, I made my own feelings known."

"You waited a year." A tear beaded at the corner of her eye. "When you could have told me from the start. I fell in love with you, James, the moment you came to my rescue. You defended me when I had only known predators. Showed me respect and care when others had treated me as if I were less than nothing. I knew it was selfish to want you, to love you...but how could I help myself? When I lost the babe, I was overwhelmed with guilt. I believed this was my punishment for killing Wilmington...and for loving you. By marrying you, I cursed you. I think that was why I pulled away. I was afraid...afraid my love would hurt you."

By Jove. This woman—she destroyed him. Even when she made no sense, even when her logic was knotty and convoluted, she managed to turn him inside-out. The knowledge that she loved him—had always loved him—reduced his defenses to ashes. With a growl of frustration, he yanked her into his arms, and she clung to him, burying her head in his shoulder where it belonged.

And finally, finally, he began to calm.

"You are not a curse," he said. "You are a gift."

"In the manner of the Trojan horse." Her voice was muffled against his waistcoat. "All I've brought you is trouble."

"A bit of trouble probably does me good. You keep me on my toes."

"Why do you have a response for everything?"

"I don't, always. But I have one now: I have loved you from the day we met, Evie, and I have never stopped."

She lifted her head, stared at him through tear-spiked lashes.

"Even now? Even knowing what I did?"

"*Ad finem fidelis*." He tucked a tress behind her ear. "But you *do* know that you are not to blame for what happened, don't you? Wilmington manipulated and abused you. Whatever you did was done out of desperation—the desperation of an adolescent girl who'd been preyed upon for years by the man who was supposed to protect her."

"I don't know how I deserve you," she said in an aching whisper.

"Then I shall tell you. By being yourself: brave, intelligent, and strong—and I didn't know the half of it. Not even half, by God." He held her gaze, wanting her to see his heart and wanting to see hers. "I admire you beyond words, Evelyn Ashewood Harrington, and I love you beyond comprehension. But I must have your word —your oath of honor—that you will be honest with me from this moment forth. No more deception, no more hiding. There must be only truth between us. Will you give me that?"

"I want to give you everything," she said fervently. "I love you more than life itself, but can you...can you truly forgive me?"

"It is done." He meant it. "Water under the bridge."

"What about the blackmailer—"

"I will deal with him."

"But how—"

"Do you trust me?"

Slowly, she nodded.

"Then allow me to take care of this for you."

She hesitated. "You must let me help. I brought this peril upon us, and I won't have you facing it alone. Please don't make the same mistake I did."

"Mistake is too mild a word for your recklessness." Reminded of it, he added sternly, "You will not put yourself at risk again. For any reason and under any circumstance. Do I make myself clear?"

"I won't if you won't. Let us work together and keep each other safe. Let us be the partners we are meant to be."

"Now she wants to be partners." He slanted his gaze toward the ceiling.

"James." Her expression was pleading.

"How can I refuse you?" He rubbed her bottom lip. "I have a plan, but it can wait until after."

"After what?"

He pulled her closer. "After I make love to my wife."

Even as he bent his head, she tilted hers, their lips meeting in a searing kiss.

⁂

Evie felt delirious—with relief, joy, and desire. She'd told James the horrible truth, and he hadn't rejected her. Somehow, he didn't despise her...didn't blame her for what she'd done.

He loves me. My husband loves me.

His mouth was warm and possessive, his taste male and delicious. And he was all hers...finally. As she was his, heart, body, and soul. The recognition made her wild with passion. She fought to deepen the kiss, tangling her tongue with his, drawing him inside her while he groaned. She managed to loosen his cravat, then flung it aside to fumble with the buttons of his shirt.

"Devil and damn." James's chuckle was husky. "Feeling impatient, are you, wife?"

"I want you, darling. I can hardly stand it."

Knowing that he had accepted the worst of her, she no longer needed to hide anything. The freedom was exhilarating. Happiness bubbled like the finest champagne, making her giddy.

Wonder glinted in his gaze. "How did I get so bloody lucky?"

"I am the lucky one. I do adore you. But could you hurry and get out of these clothes?"

"Ladies first."

He showed his gallantry by disposing of her garments in short order. The man could have been a lady's maid, she decided, with his long, clever fingers and unerring efficiency. Not even Pauline could have undressed her so quickly...and certainly would not have offered the same heated distraction. His mouth roved over her lips, her neck, her ears as he undid her layer by layer. Soon she stood before him, trembling and exposed, in nothing but her garters and white silk stockings.

"Look at you. You are so beautiful, Evie—you take my breath away."

The hungry, possessive gaze he raked over her made her *feel* beautiful. Her nipples budded and her thighs quivered as dew slickened her intimate cove. The sliver of air between them crackled with heat.

"I would rather look at you," she said breathlessly.

He cocked a brow, then disrobed with casual proficiency while she watched. His discipline and love of sporting was evident in his honed physique. His arms and chest rippled as he stripped off his shirt and removed his shoes. When he shoved down his trousers, her lungs squeezed. Perhaps he was right that Apollo wasn't the most apt comparison. For while he shared the graceful god's girdle of muscle at the hips, the shaft that hung between was far less civilized.

He was massively aroused, his cock a fleshy truncheon that looked harder than marble. Veins snaked along the impressive length, all the way to the dripping tip. His equipment was balanced by the pendulous weight of his stones and the neat, curling nest at his groin. When he stood before her in all his virile glory, his shoulders gleaming and erect member swaying between his carved thighs, liquid desire flowed in her veins.

"You are so splendid," she said reverently.

When he reached for her, she evaded his hands, and his brows snapped together in surprise.

"No," she told him. "Let me, my darling."

A half-smile touched his lips, and he let her do as she wished.

She'd touched him countless times, but the act felt different tonight. There was nothing holding her back, nothing terrifying about her desire for her husband. Tonight, her love wouldn't harm but heal, and she gave in to the pleasure of worshipping what was hers. She ran her hands over his powerful shoulders and down his taut back. When she scraped her nails lightly, his sharp breath made her smile. She caressed his chest, enjoying the sensual scratch of his wiry hair, the way his eyelids drooped when she rubbed her thumbs over his nipples. She took her exploration lower, her fingertips bumping over his ridged abdomen and the defined vee of his hips. When she curled her fingers around his rearing shaft, a feral sound scraped from his throat.

"Enough playing, Evie," he growled. "I want to pleasure you."

"No."

"What do you mean, *no*?"

If she weren't so aroused, she might have laughed at his baffled expression.

"It is my turn. My turn to pleasure you."

She surrendered to impulse, to the yearning thumping in her heart, and sank to her knees.

"Evie, are you certain you want to...by Jove."

Grasping his jutting shaft, she kissed the tip of his cock. While she'd touched him aplenty, she'd never quite worked up the courage to do *this*. He'd put his mouth on her, but being a gentleman, he had never asked for reciprocity, and she'd never initiated it. Out of fear, she realized. She'd been afraid of exposing her urges—

of enjoying carnal pleasures. Wilmington had managed to warp her thinking, making her ashamed of her honest desires.

The primal pleasure on her husband's face made her wish she hadn't held back. With him, there was no room for shame, only loving discovery. Easing back the velvety skin, she revealed the slit in his bulging dome and the pearly bead clinging to it. Going with her instincts, she licked it off.

"What a good wife you are, sweetheart."

The pride and lust gleaming in his eyes filled her with heady joy. She wanted to be his acolyte, to worship him. She wanted to give back to her husband, whose ability to love and forgive was surely divine. With him, she felt the shackles of the past fall free—and she was herself. Weightless and wanton, eager to please the man she loved. As if he gleaned her thoughts, he tipped her chin up, rubbing his thumb over her lips.

"Would you like a lesson on sucking cock, my dear?"

Gracious earth.

Her pussy quivered. "Yes, please."

He took her hands, placing them on his thighs. "Keep them there."

When he fisted his cock and brought the thick tip to her lips, she parted them eagerly.

"Wider, darling. I want to get all the way inside." He tangled his other hand in her hair, guiding her. "Ah—yes. Just so."

The feel of him sliding in, his meaty weight upon her tongue, overwhelmed her senses. She gazed up, saw his smoldering approval, and felt his fingers clench in her hair as he pushed in. Every inch she managed to take felt like an accomplishment, his guttural praise making her glow with pride. In the act of giving, she felt her own divinity—the power of the love she shared with her husband. Not perfect, easy, or comfortable...but unshakeable. Like the hold he had on her hair as he thrust into her kiss, groaning her name. The fact that she could unravel his restraint thrilled her and emboldened her to try a bit of suction.

"Devil and damn," he gritted out.

The quivering tension in his thighs told her he must be close. Sure enough, he began to pull away. She responded by sliding her hands to his hard backside, urging him deeper.

"Evie, I cannot hold back—"

Locking her gaze with his, she dug her fingers into his steely buttocks to communicate what she wanted. What he had once demanded from her. *Spend in my mouth. Let me taste your pleasure.* Understanding blazed in his eyes, and with a savage sound, he shoved deeper.

"You want it, darling? Here it is," he growled.

It was only then that she realized he'd been holding back. Now he crammed himself in, and she moaned around his girth. When he nudged her throat, she choked a little, and he went as taut as a bowstring.

"Oh, my sweet Evie." His gaze was fever-hot. "Here it comes..."

His bliss flooded her mouth, the sensation startling in its intensity. He shuddered as he shot streams of heat down her throat, and still there was more, spilling over her lips. When she sputtered, he pulled out with a groan, fisting his cock and pumping out the rest of his release while she watched, dazed by his magnificence. Tenderly, he pulled her to her feet and kissed her. The realization of what he was tasting sparked a naughty tingle between her thighs. When she squirmed, he broke the kiss.

"Not embarrassed are you, love?" he murmured.

The old Evie would have taken refuge in shyness.

"No." She squirmed again. "Not exactly."

Surprise flared in his eyes, and his smile was slow and appreciative.

"Good. Then you won't be embarrassed by the jewelry I gave you either."

Puzzled, she canted her head. "Why would I be embarrassed by the diamond necklace?"

"I wasn't referring to the diamonds, my sweet, but the pearls."

When he drew his finger over her décolletage, she looked down...and her eyes rounded at the line of pearly droplets dotting her skin.

Her cheeks burned as his meaning became clear. "James, that is *wicked*."

"I told you I was no prissy god." His wolfish grin sent tingles up her spine. "And if you think that was wicked, wait until you see what is next."

Sweeping her into his arms, he carried her to the bed.

Chapter Twenty-Four

With trembling hands, she removed the packet of herbs she'd tucked into her bodice. The pot of tea was on the table before her, lidless and releasing wisps of steam. She had brewed it strong, the way he liked it. The smoky blend would hide the taste...until it was too late.

Hate filled her as she stared at the fancy, patterned teapot. His wife liked to surround herself with luxury—and was willing to turn a blind eye to enjoy a life of comforts. She hadn't blinked when he'd sent her and their children off to London. He'd dismissed the servants for the night, knowing they, too, wouldn't dare to whisper a word.

No one would stand up against him. He was too powerful. A bully masquerading as the village's finest citizen. She alone knew the monster inside the fine clothes. She'd smelled the hot stink of his breath, felt the vicious groping of his hands, and the suffocating weight of his body pinning her down. Yet that knowledge, as heinous as it was, was not the worst pain he'd inflicted upon her. Grief surged, and she channeled it into rage.

She heard the menacing thump of boots downstairs and knew

she didn't have much time. She opened the packet of herbs, a lifetime of her mama's teaching making her hesitate.

The first rule of any healer is to do no harm, my girl.

She shoved aside the memory of her mother's warm face and gentle teachings. She was no healer; the talent of her womenfolk had skipped her. She'd failed in that as she had in so many things, yet she'd earned the love of a good man. A true gentleman, who'd given her his name... and his life. Heat pushed behind her eyes, and she blinked it back, drawing on the new force within, the part of her husband that would live on. Protecting this precious gift outweighed vengeance—outweighed everything.

Give me courage, beloved. To do what must be done. For you... and for our babe.

The footsteps grew louder. With shaking hands, she sprinkled the contents into the teapot and replaced the lid just before the door slammed open.

She spun around as the monster advanced.

"There's my good little whore," he sneered.

When she tried to escape, he grabbed her arm, twisting it until a whimper tore from her throat.

"Time to have ourselves some fun, Rose."

"Evie, wake up. It's just a dream."

Gasping, Evie opened her eyes, her vision blurred by panic. She was paralyzed by the wrenching pain in her shoulder. An instant later, James's face came into focus. He hung over her, a lock of hair dangling over his worried eyes. The phantom pain in her shoulder vanished, and she ran a confused gaze around the strange room.

"You had a nightmare." His tone was soothing, the kind one might use with a skittish horse. "We are in the gamekeeper's cottage—where we spent the night, remember?"

Everything came back to her. Last night, she'd told him every-thing...and he still loved her. They had spent the night celebrating that love in a variety of ways, from tender and slow to raw and wild and all the shades of passion in between.

"I remember. But my dream..." Her voice hitched. "It was more than a nightmare."

"There, now. You're shaking like a leaf. Whatever you dreamed, it wasn't real—"

"It *was* real," she blurted. "A memory. It was Rosalinda's memory."

He stilled. "Rosalinda...from the legend of Bloody Thom? The supposed witch who turned out to be the lover and wife of Thomas Mulligan?"

She nodded.

"Well, then."

His brows were drawn, but at least he didn't look at her as if she were mad. She was grateful that Xenia and Gigi had paved the way by sharing their visions of Thomas and Rose and that her husband, while logical, was not narrow-minded.

"You had best tell me about it," he said.

They settled side by side against the narrow headboard. Snuggled under James's arm, Evie told him about her two dreams, starting with the one that took place in the hermit's grotto.

"The grotto was Rose's sanctuary. The place took her in when she had nowhere else to go," she said softly. "She felt safe there, as if nothing could touch her."

"Extraordinary," James murmured. "And you found this place after all this time?"

"Rose led me there." Evie swallowed. "And there's more."

She told him about her most recent dream—about Rose's desperate actions and her captor's cruelty.

"When she put those herbs in his tea, I felt like it was my hand doing it. Even though she suffered worse abuses than I did, I understood her fear and grief. She wasn't a killer by nature, but she needed to protect herself...and her babe."

"She was with child?" he asked somberly.

"Yes. Even though she lost Thomas, she carried a part of him with her still."

Wetness trickled down Evie's cheek, but she was barely aware of it. Numbness was seeping through her like a fog. A chilling realization of the parallels between her and Rose.

"She loved Thomas so much. He was honorable and respected her—loved her enough to give her his name. To sacrifice his life to protect hers. Was it any wonder she was willing to kill so that his blood, the babe they'd made together, would survive? In her shoes, I would do the same."

I would do anything to defend you.

"Sweetheart, look at me."

She did, and James thumbed away her tears.

"You are not Rosalinda, and I am not Thomas," he said firmly.

"What if you come to harm because of me? I couldn't bear it. And your life isn't the only thing I fear for. The blackmailer could take away your future. He could ruin your reputation and your bid for a seat in the Commons. All the reforms, all the good you were meant to do in this world would be destroyed. Because of me."

"It wouldn't be because of you. You've done nothing wrong. Listen to me, Evie."

She was listening, but he was the one who wouldn't hear the truth. Last night, she'd been so relieved by his acceptance and unconditional love that she'd let herself believe that all would be well. Yet the dream had reminded her of the fact that nothing could alter.

I am, and always have been, a liability to James.

"You were an innocent preyed upon by Wilmington. His death was an accident, but even if it wasn't, he deserved what he got. Truth be told, the bastard got off too easily. As for the blackmailer, don't worry your head over it. I have a plan. And once he is apprehended, no one will believe the word of a criminal—of a filthy extortionist."

There were times, she thought, when James's moral certitude blinded him to how ordinary people thought. Gossips didn't care about the source of the scandal. The juicier the better, and there was nothing more succulent than blackmail and murder. Knowing it was pointless to argue, she focused on the other part of his statement.

"What is your plan?"

"I will set a trap to capture him. I have no doubt he will contact you again. This time, I shall be ready."

"That sounds dangerous," she protested. "You cannot do this alone, but I don't know how we can contact the authorities. They will ask questions, and if they discover that I killed my stepfather, even if it was by accident—"

"I agree. Discretion is necessary." He canted his head. "How do you feel about sharing this with the family?"

The notion of exposing her atrocious act to James's kin, people whom she cared for and whose opinion mattered a great deal, caused a quiver of dread. Yet she nodded.

"They can be trusted," she said quietly. "I want to tell them."

The approval in James's gaze soothed her ruffled nerves.

"They will want to help. The more hands, the better in this case. Whilst we set our trap, we will simultaneously try to hunt the bounder down. The blackmailer has highly specific information about you and Wilmington, which narrows down the list of suspects. Last night you mentioned the valet, Merrow. Who else have you considered?"

"I have been in too much of a panic to think clearly," she admitted. "I was so afraid of my secret coming out—of you being hurt because of it—that I gave the blackmailer what he wanted instead of trying to identify him."

"Your reaction is perfectly understandable and, truth be told, I am relieved that you did not go after the blackguard on your own.

From now on, you must not take risks. You are far too precious to me, do you understand?"

"As you are precious to me," she said tremulously.

The lines around his mouth softened. He kissed her hand before tucking it against his thigh. "All right, then. Besides Merrow, who comes to mind?"

She forced herself to think back. "There was the butler, Hotchkiss. Yet he was as old as the hills even then, and I cannot imagine he would have the stamina now to attempt extortion. As for the rest of the staff...no one stands out. Most did not last long in Wilmington's employ, for he was a difficult master. There were several times when the approach of a maid or footman interrupted his advances and allowed me to flee. However, I don't recall the servants' names. Perhaps Harkness might know."

"Harkness knows a lot of things."

Interpreting his pensive expression, Evie shook her head vehemently. "*No*, James. Harkness would never do anything to hurt me. She is my family, and I won't have her put under suspicion."

"All right. Who else might know enough to blackmail you?"

"Well, there is Dr. Murdoch," she said, relieved that he'd relented. "He was my stepfather's longtime physician from London and the one who attended my mama during her last days. After Wilmington collapsed, Merrow was the first to respond to my cries for help. When he couldn't revive Wilmington, he sent for Dr. Murdoch. I was terrified that the doctor would discover that my stepfather was poisoned. Instead, he ruled that a fit of apoplexy caused the death."

"Did Dr. Murdoch miss the signs of poisoning?" James mused. "Or did he see them but choose to keep the knowledge to himself?"

"Why would he do that? If he suspected poisoning, it would have been easy to identify me as the culprit. He knew I was the last to see Wilmington alive. And the brandy glass was there by the body, where Wilmington had dropped it when he fell."

"Perhaps there was no advantage in revealing his suspicions back then—the way there is now. I shall make inquiries into Dr. Murdoch. Don't worry," he said reading her thoughts. "I will be discreet in this. And in investigating the clue I found last night."

"You have a clue?" She bolted upright. "Why didn't you mention it?"

"You distracted me."

His gaze landed on her mouth, and the lazy heat in his eyes curled her toes. Merciful blossoms, she couldn't believe how bold she'd been. She couldn't wait to do it again.

"I found a glove next to the wall," he went on. "The blackmailer must have dropped it when he was getting the pearls."

"May I see it?"

As he obliged her, rising naked from the bed to fetch the item, she couldn't help but enjoy the show. He was the embodiment of virility: primal and elegant, rippling strength beneath taut skin. She had a special fondness for his backside, and the memory of those steely curves flexing against her calves gave her a pleasant tingle.

Smirking, he sat at the edge of the cot. "Keep looking at me in that fashion, and you'll fill my head with more distracting thoughts."

"Your head appears rather full already."

Her daring quip, and the sly gaze she darted at his instrument, startled a laugh from him.

"By Jove, you are a vixen," he murmured. "I don't know how I could have missed it."

She felt a bittersweet pang. "I hide myself too well."

"You are not the only one." He kissed her. "No more regrets, love. We shall do better from now on, and that is what counts."

She adored his masterful yet magnanimous nature.

"As for the glove, here it is."

She took it, shivering as she realized that the black leather had lain against the villain's skin.

"The glove appears unremarkable." She studied it with care. "In size, style, and cut."

"Plain kid, of middling quality, with indistinguishable seaming," James agreed. "The kind of glove an upper servant or tradesman might wear. However, look inside."

She did, finding what appeared to be three letters stamped in fading gold.

"The first letter looks like a *P*. The second...well, what remains of it appears to have a curved bottom. *O*, perhaps...or even *C*? And the third letter..."

"*M*, I believe."

She felt a *frisson* of excitement. "If these are initials, *M* could stand for Merrow or Murdoch. I don't think I ever knew their given names, but Harkness might—"

"We'll ask her when we return to the manor. But for now."

He plucked the glove from her, setting it aside. Then he pounced.

Trapped beneath him, she said breathlessly, "What are you doing?"

"Having my way with you." He nibbled on her ear, his breath warm and teasing. "All that talk of curved bottoms reminded me of my favorite: yours."

He slid his hands beneath her, his playful squeeze making her giggle. He kissed her, and her laughter vaporized in the heat that leapt between them. Before long, she was wriggling with need, yet when she reached for him, hard and insistent against her belly, he caught her hand. He guided it above her head, then did the same with her other hand.

"Keep them there." His gaze smoldered. "I meant what I said about having my way with you. You are delectable, Evie, and I am going to savor every part of you."

As always, he was a man of his word. His sensual onslaught was slow and steady, fanning her flames. He lavished attention on her breasts, licking and nibbling. His naughty words aroused as much as his oral skills.

"Your tits are exquisite. Will you come for me, sweetheart, if I suckle them just so?"

The answer was an emphatic *yes*. While she floated in bliss, he kissed his way down her belly. To her surprise, he continued to her legs, tickling behind her knees and pressing his lips to the arch of her foot. Then he made his way up again, and her breath hitched when he spread her thighs and stared rapaciously at her exposed flesh.

His nostrils flared. "Delectable, as I said. How I shall enjoy eating you."

Her head fell back on the pillow as he *feasted*. He brought her to the peak again and again, until she was boneless and limp. Then he turned her onto her stomach, pressing her into the mattress. The things he did were so depraved that she became hoarse from crying out with pleasure. When he entered her, face to face, his hands clasping hers above her head, the joining was as essential as their beating hearts. The world fell away. Their gazes locked, he opened her, filled her, and gave even as he took. His controlled rhythm revived her spent nerves, and she was simmering again—with passion and all that she felt for this man, her husband, the mate to her soul.

"I love you," she breathed. "I don't want anything between us. Not ever again."

"Never again," he vowed. "You are mine, and I am yours, sunflower."

He sealed his mouth over hers, and they soared into ecstasy as one.

CHAPTER TWENTY-FIVE

J ames had always admired his wife for her intellect, courage, and quiet dignity.

Yet he'd never been prouder of her than now.

It was after lunch, and they were in the drawing room of Bottoms House. Seated beside him on the settee, Evie finished telling his assembled kin about her past. Even though she hadn't gone into detail about the abuses she'd suffered at the hands of Wilmington, she'd shared enough. James saw the protective fury on the faces of his papa, brothers, and even his brother-in-law and knew he must look the same way. The women were no less affected. Gigi and Mama's eyes were bright with emotion. On Evie's other side, Xenia was dabbing her cheeks with the handkerchief Ethan had passed her.

Evie, herself, had lost her color, yet she pressed on, sharing about the blackmail: the notes and her payments, including the hundred gold sovereigns and the delivery of the pearls last night. He didn't know what it cost her to lay herself bare to his kin—to their judgment—but her willingness to do so humbled him. He made a silent promise to be worthy of her trust in him and the future they were building together.

"I know how shocking and despicable this must all sound." Despite Evie's composure, the tremor in her voice betrayed her. "I can claim no defense but fear. I have been afraid for so long—of Wilmington, of what I had done, intentionally or not, and of my secret being exposed. Most of all, I was afraid of...of losing James."

He tightened his grip on her hand. "That will never happen, my love."

The look she gave him—glimmering with love and hope—constricted his chest.

She turned back to the family. "I understand if you find it difficult to forgive me. In your shoes, I would feel the same. It was selfish and wrong of me to marry James"—she shook her head when he tried to interrupt—"but I do not regret it. I cannot regret loving him as I do. And I pray you will understand."

Rising, Mama came to Evie, who shot to her feet.

"My dear girl." Mama's voice was husky with emotion. "You love my son, and he loves you. What is there to forgive?"

James, who had also risen, saw Evie's eyes well up.

"After what I've done, I don't deserve—"

"No." Mama cut her off sharply. "Do not blame yourself. It was an accident, borne of fear and desperation. That monster Wilmington deserved what he got, and I only wish he would have suffered more. I understand why you felt you needed to keep this a secret, but the shame was his and never yours."

"Thank you," Evie whispered. "Thank you for...for standing by me. For understanding."

"My dear, I understand all too well."

James saw a flash in Mama's gaze before she drew Evie in for a hug. His wife clung to his mother, her lashes spiked with moisture. After, Mama went over to Papa, who tipped her chin up and looked into her eyes. Something passed between the two that James didn't quite understand. Then Papa kissed her, tenderly and rather thoroughly. James exchanged awkward glances with his siblings; knowing one's parents were in love was one thing, witnessing it quite another.

"Mama, as always, is quite right," Papa said, his arm around her waist. "You are not to blame, Evie, and I hope you know you may rely upon the support of this family."

The gratitude on Evie's face wrought a pang in James's chest.

Never again, he thought fiercely. *Never again will I allow her to feel alone.*

When everyone settled again, the discussion turned to dealing with the blackmailer. James took the lead, explaining his plan to set a trap. Evie told the group about the possible suspects, including the valet Merrow and the physician Murdoch. Unsurprisingly, she made no mention of Harkness, and James let it go for the time being. While he didn't like the old battle-axe, he respected her loyalty to Evie and Evie's judgment on the matter. Moreover, Evie had shown him the extortion notes, and the handwriting did not resemble Harkness's.

James passed around the glove for everyone's inspection.

"We must show the glove to Duffy." Gigi was referring to Mr. Duffield, the village draper, who was her good friend. "He is an expert in such matters and might be able to shed light on its origins."

"Whilst we are there, we could ask around and see if anyone noticed a stranger in the past few days," Xenia added. "The villagers are quite observant."

Godwin snorted. "If by observant, you mean nosy, I could not agree more."

"Be nice," Gigi said under her breath.

With a roguish wink, he kissed her fingers.

"The storm last night knocked down several trees." This came from Owen, who was folded into a wingchair and tapping his foot restlessly. "An elm blocked the main road just past Chudleigh Crest. The blackmailer might be trapped there or in Chuddums."

"Good thinking," Papa said. "Whilst the others see about the glove, why don't you and I visit Chudleigh Crest?"

Owen nodded. "Capital."

"Discretion is key," James said with emphasis. "We must not alert the villain to the fact that we are on his scent. He knows that his power lies in Evie's silence. For us to snare him, he must continue to believe that she is too afraid to speak out. If he suspects that she has confided his scheme to anyone, he will run."

"Bloody coward," Ethan muttered. "How long do you think he'll wait before contacting Evie again?"

"A fortnight separated the first two blackmail notes. The bastard knows he cannot bleed her dry all at once. He'll give her time to recuperate resources before striking again."

"A covert search for the suspects would be aided by physical descriptions." Mama turned to Evie. "I know some years have passed since you last saw Merrow and Dr. Murdoch, but could you give us your best impressions?"

"Harkness helped me to recall the details," Evie replied. "I shall start with Dr. Murdoch. A tall and long-limbed fellow, he would be in his early forties today. His hair was wavy and auburn. He had pale skin that showed his veins and watery green eyes. Wilmington claimed that Murdoch attended the *crème de la crème* in London."

"I, for one, have never heard of him," Mama said.

"My stepfather insisted that Murdoch replace my mama's longtime physician. Her health deteriorated under his care." Evie balled her hands in her lap. "His prescription of bed rest and isolation made matters worse, and she died within a year."

Despite the afternoon sun pouring into the drawing room, shadows seemed to gather around Evie. James laid his hand over hers, interlacing their fingers, anchoring her to the present. She took a breath and gave him a squeeze back before continuing.

"As for Merrow, he would be in his early thirties, a sandy-haired man of medium height with blue eyes. He had clean-cut features that some might call handsome. Harkness remembers that he had a reputation for chasing housemaids, and they all avoided him."

"That is helpful," Mama murmured.

"What do we do if we find the bastards?"

Godwin's casual inquiry landed with the subtlety of a boulder dropping into a pond.

"Not *that*." Gigi wagged a finger at him. "Get the idea out of your mind."

He quirked an eyebrow. "How do you know what I am thinking, duchess?"

"Because I know you. I know all of you"—she turned her gaze on her menfolk, who looked blandly back—"and you must not do anything that will make matters worse. The villain must be brought to the proper authorities, where he will be judged and punished for his actions."

"Spoilsport," her husband muttered.

James didn't disagree. He had to force himself to relinquish the fantasy of beating Evie's tormentor to a pulp. In the end, he would hand the bastard over to the police...but not without bloodying him first.

"Gigi is right." Mama knitted her brows. "But what if the blackguard reveals Evie's secret? Once he is captured, he will have nothing to lose."

"There is no proof that Evie did anything wrong," James said. "The physician ruled that Wilmington died of apoplexy. It is just the blackmailer's word against Evie's—the word of a criminal against that of a countess. She will deny the accusation, and that will be the end of it."

"Will it? The smallest spark can give rise to a scandal." Evie's eyes turned bleak. "What if my past harms your future?"

"Our future," he corrected. "Nothing between us, remember? Whatever happens, we will face it together."

Exhaling, she smiled tremulously before turning back to the family.

"There is something else I must share," she said. "It has to do with Thomas Mulligan and Rosalinda."

She told them about her dreams, including the most recent one.

"Dear heavens, Rosalinda was with child?" Xenia breathed. "And she was taken...by some villain? Do you know who he was?"

Evie shook her head. "I only saw flashes of him, and they were filtered by her fear and rage. I do know he was powerful, respected, and married with children."

"Did he drink the poisoned tea?" Gigi's eyes were rounded.

"I don't know. I woke up before I could find out what happened."

Remembering her terror, James put his arm around her.

"Don't think of it now, love," he murmured.

"On the contrary, I think Evie should contemplate what the dreams mean." Xenia nibbled on her lip. "These visions that she, Gigi, and I have had...I think they're meant to help us. To guide us in some way. When Ethan and I were courting—"

"Is that what we were doing, sweeting?" Ethan drawled. "I thought I was being grumpy and you were giving me indigestion with your cooking."

Xenia aimed her gaze heavenward. "As I was saying, Rose's memories uncovered not just her secrets but also my own. Her experiences helped me to overcome my insecurities where Ethan was concerned. She led me to a hiding place when I was being pursued by my enemy. The travails she endured showed me how to survive my own."

"I concur." Gigi's raven ringlets bounced with her vigorous nod. "If it weren't for my dreams of Rose, I might not have trusted my heart. I might not have married Conrad—"

"You would have, duchess," Godwin said with lazy certainty.

"I might not have married you *as quickly* as I did. And, if you'll recall, it was through Rose's memories that we discovered the caldarium, which in turn aided the revival of Miss Letty's spa and the village."

"As a matter of fact, I recall the discovery of the caldarium with great fondness."

When his sister turned red as an apple, James narrowed his gaze at his brother-in-law. The cove had grown on him. It would be a shame if he had to beat the other to a pulp for debauching his sister before marriage.

"I, too, owe a great debt to the tragic Rosalinda," Godwin went on. "For through her, I found my own everlasting love."

Godwin kissed Gigi's hand with tender devotion.

The females in the room sighed; the males snorted.

"To return to Xenia's point," Ethan said. "You believe Evie's dreams might be useful in some way?"

"I do," Xenia replied. "They might contain a clue about how to deal with the blackmailer when the time comes. Or they might help with, um, concerns of a personal nature."

James had to give her credit for her delicate reference to his marital problems. Not long ago, the idea that his family sensed the troubles between him and Evie had felt, well, humiliating. Now he realized that his pride had gotten in the way. Evie's courageous disclosures had inspired him...and made him realize that it was strength, not weakness, that led one to ask for help when needed.

"On a personal level, Evie's dreams have already helped," he said. "I admire her strength more than I can say. There is no one with whom I would rather follow the family tradition."

Seeing his wife's stunned pleasure, he did not fight the urge to kiss her. Her sweetness infused his senses, and for a mad instant, he was tempted to take more. To try to appease the insatiable appetite she roused in him. Thankfully, his restraint returned and he ended the kiss a moment later, seeing with satisfaction her flushed cheeks and dreamy-eyed gaze.

"As you were saying?" he inquired of his sister-in-law.

Xenia was doing a rather poor job of hiding her grin. "I wasn't saying anything."

"While it's all well and good that the pair of you are lovey-dovey again, the threat remains," Ethan said. "We must consider any clues in Evie's visions that could help us foil her enemy."

"One of the last visions I had was of Rose hiding her marriage license in the yew tree by the stream." Gigi sounded meditative. "After the villain killed Thomas, she knew he would come after her, so she hid the proof of her union. I remember distinctly how she waited there—how she didn't run when the bounder came for her. As if she was no longer afraid and wanted him to come."

"I know how she felt," Evie murmured. "This time, I am not running either."

"Even so, the blackguard must have been tracking her." Gigi shivered. "In that same vein, the blackmailer must be monitoring your movements. You received the first demand at Grove Hall, the second one here. He has been following you, Evie, and might have been closer than you realize. You must have a care."

James wrestled back his fear. It did no good. The only solution was to mitigate the threat: once the villain was captured, Evie would be safe once and for all.

"I will not let anything happen to my wife," he said firmly.

"The blackmailer has no reason to harm me." Evie sounded far calmer than he felt. "There is no purpose in damaging the goose that lays the golden eggs. He will want to squeeze as much out of me as he can. His greed will be his downfall, and I think we ought to capitalize upon it."

"How so?" James asked.

"If he is indeed watching me, then I should dangle a prize that he cannot resist. Something sparkly and lavish."

He caught on. "The diamond necklace?"

"Yes, but you needn't worry," she said quickly. "We will have a copy made so that when the time comes to deliver the payment—"

"I don't give a damn about the necklace." He cut her off. "I care about you. About the fact that you are deliberately baiting the bastard."

"One cannot set a trap without bait." On that cheery philosophical note, she patted his hand. "Don't worry, darling, I know you will keep me safe."

He would bloody well make sure of it.

"Moreover, I am fortunate to have an advantage that Rosalinda did not."

"What advantage, sunflower?" he asked.

She smiled, dazzling him with that inner brightness that no adversity could dim.

"I am not alone," she said.

Chapter Twenty-Six

The storm passed, and the next two days were filled with activity.

As planned, Gigi brought Evie and James to see Mr. Duffield. Discreet as ever, the dashing blond draper closed his shop for lunch, disappointing the group of matrons clamoring for his attention. He examined the glove and immediately identified the faded letters stamped inside as "*P & M*."

"How can you be so certain, sir?" Evie asked in amazement.

"*P & M* stands for 'Perry & Morris,'" Mr. Duffield explained. "It is a London outfitter located on Oxford Street and serves those of modest means. Valets and clerks are amongst the clientele, as well as respectable ladies with a mind for economy. In fact, I considered stocking Perry & Morris gloves in my own shop."

"How difficult would it be to track down the owner of this particular glove?" James asked.

"Rather like locating an eel in the Thames, I imagine. The shop on Oxford Street must sell dozens of this style on any given day—and they have other suppliers as well. This glove is the sort that any gentleman's man or tradesman might wear in Town."

While the information suggested that Merrow was a likely

suspect, making any definitive connection between him and the glove seemed unlikely. After thanking Mr. Duffield and leaving Gigi to catch up with him, Evie brought James to meet the Pickleworths. The good lady blushed when James thanked her for the herbs. While Mr. Pickleworth convinced James to have crates of delicate new asparagus delivered to Bottoms House, Evie had a moment alone with her friend.

"Did you happen to speak to your brother about a tour of his cherry orchard?" she asked.

"Indeed, I did," Loretta said. "Ned would be honored to receive you at your convenience."

"Perhaps a week from now might suit?"

"I will let him know." After providing Evie with the address of the farm, Loretta paused and lowered her voice. "I hope you don't mind my asking, but everything is well with his lordship?"

"I don't mind. Things could not be better." Evie smiled. "I have taken your advice."

A knowing twinkle came into her friend's eyes. "Picked up a broom, did you?"

"Metaphorically speaking." On impulse, Evie took the other's hand and gave it a squeeze. "Thanks to your encouragement, I decided to no longer hide my feelings, and that has made all the difference."

As James had a busy social agenda, Evie's evenings were fully occupied. She accompanied him everywhere and wore the spectacular diamond necklace in hopes of luring out her enemy. She also did her best to support James's candidacy, and the pride in his eyes gave her newfound confidence. Expressing her admiration for his reforms and his character came naturally. If the conversation fell flat, she turned to tips for reviving houseplants, a topic that never failed to find an audience. Her partnership with James had never felt stronger or more vital. Secure in their love, she even managed to be civil to Morgana Vernon.

Evie had a rare break the following afternoon and decided to spend it in the library at Bottoms House. She had her reading spectacles perched on her nose and a stack of horticultural volumes on the table in front of her. She enjoyed the tranquil space, which boasted charming green bookshelves, sage and cream carpets, and pristine floral plasterwork on the high ceiling. The bay windows framed views of the blooming springtime that the storm had left in its wake.

Not only was the library well-appointed, but it was also fully stocked. While Evie had brought along some of her own books—one never knew when a botanical guide would come in handy—she'd been delighted to find all four volumes of Loudon's *Arboretum et Fruticetum Britannicum* in the labyrinth of bookcases. She was perusing one of the books now, researching causes that might account for the disappearance of Chuddums's cherry crops. However, she found herself staring dreamily into space.

It was new to her: this feeling of peace. Although the blackmailer remained at large, letting go of her secret made her feel calmer and lighter. It was as if she'd dumped an invisible sack of bricks she'd carried for years. She was brimming with hope for the future...and she was silly with love. In fact, if she wasn't careful, she might burst into song like the returning warblers and chiffchaff. Loving James was hardly a new phenomenon, but now it felt *safe* to do so and to let her feelings show. The miracle was that he loved her back—and he wasn't hiding it either.

Evie cast a discreet glance at her husband, who was playing chess with his papa in the nearby sitting area. Sunlight polished his hair to a rich bronze, and above the elegant knot of his neckcloth, his face was set in serious lines as he discussed political strategy. He'd removed his frock coat, and his waistcoat flattered his broad shoulders and trim torso. After all these years, his splendor still caused her heart to career into her ribs, and she suspected he would always affect her this way. She would forever feel that spark in his presence, that breathless attraction and soul-deep joy that he was hers.

When he picked up his queen, stroking the piece with his long fingers, heat bloomed inside her. While the desire she felt was not new, the raw intensity of its expression was. Her honesty about the past had opened the door to honesty in all aspects of their relationship...including lovemaking. James had always been a passionate lover, but now he was exposing his naughtier appetites. It seemed that even her confident, successful husband had hidden a part of himself. Shame and guilt had motivated her to conceal her secrets, and she wondered if he had similar feelings. Perhaps he had buried his darker needs because they did not fit his image of what a gentleman and husband should be.

They had both had walls up, and together they were tearing them down. Their progress expanded her heart with joy...and sent a sizzle through her blood. She adored James's feral side. Now he was debating his papa on the merits of their respective clubs—the Reform Club versus Brooks's—and watching his lips move, she remembered how persuasive his mouth could be.

After last night's soiree, he'd shown her a novel and rather depraved position. Gripping the headboard, she'd perched atop his face, surrendering to his hot kisses and hotter words.

"Ride my tongue, love. Feed me more of your delectable cream."

She'd done both, gushing with bliss and earning more filthy words of praise.

At that instant, James caught her staring at him. Her breath hitched, blood surging into her cheeks. The knowing gleam in his eyes confirmed that he'd guessed the wanton direction of her thoughts. It was one thing to lust after one's husband, another to do so in public, and for him to be aware of it.

Mortified, she dropped her gaze to the book in front of her and pretended to read.

A few moments later, she heard the marquess say in a pleased tone, "Checkmate."

"Well played, Papa."

"Thank you, son. I was fortunate. I could have sworn you were laying a trap."

"I concede to your superior strategy, sir," James said blandly.

Pushing his chair back, the marquess rose. "Well, I promised Mama a stroll around the garden. I shall see you both at supper. Evie."

She smiled at him. "Enjoy your walk."

When James approached, she quickly bowed her head over the book.

"Interesting read?" he inquired.

"Very."

"It must be since you are so absorbed by it."

"Absolutely. It is absolutely...absorbing."

She wanted to kick herself for sounding like a nitwit.

Leaning on the table, James peered down at the page, his clean-shaven cheek close to hers. Sandalwood and musk curled in her nostrils. Desire tugged at her belly.

"I can see why this has your full attention. There is nothing quite as scintillating as the process of selecting the proper fertilizer."

Was that what I was reading?

"Fertilizing is important," she said primly.

"I could not agree more. In fact, thoughts of fertilizing you distracted me from the chess match."

"*James.* That is wicked." But she couldn't stop herself from giggling.

"Then we are a wicked pair, aren't we?"

Oh, how could she resist the stormy invitation in his eyes?

"I might have been distracted as well," she admitted. "By, um, similar thoughts."

He rewarded her honesty with a kiss that made her toes curl in her shoes. When her vision fogged up, she realized she still had her spectacles on. She tried to remove them, but James stopped her.

"Leave them on," he said.

Before she could ask why, he pulled her to her feet.

"Are we going upstairs?" she whispered.

"Too far," he said succinctly.

He dragged her into the maze of shelves.

Laughing, she said, "You cannot possibly make love to me in the library...oh, *gracious earth*."

He'd pushed her up against the shelves and tossed up her skirts. Layers of fabric rustled, crushed between them, as he found the opening in her drawers. When he slid a blunt finger along her slick crease, she bit her lip to keep from moaning.

"What were you thinking about when you were pretending to be reading?" he asked in a low voice. "What made this pussy so wet and ready?"

"You," she sighed.

"What, specifically, was I doing to you?"

Given what she was allowing him to do in a public room in the middle of the day, she didn't know how she could blush harder.

"What you did last night. When"—she squirmed against the shelves and not just because of his clever fingers—"you know."

"Refresh my memory. Give me the naughty words, Evie. The ones you were thinking when you were watching me play chess with my father."

The mention of the marquess heightened her discomfiture, yet James's intense scrutiny demanded the truth.

"I was thinking about how good it felt." She was faint with embarrassment. "When you told me to...to sit upon your face."

Approval and arousal blazed in his gaze.

"Your pussy is my favorite treat," he said huskily. "Did you like it when I licked you here, rubbed my tongue back and forth over your pearl?"

Since he was mimicking the motion with his touch, her reply was a strangled moan. He covered her mouth with his, swallowing the sound and those that followed as he fingered her to a swift climax. Pleasure spilled through her like sun-warmed honey, steaming up her lenses. Her knees buckled, but he held her securely.

"Christ, that looked sweet." His stare was fierce and ardent. "Do you want to know the fantasy I was entertaining?"

Dazed with bliss, she nodded.

"I was thinking how prim and adorable you look in spectacles. And how I wanted to make love to you whilst you were wearing them."

She blinked. "Truly? You like my spectacles?"

In reply, he reached down to unfasten himself, releasing his rearing arousal.

"Truly," he confirmed.

The knowledge that she had such power over her proper lord thrilled her. She'd always thought that her spectacles were unattractive—something to be worn only out of necessity. Although her practical side had prevailed over her vanity, she'd never felt confident wearing them. Now she tried giving her husband a coquettish look through her lenses.

"Would you care to make your fantasy come true?" she said daringly.

"I thought you would never ask."

His eyes a tempestuous blue, he notched himself to her entrance. He drove inside, a powerful thrust that thumped her back against the shelves. Stretched and impossibly full, she felt delight radiate from his incursion.

"Devil and damn." Pleasure slurred his words. "You feel like a velvet fist around my cock."

"You feel so hard. So big."

It was the truth, and she could tell he liked it.

"I'm big and hard for you. And I am about to screw you senseless."

While James was undoubtedly a man of his word, even he couldn't stop the knock on the door. She jolted at the interruption, and he groaned.

"Be quiet," he commanded, if a trifle desperately. "They'll go away."

The door clicked open.

"Lady Manderly?" The butler's inquiring voice carried into the stacks. "Begging your pardon for the interruption, but a message arrived for you."

Panicked, Evie called out, "I am, um, just locating a book. I shall be right there."

With a quiet oath, James pulled out. Hastily, she swept her skirts into place and took off her spectacles, stuffing them into her pocket.

"Stay here," she whispered.

He looked down at his glistening erection, which jutted from his open trousers.

"I am hardly going anywhere in this state, am I?"

His frustration nearly made her giggle. Blowing him a kiss, she exited the bookcase. Brunswick stood by the door, his expression impassive.

"For you, my lady. The messenger conveyed that it was a matter of some urgency."

With a nod of thanks, she took the letter from the salver. She recognized the sender immediately, and as the door closed behind the butler, she tore into the envelope.

"Who is it from?" James came up behind her. "Did the blackmailer send another demand?"

"No." Her pulse raced as she scanned the lines. "The letter is from the Botanical Society, forwarded from Grove Hall."

"Oh. What do they want?"

Astonished, she reread the letter before looking up.

"My work, it seems. They are inviting me to present my paper on *Cheiranthus cheiri, variety vespertinus* at the next society meeting."

"Congratulations, my dear," he said sincerely. "The honor is richly deserved."

"There's more. At the meeting, members will choose the most compelling presentation for publication in the society journal."

"Your victory is all but assured. When is this meeting?"

"That is the thing." She gnawed on her lip. "I am being offered the spot because of a last-minute cancellation. They want me to present this weekend in London. In *three days*."

"Well, now. That doesn't leave much time to get ready...but needs must."

She stared at him. "You think I should accept?"

"If you do not, you will regret turning down an opportunity you have worked diligently to achieve."

How well he knew her. Still, there were other pressing considerations.

"What if the blackmailer issues a demand—"

"By the time we return from London, only a week will have passed since his last note, and his pattern has been to wait a fortnight. Moreover, you should go about your business as you've always done so that he believes nothing has changed. He will think that he has kept you silenced with fear, and this will prompt him to contact you again. Then, we will seize the bounder."

Comforted by James's logic, she said hesitantly, "If you think it is all right—"

"Sweetheart, it is not about what I think. It is about what *you* want. Say the word, and I shall make the arrangements for London. In fact, while we are there, I will attend to some business of my own."

Her heart swelled with all the love she felt for him.

"No matter how horrid my past was, it was worth it," she said solemnly.

"The devil you say." James scowled. "You deserved better, Evie. You should never—"

"I am not done. What I meant to say is that everything I endured, everything I survived...I would do it all over again if it brought me here. To you."

Emotion swarmed his eyes.

"So, yes, I would like to go to London and present my work. Thank you for understanding me and being my greatest champion. For being everything I could ever want in a husband."

"You are welcome." He cupped her cheek. "Thank you for trusting me. For supporting me—with my family and my political ambitions. For being everything I want in a wife."

She fiddled with his cravat. "I can think of more interesting ways to thank one another and take care of unfinished business."

"Thank Christ. The unfinished business, as you so delicately put it, is about to burst its seams."

He held out his hand.

Fingers linked, they raced, laughing, out of the library and up the stairs.

Chapter Twenty-Seven

They arrived in London the day before Evie's presentation. The city provided a stark contrast to the pastoral charm of Chuddums. The streets were filled with noisy crowds, as well as hansom cabs, omnibuses, and carts vying to get ahead. Opening the carriage window, James was assailed by the pungent mélange of coal smoke, roasting nuts, and sewage from the Thames. The despair of the poorhouses was juxtaposed with the grandeur of the emerging Palace of Westminster, a Gothic masterpiece still under construction.

James thought that London represented the best and worst of everything. Here in the metropolis, industry was pitted against nature's order, progress against tradition. Change was around every corner, even if that corner had been there since the first days of Londinium. Many eked out a meager existence in the shadows of a privileged few. Problems abounded, and one had the choice to be part of them or part of the solution. James chose the latter. It exhilarated him to think that one day he might be part of this city's vibrant history, making his mark in the newly rebuilt House of Commons.

The next morning, he decided to stop by his club while Evie

prepared for her lecture this evening. While he was glad that she'd persuaded Harkness to stay behind—to his surprise, the old bat hadn't put up much of a protest—he did not like leaving his wife alone. He made her promise not to leave the premises and instructed the staff to secure the house. Only when he was satisfied that she was protected did he attend to his own affairs.

Located on Pall Mall, the Reform Club had been designed by famed architect Charles Barry and resembled a Renaissance palazzo with its pale stone, arched windows, and imposing entrance. The interior was equally impressive, a showcase of modernity and progress. The atrium's glass roof flooded the space with natural light, and gaslight illuminated the darker corners. The high-ceilinged rooms, redolent of coffee and cigar smoke, buzzed with talk about technological advancements, recent bills, and global affairs.

While James could have been a member of Brooks's, the established Whig stronghold favored by his father and his father's father, he'd chosen membership at the Reform instead. He had a healthy respect for tradition—for the pedigree and port atmosphere of Brooks's—but he felt more at home here amongst the intellectuals and radicals, in the often choppy but always exciting sea of change.

Immediately hailed by several peers, he took lunch with them in the dining room, which offered sweeping views of Pall Mall. The meal featured some of the best French cuisine outside of Paris, yet James found his appetite waning. As his cronies extolled his virtues and claimed that his victory was certain, the knot in his gut tightened. Even as he tried to temper their expectations, they waxed on about the importance of his win...and the dire consequences if he should fail.

After lunch, he was ready to take his leave. As he passed through the smoking room, which was fashionably outfitted with walnut furnishings and burgundy upholstery, he saw a solitary figure slumped in a wingchair in a quiet corner. Recognizing Henry Gosford, he hesitated, then decided that delaying the encounter would only make matters more awkward in the future.

As he approached, Gosford looked up. The fellow was only a few years older than James, but scandal had aged him. New lines were carved into his distinguished countenance, and his sandy hair had gone grey at the temples. His blue eyes were bloodshot, and when he put out his cigar and rose, his clothing hung loosely on his frame. He was, James saw with some shock and concern, a shadow of his former self.

"Gosford, well met."

James extended a hand, and the other shook it.

"I saw you sitting alone," he went on when Gosford remained grim-faced and silent. "I hope I am not interrupting—"

"You are not. Please, have a seat."

James could have made an excuse and declined, but the misery in Gosford's eyes made him take the adjacent wingchair.

"Drink?" Gosford waved at the nearly empty decanter of whisky on the table beside him.

"No, thank you." James wracked his brain for polite conversation. "I am surprised to see you here. I thought Brooks's was more to your style."

"It was. Until the scandal." Downing the rest of his glass, Gosford refilled it. "As it turns out, the club is entirely less agreeable when other members avoid you like the plague for fear of contracting your disgrace."

Right. No mincing words then.

"I am sorry about what happened," James said.

"Are you?" Gosford's gaze cut into him like a razor. "Are you indeed?"

"I would not wish such misfortune on anyone. Particularly not a man who I know has represented his constituents faithfully and to the best of his abilities."

"Well." Gosford held his glass in a mocking toast. "At least I was faithful at something."

James stood. "If you would rather be alone—"

"No, sit. I'm in a devil of a mood and you're a convenient target, though you've done little to deserve it. In fact, you are one of the few fellows with the decency to acknowledge my existence—to treat me as something other than persona non grata."

Taking that for the apology that it was, James returned to his seat.

"It will pass," he said. "Gossip will soon find a fresh victim, and all will be forgotten."

"Forgotten but forever changed. I have lost the respect of my peers and constituents. And my wife...well, let us say that the climate of my marriage makes the Outer Hebrides seem tropical in comparison."

"That sounds..."—James searched for a tactful adjective—"unpleasant."

"That is one way to describe it. Take my advice, Manderly, and don't invite dishonor into your life. It is a disagreeable houseguest who will destroy everything you hold dear and never leave. However bad you think it may be, the reality is a hundred times worse."

James found himself torn between pity and stirring unease. Gosford was a gentleman in his prime, who'd been at the pinnacle of his career. Even so, he had suffered the greatest of falls. True, his weakness when it came to women had led him to make choices James never would, but his was a cautionary tale.

Evie's past crept into James's head. Although he'd done his best to reassure her, she was still terrified that the business with Wilmington could ruin him. He didn't blame her for any of it—she, not that bastard, was the victim—but, if he was completely honest, a small part of him shared her concern.

Could her secret destroy everything he'd worked for and hoped to achieve?

He kept his doubts to himself. He wanted to carry his wife's burdens, not add to them. He would focus on catching the villain and having him thrown behind bars. No one would believe the word of a criminal—one who'd preyed upon a lady, no less.

Gosford took another drink. "Enough about me and my woes. How is the campaign going?"

James cleared his throat. "Passably well, given the circumstances."

"The circumstances being that I left the party high and dry, mere months before the General Election, and now that opportunist Ryerson is contesting my seat." Gosford raised a brow. "Have I missed anything?"

"That sums it up."

"I still have a few connections, and they inform me that your campaign has been gathering momentum. Preparing for a hustings, are you?"

"Yes. It will take place in Chudleigh Bottoms."

"Chuddums?" Gosford grimaced. "Why in blazes would you want to host the event in the county's armpit? Well, that's your business. I like you, Manderly. Always thought you were a decent, reasonable chap—though a bit high-minded, if you don't mind my saying."

"I don't mind."

"Sensible fellow, like I said. It is because I like you that I wish to give you some advice." Gosford leaned forward, bracing his arms on his thighs. "Principles are all well and good, but people don't vote for principles."

James frowned. "Surely that is untrue—"

"Allow me to finish. They believe they are voting in accordance with their conscience, but it is the man delivering the message and how he does so that has the greatest influence on their decisions. Take me, for instance. I am neither an intellectual nor a devoted reformer, yet I held that seat for five consecutive terms. Do you know why?"

"People like you."

"Bull's eye. Because they like me, they gave me credit for

being a better man than I am. Now take you, Manderly. You are, objectively speaking, a better man than me, but are you as well liked?"

"Popularity has never been my concern," James said indifferently.

"And that"—Gosford stabbed a finger at him—"is your problem. Lofty ideals alone will not win you the seat. Ordinary folk want to feel as if they know the man behind the politician. I portrayed myself as a devoted husband and father—which worked well until it didn't. My point is, when you are out there, don't merely speak about policy. Hold babies, pat children on the head, compliment ladies on their needlework. Voters appreciate the personal touch. And don't forget to use your lady."

"I beg your pardon?"

"Your countess—she is an asset. Her quiet charm has a way of drawing people in. More importantly, she has stars in her eyes when she looks at you—as if you stood on a pedestal and could do no wrong. You want people to share her opinion."

"I am not sure that is her opinion." Reminded of how Evie had compared him to an aloof god, he felt vaguely uncomfortable. "But I am grateful for my wife's support."

Gosford stared glumly into his empty glass. "Enjoy it while it lasts."

James planned to be deserving of Evie until death did them part.

"As for focusing less on the message and more on its delivery," he said, "perhaps you have the right of it. Lady Vernon counseled me in a similar fashion."

"Morgana Vernon is a shark."

James was taken aback by Gosford's bitter tone. "On the contrary, she has been a key supporter."

"Once upon a time, she was mine as well."

Tossing back the last of his whisky, Gosford came unsteadily to his feet.

"Here's my parting advice." He executed a tipsy bow. "Keep your enemies close and your friends closer."

Frowning, James watched the fellow stumble off, wondering what the devil he meant.

James returned home by early afternoon. Despite the strange malaise that had plagued him since the talk with Gosford, his lips twitched when he found Evie exactly as he'd left her. Bent over the escritoire in her sitting room, her spectacles perched on her nose, she was jotting notes and mumbling to herself. At the warm greeting that lit her whisky eyes, his disquiet dissipated.

He placed his hands on her shoulders and bent to kiss her cheek.

"Still busy as a bee—or moth—I see."

Removing her spectacles, she smiled at him.

"You are a sight for sore eyes. How was the club?"

"Fine." He paused. "I saw Gosford."

"Oh. How did that go?"

"It was awkward. To say the least."

"Why don't I pour you a drink and you can tell me about it?"

He decided that some of life's greatest pleasures were the simplest. Or perhaps he was just a simple fellow who enjoyed basic comforts like coming home to his wife and being able to tell her about his day. They settled on the settee, and with his arm around her, he described the interaction with his disgraced colleague.

"What do you think he meant by keeping your friends close?" she mused.

"I suspect he thinks Lady Vernon betrayed him. The moment the scandal hit, she jumped ship."

"She jumped from his ship onto yours."

When he raised his brows, Evie shook her head.

"I didn't mean that in a jealous way. I know you have no intention of dropping your anchor in her port, so to speak."

He had to grin. "Careful, sweetheart. These nautical references might give me ideas."

"Oh, do keep your mast down," she quipped.

He wondered if she knew the effect her cheekiness was having on him. Hearing his shy darling refer to his "mast" was making his trousers uncomfortably tight.

"Regardless of my personal feelings about Lady Vernon, I think you should heed Gosford's warning. She shifts her favor with the wind. What she did to Gosford, she can and will do to you." Evie gnawed on her lower lip, her eyes troubled. "If she catches even a whiff of the scandal from my past—"

"She won't," he said. "And I have no illusions about her loyalty. I am not as gullible as people seem to think."

She tilted her head. "Who thinks you are gullible?"

He wasn't certain he wanted to have this discussion. Since the thoughts had been niggling at him like a toothache, however, he gave in.

"You do," he told her.

"I never said such a thing." She looked genuinely shocked.

"Perhaps you did not use that exact word. But when you compared me to Apollo, you said I have lofty ideals, and more than once you've called me high-minded."

"Those were meant as compliments." Her brow pleated. "If you took them in some other fashion—"

"I know what you meant." Feeling like a fool, he sat forward and rubbed his hands over his face. "It has been a long day. Forget I mentioned it."

"I will not. Something I said bothered you." She studied him with disturbing acuity. "You've never liked that comparison with Apollo. You think it implies that you are prissy—feeble and not as manly as the great Zeus."

"That is not the part that bothers me," he averred.

"Then what is it, James? Tell me."

He exhaled. "I am not perfect."

"All right," she said slowly.

"And I don't want you to think that I am."

"You needn't worry on that account."

He ignored her gentle jibe. "Gosford disagrees. He says you've placed me on some sort of pedestal, and I should play up your wifely adulation. He says your view of me will help convince constituents that I am a worthy candidate. But I don't want you to think of me as some aloof and impeccable god. I'm not. I am just a man who has flaws like everyone else—"

"I am perfectly aware of your flaws," she said. "You are stubborn and idealistic to a degree that sometimes puts you out of touch with ordinary folk. You prefer to keep your own counsel, which is usually sound, but you also risk brooding and stewing over things you would have been better off discussing. You have exceedingly high standards, especially when it comes to yourself."

Her assessment stopped him short. And made him feel like an even bigger idiot.

"Well," he muttered. "As long as we have that clear."

"I didn't mean to insult—"

"You didn't." He gave her a wry look. "I asked for your opinion and now I have it."

"You have *part* of my opinion," she corrected. "I also think you are honorable, loyal, and kind. Your intelligence is tempered by humor, and while you are hard on yourself, you are generous with others. You are not perfect...but you are perfect for me. I could not imagine a better husband—a better lover or partner. Which is why I am madly, irrevocably in love with you."

Touched, he kissed the back of her hand and tucked it against his thigh.

"I wasn't fishing for compliments but thank you. You must know that I love you outrageously in return. Enough about my day. How is your speech—"

"Not so fast. We are not done discussing what put you in a mood."

He started to deny that he was in a mood but realized it was pointless. Moreover, hadn't he been the one to insist on honesty in their marriage? If he couldn't be truthful with his wife, then who could he share his troubles with?

Searching for the right words, he said, "I don't want to be thought of as infallible."

Understanding came into her eyes. "Perfection is a heavy burden to carry."

"At the club, people were all but celebrating my victory. They alluded to my past successes and what they perceive as my winning qualities. Yet the outcome is far from certain." He heaved out a breath. "Ryerson has been gaining momentum. While his tactics involve fearmongering and smearing his opponents, one cannot deny that they are effective. I am beginning to wonder if they might be more persuasive than my approach. What if voters don't care about my policies and plans?"

"The fact that you take the moral high ground is admirable and signals that you are a man of character and honor. While Ryerson has found success attacking his opponents on a personal level, your strategy has better staying power. People will vote for you because you have the best ideas—because you care about their welfare and wish to create real and lasting change."

"What if I lose?" He forced himself to give voice to his fear. "What if I don't get the opportunity to implement my ideas?"

"Then you lose. But you will lose knowing that you have done your best, and I know for a fact that the best of James Harrington is no trifling tide."

He huffed out a laugh. "Back to the nautical metaphors, are we?"

She squeezed his hand. "Fear of failure is natural and more so when expectations are high and consequences great."

At her perceptiveness, he felt his chest tighten. "There it is, in a nutshell."

"I know you don't like the comparison, but that is partly why I thought of you as Apollo: you are the golden one, the dutiful heir and brother whom everyone can rely upon. You wear responsibility so effortlessly that sometimes it seems as if there is no cost to you. Yet there is, isn't there?"

His eyes heated. Appalled, he stared at his shoes, fighting to regain control.

"I don't want to fail," he said at length. "I don't want to be a disappointment. To let down those who have put such faith in me."

"If you put your best effort forward—and I know you could never do anything less—then you have fulfilled your promise to them and yourself. You do not need to be perfect, James," she said gently. "You need only be yourself."

"What if it is not enough?"

She brushed her fingers along his jaw, angling his face so that he was looking at her.

"No matter what happens, I could not be prouder of you. I know the rest of the family feels the same way. James, my darling, you are, and have always been, enough."

Christ.

Crushing her against him, he buried his face in her hair. She held him, giving him what he needed. He realized then that she had always given him this, since the early days of their marriage. He'd appreciated what he had thought of as her steadying presence, but it was more than that. She understood him like no one else. Even when she had kept secrets and withheld romantic sentiments because she felt herself unworthy, she had offered him her sweet and unconditional love. With her, he'd never had to be anyone but who he was.

He drew back, gazing into her warm eyes.

"Thank you for listening. For understanding."

"What are wives for?"

"As to that. I have a few ideas."

He leaned in to kiss her...and was surprised when she placed a finger to his lips.

"I am glad you are not perfect or infallible," she said softly. "It makes you more suited to a mere mortal like me."

"There is nothing *mere* about you, Evie." He took her face between his hands, needing her to recognize the truth. "You are my world. You've said that I rescued you from ruination, but the reverse is true. You saved me. You ease my burdens and balance me —remind me that life is about more than duty. Without you, I am lost."

Her gaze shimmered, and he hoped she finally understood what she meant to him.

"Then I suppose," she said, "that you should be thanking me."

He raised his brows. "What sort of payment comes to mind?"

"I have a few ideas."

A smile flirted at the corners of her mouth. In a blink, she'd gone from his wise and steadfast spouse to his sweet and seductive lover. He marveled at her complexity. She knew his virtues and his failings and, by some miracle, loved him as he was. Gratitude amplified his need for her, which felt as vital as his next breath.

"If I may, I do have a request," he said.

Her eyes lit up. "The spectacles?"

Yes, she knew him well.

Tenderness became a tempest, a roiling sea of desire. And when she cried out her love for him, her spectacles sparkling and incomparable breasts jiggling with his thrusts, he let his emotions sweep him away. Trusting that what they'd built together would hold and keep them safe, he surrendered to the storm.

Chapter Twenty-Eight

"By day, the *Cheiranthus cheiri, variety vespertinus*, is cloaked in modesty. At twilight, it spreads its petals and guides the night-flying moth with its seductive perfume. Thus, this overlooked wallflower is not waiting to be noticed: it is adapting, surviving, and blooming on its own terms."

Evie held her breath...and released it as applause filled the room. A moment later, the clapping turned thunderous, most of the audience surging to their feet. As the President of the Botanical Society, Mr. Brixley, came to the lectern and thanked Evie for her remarks, she looked out at the crowded hall. James sat near the back, a place he'd chosen so that he could support her without being a distraction. Their gazes met, and his gleaming pride dimmed everything else. When he winked, her heart tumbled helplessly, and she had to force herself to concentrate as Mr. Brixley invited questions from the audience.

After the presentation, she was swarmed. She was pleased to find that her lecture had drawn an unusual number of female attendees, and she took the time to answer their questions and converse about their interests. As icing on the cake, Sir Richards, a longtime society member and former president, came to pay his respects. He was known as a curmudgeon, but she'd always liked how he treated her as a botanist first and lady second.

"You have outdone yourself, Lady Manderly." His hazel eyes were sharp, his features weathered by his passion for the outdoors. "Your presentation was the evening's pièce de résistance, and I daresay it will earn you a spot in our next publication."

Delight and triumph rushed through her. "You are too kind, sir."

"I am too old for niceties," he said with a harrumph. "You have earned your place in the society—and the post of secretary, if our less progressive colleagues can see beyond their prejudices. Mr. McAllister's term is coming up, and you have my vote to take his place."

"Take his place? As secretary?" The notion of occupying the prestigious position stunned her. "The idea...to be frank, it never occurred to me."

"It ought to. You need to be as clear-headed about your own merits as you are about *Cheiranthus cheiri, variety vespertinus*." He was diverted by the waitstaff entering with trays. "Ah, here come the refreshments. I hope they don't run out of the macarons like last time. If you'll excuse me."

Without further ado, Sir Richards hurried toward the refreshment table. His haste alerted the other guests, who raced there as well. Scuffles ensued, leading Evie to conclude that botanists and food made for a dangerous combination. Then James approached, and her mind emptied of all else save him. He was the picture of elegance—so perfect, in fact, that she wanted to muss him up a little. To run her hands through his hair and tear off that starchy, precise cravat. With a flash of heat, she wanted him the way he'd been this afternoon: naked and undone as he shoved inside her, growling her name.

"We will do that later," he said.

"How do you know what I was thinking?"

"Because I was thinking the same thing." His grin was brief

and devilish, and the kiss he brushed over her knuckles set her aquiver. "You were brilliant, my love. From now on, no one in the audience will see a wallflower as anything but extraordinary."

"Do you think so?" she said happily. "I was nervous and stumbled at the beginning. But I gained confidence as I went on, and by the end, I felt more at ease."

"You were a smashing success. If I'm not mistaken, Sir Richards agreed with my assessment."

"He did. Oh, James"—she couldn't hold back a sigh of elation—"he thinks my paper will be chosen for publication."

"As it should be. The other presentations couldn't hold a candle to yours."

"There's more," she said excitedly. "He says he would vote for me to become—"

She was interrupted by the arrival of Lawrence Whetham, a wiry fellow whose hair was slick with pomade and whose unctuous manner hid sharp claws. In the past, he'd been rather dismissive of her work, and she remained wary as they exchanged pleasantries.

"Lady Manderly, how enchanting you look," he drawled. "The hue of your gown is quite becoming."

Gigi had insisted that Evie have something new to wear for the occasion. Given the short notice, Mrs. Sommers had worked her dressmaker's magic and cleverly remade Evie's slate-blue silk poplin, bringing its silhouette in line with the latest fashion. The frock was freshly trimmed with narrow black velvet bands at the cuffs, its muslin chemisette newly edged with lace. Likewise, Evie's coiffure projected femininity without frivolity: the front had a smooth middle part, and the back was arranged in interwoven braids. A small jet comb, shaped like leaves, secured the coil at her nape.

"Thank you, sir," she said.

"And your study of wallflowers was quite...thorough." The praise was backhanded and patronizing. "It is unusual for a lady so fair to possess a hint of intellect as well."

A hint of intellect is more than you possess, you condescending prig.

With great restraint, Evie did not take the bait.

"I enjoyed your demonstration of the *Selaginella lepidophylla*," she said.

Whetham had shown the audience a desiccated *Selaginella*—known colloquially as a resurrection plant. The brittle brown tangle had appeared quite dead...until he placed it in a bowl of water. With the faintest quiver, the clenched ball had softened. As if by magic, its branchlets unfurled, revealing tiny leaves that turned plump and green. Revived, the plant had resembled a small, lush fern. As astounding as the phenomenon had been, Evie thought that Whetham had presented it like a parlor trick. He'd basked in the crowd's amazement but offered none of the true science behind the plant's resurgence.

"It went over well, didn't it?" Whetham's smile was smug. "Nothing captivates an audience more than a mystery."

"Resurrection isn't a mystery. It is a process," Evie said. "If one observes the steps, one will understand the phenomenon."

"Yet science can be so dry. Miracles draw far more interest." Whetham's expression turned sly. "In point of fact, I was talking to our esteemed president—Mr. Brixley and I go back to our Eton days. We both agreed that increased public attention would benefit our society greatly. To that end, I offered to write up my presentation for the next journal and received his hearty endorsement. All for the good of the society, of course."

His revelation punctured her hopes like a thorn.

"Of course." Evie forced herself to add, "My congratulations."

"Thank you. As I said, your presentation was charming. I daresay the earl lent you a few pointers, eh?"

Whetham turned to James, his manner ingratiating. "Your reputation for eloquence precedes you, my lord, and your lady's efforts bear your polish. Quite generous of you to help her make a splash."

The pressure rose in Evie's veins. It was bad enough that he should inveigle his way into the journal—that he should displace her study with his trifling exhibition. But to imply that her success was due solely to James... Rejoinders proliferated like weeds in her brain, none of them fit for public consumption. As she struggled to find a suitable response, James spoke.

"My wife needs no polish."

His eyes were cold—so chilling that Whetham took a step back.

"She rests on her own merits, and her accomplishments are entirely her own."

"I meant no offense, my lord." Whetham licked his lips. "I misspoke, that is all."

"One ought to be careful in one's choice of words. Especially when they insult a lady and diminish her achievements. Do we understand one another?"

"Completely. I beg your pardon again for the misunderstanding." Sweat beaded on Whetham's forehead, his gaze darting. "Ah —there is a crony I must speak to. If you'll excuse me."

He fled as if the hounds of hell were on his tail.

"You put the fear of God in him," Evie said in awe.

"The pompous worm deserved it." James brushed a speck of lint off his sleeve. "I know you could have handled the situation yourself, but you should not have to deal with such irritants on your special occasion."

Is it any wonder that I adore this man?

"What would you like to do next, love?" James smiled at her. "Should we have a *tête-à-tête* with Brixley? It should not be diffi-cult to convince him that your study far outweighs Whetham's parlor trick in terms of scientific merit and deserves to be published in the next journal."

Happiness dazzled her. Suddenly, she knew what she wanted— what truly mattered. While she valued achievement and scientific inquiry, her deepest desire was to be seen. She longed to be understood and loved for who she was.

Now I have that. Which means...I have everything.

She slipped her hand into James's.

"That can wait," she whispered. "Right now, I want a private celebration with you."

His eyes smoldered. "I'll summon the carriage."

"Well, now," James murmured. "What have I done to deserve this?"

The carriage had barely started moving when Evie knelt gracefully between his legs. His blood rushed in his veins as his lovely lady scientist unfastened his trousers with the same care she used when gathering her specimens. In the lamplight, her hair was spun gold, and her eyes were mysterious amber pools. When she freed the last button from its hole, his cock sprang free, hard and ready.

"This is for being you," she said. "I adore the man you are."

He didn't know what aroused him more: her passionate avowal or the way she gripped him with her gloved hands. The sight of her delicate fingers, encased in pearl-grey kid, frigging his rampant pole was an inexpressible delight. She used his own arousal to lubricate her decadent pumping, her expertise bringing forth more liquid desire.

"Shouldn't our positions be reversed?" He toyed with a tendril at her temple. "We are celebrating your accomplishments, after all."

"You may have your turn. After I have mine."

Her feminine hunger beguiled him. She eyed his cock as if it were her favorite treat, and when she darted out her tongue, rimming his tip, he grunted with pleasure. His wife had become an expert at tormenting him with her mouth. She took her time, her teasing flicks and voluptuous suction making him grip the edge of the seat. When he judged she'd had her fun, he threaded his fingers in her coiffure. Pins pinged to the carriage floor as he guided her head.

"Deeper," he instructed.

Her hum of assent sent a delicious vibration down his turgid shaft. She dove down with a cheerful enthusiasm that caused his hips to buck. Knowing that she enjoyed this as much as he did—well, perhaps not *quite* as much—was a potent aphrodisiac. As carnal heat blazed through him, he had a flash of insight: he and Evie had earned this. Their physical intimacy was rooted in the trust they'd built. Love made it safe to express their deepest desires, to be who they were, without fear of judgment. With her, he didn't have to be the perfect gentleman or heir...it was enough to be himself.

The recognition stripped away the layers of civility, baring his primal self. Dark impulses pounded in his blood. He unleashed the desires that could only be sated by his mate.

"Take more of my cock." He fisted the silken ribbons of her hair. "I know you can do better."

He knew Evie enjoyed a challenge, and her moan of excitement proved him right. That sound, muffled by his meaty rod, churned his lust, and he pushed her head toward his lap. The lush glide of her tongue set fire to his blood. She bobbed on him, hollowing her cheeks with such alacrity that he spurted a little. When the carriage hit a bump, he felt the ripple of her throat and groaned in bliss.

She sputtered but continued her ministrations, taking him to the precipice.

"Do you want it, darling?" he grated out. "Do you want me to spill down your throat?"

Her eyes, huge and watery with effort, gave him the answer.

"Then take it, sweet wife. Take it all."

His fingers digging into her scalp, he let himself go. Bliss seared him as he erupted with a shout. His stones pulsed, releasing their hot load into his wife's loving kiss. She accepted his offering and tidied him with gentle licks. Panting, he drew her into his lap, kissing her thoroughly. Like before, she squirmed at sharing the earthy flavor.

"I like it," he growled against her lips. "I like tasting what you give to me. I like that you are as gifted at giving a lecture to a learned society as you are at sucking my cock in a moving carriage."

"James." She wriggled again, her eyes filled with helpless need.

Understanding, he smiled. "Your turn, sweetheart."

Lifting her off his lap, he bent her over the opposite bench. As she balanced her arms on the velvet squabs, he went to one knee, grabbing a fistful of her skirts. The rustling layers resisted his command, but he was resolute and achieved his goal. With her skirts spilling over his head, he widened the slit in her drawers, exposing her swollen crease. Her fragrant arousal made him heady. He drew his tongue slowly, lazily over her plump folds.

"Ripe as a peach," he murmured. "How I shall enjoy eating you."

She made an incoherent sound and pushed her pussy against him. As carriages clattered past and hawkers shouted their wares, he feasted on his countess with leisurely delight. He sheathed his tongue in her cunny, grunting when her muscles clenched around him. Rubbing her nubbin, he ate her thoroughly, uncaring if he gorged himself. Eventually, his desires took him higher—to her naughty rim. She gasped when he tongued her there, slowly and deliberately. Between them, they'd discovered that no pleasure was forbidden, and he took his time playing with her lovely hole. When she came, her cry was as sweet as her gushing honey.

He rose, shoving her skirts out of the way and notching his ready member to her slit. He drove inside, panting at the snug fit.

"Please, James."

Evie twisted her head to look at him. Her mouth was slack with desire, her gaze glassy with need. She was as far gone and desperate as he was.

"Love me," she pleaded. "Don't stop."

"Never. I'll never stop."

He slammed his hips, giving her his all. When the carriage bounced, he grabbed the strap for balance, continuing to plow her with determined force. Her mewls of pleasure and the soaked velvet of her pussy became his world. Her bunched skirts obscured his view of their joining, but he felt everything.

With her, he always had.

"I cannot get enough of you," he rasped. "My Evie. Mine."

"I want you, James. All of you," she cried.

"Then take me."

Holding fast to the strap, he hammered into her. He took her like the animal he was—the animal he could only be with her, the mate to his soul. She arched her spine, her fingers digging into the cushions as she cried out again. Her sheath milked him, but he resisted heaven's pull. He slowed his pace, prolonging her shivers. When she descended from the heights, he took her up again.

And again.

Only when she was boneless with satisfaction did he seek out his own.

"Look at me, sunflower."

She did, and the love in her eyes spurred his race to the finish.

"I am going to spend so hard for you."

"Do it, darling. Fill me." Her face glowed with naked longing. "Give me another babe."

The need to give her what she wanted—what was in his own heart—rushed through him. With a hoarse shout, he planted himself as deep as he could go and gave her everything he had. Everything he was. When his shudders eased, he remained buried in his wife. They exchanged tender words and kisses, soaking in the perfect ecstasy of the moment...and the blossoming hope of the future.

Chapter Twenty-Nine

After the triumph of Evie's lecture, she and James attended to darker matters. They had planned to use their final day in London to learn more about Dr. Murdoch and the blackmailer's glove. Since the tasks were delicate—they could not risk alerting the villain that they were on his trail—they'd decided to go incognito. Xenia had given Evie brown hair dye to darken her locks, as well as a drab gown she'd worn as a house-keeper. Evie had added a plain bonnet to the outfit and was satis-fied that the woman in the looking glass could pass for a lady's maid.

When James strode into the bedchamber, she burst into giggles.

"What are you laughing at, young lady?" he drawled.

"You, of course."

He'd darkened his hair as well and added side whiskers and a dashing moustache. He wore a rakish frock coat of plum broad-cloth, a waistcoat glimmering with gold thread, and a striped cravat tied in a fussy knot. In other words, he'd succeeded admirably in his goal: no one was going to recognize him as this boulevardier.

"The moustache makes you look like a villain from a Gothic novel," she teased.

He swept her into a dip, his dramatic flair making her shake with laughter.

"Do not disparage the moustache, madam, until you have experienced its power."

He nibbled the length of her neck, and her shaking took on a different quality as the bristly hair scraped sensually over her skin. He stopped, giving her a knowing look.

"After our errands, I shall keep this on and kiss you all over," he murmured. "We'll see where you like it best."

"That is wicked." Her lips curved. "I shall hold you to your promise."

They headed to Perry & Morris first. Located on Oxford Street, the shop was narrow and neat, with plate-glass windows displaying gloves on velvet stands. Evie entered first. The place smelled of leather, dried lavender, and wood polish. Gleaming mahogany counters topped glass cabinets, where gloves were sorted by size, material, and color. Female assistants dressed in black were helping customers.

When the doorbell tinkled, Evie stifled a smile as James sauntered in. Her husband was enjoying this bit of intrigue more than she would have expected. Indeed, he seemed lighter and more playful in general. With her, he was not just a duty-bound husband and politician—or an untouchable god—but a flesh-and-blood man whose flaws and wicked desires made her love him more.

She liked to think that their reconciliation had helped them to grow. She felt comfortable in her own skin—felt free to love and play. Once the blackmailer was apprehended, she hoped she might shed the albatross of her history once and for all.

A young brunette approached. "May I be of service, ma'am?"

"Yes, indeed."

As rehearsed, Evie posed as a lady's maid whose employer had purchased gloves here some months ago and misplaced them.

"My mistress was ever so fond of those gloves," Evie said, "and would like to purchase another pair. Alas, neither she nor I can recall the name of the model. She sent me to inquire if you might have a record of her purchase?"

"Certainly, if the purchase was made on her account. If you give me her name, I will consult our ledger," the assistant offered.

"My mistress bought the gloves with ready money."

"I see." The assistant's mien was rueful. "Unfortunately, we do not keep records of clients who pay in cash. Unless she has an account, I would not be able to identify which model of gloves she purchased."

In other words, if the blackmailer paid in cash, we will not be able to trace his identity.

Thanking her, Evie left the shop, and James joined her in the carriage a few minutes later. She told him what she'd learned, and he shared his findings.

"I told the clerk I wished to replace several items obtained under the account of John Merrill. When said account was not found, I made a fuss, and the manager came and showed me the ledger. I insisted on flipping through the pages myself—and saw neither Merrow nor Murdoch listed under the surnames starting with 'M.'"

"I suppose it was always a remote possibility that the glove would lead to the blackmailer."

"Don't lose hope, sweetheart. We may yet discover something at Murdoch's offices."

The physician's fall from grace was evident in his address. Rather than fashionable Harley Street, Dr. Murdoch consulted from a building of shabby gentility on a narrow Bloomsbury lane. The office was surrounded by boarding houses and minor businesses.

"Wait here," James said. "I shall be right back."

He saw Evie struggle between desire and good sense. She wanted to accompany him, and she knew it was a bad idea, given that Murdoch might recognize her.

She sighed. "Be careful, darling."

He kissed her before alighting. The building had three doors, and on the farthest left, he made out the words *Dr. Ezra Murdoch, Physician & Surgeon* engraved on a brass plate eroded by time. The knob squealed as he opened the door, revealing a steep staircase to the third floor. He made a rapid ascent, the floorboards creaking beneath his shoes.

The waiting room was furnished with chairs and a desk. The latter was blanketed by dust. The air was musty, with an underlying hint of rot. As the hairs on his nape rose, James headed toward the door to the consulting rooms. He pressed his ear against the wood—no sound came from within. Grasping the knob, he turned it. The door opened, releasing a smell that churned his stomach. Not a hint of rot, but putrid, full-fledged decay.

The origin required no deduction.

The body lay next to the desk, the hovering insects lending an illusion of movement. Holding a handkerchief over his nose, James forced himself to walk into the shuttered room and look down at what had once been a living man. Murdoch, as described by Evie, was still recognizable from his auburn hair and long-limbed figure, his garb that of a professional man. However, decomposition had distorted him, melting parts and blackening others. His eyes had lost their color, sunken into what remained of his face.

A cursory examination did not reveal a wound that would have caused Murdoch's death. Something glinted on the floor by the desk chair: crouching, James saw it was a rather fine cut-crystal tumbler. Murdoch might have been drinking from it when he collapsed, which explained its current position. James picked up the crystal vessel, turning it in his gloved hands, noting the dried amber film on the side where it had landed.

Replacing the tumbler, he headed to the mahogany cabinet against the wall. The piece's grandeur hinted at better times: the bottom half was fashioned as a sideboard and upon it was a tarnished tray holding crystal glasses that matched the one by the chair. There were two decanters, one of brandy, the other of sherry. Above the sideboard was a deep glass-fronted cabinet, and when James opened it, he saw an army of brown tincture bottles placed in exact rows. They were filled with murky liquids and labeled in precise copperplate. One bottle stood out from the rest—as if it had been recently disturbed.

James lifted it, and his blood chilled as he read the label:

Atropa belladonna.

Chapter Thirty

When Evie and James returned to Bottoms House the next day, Xenia and Gigi dashed into the entrance hall to greet them, their voluminous skirts swinging with their haste.

"There you are!" Gigi exclaimed. "What took you so long? We've been waiting for ages."

James turned to Evie. "My love, why do I feel as if we have been run to earth before we've even crossed the threshold?"

"Come quickly." Xenia, whose temperament was generally less excitable than Gigi's, looked as if she were about to burst at the seams. "Mama is waiting for us."

Evie's curiosity was further piqued when they were led to Xenia's private sitting room. Mama was there, sipping tea in the cozy chamber overlooking the garden. After greeting her, Evie and James settled on an overstuffed chintz sofa.

"The pair of you look refreshed." Mama's gaze was warm. "How was your lecture, dearest?"

"It went as well as I could have hoped." Smiling, Evie interlaced her fingers with her husband's. "James was a great support."

"You shone on your own merit." He kissed her hand before adding somberly, "We made some discoveries as well."

He described the visit to the glovemaker's shop and to Murdoch's consulting rooms. The description of the physician's death did not improve with a second telling, and Evie shivered.

"Heavens." Gigi paled. "What did you do?"

"I sent an anonymous note to the police with Murdoch's address," James replied. "I couldn't risk further involvement. To do so might alert the blackmailer to my activities—or stir up scandal I cannot afford."

"Do you suppose that Murdoch was involved with the blackmail scheme?" Gigi asked. "And someone—his partner, perhaps—murdered him to ensure his silence?"

"Or to take his share of the payment," Mama said coolly.

Xenia's forehead pleated. "Do you think Merrow is responsible for both the extortion and the murder?"

"It is possible," Evie said. "He struck me as a scheming fellow —one who would do anything to get ahead. His devotion to Wilmington was likely self-serving: he viewed his master as a ladder to reach his ambitions. By taking Wilmington's life, I deprived Merrow of his livelihood and foiled his plans. I still remember how he cornered me, shouting, '*What have you done?*'"

With flooding terror, she felt him shoving her against the wall, his eyes blazing with violence, his spittle stinging her face. Warmth encircled her shoulders—James's arm. His strength drew her back into the present.

"All right, love?" he murmured. "Perhaps we ought to take a break—"

"No, let us finish this." Composing herself, she shared the theory she and James had deliberated upon. "It is possible that Merrow persuaded Dr. Murdoch to keep the poisoning a secret. Accusing me would have gained him nothing save perceived justice for his employer. But I don't think loyalty was his driving motivation—self-interest was. He might have decided that while I was useless to him as a penniless adolescent girl, perhaps one day I would be worth something. Perhaps one day I could give him the wealth he'd been robbed of...and he would have an unbreakable hold on me. He could get whatever he wanted because he knew my secret."

"He played a long game." Mama nodded briskly. "That takes intelligence and self-control, which makes him a dangerous nemesis indeed."

"Should we keep to the plan and try to lure him out?" Gigi bit her lip. "Before, we didn't know Merrow was capable of murder, but now..."

"Now we need to stop him more than ever," Evie said. "James and I have discussed this."

"I wouldn't say we are in full agreement on using you as bait to capture Merrow," James muttered. "But, yes, in principle, we agree: he must be stopped."

"I won't be in danger with everyone looking out for me," Evie said soothingly. "By the by, we picked up the necklace from Garrard."

Reaching into her traveling bag, she removed the velvet case and opened it. The fine paste diamonds sparkled in the sunlight, the riviere pattern an exact replica of her original necklace.

"Quite convincing," Mama said. "It would fool most people."

"I plan to wear the genuine article at every affair. If the black-mailer has eyes on me, he will see it and hopefully be enticed to make another demand."

A sudden silence descended upon the room, and she caught the glances traded between the other ladies. A sense of foreboding quickened her pulse.

"What is it?" she asked.

It was Mama who spoke. "There is a reason we wanted to speak to you in private upon your return. We made a discovery ourselves. I am afraid it has to do with Harkness."

Disquiet spread through Evie. "What about her?"

"After you left, she was acting strangely. There was a certain furtiveness to her behavior that caught my attention. One day, I followed her," Mama admitted.

"You did what?" James frowned. "Were you alone?"

"Dear boy, you ought to know by now that I can take care of myself. I could hardly bring a coterie with me on a covert mission, could I?" She waved off his concern. "At any rate, I followed Harkness to Chudleigh Crest, where she visited a coaching inn. From what I could ascertain, she was inquiring about the schedule to the Reading train station."

The lines deepened on James's face. "Evie, did you know Harkness was planning a trip?"

"No." Her dread turned into denial. "However, I am sure there is a good explanation—"

"I did not wish to say it then, but I must now."

Seeing Mama's sober countenance, Evie shook her head, as if she could ward off what was coming.

"Back when you discussed potential suspects—those who were present at the time of Wilmington's murder and knew your secret —you missed one key person."

"I had the same thought," James said quietly. "And I mentioned it to Evie."

"No." When the word emerged as a hoarse whisper, Evie said it again. "*No.* You're both mistaken. Harkness has taken care of me my entire life. She would never—"

"I know it is hard to contemplate the possibility, but you must," Mama insisted.

Evie's head whirled. "Inquiring about train schedules is not an indication of guilt. Harkness might just want a holiday—"

"There is more." Xenia's brown eyes shimmered with empathy. "I am sorry, Evie, but after what Mama discovered, I...I searched Harkness's chamber."

"While I distracted Harkness," Gigi added. "We had to do it, Evie, for your safety."

Evie said faintly, "Did you find something?"

"Fifty gold sovereigns," Xenia blurted. "And a pair of lady's gloves from Perry & Morris."

"Those are coincidences. They mean nothing." The knots in Evie's chest made it hard to breathe. "Harkness has always practiced economy. She has scrimped and saved since I was a girl. With the wages James provides, it's perfectly possible that she saved—"

"You gave the blackmailer a hundred sovereigns." James's jaw was granite-hard, his gaze full of steel. "Now Harkness has half that amount in her possession...which could be her share if she is working with a partner. And don't forget Harkness knows Merrow. They worked together for years."

"She would never hurt me," Evie said desperately. "You know what she has done for me."

"I know she resents me," James countered. "She has never hidden her animosity. It is not much of a leap to suppose that she might act upon it. Perhaps blackmailing you is a way of gaining revenge on me for taking you away."

"She would never do such a thing." Evie was appalled. "As for the money, that must be her own savings. And countless people own gloves made by Perry & Morris—"

"Harkness has large hands for a woman," Mama said. "Xenia took one of her gloves, and now that you have returned, we may compare it with the blackmailer's."

"You are wrong, all of you." Evie shot to her feet, her voice shaking. "Harkness would never betray me. For years, she was the only family I had—"

Suddenly, she was weeping. An instant later, James was holding her.

"There now." His voice gentled. "It is true that we don't know for certain if Harkness is involved. However, we cannot ignore the evidence."

"Sh-she stood by me."

Evie drew back, her chest twisting when she saw his stark expression.

"When I was alone in the world, Harkness was my only friend. I cannot lose her."

"If she is innocent, then you will not lose her," he said. "Yet we must take precautions."

"What sort of precautions?"

Mama spoke up. "You cannot confide in her any longer. About anything."

"If Harkness were conspiring with Merrow or whoever the blackmailer is," Evie said miserably, "wouldn't she have told him about our plan? He would know that I shared my secret with you and that we are setting a trap to capture him. Wouldn't he have exposed my secret by now?"

"Perhaps she hasn't had the opportunity to share the information," Gigi suggested. "Or perhaps he has a contingency plan of some sort. From a practical viewpoint, exposing you doesn't do him any good: better to wait and see if he can gain leverage in another way."

"If the blackmailer does not make contact this week," James said grimly, "that would support the theory that Harkness tipped him off."

"In any case," Mama said, "you must play along, Evie. Act as if you suspect nothing. When Harkness asks about London, you will say that your lecture was a success, but you learned nothing about the blackmailer."

"In other words, I must keep secrets again." With palpitating anguish, Evie said, "I must lie to my oldest friend...who may have betrayed me."

Evie spent the next few days accompanying James to various events. From charity functions to hospital visits, she played the role of loving wife and helpmeet as best she could. While her support of her husband was genuine, the fact that she might have compromised his future by trusting the wrong person—the person who'd been her confidante, whom she thought of as kin—weighed as heavily as the diamond necklace she flaunted to lure the blackmailer.

One bright spot was her visit with Loretta Pickleworth's brother, Ned Lydell. At James's insistence, she took a pair of footmen for protection since he was detained at a meeting. Their presence seemed superfluous on such a beautiful spring day. The sky hung like a bright blue banner, while the fields of wheat and barley formed a patchwork of silky greens. Mr. Lydell proved a gregarious host, giving her a tour of the farm that had been in the family for generations. When they came to the cherry orchard, which consisted of a few rows of straggly trees, his broad face turned mournful.

"Used to be the pride of the farm and the county, the orchard was," he said. "My grandpapa—the last to taste the cherries—said they were unique and unlike any other. Sweeter and tarter, with a finish that reminded him of flowers. He said it had to do with the clime and the shelter of the valley. The trees had white blossoms that gave off such a strong fragrance at night that you could smell them from the farmhouse. Grandpapa used to joke that at peak season, our farm smelled like a broth—er, a house of ill repute. No offense, my lady."

"None taken."

Evie spoke absently as she examined the lichen-covered trunks, gnarled branches, and sparse crowns. She touched a stunted blossom—small and pale, it was clear that it would never bear fruit. Others like it had already fallen, lying like tiny, crumpled ghosts upon the ground.

"Did anything change around the time that the trees stopped producing fruit?" she asked.

Mr. Lydell scratched at the tuft of straw-colored hair sticking out above his ear.

"Not from what I've been told. The weather didn't change, nor our tending of the orchard. Of course, the land around us changed—the building of factories and the railway and so forth. But the farm, it stayed the same."

She took out a small notebook. Donning her spectacles, she began jotting notes.

"There continued to be a healthy population of bees?" she asked.

"I think so. But as the orchards died off in the area, the bees left too."

"What about moths?"

"Moths?" He frowned. "I don't reckon anyone paid them much attention."

"That is hardly surprising," Evie murmured. "Yet it is often the smallest, most easily forgotten creatures that hold the world together. Do you remember ever seeing moths in the orchard—at night, perhaps?"

"Well." The farmer braced his hands on his hips. "I can't say that I have. My grandpapa and his papa before him collected almanacs and added their own notes. Maybe you would like to have a look at them?"

With a spark of excitement, she said, "I would indeed, sir."

She left the farm with a small trunk of dusty almanacs and a pie freshly baked by Mrs. Lydell. Unfortunately, her desire to delve into the handbooks was thwarted by the evening's obligation: a ball hosted by Lady Vernon. Pauline was putting the finishing touches on her outfit when Harkness came in.

Tension gripped Evie. She hadn't invited Harkness to accompany her on the farm visit. Indeed, she'd been avoiding her companion all week because it was too hard to keep up the pretense that all was well between them. Knowing what was at stake—what the blackmailer could do to James's future—she dismissed her maid and forced a smile.

"How was the visit to the farm?" Harkness asked.

"Fine."

Feeling nervous, Evie turned to show off her new ball gown. It was the shade of blushing peonies, with a square neckline and tiered skirts that twirled gracefully.

"What do you think? Will I do?"

"The frock is pretty enough." Harkness's mien was as dour as her charcoal-grey bombazine. "More importantly, it shows off the necklace. If the dastardly villain is watching, he won't be able to resist the diamonds. He'll send the next note, and by God's mercy, we shall capture him and be done with this dark business."

Conflict tore at Evie. If Harkness was indeed in cahoots with the villain, would she bring up the plan to seize him? If he were caught, surely she would be implicated as well? Or was this some sort of reverse ploy...to manipulate and maintain Evie's trust?

Please be who I think you are, Harkness. Please be a true friend.

Evie's temples throbbed. "I will be very glad when all this is done."

"Is something wrong, lambkin?"

The familiar endearment twisted her heart. "No."

"You haven't been yourself since London." Harkness's gaze slitted. "Did something happen while you were there?"

Is she probing? Acting as an accomplice to the villain? Or is she being a concerned friend?

"As I've said, my lecture went splendidly." The ache spread to the back of her skull. "Were you referring to something else?"

After a pause, Harkness said grudgingly, "I was wondering about the state of affairs between you and the earl. If your reconciliation has lasted."

"It has." Thinking of James—of all he was willing to risk for her—ignited a spark of defiance. "Our love has grown stronger, and this time, it is going to last. Forever."

"Forever is a long time, pet. Sure of him, are you?"

"I am sure of my husband. What I am less certain of is you."

The words slipped out, driven by anxiety Evie couldn't contain.

Harkness jerked her head, her steel-grey curls bouncing like springs. "You would question my loyalty? After everything we have been through together? Is that why you've been avoiding me?"

The hurt in her companion's eyes would have made Evie scramble for an apology—but a flash of guilt followed. Evie felt as if someone had suddenly yanked on her corset strings. Her lungs constricted, despair suffocating her.

No, no, no. Not you, Harkness. I can't bear it.

Yet she couldn't ask what she wanted to and had probably revealed too much already.

"You misunderstand." It took all her willpower to summon a contrite tone. "What I meant was I am uncertain about how you are faring these days. Our recent talks have revolved around my problems, at the expense of any you may have. I have noticed that you haven't seemed yourself. Is there...is there something amiss? Anything you wish to discuss?"

Loyalty and love made her open the door. If Harkness confessed now, then perhaps the situation could be salvaged. Or perhaps there was another explanation for the incriminating evidence—

"Nothing is amiss." Harkness's denial came as swiftly as a blade in the back. Her gaze darted to the side before returning to Evie's. "It is kind of you to inquire."

"Of course." Evie smiled, her heart cracking. "What are friends for?"

Chapter Thirty-One

"There is no need to be nervous," James murmured.

"Isn't there?" Evie whispered back. "All eyes are upon us tonight."

They stood at the top of the stairs that descended into the boisterous ballroom. The mirrored walls magnified the size of the crowd. Skirts in a rainbow of hues swirled, jewels glittered, and voices and music blended into a dull roar. As they waited to be announced, guests studied them with open curiosity.

Taking his wife's gloved hand, James kissed it.

"Beauty such as yours will always draw attention," he said.

She was a vision in her vibrant pink gown, which complemented her fair coloring and made her look like a shy angel. In contrast, her eyes brimmed with sensual warmth and lively intelligence. Her neckline was more daring than usual; he knew she'd chosen it to draw attention to the diamonds, but he thought the creamy mounds of her breasts were far more enticing than any jewels. In short, she was exquisite, and any hot-blooded man would look twice.

Protectiveness surged through James. He would stay close to her tonight.

"They are looking at you, not me," she said. "You are the cele-brated personage. I am merely an accessory."

As endearing as he found her lack of vanity, she was utterly wrong.

"You are no one's accessory," he said. "As fellows will be vying for a place on your dance card the minute we get down there, I wish to reserve the waltzes now."

"Well, then. I shall see if I can fit you in."

At her impish smile, he couldn't resist bending to her ear.

"You fit me in fine last night," he said in a low voice. "In fact, I seem to recall you requesting that I go even deeper."

To his delight, Evie's cheeks pinkened and matched her gown. As she wore this most charming of blushes, they were announced. They descended into the gilt-and-marble pit and were immediately swept up in the social tide. Knowing how the game was played, James sought out the influential members of his party. He danced with their wives while they danced with his. Although he would prefer to monopolize Evie's dance card—an impulse his mama would undoubtedly chide him for—he was proud of her poised performance.

She danced, smiled, and yes, dazzled. Since their reunion, she had gained confidence, and her intellect and modesty made her a force to be reckoned with. He couldn't ask for a better countess, wife, or political partner. She was everything he'd dreamed of...and more. He wouldn't let anyone—or anything—threaten her.

The awareness that the blackmailer might have eyes and ears on her at this very moment prompted James to continuously scan the throng. Did the footman who was serving the champagne look overly long at Evie's necklace? What about the one manning the refreshment table...did he seem to be monitoring her movements? The problem was that everyone began to look suspicious. Distracted, James had difficulty focusing on his own conversations.

"Lord Manderly, I was looking for you."

Like a Biblical sea, the throng parted for the hostess. Lady

Vernon glided toward him in a silver gown, a matching plume bobbing in her hair. Despite her glittering appearance, James's attention shifted from her to her escort.

What in blazes is Ryerson doing here?

On the surface, Eustace Ryerson was the picture of respectability: tall, robust, and composed to the last button. His dark hair was carefully pomaded, his cravat flawless. His expression was mild and polite...if one failed to notice the tiny smirk on his thin lips. His wintry eyes were a window into his character. Cold and hard, they were convinced of their own clarity.

"I have brought you a surprise, my lord," Lady Vernon said lightly. "I thought the two of you ought to get better acquainted before the hustings."

Her charm did not cover her ruthless stratagem. Wanted to throw two gladiators into a ring, did she, and see who emerged victorious from the match? James felt the excitement of the surrounding guests, who watched the exchange like Roman spectators, sampling canapés and sipping on champagne. Lady Vernon was not only testing James's mettle, but she was doing so publicly: to make sure she'd picked a winner this time and not a loser.

Gosford's warning surfaced. *Keep your enemies close and your friends closer.*

That was the way of politics, and James had to accept it. Even if it went against the foundation of who he was. The honor and decency he espoused.

"A pleasure to meet again, sir," he said with a bow.

"The pleasure is mine," Ryerson replied. "I was not certain you would be present this eve."

"Why would I miss such an agreeable event?"

"Not by choice, of course. But I heard you were struck down by illness after visiting the parish infirmary." Malice glinted in Ryerson's gaze. "A well-intentioned act, no doubt, but it serves to remind us that man's remedies are not God's. Disease, like poverty, will not be cured by Acts of Parliament but by acts of Providence."

"I do not believe God intended men to die for want of medical treatment," James said evenly. "My illness and recovery only reinforced what I know to be true: the privilege of good health should be available to all—not just those who can afford it."

"My lord, I fear you grow impassioned. Perhaps it is the aftermath of your illness—fever is known to erode rationality." Ryerson's sharp barb earned muffled laughter from the audience. "Yet we cannot forget where we are. All this talk of contagion and death will surely offend the sensibilities of these esteemed guests. I know you are new to politics, sir, but never forget the importance of delicacy and respect."

The nerve of the bastard, taking refuge behind civility, when he advocates for barbaric measures that punish the poor and leave the sick to die.

"The truth may not be pleasant or polite, but it is, nonetheless, the truth. Given the choice, I would deal with honesty, in all its forms, rather than falsehoods, no matter how pretty."

"Quite the idealist, are you not? Cut from the same cloth as Gosford."

"While Gosford has my respect for his many years of serving the public good, he and I are not the same," James said evenly.

"That is true. Scandal has ruined him, but you are an honorable fellow. One from an impeccable lineage and whose reputation is untarnished. Have a care, however: no man is impervious to rumor and gossip."

Something flickered in Ryerson's eyes—glee. Though the gloating light vanished the next instant, it left unease coiling in James's gut.

Does Ryerson know something? Has he somehow caught wind of Evie's past?

"The higher one rises, the harder the fall, as the saying goes," Ryerson said airily.

James's suspicion grew, and he was scrambling to counter when Evie emerged at his side.

"Darling, you promised me a dance." She turned a guileless look upon Ryerson. "Oh, forgive me. I see you are otherwise engaged."

Lady Vernon made the introductions.

Ryerson bowed over Evie's hand with a flourish.

"My lady, every great man must have his guiding star," Ryerson said grandly. "Lord Manderly is fortunate to have found his in you. I daresay your charm and steadiness keep his enthusiasms in check."

The condescension—and the fact that he was using Evie to deliver the dig—shot up the pressure in James's veins.

"How kind of you to say, sir." Evie's manner was honey-sweet. "However, my husband keeps his own counsel. Indeed, his enthusiasms, as you put it, are quite catching and have won him many admirers, of which I am one."

"Your devotion is admirable," Ryerson said with a brittle smile. "As you undoubtedly nursed Manderly back to health during his illness, you do so now with his reputation."

"My husband's reputation needs no nursing. It is, and has always been, in the pink of health."

"No man is perfect," Ryerson said shortly. "In reputation or in health."

"From the way you queried my husband about his illness, I assumed that *you* had never suffered an ailment." She widened her eyes like an ingenue. "I envy you such robustness, sir—and such conviction."

Ryerson sputtered as smothered laughter rippled through the crowd. Lady Vernon, James saw, was gazing at Evie with dawning respect.

Pride and gratitude blazed through him. *What a woman fate has bestowed upon me.*

"Come, my dear." He offered Evie his arm. "I was promised a dance, and I shall claim this waltz as my due."

"Of course. If you'll excuse us?" she said politely.

With a demure curtsy, her eyes sparkling brighter than the diamonds, Evie went with him to the dance floor.

Evie exited the retiring room.

Despite the late hour—and her sore toes from dancing—she buzzed with energy...and happiness. It wasn't often that James needed her help, but tonight she had proved her worth. She'd stood for him as he'd done for her countless times. How dare that worm Ryerson insult him? James had been holding his own, but her wifely instincts had led her into the fray. Afterward, she'd fretted that he might resent her interference.

She needn't have worried.

"Thank you for coming to my rescue," James had murmured during their waltz. *"What a brave little wife I have."*

"I didn't mean to interfere—"

"You didn't. And I shall have to think of some way to thank you —say, by putting you on your hands and knees tonight."

The quiver of heat had made her stumble. James caught her, of course, steering her smoothly through the turn.

Recovering, she'd muttered, *"Would that be thanking me—or yourself?"*

Laughter had gleamed in his gaze. *"Let us call it an act of mutual appreciation."*

The thought of mutually appreciating one another caused Evie to hasten her steps. Having made the rounds, she and James could leave...and commence with the evening's true festivities. She was about to pass through the marble colonnade that circled the ballroom when a footman approached. Blond and strapping, he looked as new and shiny as the brass buttons on his livery.

"Do I have the honor of speaking with the Countess of Manderly?" he asked tentatively.

She gave him a puzzled smile. "Yes."

"I have a message for you, my lady."

He extended a silver salver, and dread slithered up her spine when she saw the familiar penmanship. She picked up the sealed note as casually as she could.

"Who gave you this?"

"I am not certain. My duty is to deliver messages, and this one, um, appeared on my tray. It might have been there for some time before I noticed it," he said apologetically. "If you wish, I could ask the butler whether he saw—"

"That won't be necessary." The last thing she wanted was to draw attention to the note. "I'm certain it is from my husband, announcing that he is ready to depart."

"Yes, my lady." The footman looked relieved. "I've conveyed many such messages this eve."

Evie waited until he left to break the seal.

Deliver the diamond necklace to the hermit's grotto at midnight tomorrow. Place it in the niche at the entrance. Come alone—or I will destroy the Earl of Manderly's reputation and future.

CHAPTER THIRTY-TWO

"I have to be the one to deliver the necklace," Evie insisted the next morning. "Otherwise, the blackmailer will sense a trap."

"I will not have you endangering yourself," James growled.

And yes, he *was* growling—because they'd been going around and around since she'd received the note, neither willing to concede ground. Now they had an audience. His family was gathered again in Xenia's sitting room to avoid prying eyes. He and Evie stood in front of the hearth, arguing their points.

"I won't be in danger. He wants the jewels, not me. In fact, he is probably toasting my good health since it is tied to his growing fortune."

Evie's blasé attitude tested his patience to its limits.

"You wanted to flush out the bounder—I agreed," he said grimly. "You wanted to be the bait? I permitted it. However, I will not allow you to prance into the bloody woods at midnight to rendezvous with a villain who, might I remind you, has committed murder!"

"*Allow* me?" Outrage flared in her eyes.

"Children, please." Mama, seated on the sofa, used a calm yet firm tone. "There is no point in quarreling. Our time and energy would be put to better use coming up with a plan."

"Mama is right." Standing behind her, Papa added his authority. "When tensions are high, cool heads must prevail. James is correct—Evie cannot go into the woods alone."

"Actually, I agree with Evie." Mama twisted around and frowned at him. "If anyone else goes in her stead, the villain will know the game is up."

"But should danger arise, Evie would be ill-equipped—"

"Why? Because she is a female?"

James exchanged uneasy glances with his brothers. Growing up, they'd all heard this whisper-soft tone from their mama and knew it was the laying of a trap. Ethan subtly shook his head at Papa, trying to warn him.

"Well, yes, partly." Papa drew his brows together. "But that is not the only—"

"I am a female."

Papa cleared his throat. "Of that, I am well aware."

"And during the conflicts with Boney, did I not successfully navigate perilous situations?"

James stilled. Mama rarely discussed her experiences during the war, and to this day, neither he nor his siblings were quite clear about the role she played. Papa would only say with pride that she was a true heroine.

"You are an exceptional woman, my love," Papa muttered.

"Evie is as well. Come sit with me, dear girl."

At Mama's beckoning, Evie went to join her on the sofa...but not before giving James a smug *Mama-agrees-with-me* smile. He sighed, torn between irritation and fathomless love for his hard-headed spouse. As requested, she sat next to Mama—at least she heeded someone—and James had the sudden recognition of how alike the two were. Not on the surface, for Mama's beauty was sultry and dark while Evie's was solemn and fair, but at the heart of who they were.

Strong, intelligent, and brave women who loved fiercely and were loyal to the bone.

Mama patted Evie's hand. "During the prior deliveries, did you see the blackmailer?"

"Neither hide nor hair of him." Evie hesitated. "But he must have been there...watching."

"Yes," Mama agreed. "And he will be there again tonight. To flush him out and run him to ground, you must make an appearance. However"—she held up a hand to cut off James's protest—"you won't be alone. This morning, we will send scouts to find the best places to keep watch without the blackmailer's awareness."

Xenia and Gigi volunteered simultaneously.

"I will go!"

Ethan and Godwin groaned.

Now they know how I feel.

"By all appearances, Xenia and Gigi will be two ladies taking a morning constitutional through the woods." Mama gave a pleased nod. "Once they determine the best places of concealment, the men will take their places. Tonight, Evie will bait the trap, and when the villain appears, the men will make their move—and capture him. Evie will always be under watch and protected, but as an extra precaution..."

Picking up the knitting bag at her feet, Mama pulled out a pearl-handled pistol as if it were a harmless ball of yarn.

"She must also be able to protect herself."

It was nearing midnight. Concealed in the recessed alcove of the hermit's grotto, which gave him a view of the entrance, James saw the approaching glow of a lantern. His muscles stiffened for he knew it was Evie walking through the dark woods alone. The fact that he and his kin had the grotto surrounded and that Evie herself carried a pistol that Mama had taught her to use did little to alleviate his tension. His wife should not be undertaking this dangerous errand. Yet his protectiveness was tempered by his understanding of her: she needed to see this business to the end. Fiercely proud of her courage, he was determined to help her defeat the demons of her past.

The light of the lantern dazzled his pupils as Evie entered the grotto. He had to leash his impulse to pull her into his arms and hold her tight. Instead, he stayed hidden in case the blackmailer had eyes and ears nearby. He heard the swish of her skirts and the soft sound of the jewelry box being placed upon the niche.

Then she was gone, leaving him in darkness.

The shadows seemed to grow deeper as he waited. He hadn't worn a watch for fear that its ticking might give him away. Minutes felt like hours as he awaited his adversary. His mind wandered—from the consoling knowledge that Evie would be safely back at the manor by now to the satisfaction he would feel when he finally captured the blackguard. He thought about the grotto, too, and its mystical connection to Evie's dreams.

A rational man, he didn't believe in ghosts. Yet he couldn't deny he felt something—a presence or energy—in this strange hollow. Before the light had died, he'd seen the spiral of shells and the inscription on the wall that Evie had described.

You are mine, and I am yours. Not only for ease, but for every trial. This is the way of love: to stay, to forgive, to begin again.

Was it Rosalinda and Thomas's version of *Ad finem fidelis*? Whatever the case, he couldn't argue with it. His marriage had taught him that love was about committing to one another and taking chances despite mistakes.

He set aside sentiment and focused on monitoring the grotto's entrance. At times, his vision played tricks on him, picking up movement where there was none. Then he saw a faint flicker; he blinked, and it was still there—growing brighter, getting closer. He made out a lantern held by a cloaked figure.

James's muscles bunched in readiness as the shadow moved into the grotto. The man set the lamp down and picked up the jewelry box. He checked the goods, then stowed the box in the satchel strapped across his chest.

James pounced.

"What the bloody—"

He wrestled the villain to the ground. It was like grappling with a lamprey. The man was slippery and strong, and just when James thought he had the upper hand, the bastard kneed him in the groin. The dirty move made him see stars. His grip loosened, and the bounder broke free, making a run for it.

Staggering to his feet, James caught his breath and yelled, "Grab him! He's getting away."

He heard the answering shouts of his brothers and Papa. Grabbing the blackmailer's lamp, he shoved aside the pulsing agony and dashed out of the grotto. He saw dark figures racing through the woods and joined the chase, passing Papa and reaching Ethan.

He sprinted side by side with his brother.

"The bastard has the speed of a bloody thoroughbred," Ethan panted.

"We cannot let him escape," James bit out.

Pumping his arms harder, he propelled himself forward. He ran as if his future depended upon it. His muscles burned, sweat stinging his eyes as he gained ground. The sound of rushing water grew louder, and the trees thinned, the forest opening into a clearing eerily lit by moonlight. Swollen by recent storms, the stream cut through the land in a dark, frothing rush. Spotting Owen and the blackmailer running up the sharply inclining bank, James followed. He fought for balance on the slippery grass, mud sucking at his boots. One wrong step would send him toppling into the churning waters.

He was less than a hundred feet away when Owen caught up with their foe, tackling him from behind. James's heart shot into his throat when both men pitched toward the water's edge. They caught their balance, locked in battle, moonlight dashing their shadows over the churning waves. Owen fought like a man possessed—with a blind and brutal ferocity that had been foreign to his nature before the war.

James raced toward them, but the villain managed to twist free of his brother's hold. With an inhuman howl, Owen lunged at him, and the pair wrestled ever closer to the stream's edge. James was close enough to see the wildness of his brother's eyes when the earth gave way beneath the blackmailer's feet. The man fell into the water, screaming, his grip tightening on Owen and dragging him to his knees.

"Let go, Owen!" James yelled. "For God's sake, let go!"

But Owen didn't. He remained where he was, kneeling on dissolving ground, holding onto the enemy's hand—as if he could not bear to let another soul slip away. Or as if he were ready to follow the other... James hurled himself forward, grabbing Owen by the waist. In that instant, he saw the villain's hand slip from his brother's. The bounder's shout was lost in the roar of the water, his body disappearing in the vicious current.

Feeling Owen's shuddering tension, James said hoarsely, "He's gone, brother. There is nothing more we can do. Come with me now."

For a heartbeat, Owen didn't respond. Then his breath hitched in the softest of sobs...and he allowed James to haul him back from the edge. They reached solid ground just as the bank rumbled, collapsing into the thunderous tide.

CHAPTER THIRTY-THREE

Three days later, Evie groggily reached for James.

He wasn't in bed beside her. As she came fully awake, blinking in the watery light, she realized where he was. The finale with the blackmailer—Merrow, as it turned out—had been grim and shocking. Yet while that matter had been laid to rest, another problem had reared its head. The deadly struggle with Merrow had revived Owen's demons. By day, Owen was jittery and withdrawn, his spirits low; at night, he fought his way out of nightmares. An unspoken fear gripped the family: had the dark business reopened the invisible wounds of war?

Everyone was determined to do their part to prevent Owen from regressing to his former state. James and his siblings had taken turns spending the night with him. Mama and Papa hovered, as much as Owen allowed, and Evie tried to provide cheerful distraction. She had to drag him into the garden, but once there, he talked with her about their shared interest in plants. In her efforts to engage his mind with something harmless, she had even shared her latest botanical puzzle. He listened, if somewhat half-heartedly, as she discussed her theories regarding the disappearance of Chuddums's cherries. In the Lydells' almanacs, she'd found mention of the "Widow's Weeds Moth," a dull grey creature that had once been commonplace but had disappeared around the time the cherry crops had begun to dwindle.

Coincidence? Evie thought not. She had asked Owen to join her on her next visit to Ned Lydell's farm, and when he didn't turn her down, she considered it a victory. However, that didn't assuage her gnawing guilt. This was her fault. She had embroiled Owen in her troubles, and he was paying dearly for helping her—the whole family was. James, who ought to be preparing for the approaching hustings, had instead been cleaning up the mess she'd caused.

After Merrow had fallen into the stream, James and his papa had gone to the magistrate and given an account of what happened. The story, while altered to protect Evie's secret, remained faithful to the truth. A villain had stolen Evie's necklace. James and the others had caught him in the act and given chase. He'd fallen into the water and appeared to have drowned.

The magistrate and his men found the body the next day, tangled in a thicket of reeds downstream. When Evie had been called upon to identify the thief, she'd looked at the still, clean-cut features and sandy hair and recognized Merrow immediately. She'd verified that he was the one who'd taken her necklace...and that had been that. Now her blackmailer was dead, the threat gone. Yet relief remained elusive, and she was plagued by restless unease. An inner voice whispered that darkness would always follow her and she could never outrun it.

Another death. More suffering. Am I cursed to bring misfortune to those dearest to me?

Pushing aside her fears, she resolved to adopt a better frame of mind. She would help James with the hustings and the campaign he was sure to win. Perhaps she could even talk him into relaxing this evening. He was under a great deal of strain, and although he hid it well, she saw the lines of fatigue around his eyes. What he needed was pampering—a long hot bath, she decided. To help him unwind, she would rub his shoulders and perhaps other parts of him...

With a warm flutter, she got out of bed, and Pauline readied her for the day. She decided to tackle the task she'd been avoiding: making amends to Harkness. The fact that she'd suspected her dearest friend of being involved with the blackmail scheme filled her with remorse.

It was clear now that Harkness had done nothing to warn Merrow. Had she been his accomplice, he would not have come to claim the decoy necklace. A man forewarned does not walk straight into a snare. Merrow's unguarded arrival, his shock when confronted, and his desperate, solitary struggle for survival all proved he had acted alone.

In retrospect, every scrap of "evidence" against Harkness dissolved into mere coincidence. The sovereigns were her savings and her gloves commonplace. Her wish to travel was just a longing for a holiday. None of it pointed to treachery. Yet Evie had doubted her companion, who'd been there for her through thick and thin. While she'd never accused Harkness directly, her cold behavior had damaged their relationship. She needed to confess her terrible suspicions and offer her abject apologies. Thinking of how her well-meaning family had violated Harkness's privacy, she winced. No, apologizing would not be sufficient. If need be, she would grovel.

At Harkness's chamber, she found the door ajar and knocked softly before entering.

"Good morning, Harkness. I was wondering if you might be..."

She trailed off as she saw Harkness sitting in a chair, dressed in traveling clothes. Her companion's battered trunk and valise were packed, waiting to be carried out.

"I...I wasn't aware you were taking a trip," Evie blurted.

"I am leaving." Harkness's gaze was hard as obsidian. "You will find my letter of resignation on the desk. I thank you for the years of employment—"

"No." With a cry, Evie flew over, kneeling and putting her head on Harkness's lap as she had when she sought comfort as a child. "I am sorry for my behavior of late. I have much to explain, I know, and I came here to do it. To apologize for being distant and cold and—"

"You misunderstand." Harkness's voice was harsh, the scrape of steel against steel. "I am not leaving because of anything you did. But after last night, I can no longer pretend that my presence is of benefit to you."

"I know you are angry at me and deservedly so. You have always been my confidante, and I shut you out. If you'll let me explain—"

"No, my lamb." Harkness lifted a hand, running it with unexpected gentleness over Evie's hair. "You don't need to explain anything. For I failed you, you see. I promised your mama I would look after you and never let you come to harm. Yet I kept secrets from you...kept you in the dark about so many things."

Looking up, Evie saw that Harkness's eyes were glittering, not with anger...but remorse?

A cool droplet slid down her spine. "What do you mean?"

"I did it to protect you," Harkness said bleakly. "You were a young girl, and I didn't think you could handle the truth. I told myself I would tell you someday, when the time was right and you were ready...yet I kept putting it off. It was cowardice, I suppose, for I dreaded the very thought of revealing this terrible secret. As the years passed, it became more difficult to bring it up—"

"Bring what up? Harkness, please, you are frightening me," Evie pleaded. "What have you hidden from me that I should know?"

"When it happened, you were so young—only fourteen. I was afraid you would say something to Wilmington. You were dependent on him, for everything, and the knowledge...it would only put you in danger. I did what I thought was best: I stayed, looked after you, and kept my silence. Everything I did, I did to protect you—do you understand?"

"I *don't* understand. You're not making any sense. What is this secret? *Tell me.*"

"He didn't know that I was there." Harkness's eyes took on a faraway gleam. "He should have known because I was always there by Beatrix's side. I was in her sitting room when he came in, with such stealth that I didn't hear him."

Dread curled in Evie's belly. "He...you mean Wilmington?"

"Yes. It was Wilmington. He was alone with Beatrix, and I didn't know. I was busy searching for a book she liked. When she was a girl, she begged me to read to her, and during her convalescence, I wanted to give her comfort." Harkness's voice broke. "Instead, I let her come to harm."

Evie gripped her companion's arm. "What happened?"

"I found the book. I'd taken but a step into the bedchamber when I saw him standing by the side of the bed. Instinct made me retreat behind the doorway; I was not one to interrupt a private moment between a man and his wife. Yet the silence that ticked by stirred the hairs on my nape and prompted me to peer around the doorway."

"What did you see?" Evie asked through numb lips.

"Wilmington...he was lifting a pillow from Beatrix's face. She was waxen and still—and I knew. I knew what he had done. He murdered her—killed my darling girl."

Evie felt as if she were floating. Her voice sounded as if it came from someone else.

"What happened next?"

"He...he put the pillow back in place." Tears dripped over the worn folds of Harkness's countenance. "He fluffed it, the weapon he used to kill my dearest Beatrix, and then left without a second glance. I remained where I was, half-hidden in the doorway, her book clutched to my chest. I didn't know what to do. Who would believe me if I reported what I saw? Who would take the word of a servant over a man as powerful as Wilmington?"

"Why didn't you tell me?"

"What good would it do for you to know the depth of his depravity? Having gone through your mama's money, your stepfather killed her to gain control over the one thing she refused to relinquish: your dowry. Yet you were dependent upon him—you had no means of escape. The knowledge would have haunted you, the way it has haunted me, and I wanted to protect you...the way I failed to protect Beatrix."

Evie felt herself unraveling. Harkness's revelation tore at the fabric of who she was. She had finally convinced herself she was made of strong and worthy stuff—but now she was reduced to a pile of shapeless string.

"Wilmington killed Mama because of me." She rose, staring down at her trusted companion. "She died protecting my future. And you kept this from me?"

Harkness came stiffly to her feet. "Pet, Beatrix's death was not your fault. I knew you would blame yourself, and that is why I didn't—"

Another thought assailed Evie.

"Did you kill him?" she whispered. "Did you switch the bottles of valerian and belladonna?"

"No."

Harkness's vehemence seemed like the truth—but Evie was no judge of that, was she?

"I hated that monster," Harkness said fervently. "When he died, I shed tears of joy because you were free of him at last. But I lacked the strength to do nature's work."

The relief felt like a speck in the swirling void of Evie's reality.

Mama died because of me. Died trying to protect me. I am a curse.

The knock on the door jolted her. Disoriented, she saw Gigi hurry in.

"Heavens, Evie," Gigi said breathlessly. "I've been looking all over for you!"

"You have?" Evie's head was spinning. "Why?"

The apprehension in Gigi's gaze filled Evie with foreboding.

"You must come quickly. I'll explain on the way."

CHAPTER THIRTY-FOUR

"Ryerson is behind this slander."

Despite the pounding in his chest, cold fury focused James. He was in Ethan's study, along with the rest of the family, as well as Friend and Dunsmuir, who had delivered the catastrophic news. On the desk was the most recent copy of *The Morning Post*, and he stared with burning eyes at the story blazed across the front page:

A Lady's Past Shadows Her Husband's Ambition

Rumors of an unsettling nature now circulate regarding the wife of a rising parliamentary hopeful. According to a source within her late stepfather's household, certain indiscretions in the lady's youth have been misrepresented to avoid scandal. While details are still unfolding, the implications cast a troubling shadow over the candidacy of her husband, a nobleman of distinguished lineage, whose papa was known for his valor fighting Boney.

While the article named no names, it might as well have. Everyone would know that the story was about James and Evie.

Over scandal broth, the wags would be speculating upon the nature of Evie's "indiscretions."

Enraged, James bit out, "The dirty bastard knew he was losing and started these rumors to ruin my campaign. At the ball, he intimated that he would use scandal to smear me—"

"His strategy was effective," Dunsmuir said soberly. "Being a mudslinger pays off, I'm afraid. Ryerson has brought down many an opponent in this manner."

James tried to calm himself—to not let anxiety muddle his logic. Before his death, had Merrow sold this piece of filth to Ryerson? Had he calculated that his blackmail scheme would soon run dry and found another way to turn a quick profit? How much had Merrow told Ryerson? The article, while sensational, damned through insinuation rather than fact. Details were vague, which led James to believe that Ryerson did not know about Wilmington's poisoning. If Ryerson did know, he would have undoubtedly accused Evie of murder—and James of being an accomplice who covered up her supposed crime.

No, Ryerson doesn't know. Maybe Merrow was selling him information in pieces. Yet now Merrow is dead—and perhaps Evie's secret will die with him.

The coil in James's gut told him that the danger was far from over. Scandal was rising like a tide, and he had to protect Evie from its lethal undertow. He had to keep an eye on Owen, who hadn't slept for days and seemed to be falling to pieces. He had to win his campaign—to make good on his promise to bring justice, health, and honor to all.

By God. How will I accomplish all of that and still stay afloat?

His cravat suddenly felt as if it were strangling him, his lungs pulling for air.

"People will see through this." He dragged a hand through his hair. "This is naught but rumor and idle speculation. Once voters are presented with the issues—"

"You overestimate people," Friend said in disgust, "and their interest in issues that impact their daily lives. It is done, Manderly."

He stilled. "What do you mean?"

"I mean the campaign is over. Time to hoist the white flag and move on."

The matter-of-fact words plowed into him like a fist, knocking out his breath.

"Now wait just one bloody minute," Papa spoke up, his posture rigid and eyes flashing with outrage. "The pair of you convinced my son to run for this seat because you know he is the best man for the job—a man of honor who will do his best to represent his constituents. Now this...this scoundrel, Ryerson, has the gall to insult James and his wife, and instead of closing ranks and defending him, you fall out of formation and *desert*?"

"We are not deserting him, sir," Dunsmuir said hastily.

"Then what else do you call abandoning my son and fleeing like a pair of lily-livered curs?" Papa barked.

"Marcus," Mama murmured. "It is not their fault."

"Mama is right." James found his voice. "Friend and Dunsmuir are not to blame."

I am. I failed to do my duty. I failed Evie and my campaign.

"We aren't abandoning you, Manderly," Dunsmuir said earnestly. "You will have our friendship, always. However, it is in your best interest to end the campaign. You saw what Ryerson did to Gosford. When Gosford resisted resigning, the rumors Ryerson circulated became increasingly lurid." He cast a nervous glance at Xenia and Mama. "Things were said about him that I cannot repeat in polite company. When Gosford finally yielded, his reputation was in shreds. He will never recover."

Gosford's warning rang in James's head.

Don't invite dishonor into your life. It is a disagreeable house-guest who will destroy everything you hold dear and never leave. However bad you think it might be, the reality is a hundred times worse.

Invisible bands tightened around James's chest.

Is that where I am now headed? Is my reputation—my honor as a gentleman—destroyed? Is it my fate to be scorned in clubs, to be torn to shreds by gossipmongers, to be a blemish on my family's good name?

Such an existence seemed unthinkable. Unbearable. As James began to grasp the enormity of the situation, Evie and Gigi entered the study. One glance at his wife's bloodless face told James that his sister had broken the news.

Soon after Evie arrived, the others left to give her and James privacy. She had heard enough, though, and read the article in *The Morning Post* condemning her and destroying James in the process. Now her husband stood by the window, looking out at the gardens, his hands braced on his hips. Tension radiated from him. He didn't say anything—didn't have to. His silence shouted at her louder than he ever would.

"This is my fault," she began.

"It is not." He spoke curtly, without turning. "This is Ryerson's doing."

"He couldn't have done it without my participation."

The truth battered her down. There was nothing left in her—no fight, not even an instinct to flee. She wanted to admit defeat... to apologize for ruining everything that was good. For allowing her cursed existence to drag down her blameless husband.

"As we have worn this subject threadbare, there is no need to linger upon it." James twisted his head to glance at her, his handsome countenance aged by harsh lines. "God knows the public will be doing enough of that."

"Do they...do they know what I did to Wilmington?"

Clenching her hands, she almost wished they did. The guilt of holding her secret—of witnessing how it was affecting James—was more painful than facing the consequences.

"It is unlikely. If Ryerson knew the specifics, it would be all over the papers."

"The scandal is worse than you know. Worse," she added, "than I even knew."

She was still coming to terms with Harkness's revelation. There had been two murders in her family: one accidental...and one intentional. The fact that Wilmington had killed Mama overwhelmed her ability to cope. She felt numb and detached—like a mere observer in the unfolding tragedy of her life.

"It doesn't matter," James said wearily. "In a few hours, I will announce my resignation, and all of this will go away."

"You are going to resign?"

He turned fully to her then, an angry god bathed in golden light.

"What do you expect me to do?" he said. "Let them rip your reputation to pieces and label me an accomplice? Invite them to excavate your past and see how much dirt they can dig up?"

His words sliced into her, sharper than any blade.

She swallowed. "But...but the campaign means everything to you—"

"The campaign, as my cronies so succinctly put it, is done. And so am I."

"Surely there is something that can be done—"

"What, precisely, would you have me *do*, Evie?" he gritted out. "Can't you see I am out of options? Contrary to what you seem to believe, I am not some damned deity. I do not possess divine powers that allow me to solve all problems."

"I never said you had such a power," she said with stunned hurt.

"Your actions have implied it," he snapped. "Why else would you come to me with your troubles and expect me to manage them?"

The unfairness of his accusations ignited her temper.

"I didn't want you to have to deal with my troubles," she said in a shaking voice. "That is why I kept them a secret all these years."

He clenched his jaw. "Now is not the time to remind me of your lies."

"No? Then let us talk about yours."

His eyes flashed ominously. "I have never lied to you."

"I beg to differ. You said I was not to blame for what happened, yet you *do* blame me, don't you? It is only logical, and you are nothing if not that. Things in your campaign were going swimmingly, then—*voilà*. My past raises its ugly head. Disaster and devastation ensue."

He scowled. "That is hardly fair—"

"You are thinking to yourself that if you had married someone else, you would not be in this predicament."

"Don't presume to know what I bloody think."

"A proper lady is a credit to her husband and helps him to achieve his ambitions. I, on the other hand, have lied to you, lost your babe, made you hunt a blackmailer, traumatized your brother...oh, and destroyed your good name. Am I missing anything?"

"What do you want me to say?" James's voice went frighteningly soft, the way it did when he was pushed past his limits. "This isn't all about you, Evie. Not everything is—although you seem to forget that."

"I beg your pardon?" she said coldly.

"Your self-pity grows tedious. Everything I have been working for—that I wanted—lies in shambles, and all you can talk about is you. About *your* past, your shame, your guilt. So yes," he said scathingly. "Perhaps you have the right of it. Perhaps I did have the thought that it would be nice to be married to someone who didn't just come to me with problems but also supported me in my time of need."

There it was: the truth lay bare. She'd known it all along, yet hearing him say it, feeling his anger and resentment, was more painful than she could have imagined. Every breath hurt, as if she had razor blades in her chest. As if her emotional calluses had been shaved off, her husband's disdain pressed upon her every tender shortcoming.

A rapping sounded on the door.

"What is it?" James snarled.

Ethan edged inside, his gaze darting warily between them.

"I am sorry to interrupt." He cleared his throat. "You have a visitor, brother."

"Tell them I am indisposed—"

"It is Lady Vernon. She says she wishes to help."

Of course she does. I ruin things; she fixes them. She is exactly the sort of woman James ought to have married, and he finally recognizes it.

The gleam of hope in James's eyes was more than Evie could bear.

"I'll leave you to her," she said.

She fled before the tears could fall.

CHAPTER THIRTY-FIVE

Evie slipped out of the manor as the sun was dipping toward the horizon. It was the first opportunity she'd had to leave without anyone noticing. Xenia, Gigi, and Mama had taken turns checking on her, and their concern added to her guilt: after the wreckage she'd made of James's life, she didn't deserve such care.

"This is the blackmailer's fault, not yours, Evie," Mama had insisted. *"Once the dust settles, we shall put our heads together and come up with a solution."*

The solution was simple. If Evie disappeared from James's life, his troubles would be over. The scandal was hers—and she would take it with her. Then he would be free to pursue his dreams...with whomever he chose. Maybe he would even forgive her one day and not look back at their time together with anger and contempt. Evie's mama had sacrificed everything to protect her, and she would not allow James to do the same.

She'd gathered a few essentials in her valise and donned her cloak. Harkness had left, so she would travel alone. She didn't know where she was going, only that she needed to leave. She had a vague plan to catch a coach to the nearest railway station, but as she walked in the crisp spring air, she felt a yearning to see the woods one last time. Her feet took her there, and when she entered the forest with its mossy carpet and budding canopy, the knot in her soul unraveled. Pain poured out, hot and liquid, down her cheeks.

She didn't know how long she wandered. As the shadows deepened to a violet dusk, she found herself at the hermit's grotto. Entering the little hollow, she felt a tremor in the ground as if the earth had sighed. It felt natural to set down her valise and sit in the alcove, letting the bench take the weight of her woes. She rested her head against the stone and gazed at the spiraling shells until her eyelids fluttered.

"Why are you here?" a familiar voice asked.

Opening her eyes, Evie saw that she was no longer alone in the dark.

"Rose?" she whispered.

The beautiful woman nodded, her hair rippling like a dark river over her shoulders. She was dressed in white, like an angel, but her eyes glowed with earthly secrets.

"Tell me why you are here," Rose repeated. "When your heart is elsewhere."

"Because I must be alone." Evie's voice cracked. "Because I committed the gravest of sins, I am cursed. And I cannot let that curse hurt the people I love—not again."

Rose gave her a pitying look.

"The only curse you bear is the one you placed on yourself. Beliefs are stronger than truths. I know a thing or two about that." A smile, nearly sly, curved her lips. "Now don't make the same mistake I did. Go after him, grab him with both hands, and tell him, '*You are mine, and I am yours. Not only for ease, but for every trial. This is the way of love: to stay, to forgive, to begin again.'"*

"You...you etched that on the wall?"

"Thomas did." Rosalinda's gaze was as brilliant as gems. "He always was a romantic."

"I am sorry...for how things ended," Evie said falteringly. "The pair of you deserved better."

"We did. We do," Rose added significantly. "As do you."

"No." Evie's voice trembled. "I've done a terrible thing, and even if it was an accident—"

"There are no accidents, Evie," Rose chided. "You are a scientist, and you must look to the facts. Do not be distracted by illusions—by the lies we tell ourselves. Look at the shells and see what is there."

Frowning, Evie turned her gaze to the spiral on the wall. To her astonishment, it began to move, to spin. Round and round, until she grew dizzy and nauseous.

"Don't avert your eyes, Evie. Look beyond your fears. *See the truth.*"

She fought back distress. Soon the spiral began to change, the shells rearranging themselves into a different shape, curling inward, then expanding...into a flower? No, not a flower—it was *Selaginella lepidophylla.*

Resurrection isn't a mystery. It is a process. If one observes the steps, one will understand the phenomenon.

"You're getting closer," Rosalinda whispered. "Now, what holds you back—what stops you from examining the truth?"

"I...I don't deserve it." Guilt, familiar and worn, smothered her. "Because of what I did. Because I took Wilmington's life."

"What if that is the illusion?"

"What do you mean you have no idea where Evie is?" James demanded.

After Lady Vernon's departure, he had gone in search of his wife. When he couldn't find her, he'd asked the others if they had seen her. Now his family was gathered in the drawing room...and their concern threw tinder on his own.

"She is not here." Xenia wrung her hands. "The servants have looked everywhere—we've all been looking—and she's gone."

Beneath James's frustration, panic began to drum.

"She would not have left without telling anyone," he said curtly. "Are you certain all the servants have been questioned?"

Ethan moved to stand in front of his wife.

"You are upset, brother, and understandably so," he said evenly. "But do not take your temper out on Xenia."

James exhaled. Ethan was right. This wasn't Xenia's fault—it was his.

"I pray you'll forgive my rudeness, Xenia," he said heavily.

"There's nothing to forgive." His sister-in-law's eyes shone with an empathy he didn't deserve. "You are only worried about Evie. Do you think it is possible that she went for a walk? To clear her head after...um, today's unfortunate events?"

Xenia's tactful reference made James feel like the lowliest scoundrel. While the scandal had rocked him, he wasn't proud of how he had handled the situation, specifically with regards to Evie. He had lashed out at her because he'd been angry and upset. Because he hadn't been prepared for how devastating failure would feel. He knew the guilt Evie carried, yet he'd twisted the responsibility she felt into something far uglier. Thinking of how he'd accused her of being self-absorbed and unsupportive, he wanted to punch himself...the way Evie ought to have.

Instead, she'd looked at him like a whipped puppy. His throat grew scratchy as he recognized that her response to his vitriol hadn't been one of anger but acceptance. She felt she deserved his scorn—when, actually, she had the right of things. He *had* lied to her. And to himself as well. She had concealed her past because she was afraid of losing his love and ruining his future. When she'd finally trusted him with the truth, he had assured her that it didn't matter. He had promised to find a solution. Yet when he failed to do so, he had blamed *her* for the collapse of his campaign...because his pride and ambition had blinded him to what mattered most.

Ad finem fidelis.

Evie had given him her love and loyalty, and she deserved his in return. Sudden fear spiked as he considered how far she might go to protect him. Would she leave him?

She is welcome to try.

She was his wife, and she belonged by his side. If he had to hunt her down and grovel to get her back, then so be it. Looking at his assembled kin, he knew that he needed their help.

"Evie may have left. I certainly gave her reason to," he said with self-loathing. "I would like to organize a search for her."

"We shall find her." Papa clasped his shoulder. "Do not judge yourself too harshly, son. It has been an eventful day. Once you and Evie are reunited, you will sort things out."

James nodded, though he felt far from reassured. Looking out the windows, he saw darkness had fallen. At this very moment, Evie was God knows where, alone and unprotected.

"We will split up," he said urgently. "We must search Chuddums, the neighboring villages, and the nearest railway stations. Anywhere you can think of that Evie might have gone."

A few hours later, James's worry turned into full-fledged panic.

They had looked everywhere for Evie. In Chuddums, they'd knocked on the doors of everyone they knew and some they didn't. None of the villagers had seen Evie, but several—including the Pickleworths, Mr. Duffield and his companion the blacksmith, and Wally and his group of cronies—volunteered to join the search.

They widened the circle to Chudleigh Crest. Evie had not been seen at the coaching inn or anywhere else. James's siblings and their spouses had continued to other villages. Mama and Papa were on their way to Reading in what was rapidly becoming a wild goose chase. James had wanted to take charge of one of the searches, but everyone insisted he should be at Bottoms House in case Evie returned on her own.

What if Evie doesn't come back? What if she has truly left me? What if my despicable behavior drove her away for good?

He was riding back toward the manor, so drenched in despair that he didn't feel the rain as it began to fall. His horse did, shaking its head in displeasure. When thunder boomed, it reared and whinnied; James gripped the reins, fighting to stay seated. Panting, his face slick, he managed to calm the animal...but not the beast howling within him.

Right now, Evie could be cold and wet because I was a bastard to her. She could be lost and alone in the dark, with no place to go—

The flash of clarity was brighter than the lightning that cracked the sky.

The place took her in when she had nowhere else to go. She felt safe there, as if nothing could touch her.

"Devil and damn," he said, stunned. "Could Evie have gone there?"

With a surge of hope, he turned his horse around and galloped toward the woods.

With a gasp, Evie surfaced in the darkness of the grotto.

As the storm raged outside her cozy hideaway, she knew that

she was alone. Rosalinda was gone...but she had left a priceless gift: knowledge.

"By the blooms," Evie whispered. "I know who is behind everything."

As the truth swept through her, a dark shape emerged in the doorway.

A scream tore from her throat, echoing in the cave.

CHAPTER THIRTY-SIX

"Sweetheart, it's me," James said in a rush.

A flash of lightning illuminated Evie standing by the stone bench. He hurried over and was relieved beyond measure when she threw herself into his arms. The feel of her softness and the scent of her hair steadied him. His love was safe. Nothing else mattered.

"I have you now," he murmured. "I am never letting you go again."

"You g-gave me a fright."

He hugged her tighter against his own thundering heart.

"I'm sorry for frightening you," he said hoarsely. "And sorrier still for behaving like a scoundrel. Can you forgive me?"

"I was at fault as well—"

"No, the fault was mine entirely. I had no business speaking to you the way I did. I didn't mean any of it. The news of the scandal made me angry and panicked, and I lashed out at you because you were a convenient target." Self-recrimination clogged his throat. "You deserve better, and I beg your forgiveness. If you give me another chance, I vow to be worthy of it."

"I forgive you," she said tremulously. "However, we were both under duress, and I played a part in our argument. I came to you already certain of my own unworthiness and would not let you contradict it—no, darling." She cut him off. "You must hear me out."

"I will," he promised. "I will do anything you want, my love. But I'm getting you soaked, and I don't want you to catch a cold. Why don't I get a fire going in the hearth and then we can talk while we wait out the storm?"

"A fire would be nice," she agreed. "There is kindling in the hearth."

Using the matches he'd brought and oil from his lamp, he soon had a blaze going. The grotto warmed quickly, and he removed his outer garments, letting them dry while he settled on the bench next to his wife. With his arm around her, her head tucked against his shoulder, he took a full breath for the first time that day.

"Now what did you want to tell me?" he asked.

Evie tilted her head to look at him, and her somber expression made him brace.

"I don't know how to put this without sounding mad." She drew a breath. "So I will say it directly and let you be the judge."

"Say it, sunflower. I won't think you mad."

"I believe Wilmington is alive."

He drew his brows together, trying to fathom what she meant.

"And I think he is behind the blackmail," she blurted.

James exhaled. "Why don't you explain how you arrived at this conclusion?"

He listened as his wife laid out the facts with a scientist's logic. The notion that she'd been inspired to do so by a ghost in a vision added a certain irony, but everything she said made perfect sense.

"*Resurrection isn't a mystery. It is a process. If one observes the steps, one will understand the phenomenon*—those were my own words," Evie mused. "It was as if I knew all along that something was not right. Yet I was blinded by the years of guilt—by the assumption that I had somehow accidentally poisoned Wilmington...which, if I allow myself to think about it, makes little sense. I *know* which bottle I took with me that night. I know it was the valerian, for belladonna was dangerous and I never touched it. How could I have switched the bottles without knowing?"

"You didn't switch them," James said slowly. "Someone else did?"

Evie nodded. "Once I allowed myself to consider the facts— the possibility that I did not make the grievous mistake I'd blamed myself for all these years—I began to wonder how the bottles could have been switched. I left my chamber with valerian in my pocket. Sometime between then and after Wilmington collapsed, when I had the wherewithal to check my pocket again, the bottles were changed."

"Who was near you...Merrow." A tingle crossed James's nape. "You mentioned he was the first to come in when you called for help. He cornered you, pushed you against the wall, and demanded to know what had happened."

"You have a memory for detail." Evie looked impressed.

"I remembered the details because I wanted to plow my fist into Merrow's face for threatening you," he said bluntly. "But also because the behavior struck me as odd. Why not rush to his master, try to revive him first? That is what anyone would do unless...unless he knew that there was nothing to worry about."

"Exactly." Excitement glittered in Evie's eyes. "Suppose this was all staged—all part of an elaborate ruse. Merrow knew Wilmington was not in any real danger, so he trapped me first. In my state of panic, I didn't notice him switch the bottles. He took the valerian, leaving me with the belladonna...so that I would believe that I had poisoned Wilmington."

"To what end?"

"Wilmington was up to his ears in debt. He married my mama for her fortune, and he gambled it away. When she refused to hand over my dowry, he...he, oh James." Evie's voice broke. "I think he killed her."

Evie told him what Harkness had witnessed.

"The murderous blackguard," James said with quiet fury. "I hope he is, indeed, alive, for I shall enjoy tearing him limb from limb."

"My mama died to protect me from that villain."

The tears that spilled were cleansing. Evie's rage was equal to James's, if not greater. For now that the illusion was gone, she saw with crystal clarity how diabolical Wilmington was.

"Afterward, he not only foisted his unwanted attentions on me, but he also tormented me, twisting my thinking so that I believed I was faulty...that I somehow deserved pain and misfortune."

"Dying is too good for him. He will suffer," James stated. "Greatly."

"I think he must already be suffering. As I said, he spent my mama's fortune. After her death, he took over my dowry and squandered that too. I remember him hiding when creditors came to call...and they weren't the usual merchants. Unsavory characters would visit the manor, the kind that carried weapons and left a trail of broken things in their wake."

"Moneylenders." James's gaze blazed with understanding. "The bastard went to the cent-per-cent men and dug himself a hole so deep that his only means of escape was—"

"Faking his own death," Evie finished. "While doing so, he saw an opportunity to keep me under his thumb. He must have figured out I was lacing his drinks with valerian. So he made me think I'd given him the wrong herb—the deadly herb—instead. Then he lay in wait until the time was ripe to manipulate me again."

"He probably thought my political aspirations gave him lever-age," James said. "But he underestimated you. You are no longer a frightened young girl under his power. You are a strong and intelligent woman, and you figured out his dastardly scheme."

"I wish I could have figured it out sooner," she said wryly. "But, yes, I think I have most of the pieces. Merrow was a part of this from the beginning, as was Murdoch. After Wilmington collapsed, the two were the only ones to tend to him. Murdoch signed his death certificate, and before the ink was dry, they carted him off, saying it had been Wilmington's wishes to have a quick burial."

"Only, instead of dying, he did the flit. Years later, he is in need of money again and initiates the blackmail scheme, sending Merrow to do his dirty work. And Murdoch..." James gave a decisive nod. "He had come down in the world. He must have discovered what Wilmington was up to and demanded a cut—probably fancied he deserved it. Perhaps he even threatened to expose Wilmington."

"And Wilmington did what I *didn't* do," Evie said with satisfaction. "He killed using belladonna. You do know what this means, don't you?"

"That I admire and love you beyond words?" James said fiercely. "That I wish I could have protected you from all of this, but that I am bloody glad—and proud—that you have the courage and strength to not only survive such dark machinations, but to look past the lies and parlor tricks to see the heart of the truth?"

"Those are lovely sentiments." Evie smiled tremulously. "However, I was referring to the fact that if Wilmington is alive—"

"He is," James said with cold certainty. "Cockroaches like him can withstand anything. How I shall enjoy crushing him."

"Do leave some crushing to me, darling. I think I'm entitled. But back to my point: Wilmington's continued existence means that there is no scandal."

Seeing James knit his brows, she was surprised that he had not made the connection already. This was simple deduction compared to the more complicated scheme he'd had no trouble following.

"I didn't kill Wilmington," she explained. "You are not married to a murderess. Ergo, there is no scandal—only the gossip circulated by Ryerson and his ilk, gossip that will be proven false. Ergo, your campaign still has a chance. You can and will win—"

"Do you honestly think"—James's gaze burned, and he seemed to struggle for words—"that after everything you just told me, after everything you've been through, that I give a *damn* about my blasted campaign?"

"Oh." She blinked. "Is this a trick question?"

He swore vehemently and with colorful vocabulary she didn't know her proper lord would have knowledge of, let alone use. He took her by the shoulders.

"This is not a bloody trick but a fact," he growled. "I want you to hear me. I mean it, Evie—pay attention."

"I am listening," she whispered.

"I love you, Evelyn Harrington—with every cell of my being. It was that way for me from the start, and it will be that way until I depart this earth. You understand and accept me better than anyone: my pride and ambition, my fear of not being enough. You are my anchor, and when I thought you had left me, I was in hell —utterly lost without you. So how important do you think you are to me?"

Her pulse thrumming, she said, "Very important."

His expression had never been more intense. "Try again."

"The most important."

The recognition pruned away her insecurities. There was nothing to stop her from being who she was meant to be. She felt herself unfurl, then burst into full bloom.

"I am more important than your campaign," she said.

"Bloody right you are." He cupped her cheek, rubbing his thumb along her cheekbone so tenderly that her heart stuttered. "Nothing matters to me more than you. Nothing."

He pressed his mouth to hers. The kiss was gentle and deep, a reminder of the promises they had made and how, this time, they had kept them. Knowing they would spend the rest of their lives cherishing and honoring one another, Evie felt happiness flood her like sunlight, reaching every dark corner and banishing her doubts for good.

"I appreciate the sentiment, I do," she said. "And I adore you with everything that I am. But you would not be the man I love without your ambition and desire to improve the lives of others. I believe in you, James—in the honor and decency you stand for. I believe you can win this election and be a force for progress. I intend to support you in any way I can, starting with seeing justice served to Wilmington. Together, we can put that scandal to rest once and for all."

"Together, we can do anything, my love." James's mien was equal parts fierce and solemn. "You are mine, and I am yours. Not only for ease, but for every trial. This is the way of love: to stay, to forgive, to begin again."

Emotion welled as he spoke the vow written on the wall—and she finally understood what it meant. Their love, like Rosalinda and Thomas's, had never been an easy thing, but the trials they endured had strengthened their bond. They had taken risks for one another—staying, forgiving, and now starting anew—and she would make that same choice, over and again, if it brought her back to him.

"I choose you," she said. "I will cherish you, always and forever."

They sealed their promises with another kiss, and instant heat flared between them. He shoved his fingers in her hair, his mouth consuming hers with sweet intensity. Soon they were breathless, laughing at their haste as they tore away the layers between them. It wasn't long before he laid her upon his coat, naked and trembling with passion, her nipples budded and glistening from his passionate ministrations. He knelt between her spread thighs, her

Apollo gilded by firelight, who wasn't perfect but something far better.

"You are mine," she breathed. "My husband, my love. Come to me."

At her summons, a savage light came into James's gaze. He fell upon her, and she gasped at his bold and relentless penetration, the sensation of his thick heat drilling into her core.

"Devil and damn, I love being inside you," he said in a guttural voice. "The way you hold me so tightly—*yes*, exactly so. Squeeze me like you never want to let me go."

Moaning, she did. The sensual sounds of their mating filled the grotto. Gazing at his precious countenance, she ran her hands over his flexing back, savoring the feel of him so hard and strong, inside and over her. She hooked her legs around his muscled hips, arching to draw him deeper, digging her nails into his shoulders.

"By Jove." Sweat sheened on James's brow, his face taut with restraint. "You're taking me so deep. I can't hold on much longer—"

"Let go," she whispered. "Give it to me. I want everything from you."

She saw the instant his control snapped. He reared back—and *slammed* into her. Cries jolted from her lips as he pounded into her, his stones slapping her pussy with weighted momentum, the pleasure raw and wild. Their bodies strained together, their eyes locked, and she was nearly there when his neck arched, and he roared her name.

Drawing back, he rammed in. His face contorted as he spent, a forceful eruption that scraped feral sounds from his throat. He coated her insides with heat, and each time she thought he was done, he surged again until she was overflowing. He collapsed atop her, burying his face in her neck. Stroking his hair, she was happy to bask in his contentment even if she hadn't quite reached her own zenith.

"Thank you, my love." He lifted his head. "Now it is your turn."

"My turn...oh, you needn't."

She squeaked in shock as he kissed an intent path down her body. Surely he didn't mean to kiss her *there*, right after he had—

"James. You mustn't—oh, *by the blooms*."

He swiped his tongue through her folds, his gaze smoldering and roguish.

"By the blooms, indeed," he murmured. "What a pretty bud I've found. And it's begging to be tended."

He closed his lips around her, drawing her sensitive peak into his mouth. He sucked and licked and tended to her with such nonchalant depravity that she soared over with a blissful cry. Then he crawled over her, her wicked god of a husband, and kissed her thoroughly.

"I love you, wife," he said with satisfaction.

A sigh stole into her heart. "And I you, husband."

His gaze glinted. "Ready for more?"

The sigh became panting.

"Always."

Chapter Thirty-Seven

As soon as the storm ended, James and Evie returned to Bottoms House. He sent word to the others that Evie was with him and safe. As he had kept her awake—and vice versa—most of the night, he was feeling sleepy. Before he could suggest a quick nap, Gigi and Godwin arrived.

"Thank heavens you are back!" Gigi hugged Evie.

"I am sorry to have inconvenienced everyone," Evie said sheepishly. "It was inconsiderate of me to wander off without leaving word. I was waiting out the storm in the hermit's grotto when James found me."

"Never mind, we are just relieved that you are well." Gigi paused for a heartbeat. "All *is* well, I trust?"

In answer, James held out a hand to his wife. She took it, her glowing smile affirming what was in his heart.

"All is well," she said.

"Well, we had quite an adventure of our own," Godwin said. "We were checking roadside inns when the storm struck. We ended up taking shelter at a rustic place off the beaten path, the Stag & Harrow—"

"And you will never guess what we discovered," Gigi exclaimed.

Seeing his sister's effervescent excitement, James said, "We won't have to guess. The answer is about to pop from you like a cork."

When Conrad snickered, Gigi nudged him with her elbow.

"Why am I in trouble?" he asked. "Your brother was the one who was teasing you."

"You are supposed to take my side."

"All right, then. I shall."

He slung an arm around her waist, dragging her against him while she giggled.

"This is better," he drawled. "At the very least, my ribs are protected."

With roses in her cheeks, Gigi said, "*As* I was saying. We were chatting with the innkeeper at the Stag & Harrow, asking if he'd seen a lady matching Evie's description. He said he hadn't, but then he added, *I'll pray for her swift return—unlike that poor fellow the constables found in the stream. He was here but a few nights before he disappeared. At first, I thought he'd left without settling his bill, but then I heard the news. Dreadful business.*"

James stilled like a bloodhound catching the scent. "Merrow stayed at the Stag & Harrow?"

Gigi and Godwin nodded.

This is it. The trail to Wilmington.

The anticipation in Evie's expression reflected his own.

"I'll send for the carriage," he said.

As he headed off to handle the details, he heard his sister ask, "What is going on?"

"It's a long story," Evie said. "If you wish to join us, I will explain on the way."

James, Evie, Gigi, and Godwin arrived at the Stag & Harrow around noon. The innkeeper, an amiable fellow named Mr. Rudwick, was supervising the busy taproom and promised to assist them as soon as he could. He offered them "a plate of the hot" while they waited; realizing that he and Evie had skipped several meals, James gratefully accepted. When the food arrived—a generous spread of roast beef smothered in gravy, mashed potatoes, and herbed carrots, accompanied by thick slices of bread—they both ate heartily, washing it down with strong tea.

"The pair of you have worked up quite an appetite." Godwin smirked as he buttered his bread. "Busy night, Manderly?"

Luckily for Godwin, the arrival of Mr. Rudwick prevented James from responding. James introduced himself and gave the story he'd prepared, which adhered to the facts as much as possible. He said that Merrow had robbed his wife and was part of a criminal organization based in London that preyed on unsuspecting country folk. He was looking for clues that might enable the authorities to locate and capture Merrow's gang.

"I would be glad to be of service, my lord," Mr. Rudwick said at once. "I never liked the look of that Merrow fellow. He had a shifty way about him and bothered my barmaids. If you don't mind my saying, it is about time someone took the interests of country folk to heart, and you'll find me on your side at the hustings."

James thanked him, and the innkeeper showed them the chamber that Merrow had occupied. Another guest had stayed there the night before, and a search yielded no helpful clues. Then Mr. Rudwick led them to his office, a cramped closet off the taproom. He took a basket off a shelf and set it on his desk.

"These are Mr. Merrow's belongings," he announced. "I meant to sell them to settle his account."

"Allow me to compensate you, sir," James said.

After Mr. Rudwick left them to their privacy, the group began sorting through the basket. James started with the battered leather satchel, which held a change of clothes, a cracked shaving kit, and a familiar item.

James held up the single glove. "It bears the stamp of Perry & Morris and matches the one I found by the gate. It's evidence that Merrow collected the pearls."

"So is this," Evie said.

Her eyes wide, she showed them what appeared to be half of a pawn ticket. The voucher was smudged from handling and torn along the right edge. Luckily, the red stamp on the corner could be read in its entirety:

Doolittle's Emporium of Wonders, Whitechapel, London.

A clerk's neat hand noted the pledged item, and even though half the description was missing, what was there was enough: *Necklace, pearls, gold filig—.*

Evie's bottom lip quivered. "He pawned my mama's pearls."

"You will have them back, my love," James promised. "My guess is that Wilmington was using the necklace as payment. He gave Merrow half the ticket, promising the other half when the job was complete."

"What other infamy did that bounder have in mind?" Evie clenched her hands. "How much did he think he could bleed from me?"

"You were not the only one paying him."

This came from Godwin, who was reading a letter he'd sifted from the pile.

"You're not going to like this," he said, passing it to James.

James read the message aloud:

Dear Mr. Ryerson,

I pray the information you purchased has served you well. Give the other half of my fee—five hundred pounds—to my man, Merrow, as you did before. In return, he will furnish you with the rest of the details, and the scandal will destroy your opponent once and for all.

Yours,
  C. Wilcott

Scarlet flared in James's vision, and he had to restrain himself from crumpling the note.

"Ryerson purchased filth from this C. Wilcott—who must be Wilmington using an alias—to destroy my campaign," James clipped out. "He didn't have all the details yet, which was why the gossip was vague. The fact that Merrow was still in possession of the note suggests that he hadn't delivered the rest of the information to Ryerson."

Evie placed a hand on his arm. Her eyes were as furious as his.

"Think of it as killing two birds, darling." His lady scientist spoke coolly. "When we bring down Wilmington, we will also expose Ryerson's corruption. The world will soon see their true villainous colors."

CHAPTER THIRTY-EIGHT

The next day, Evie and James traveled to London. Their family had insisted on accompanying them and now kept watch as they approached *Doolittle's Emporium of Wonders*. Located in bustling Whitechapel, the pawnshop was situated on a narrow street crammed with businesses, which ranged from disreputable to more disreputable. The emporium itself bore a gilt sign that looked freshly painted, and its plate glass window displayed a mishmash of goods, from a stuffed monkey to a fashionable top hat.

As Evie and James entered, they were greeted by a chorus of wailing babes. They made their way through a maze of cabinets and shelves teetering with bits and bobs to the main counter, where a harassed-looking blonde was tending to three toddling triplets and a pair of older, freckled twins. While the triplets raced about like pups escaped from the whelping box, the woman was trying to separate the twins, who were locked in a battle over a wooden horse.

"Stop it," she hissed. "Or I'll break this toy in 'alf, leaving one o' you wif the 'ead and the other wif the arse!"

"I want the arse," the taller twin said.

"Alfred the Second said a bad word," the other reported.

"Mum said it first," Alfred the Second muttered. "You're such a tell-tale."

"Pardon, ma'am."

James's pleasant inquiry cut through the mayhem. All eyes turned to him. Then a massive shaggy brown dog came charging through a curtained doorway, and Evie's breath caught as it headed straight for James.

"Sit," James commanded.

The dog skidded to a halt and sat, its tail thumping against the floor.

"Gor." The blonde turned huge eyes to Evie. "If your pot-and-pan manages tots the same way, I may 'ave to steal 'im for meself."

Recognizing the Cockney slang for "husband" and the harmless nature of the woman's admiration, Evie smiled. "I think I will keep him, thank you."

"You would be a fool not to, and you don't strike me as a fool, luvie. I'm Sally Doolittle, proprietress o' this madhouse. Anyfing I can 'elp you wif?"

"As a matter of fact." Removing the half-ticket from his coat pocket, James showed it to Mrs. Doolittle. "We are looking for this item, which we believe is in your possession."

"Looks like my old man's handwriting. Please wait while I fetch 'im." Opening her mouth, Mrs. Doolittle let out a bellow that rattled the cabinets. "*Alfred-kins!* Get your behind out 'ere. Customers need attending, do you 'ear me?"

After a delay, the curtain parted, and a slight fellow with a mop of brown hair strolled through.

"The dead could 'ear you, Sal," he said, yawning. "Is there a law against a bloke getting some shut-eye?"

"Papa!" The children swarmed him.

"There are my good tots." Patting each of them on the head, he handed out boiled sweets as his offspring cheered. "Nothing like candy to calm the spirit, eh? Now be off and play quietly while the adults talk."

After the children barreled off like locomotives under full steam, he turned to Evie and James and performed a sprightly bow.

"Alfie Doolittle, at your service."

James introduced himself and Evie.

"We are in search of this item," he said, "which we believe is being held in your shop."

Glancing at the stub, Mr. Doolittle shrugged. "I hold a lot o' things, guv."

"This pearl necklace belonged to my mama," Evie said. "It was the only thing I had of hers, and it was stolen from me by the man who deposited it here."

Mr. Doolittle drew himself up. "If you're accusing me o' handling ill-gotten goods—"

"We are not accusing you of anything. Yet." James's warning was clear. "We see no reason to summon the police when this matter can be handled discreetly—and advantageously."

When he took out his pocket-book, Mr. Doolittle's manner turned speculative.

"I offer a service," he said smoothly. "Patrons deposit their goods wif me for safekeeping, and I issue them a ticket like the one you 'ave there. When they return wif the ticket and pay the holding fee, I return the item. My trade is as clean as a nun's conscience."

"I assume you keep a record of the depositor's information?" James asked.

"Weren't born yesterday. Keep my records and my business straight, don't I."

Rifling behind the counter, Doolittle emerged with a thick ledger and thumped it onto the counter. He thumbed through the volume and tapped his finger on a page.

"'Ere's the transaction you're after. *One necklace, graduated pearls o' exceptional quality, gold filigree clasp—valued at two hundred pounds.* Deposited by one Charles Wilcott. And let's see...

I made a note. Wilcott paid the holding fee up front and said the necklace was to be given to the man who brought in both halves o' the ticket."

"Do you have Wilcott's address?" James demanded.

"That's confidential."

James placed a twenty-pound note on the counter.

"14 Burton Crescent in Bloomsbury. A lodging house, and not a very fine one."

A thrill chased up Evie's spine.

"Now, you will return my wife's necklace," James said.

"That I cannot do, guv. For any price." Mr. Doolittle shut the ledger. "I'm bound by the pledge o' my trade. If word got out that I relinquished a patron's deposited goods wifout proper authorization, my reputation won't be worth dirt."

"Your patron is a murderer and extortionist," James stated. "If the police get wind of your involvement, your reputation will be the least of your worries."

"Let the Peelers come." Mr. Doolittle folded his arms over his chest, a slight sneer on his face. "I ain't afraid o' a pack o' blue-bottles."

"But you should be afraid of me," James said in a dangerous tone. "My wife has suffered enough losses, and I will not stand by while you keep what is rightfully hers."

Evie stopped him before he could follow through with his threat.

"Leave the necklace for now, darling." She kept her gaze steady on the burning blue of his. "When we capture Wilmington, we will get the other half of the ticket. I shall have my pearls—and justice at last."

Dusk had settled over Burton Street like a shroud. Gas lamps dotted the terrace, their flickering halos doing little to relieve the misery of the surroundings. Evie shivered as they drove past the bleak lodging house at number fourteen: its sunken roof and crumbling brick facade gave the impression that it was rotting from within.

In a nearby alleyway, Evie and James rendezvoused with his family.

"Are you certain the two of you should go in alone?" Papa asked.

"If we barge in as a group, the commotion might alert Wilmington," James said. "I will handle the coward. But in case he makes a run for it, the rest of you must cover all exits."

"You can count on us," Ethan said.

"Evie, you are prepared?" Mama inquired.

"Yes, Mama." Evie removed the pearl-handled pistol from the pocket of her cloak. "Wilmington is no threat to me."

"Not physically," Mama murmured. "Yet facing one's demons is never easy. You must confront him together, my dears, and let your love strengthen your purpose and resolve."

The group split up, and hand in hand, Evie and James entered the lodging house. It was supper time, and from the distant clatter of dishes and hum of conversation, most of the guests were occupied with the meal. The shabby foyer was manned by a single clerk, who was as weathered as the décor. His gaze widened as he took in James's elegance and commanding presence.

"We are looking for Charles Wilcott," James said softly. "We don't wish to cause any trouble for you or your occupants. If you cooperate, there will be no need to summon the authorities."

Sweat dotted the clerk's upper lip, his gaze darting as he made the calculations.

"I believe Mr. Wilcott is in his room. Top floor, room f-four," he stammered. "Up the stairs to your right, my lord."

James held out a gloved hand. "The key, if you please."

Fumbling, the clerk unhooked the key from a jangling chain and handed it over.

James deposited a coin on the desk, and he and Evie headed up the stairs. Each creak of the floorboards quickened her pulse; when they arrived at the appointed door moments later, she felt as if she had run a mile.

I have been running—all my life, it seems. But that stops here and now.

"Ready, my love?" James lifted his brows.

"As ready as I shall ever be."

He inserted the key and opened the door.

"How many times must I tell you that I don't want that slop you call supper?" The man hunched over the table continued scribbling in a journal and didn't bother to look at them. "Go away and leave me to my privacy."

"Hello, stepfather," Evie said.

The man jerked up, stumbling from his chair, his face shocked...and menacingly familiar. The intervening years had added grey to his hair, deepened the lines of discontent on his noble brow, and added a sag to his jowls. But the eyes...the eyes were the same. Under slashing dark eyebrows, the pale, hard orbs sent a chill down Evie's spine, and she braced against the instinct to run and hide.

"Evelyn." Recovering his composure, Wilmington managed a sneer. "My, you have grown up, haven't you?"

"And you are not dead."

"What can I say? I experienced a miraculous recovery."

When he sauntered toward a dresser, James pulled out a pistol. Cocked it with cool intention.

"Stay where you are," he said.

"Is that any way to greet your father-in-law?" Wilmington spoke in mocking tones, but he stayed where he was. "You should know that Evelyn has always had an active imagination. Whatever she told you—"

"I would believe it. My wife has my full confidence. You will rot behind bars for your crimes."

"You killed Mama."

A floodgate opened, fury pouring through Evie. She advanced toward him, her shoulders set, her hands balled at her sides.

"You smothered her to gain control of my dowry. Then you abused me and tricked me into thinking I had poisoned you. I suppose you didn't think I was useless after all, for you planted the seed of guilt in me so that you could reap the rewards. So that when the time was right, you could threaten, terrorize, and extort me from beyond the grave."

"Rather clever of me, wasn't it?"

Wilmington smiled—then lunged.

He clamped his hand on Evie's throat, yanking her back against his chest, using her like a shield.

"Put your pistol on the ground," he snarled. "Now. Or I'll snap her neck."

The promise of retribution flashing in his eyes, James crouched and laid down the weapon.

Gasping, Evie clawed at Wilmington's iron grip with one hand. She slid the other into the pocket of her skirts, closing her fingers around the pistol's handle. Blindly, she rotated the pistol until the barrel pointed backward.

"Hurt her, and you will die slowly," James said.

"Kick over your pistol," Wilmington barked.

James flicked his gaze to Evie—and she acted. Tightening her grip, she pulled the trigger. The *crack* of the bullet, muffled by the layers of her gown, was followed by Wilmington's guttural howl. His hand spasmed around her throat, and she broke free as he collapsed to the floor. Lying on his back, he clutched his bleeding thigh, whimpering in agony.

Evie stumbled over to look at him, her bosom surging and pistol drawn. Drawn and ready to fire the second round. On the ground, Wilmington writhed, pale and sweating, hatred twisting his features.

"Finish it," he spat. "Do it, you worthless cunt."

Evie's finger trembled on the trigger. For an instant, she imagined the sweetness of vengeance—of paying back Wilmington for all the pain he'd inflicted. With a gentle motion, no more force than she would use to pluck a spent blossom from a stem, she could put an end to him and his villainy. She felt James standing behind her—felt his strength and support, the gift of his love.

"I make my own choices. I always have."

She lowered her weapon.

"Well done, my love," James murmured. "I shall secure him."

Striding past her, James used a bedsheet to tie Wilmington's hands.

"Where is the other half of the pawn ticket?" he demanded.

"For God's sake, I'm bleeding to death—"

Wilmington screamed when James clamped a hand over his wound and squeezed.

"The cabinet," the bounder gasped. "In the...the lining of my hat."

Retrieving the ticket, James presented it to Evie. Then he returned to Wilmington and used his cravat as a tourniquet to staunch the bleeding.

"Bloody hell, are you trying to kill me?" Wilmington moaned.

"Death is too easy for the likes of you."

James knotted the linen with savage force. Wilmington screeched and lost consciousness. His job done, James went to Evie and took her gently by the shoulders.

"Are you all right, my love?"

She smiled. "Yes. Are you?"

"I lost a few years of my life when that bastard had his hands on you. Other than that, I am fine."

Seeing the lingering shadows on his face, she moved closer.

"I was never in any danger. Not with you to protect me."

"You protected yourself. With the pistol Mama gave you." He tucked a stray tress behind her ear. "Let that be a reminder to never cross the females in this family."

"I was referring to more than your physical protection," she said softly. "Your love, James, has always been my shelter. Because of you, I had the courage to confront my greatest fears and now I am finally free. Free to be the wife you deserve—and the woman I was meant to be."

"I could not be prouder of the woman you are," he said fiercely. "My sunflower, my love."

They kissed, and were still kissing, when their family arrived.

Chapter Thirty-Nine

Releasing her arm, he shoved her aside.

"Dirty whore," he said with a leer. "Remove your dress and do it slowly. I have a fancy for a show while I enjoy my tea."

Panting, her arm pulsing with pain, Rose watched as he went to the table. He picked up the pot of tea that she had poisoned. Pouring the liquid into a cup, he grunted with approval at the darkness of the brew—strong, the way he liked it. He added cream and sugar, his every movement speeding up her heart.

He must pay. For what he did to Thomas. For what he will do to our babe if I do not stop him now.

She held her breath as he raised the cup to his mouth.

Let him drink it. Let him die. Let his death be as painful as the abuses he has visited upon me.

"No." The word broke from her lips.

"What?" He snapped his head in her direction. "What did you say to me?"

"No," she repeated...but it was to herself, not to him. "Not this way."

He slammed down the cup with enough force to shake the table. "Do you dare to tell me what to do, you slut?"

She stared at him, the monster of her nightmares, and realized she was no longer afraid. She had known the love of a good man and carried his strength inside her. No matter what this brute did to her, she would prevail—because love always won. Love taught her to make the right choices, to fight for what mattered, and to know that no matter what, it would always be there for her.

You are mine, and I am yours.

She heard Thomas's vow, felt it in her marrow, and knew that she would never find him again if she had a stain on her soul.

The monster came toward her, halting when she pointed a finger at him.

"I curse you," she said.

His eyes slitted. "What tricks are you playing?"

"I curse you, and all the generations of your blood that follow in your footsteps."

As she said the words, she felt a jolt of energy—of power that seemed to come from a place beyond her. It rushed through her veins, and she felt taller, stronger. Her voice rang with authority as the prophecy flowed from her.

"Your trespasses will cause you to suffer, the way you have caused others to suffer."

He blinked like a bully faced with a more powerful adversary for the first time.

"For every abuse you have inflicted, you will feel the same pain inflicted upon you."

The color drained from his face. His expression went from uncertain to frightened as he suddenly gripped the left side of his chest.

"You know what you have done," she intoned. "Now you will feel it: the crushing weight upon your breastbone, the vise closing around your heart. Every breath you take causes the agony to spread."

"I...I cannot breathe."

Clutching his chest, he staggered, then fell to his knees.

"There is no air for you," she said calmly. "Only pain. You will leave this earth feeling the pain you have caused and knowing that you will not be mourned."

He gave a great, gasping groan—then fell over onto his side.

Blinking, Rose shook away the haze. She approached the unmoving figure cautiously. The monster's eyes were open and shocked, his last expression one of terror. He was dead...but not from her poison. It was from the poison in his own soul: the act of a guilty conscience exacting payment.

Closing the door, Rose left the manor without looking back.

That night, James sat against the headboard next to Evie, holding her as she shared the rest of her dream.

"Rose didn't kill her abuser after all," he murmured.

"No," Evie said tremulously. "He did it to himself. For despite the pain he had caused her, it was not in her nature to do harm."

"As it was never in yours." He pressed his lips to her forehead. "Does it give you peace, knowing that Rose was innocent?"

"It does. But I wonder what became of her." Evie bit her lip. "Of the child she carried."

"Perhaps we shall never know. However, I am certain of one thing."

"What is that?"

"She was a survivor. A fierce and resourceful woman who would do anything to protect the child she made with the man she loved."

"Yes." Evie smiled slowly. "While we are on the subject of children."

With a graceful motion that stole his breath, she swung a leg over his lap, sitting astride him. Her night rail bunched at her waist, and when he felt her warmth pressed against his groin, he went instantly hard.

She brought her lips close to his. Her every word made him quiver with anticipation.

"I do believe you have a promise to keep," she said.

Chapter Forty

Several months later

"Friends, I thank you for the trust you have placed in me this day," James said from the dais. "I accept your charge with humility, gratitude, and an unyielding sense of duty. Throughout my campaign, I have argued that every life—whether shaped by labor, devoted to service, or marked by suffering—deserves dignity. That conviction will guide my every step in the Commons."

As applause thundered through the Reading Town Hall, Evie beamed with pride from the front row, where she sat with the rest of the Harrington clan. The assembly room was packed with supporters, including many of the good folk from Chuddums. All had come to hear James's victory speech. His opponent, Ryerson, had been enveloped in scandal for spreading slander purchased from a criminal but had refused to concede defeat. In the end, the people protested Ryerson's disgraceful behavior at the polls, where James had beaten him by a resounding margin.

"The measure of a nation is not found in the strength of its wealthiest, but in how it treats its most defenseless." James's voice, deep and resonant with conviction, filled the hall. "These ordinary, hardworking people are not guilty of some moral failing. No, they toil with dignity and diligence yet find it difficult to feed their families and afford a roof over their heads. This is not part of some ordained order but a reflection of an unjust system that must be changed."

The cheers that went up were even louder than before.

"You have to give my brother credit," Ethan muttered to Xenia. "He knows how to pour on the butter."

"Shh." This came from Harkness, who sat in the row behind them. With prim censure, she said, "The earl is giving an important speech."

Ethan rolled his eyes at Evie, who responded with a rueful smile. She and Harkness had long since reconciled; she couldn't hold a grudge against her dear companion when she, herself, had kept secrets to protect those she loved. Their relationship had resumed its normal course—with one exception. After James had helped to capture Wilmington and stood by her side during the brief trial that found the villain guilty of extortion (murder had been too difficult to prove, and it was unlikely Wilmington would survive his sentence of penal servitude), Harkness had taken a liking to Evie's husband. In Harkness's eyes, James could now do no wrong, a shift that relieved and amused Evie.

As James continued to speak, his siblings and parents glowed with pride. In the weeks leading up to the election, they had all pitched in to help him clinch this victory. His parents had hosted events on his behalf, and his siblings had helped to spread goodwill.

"I shall not forget the hardships you have confided to me nor the aspirations you have shared," James was saying. "In particular, I would like to extend my gratitude to the people of Chudleigh Bottoms, who have inspired me with their perseverance, ingenuity, and commitment to one another. The resurgence of their village, after years of hardship, has demonstrated that success is possible, even for those deemed unlikely to win."

"We are losers and proud of it!" The contribution came from Wally, egged on by his ancient cronies, who stamped their feet and thumped their canes in agreement. "Long live Chuddums!"

"*Long live Chuddums!*" the crowd began to chant.

His lips twitching, James waited for the enthusiasm to die down.

"I would be remiss if I did not acknowledge my family. My parents and siblings have been stalwart supporters of my campaign and throughout my life. I owe them a debt of gratitude."

Evie saw the tears in Mama's eyes, the approval in Papa's. Ethan, Gigi, and Owen exchanged grins, as if to say, *We shall be collecting on that debt, dear brother.*

"And to my wife, Lady Evelyn Harrington."

James's gaze found hers, and she basked in the emotion she saw there.

"No speech can fully convey my appreciation. She has been the quiet hearth at which my spirits are restored, and the bright mind that illuminates the world of those around her."

"Bright mind, my foot. Lady Manderly is a natural genius," Wally shouted. "She figured out a way to bring the cherries back!"

Blushing furiously, Evie wanted to demur: a new crop of cherries was far from assured, yet her reintroduction of the Widow's Weeds moth to Mr. Lydell's orchard had led to prodigious blossoming not seen for decades. She was hopeful that the fruit would follow. In the meantime, she was working on a paper—a follow-up to her recently published work in the Botanical Society's journal. She was tentatively titling it, "*The Curious Case of Chuddums's Cherries.*"

"To my wife," James said with tender pride. "Whose presence is a beacon to all of us."

Since Evie could not reply, she answered with action. She brushed one hand over her mama's pearl necklace and the other subtly over her waist, where the new life she carried had yet to show. James had given her these gifts—one from the past, the other for the future—and she wanted him to know how precious they were to her. How precious *he* was.

She saw his subtle nod of recognition before he delivered the closing.

"With your continued support, I will strive to bring about progress that will be felt in the lives of every man, woman, and child in this district. I thank you again for this great honor. Today, let us celebrate; tomorrow, we begin the work."

As the audience surged to a standing ovation, James stepped down from the dais. He moved toward her with single-minded purpose. When he reached her, he simply extended his hand, and the rest of the world fell away. Rising, Evie slipped her fingers into his. Their connection was such that the crowd stayed at a respectful distance, yielding them a few moments alone.

He kissed her hand, a decidedly proper gesture. However, the brush of his lips over her skin reminded her of the celebrating they'd done during the carriage ride over. The wicked flicker in his gaze held the promise of more private festivities.

"Did I speak clearly enough?" he asked.

She smiled at his earnestness. It was so *James* to question his own perfection.

"You were flawless," she said warmly. "I heard every word you said."

"I hope you heard what I couldn't say as well."

Since honesty and openness were now cornerstones of their marriage, she knew exactly what he meant.

"You are madly and irrevocably in love with me." She tilted her head. "I hope you heard my reply."

His eyes were bright. "You are mine, and I am yours."

"That about covers it. Now, shall we circulate and celebrate your triumph?"

"Our triumph," he said gently. "Are you certain you are up for it, sunflower?"

Knowing he was referring to the babe, she blushed.

"There is no need to fuss, darling," she said. "I am perfectly well and have been since the last time you asked—which was about an hour ago, before your speech. With seven months remaining, you shall tire yourself out if you continue to be this overprotective."

He merely smiled and bent to kiss her cheek. Then, their arms linked and hearts in unison, they moved into the crowd. While the newspapers the next day held varying opinions about the outcome of the general election, there was one universal note of agreement: the Earl and Countess of Manderly dazzled with their elegance, decorum, and accomplishments, and a couple so united in passion and purpose would surely go far.

Epilogue

Gazing at the spiral of shells, she waited for him. When his ethereal light filled the grotto, she spun around. She ran to him with the delight of a bride greeting her new groom—which he was and would forever be.

"Thomas," she said in an aching whisper.

He was as handsome as ever, his typically somber countenance lit with excitement.

"I should not have doubted you, my darling Rose," he said. "You were right. They are the ones destined to free us."

"We are close, my love," she agreed.

Although she knew they were beyond corporeal touch, she brushed her fingertips along the glowing outline of his jaw. She felt the intimacy—the invocation of their bond. When his eyes brightened, she knew he felt it too: their love that defied time and place, that would not bow to so paltry a thing as mortality.

"Only one more trial to go," Thomas said fiercely. "If he succeeds, you and I will be free of this plane. Free to be together—for eternity."

"Yes."

Rose's longing was like a captive bird, fluttering against the ribs of her soul. Yet the decades had taught her patience and the wisdom of allowing things to unfold in their time. She did not want Thomas to be disappointed if destiny had different plans than the ones they hoped for.

"This last brother...he is different from the others," she said softly. "His demons are strong, and he may not be ready to slay them."

"She will help him," Thomas said confidently. "Their love will prevail."

"Like ours?" Rose teased.

"Like ours, for this is the way of love." His smile was tender. "To stay, to forgive, and to begin again."

From Grace's Desk

Dear Gentle Reader,

James and Evie's story is one I hold especially close to my heart. Their quiet devotion, even when they were estranged, spoke deeply to me. Second chances require courage, vulnerability, and the willingness to hope again—and I hope you enjoyed their journey back to each other as much as I did.

While three of the Blackwood siblings have fulfilled the family legacy, the youngest brother still walks a lonelier path. Owen returned from war changed—guarded in ways that have shaped this entire family. But when a dodgy miss with a wicked smile and secrets of her own refuses to treat him like a broken man, everything he believes about love—and himself— begins to unravel.

Owen's story is one of redemption, sparkling desire, and a love that asks for everything. It will also be the final chapter in the Blackwood Legacy.

Thank you, as always, for reading and for loving this family as deeply as I do.

Owen's story, *Four Promises to Love*, is available for preorder and will release in September 2025.

Hugs and happy reading,

Grace

Author's Note

James, the Harrington heir, has intrigued me for some time. I adore quiet, honorable heroes, and to me, his story is, at its heart, one of conscience. Unlike some of the conflicts faced by his siblings, his is not forged on a battlefield or born of scandal, but shaped by ideas—by the uncomfortable realization that the world is far from just, and he ought to do something about it.

One of the central political debates of the era involved the Corn Laws, tariffs imposed on imported grain that were designed to protect British landowners from foreign competition. While these laws were presented as a means of preserving rural stability, in practice, they kept food prices artificially high, placing the greatest burden on those least able to bear it. James's opposition to the Corn Laws reflects his belief that policies benefiting the wealthy at the expense of the working poor cannot be justified, no matter how well they are dressed in rhetoric. History has an unfortunate tendency to repeat itself in this regard, and I will leave it to the reader to decide how much—or how little—has changed.

If James's moral compass points him outward, toward society and reform, Evie's turns inward, finding meaning and solace in the natural world. Her fascination with botany is not accidental; for her, science offers both order and hope. While I freely admit that I invented Evie's particular subspecies of wallflower—the metaphor was simply too tempting to resist—the resurrection plant that appears in this story is real. It was brought to England from arid regions abroad and used in scientific demonstrations to great effect. A plant that appears dead, only to bloom again under the right conditions, captured the imagination of Victorian audiences...and my own.

Another feature of the landscape that fascinated me was the hermit's grotto. These structures, popular on grand estates, were meant to evoke spiritual reflection, solitude, and communion with nature. Yet most were imitations, and some landowners even hired "hermits" to inhabit them, lending an air of romantic mysticism to what was, in fact, a curated illusion. I found the irony irresistible. The tension between appearance and authenticity—between what is constructed and what is sincere—felt fitting for the story and Evie's journey of empowerment and self-discovery.

As ever, what draws me most to the Harringtons is their resilience. They do not shy away from difficult questions, nor do they emerge from them unchanged. Happiness, for this family, is never simple and never guaranteed. It must be earned, defended, and sometimes reimagined. Yet they persist—with love, courage, and loyalty—just as they always have.

Ad finem fidelis.

Thank you, as always, for reading.

About the Callawayverse

Grace Callaway's novels are all **standalone romances**, set in an interconnected world of families, friendships, and intrigue. You can read them in any order—or follow the chronological series order below.

Chronological Series Order

1. Mayhem in Mayfair

2. Heart of Enquiry (The Kents)

3. Game of Dukes

4. Lady Charlotte's Society of Angels

5. Blackwood Legacy

Series you are currently reading:

BLACKWOOD LEGACY

One Kiss to Desire (Book 1)

After an accident destroys the dreams of musician Lord Ethan Harrington, he takes refuge at a supposedly haunted manor in the downtrodden village of Chudleigh Bottoms. He hires mousy housekeeper Xenia Loveday who, instead of making his life easier, ignites his darkest desires. As their forbidden romance blossoms, they must face the dangerous secrets of Xenia's past...and unravel a century-old curse. *Winner of the National Excellence in Romance Fiction Award* & the *Passionate Plume*

Two Secrets to Surrender (Book 2)

Spirited debutante Lady Gigi Harrington wants to help revive a fading business in the quaint village of Chudleigh Bottoms. The arrival of a wealthy and arrogant industrialist jeopardizes her plans...especially since they share a sizzling secret. The pair lock horns, drawn together by scorching animosity and even hotter passion. Will their enemies to lovers romance lead to happily ever after...and unlock the secrets of an ancient prophecy?

Three Chances to Cherish (Book 3)

When a hidden enemy shatters the fragile peace between Lord James Harrington and his shy, brilliant botanist wife, Evie, long-buried secrets and an ancient village prophecy rise to test their marriage. Their slow-burn love flares into heady, undeniable passion as James longs for the wife he vowed to protect, while Evie fears yielding her heart to the honorable man she feels she has never deserved. As danger closes in, they must choose whether to fight for their hard-won happiness—or lose each other just as love begins to bloom.

Four Promises to Love (Book 4)

Owen's story and the series finale—coming Fall 2026

And in case you missed the story of Marcus and Pandora Harrington, the Marquess and Marchioness of Blackwood...

The Lady Who Came in from the Cold (Heart of Enquiry series, Book 3)

Former spy Pandora Hudson gave up espionage for love. Twelve years later, her dark secret rises to threaten her blissful marriage to Marcus, Marquess of Blackwood, and she must face her most challenging mission yet: winning back the heart of the only man she's ever loved.

Acknowledgments

This book, like the family at its heart, exists because of a village.

To my readers: thank you for returning to the world of the Blackwoods yet again. Your enthusiasm, reviews, and quiet loyalty are the reason the Callawayverse continues to grow. I write my stories for you, and I never take for granted that you choose to spend your time here with me.

My heartfelt thanks to my editor, Peter Senftleben, whose insight and care continue to elevate my work, and to Alyssa Nazzaro, whose thoughtful proofreading helps ensure every detail shines.

I am endlessly grateful to the people who make it possible for me to write at all—my assistant, Jill Glass, and my son's caregivers, whose support creates the space for these stories to exist.

Special thanks to my friend Shellei, for sharing her profound knowledge of flora and fauna.

To my family, and especially to my husband: thank you for your love, patience, and unwavering belief in me. None of this would be possible without you.

It truly does take a village. I am fortunate to have mine.

About the Author

Grace Callaway is a *USA Today* and international bestselling author of hot, heart-melting historical romances filled with mystery, adventure, and swoon-worthy happily ever afters. A multiple-time winner of the Daphne du Maurier Award, the National Excellence in Romance Fiction Award, and the Passionate Plume, she is known for blending emotional depth, danger, and passion into deeply satisfying love stories.

She holds a doctorate in clinical psychology from the University of Michigan and lives in Northern California with her family and beloved rescue dog. When she's not writing, Grace enjoys dancing, discovering hole-in-the-wall restaurants, and going on adapted adventures with her special son.

STAY CONNECTED WITH GRACE

Newsletter:
gracecallaway.com/newsletter

Website & Shop:
gracecallaway.com

Reader Group:
facebook.com/GraceCallawayBookClub

Instagram:
instagram.com/gracecallawaybooks

Facebook:
facebook.com/gracecallawaybooks

www.ingramcontent.com/pod-product-compliance
Lightning Source LLC
Chambersburg PA
CBHW030127310726
48970CB00005B/1330